Raves for Marshall Ryan Maresca's
***The Thorn of Dentonhill*:**

"Veranix is Batman, if Batman were a teenager and magically talented. His uncompromising devotion to crushing the local crime boss encourages him to take foolish risks, but his resourcefulness keeps our hero one step ahead of those who seek to bring him down. Action, adventure, and magic in a school setting will appeal to those who love Harry Potter and Patrick Rothfuss's *The Name of the Wind*." —*Library Journal* (starred review)

"Maresca brings the whole package, complete and well-constructed. If you're looking for something fun and adventurous for your next fantasy read, look no further . . . an incredible start to a new series, from an author who is clearly on his way to great things."
—Bibliosanctum

"Books like this are just fun to read."
—The Tenacious Reader

"This is hang-on-to-your-toothpicks adventure with a mystery bent as Veranix tries to learn how to control the new magic he has and discover why some powerful people want to kill him for it. It's action-oriented—swashbuckling Indiana Jones meets the burglar Bilbo Baggins of *The Hobbit*—but the characters have a warmth and conflicting goals and attitudes that make them worth following."
—Kings River Life Magazine

"I loved every minute . . . this was a great debut novel and I can't wait to see more of Maresca's work"
—Short and Sweet Reviews

"Maresca's debut is smart, fast, and engaging fantasy crime in the mold of Brent Weeks and Harry Harrison. Just perfect."
—Kat Richardson, national bestselling author of *Revenant*

DAW Books presents the
novels of Marshall Ryan Maresca:

THE THORN OF DENTONHILL

*

A MURDER OF MAGES

A MURDER OF MAGES

A novel of
The Maradaine Constabulary

MARSHALL RYAN MARESCA

DAW BOOKS, INC.

DONALD A. WOLLHEIM, FOUNDER

375 Hudson Street, New York, NY 10014

ELIZABETH R. WOLLHEIM
SHEILA E. GILBERT
PUBLISHERS

www.dawbooks.com

First Printing, July 2015
1 2 3 4 5 6 7 8 9

DAW TRADEMARK REGISTERED
U.S. PAT. AND TM. OFF. AND FOREIGN COUNTRIES
—MARCA REGISTRADA
HECHO EN U.S.A.

PRINTED IN THE U.S.A.

Acknowledgments

This book would not exist without the assistance of quite a few people.

First of all, there is my amazing and incredibly patient wife, Deidre Kateri Aragon. She has been an anchor in my life for the past fifteen years, giving me the ability to pound away at a keyboard day after day to make this book happen. But more importantly, she got me on task in the first place, moving me from being that guy who just talked about "writing a book at some point" to actually making writing a real focus in my life. She, as well as my son Nicholas, have been a source of constant support and strength through the process of becoming a novelist.

No less important to thank are my parents, Louis and Nancy Maresca, and my mother-in-law, Kateri Aragon, all of whom have contributed in innumerable ways to make it possible for me to write this book.

Next, there are all the many people who read versions and drafts of *A Murder of Mages*, and gave useful advice that helped shape it into a stronger, better work. This includes Anne Soward, Amy Sterling Casil, Miriam Robinson Gould, and the Bat City Novelocracy crew: Kevin Jewell, Abby Goldsmith, Ellen Van Hensbergen, Katy Stauber, Nicole Duson, and Amanda Downum. And a huge portion of those thanks have to go to Stina Leicht, who has been running the ArmadilloCon Writers Workshop for many years, and after I had attended it several times, brought me on board to run it with her. Stina has been a friend, a mentor, a sympathetic ear, and a good source for the occasional much-needed whap upside the head, which is exactly what every writer needs.

I can't emphasize enough how much is owed to my agent, Mike Kabongo. He's handled with grace and humor the arduous task of dealing with my constant harassment while shopping my work. Back when he first responded to an unsellable draft of *Thorn of Dentonhill*, he said, "Clearly you are a writer I want to watch. Even if you decide I'm not the agent for you, do let me know when you hit the shelves, I want to buy something with your name on it." So far he's continued to show the same enthusiasm for each manuscript I've sent him, and I hope to not let him down.

Further thanks are owed to my editor Sheila Gilbert, Joshua Starr, and everyone else at DAW. I am deeply grateful for all the hard work they've done to make this the best book it can possibly be.

Finally, there is my dear friend Daniel J. Fawcett, who has been my sounding board and bent ear on everything creative I've done since the seventh grade. Nothing in this book would be what it is without his influence. I wouldn't be who I am today without his friendship.

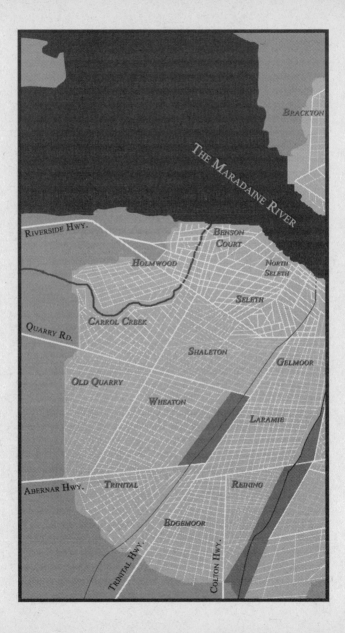

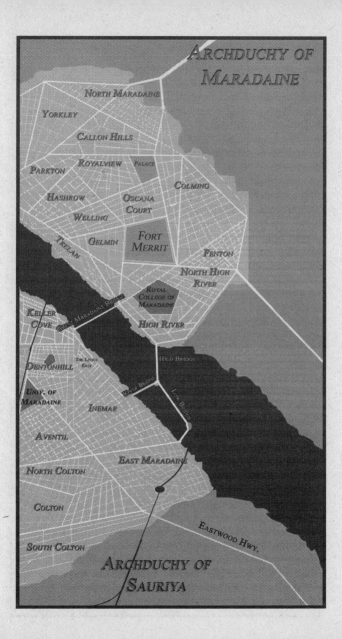

ARCHDUCHY OF MARADAINE

NORTH MARADAINE

YORKLEY

CALLON HILLS

ROYALVIEW   PALACE

PARKTON

HASHROW   OSCANA   COLMING
            COURT

WELLING

TRELAN   GELMIN   FORT
                    MERRIT   FENTON

                    NORTH HIGH
                    RIVER

KELLER
COVE   GREAT MARADAINE BRIDGE   ROYAL
                    COLLEGE OF
                    MARADAINE

            HIGH RIVER

            THE LITTLE   HIGH BRIDGE
DENTONHILL   EAST

UNIV. OF   RIVER BRIDGE
MARADAINE   LYN BRIDGE

            INEMAR

AVENTIL

NORTH COLTON   EAST MARADAINE

COLTON

SOUTH COLTON   EASTWOOD HWY.

ARCHDUCHY OF SAURIYA

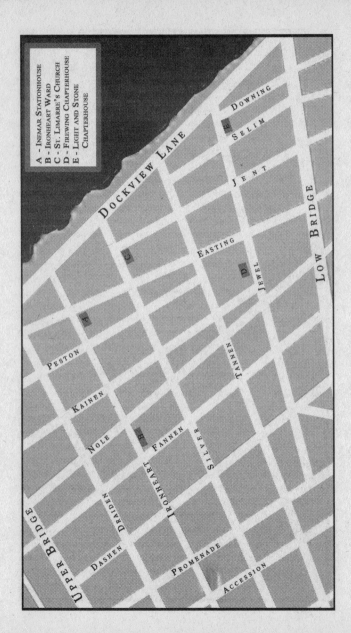

Chapter 1

SATRINE RAINEY WALKED TO the Inemar Constabulary House carrying a lie. It gnawed at her, every step she took across the bridges to the south side of the city. Taking it across the river would help it pass. The one person who knew the truth was up in North Maradaine, and he almost never crossed the river. The Inemar Constabulary House, on the south bank, might as well have been in another city.

The lie would pass. It was wrapped up in enough truth to pass.

The wind whipped past Satrine, cold and riddled with wet. She pulled her coat tight around her and quickened her pace, overtaking a pedalcart that trundled along one side of the bridge road. The path split on a tiny jut of rock in the middle of the river, the water below choked with sails and barges. Satrine turned onto the Upper Bridge, leading to the neighborhood of Inemar, the heart of the south side of Maradaine.

Satrine hated Inemar. She hated everything south of the river. Not that it mattered. She had to go. And if all went well, she would come back tomorrow, and every day after that.

The steps at the end of the bridge were crowded, people shouting at everyone as they went down to the street level. Dozens of voices selling useless trinkets, witnessing stories of saints, pleading for coins. Two newsboys from competing presses called out lurid stories over each other. Satrine pushed her way through the throng and pressed her way down to the street. She dodged through the traffic of horse carriages and pedalcarts, without missing a step. Muscle memory.

Gray stone dominated Inemar. Gray and tight, this part of the city didn't waste an inch, buildings pressed up against each other. Not a bit of green in this neighborhood. No trees shading the walkways. Iron grates bordered properties instead of hedges. Even the weeds between the cobblestones were trampled and dead.

"Hey, hey, Waish girl! Waish girl!"

Satrine grimaced. She knew someone was calling her. Most people presumed she was Waish. Here in Maradaine, people forgot that red hair was a common trait in the northern archduchies of Druthal.

"Waish girl! I'm talking to you!" A hand clasped her shoulder.

People had no damn manners in Inemar.

Satrine spun around and swatted away the offending hand. Its owner was a young man with beady eyes and ratlike teeth, wearing a threadbare coat and vest and bearing a disturbingly wide grin.

"Not Waish," Satrine said. "And not a girl."

The young man didn't blink, he just charged on into his spin. "You're new down here, though, don't know your way around, just crossed the bridge, am I right? You need yourself a guide and escort, am I right?"

"Not right." Satrine had already said eight more words than she had planned to say to anyone on the street, and she turned to head back on her way.

"That's all right, that's all right." The young man kept pace with her. "Even if you know your way about, it's always good for a girl like—lady, I mean—a lady like you to walk with someone, don't you know. Lot can happen in these streets, you know."

"I know."

"So there you have it, miss," the young man said,

crooking his arm through hers as he spoke. "You walk with me and—"

He got no further in his speech. Satrine twisted his arm behind his back, and a moment later she had him on the ground, face pressed into the cobblestone.

"I know where I'm going," Satrine growled into his ear.

He only grunted in reply. Satrine released him and walked away at full pace, giving only a glance out the corner of her eye to see that the young man was not following her. He had probably slunk back to the bridge to harass another newcomer.

She pushed through the crowd, the usual diverse mix of folks seen in Inemar; most were Druth, with fair skin and brown or blond hair. There was a smattering of greasy-haired Kierans, tanned Acserians, and a handful of other exotic faces, having wandered out of their enclaves in the Little East.

The Constabulary House was only two blocks from the bridge, a small fortress of stone and iron towering over the corner square markets. The building itself had to be ancient. Inemar was full of relics, both buildings and people.

Satrine passed through a gated stone arch where two Constabulary regulars stood at attention, their dark green and red coats crisp and clean in sharp contrast to the gray and rust surroundings.

The regulars just gave her a nod as she passed. And why wouldn't they? She was a respectable-looking woman, her hair tied back, her face clean. She wore what any decent woman in Maradaine might wear, though her canvas slacks and heavy blouse were hardly what anyone would consider fashionable.

Satrine entered the building itself, into a small lobby, where a wooden counter restricted her from the cramped and crowded Constabulary floor. Desks and benches shoved into every corner, men in Constabulary coats on the benches, behind the desks, pushing through the narrow spaces. Some of the men were Constabulary regulars, some officers.

One woman pressed her way through to the counter. She wore the Constabulary coat, but Satrine noticed a key difference in her uniform. She wore a skirt that stopped just below the knee. It conformed to standards of decency, but it was more like what a schoolgirl should wear rather than a constable.

"Ma'am, can I help you?" The woman's hair was pulled back tight, which matched the stress in her voice.

"I'm looking for Captain Cinellan?" Satrine asked.

"Second floor," the woman said, pointing to a narrow corridor to her left. "The inspectors' offices are up there." Someone else dropped a pile of papers in front of the woman, and her attention left Satrine immediately.

Satrine went down the corridor, which ended in a tight spiral staircase, solid stone masonry. Satrine went up the steps, running her fingers along the cool wall, her thoughts filled with the paper that felt like it was burning a hole in her coat pocket.

She came out of the stairway to a wide room, bright sunlight streaming through the windows along the eastern wall. The far wall was lined with cabinets and slate boards, and there were desks sparsely placed about the floor, each one with an oil lamp—unlit—hanging above them. Men wearing Constabulary vests worked at the desks while a handful of boys ran through the room. Two boys bolted past Satrine as she came up, racing down the stairs.

A fair-haired woman at the closest desk—the only other woman Satrine saw on the floor—smiled brightly when Satrine approached. "Careful of them."

"Fast runners," Satrine said.

"Fastest we have. Did they send you up here with a report?"

"A report?"

"For one of the inspectors?"

"No." Satrine took a deep breath. This close, the lie was a weight pressing on her chest. "I'm here to see Captain Cinellan."

"All right," the woman—Miss Nyla Pyle, based on her

brass badge and lack of marriage bracelet—said. "Can I have your name?"

"Rainey. Satrine Rainey."

Miss Pyle's eyes flashed with recognition. She gave a small nod as she bit at her bottom lip. "This way, all right?"

The woman led Satrine through the inspectors' work floor, past various men discussing the cases they were working on. Satrine only caught snippets of conversation before reaching the door with a brass plaque on it: CAPTAIN BRACE CINELLAN.

Miss Pyle knocked and opened the door simultaneously. Captain Cinellan's office was dim, no windows, only burning oil lamps and candles on his desk. The man himself was hunched over the desk, the muscular frame of an old soldier, beat down and bent with age. Not that he was that old; his face had few lines and his hair untouched by gray. But he held himself like an old man. A tired man.

"Yes, Miss Pyle?" he asked.

"Missus Satrine Rainey to see you, Captain," Miss Pyle said, putting a strong emphasis on Satrine's last name. Captain Cinellan's weary eyes glanced over to Satrine, and they sparked with sympathy.

"Yes, of course," he said. He got up from the desk and crossed over to Satrine, extending his hand. "Missus Rainey, very good to meet you."

Satrine took his hand and shook it, giving him a strong, solid grip. She wasn't going to give him anything less, give him any cause to doubt her resolve.

Cinellan gestured to her to take the chair on the other side of his desk, despite it being full of books and ledgers. Miss Pyle grabbed them off the chair before anyone else spoke.

"Return these to the archives, Captain?"

"Yes, Miss Pyle. And, um . . . tea with—"

"Honey and cream," Miss Pyle finished. "Anything for you, Missus Rainey?"

"Tea, yes," Satrine said. "Cream only."

Miss Pyle nodded and left the office as gracefully as

possible with her arms full, deftly shutting the door with a swing of her foot.

Captain Cinellan sat down behind his desk. "So, Missus Rainey, let me just say . . . when we all heard about what happened to your husband, well . . . most of us didn't know him down here on the south bank, of course, except by reputation. And when something . . ." He faltered, biting at his lip.

"Devastating occurs?" Satrine offered. That was the best word to describe what had happened to Loren.

Cinellan nodded. "Absolutely. It gives a man pause. Especially for all of us here in the Green and Red."

"What happened to my husband was—is—tragic, Captain Cinellan, but I have to . . ."

"Yes, I know," Captain Cinellan said. He dug through the papers on his desk. "I received word from Commissioner Enbrain that you would be coming here."

Satrine's heart jumped to her throat. If Enbrain had sent a letter here as well, then that would ruin everything. She couldn't have that. Loren needed her to succeed. The girls needed it.

"He sent you my orders?"

"Orders, what?" Cinellan looked confused. "No, he just sent a runner with word you were going to be coming in here today."

"So you don't have the orders?" This was the moment. She forced the words out despite the rising bile in her throat. "You're to give me a position here." She pulled the letter out of her pocket.

Cinellan glanced at the letter, waxed shut with Commissioner Enbrain's seal. Or, more correctly, an excellent forgery that Satrine had spent hours copying. Cinellan gave it no more than two seconds of regard before cracking it open and reading the letter.

"I'm to make you what?"

Satrine almost answered, but she bit her tongue before she revealed that she knew the contents of the sealed letter.

"This can't be serious!"

"What is it?"

"According to this, I'm to make you an inspector."

Inspector Third Class, to be precise. Satrine dared well enough putting that on the letter.

She had worked on her expression in the mirror for an hour. Old skills, long unpracticed, but still in her muscles. She needed to convey just the right degree of pleasant surprise without approaching shock. She opened her eyes wide and drew her breath in sharply. She put her hand over her chest, as if her heart was racing, and asked, "And what would the salary be?"

"Salary!" Cinellan snapped. "Missus Rainey, do you have any experience related to investigative work?"

"Beyond having a husband who was an Inspector First Class?"

"That is not a qualification, Missus Rainey. My wife plays the flute excellently, yet I'm only thumbs."

"Fair enough." Satrine knew that wasn't going to keep this wagon rolling. "Prior to my marriage, I was an agent in Druth Intelligence."

Cinellan raised his eyebrow. "For how long?"

Satrine knew she had intrigued him, at least enough that he could be reeled in. "Four years." She held her breath for a moment, letting a small smile form. "Officially."

"I don't suppose that's verifiable."

Satrine knew that was coming. "We don't get tattoos like army or navy does."

"You understand I can't just take your word . . ."

"Of course," Satrine said, pulling another letter from her pocket, this one completely legitimate. "I know it isn't exactly—"

He gave it a quick glance. "I've seen enough 'thanks for service to the Crown' letters to know what they really mean." Cinellan grunted in something sounding like disapproval. "Most inspectors have several years walking the streets first."

"Do you need my whole history, Captain?"

"I need some reason why I should make inspector some—no disrespect to you, Missus Rainey—some random woman who walks off the street over the heads of several men who've earned the posting!"

Satrine had been expecting this. Her forgery, as impeccable as it might be, wouldn't be enough to convince any captain worth the crowns he was paid to take her on.

"Leaving aside that I am not some 'random woman,' but the wife of a dedicated constable—a man who all but died for this city—I do have the skills and training necessary to serve as an inspector."

"I'll grant four years in Intelligence is nothing to scoff at. Even still, no formal training is a substitute for knowing these streets."

"Streets of Inemar?" Satrine asked. She didn't bother to hide her grin. "I grew up not three blocks from here."

Cinellan chuckled. "You can't try and trick me with that. You're a North Maradaine lady if ever I met one."

"Oy, that what you think?" Satrine slipped into her old accent like it was a comfortable shoe. "No surprise sticks like you never clipped any of us."

Cinellan's eyebrow went up. "What corner?"

"Jent and Tannen."

"No chance! When I first got my coat, I knew every rat and bird in that part of the neighborhood. The only Waishen-haired girl back in the day was—"

"Trini 'Tricky.'"

"Exactly! And she . . . she . . ." His eyes went wide. "Impossible!"

Satrine bowed her head gracefully. "It was another life."

"I know for a fact that there is a report down in the archives on the investigation of her . . . disappearance."

Satrine shrugged. "My recruitment into Druth Intelligence was . . . unorthodox. I didn't have a chance to tell anyone I was going."

Cinellan laughed out loud. He was warming to her. That was always her gift—to survive on the street, to thrive in Intelligence, she made people fond of her. She used to wrap herself in lies on a daily basis, but to sell one to a man like her husband, a man just doing his job honestly, it made her ill.

"I'm intrigued, Missus Rainey, and the commissioner notes that we should be giving more positions in the

Constabulary force to women." He shook the letter casually. The commissioner had written that very point, but as an argument to make Satrine a clerk. A position that paid five crowns a week. That salary would put her family on the street; she would never let that happen to her daughters. Her girls would never have to do what she lived through.

Miss Pyle came back in with a tea tray. Cinellan dropped his light demeanor while Miss Pyle was there, thanked her for the tea, and waited for her to leave before sipping it. He sat at his desk, teacup in hand, for some time in silence. Satrine picked up her own, but didn't drink any, not yet. She didn't think it would be particularly good, anyway.

"I'll be frank, Captain," Satrine said. "I'm not a widow, though I may as well be. I have two daughters whom I am putting through school, a husband who needs caring for, rent, city taxes, and several other expenses. If I'm not bringing home twenty crowns a week, then it all falls apart."

"Standard pay for Inspector Third Class is nineteen crowns five."

"I can start with that." There was enough saved up—especially with what the boys at Loren's district house had scraped together for her family—to last on nineteen-five for a few months. Come the summer, she would find some way to earn those last fifteen ticks.

"Ambitious, good," he said. "Still doesn't sit right, even with the commissioner pushing it."

"I'd be happy to be put to the test."

"Hmmph," Cinellan snorted. "What sort of test?"

"Give me a week," she said. "Any floor sergeants grouse, you tell them you got pushed by the commissioner."

Cinellan tapped the letter on his desk. "Which I have."

"If you don't think I measure up at the end of the week, you send me on my way. You can tell the commissioner you tried and it didn't work."

Satrine's heart pounded like a hammer, threatening to smash through her chest.

"Fine," Cinellan said. "Though I got to tell you, it's mostly so I can pull your old file from the archives and write in it that I solved a twenty-year-old case."

"Thank you, Captain," Satrine said. Most of the tension in her shoulders relaxed. Not all, not until she had the job secure. She took a drink of her tea. It was, as she had predicted, awful.

"Don't thank me yet," he said. "You haven't met your partner."

⬥

Satrine was brought to a pair of desks shoved to a far corner of the inspectors' floor, away from the windows. Two large, rolling slateboards had been wedged in front of the desk, giving it some illusion of privacy. Cinellan knocked on one of the slateboards.

"Welling? Your partner's here."

"Don't have a partner," came the reply from behind the boards.

"Every Third Class has a partner. That's how it goes."

The man behind the boards stood up, though Satrine could only see the top of his head. "Then make me Second Class."

"Not on the table, Welling."

"Very well." The man came out from behind his slateboards.

The first thing Satrine noticed was his eyes. Blue and enormous, almost too big for his head. He stared long and hard at her, unblinking. She then realized that it wasn't that his eyes were large, but that the rest of his face, while youthful, was drawn and sharp. He wore a crisply pressed inspector's vest, though the rest of his clothes showed a slovenly disinterest in his appearance. His heavy leather overcoat was splattered with mud, as were his boots, and his dark shirt bore more than a few stains.

He stared hard at her while deliberately flicking his fingers, as though counting.

Captain Cinellan gestured to Satrine. "Welling, this is—"

"Missus Satrine Rainey, wife of Inspector First Class Loren Rainey, currently inactive due to severe injuries." Welling nodded crisply and extended his hand. "Condolences." He said the last word with no inflection or emotion.

Satrine took his hand and shook it, though he only allowed her the briefest contact before withdrawing his hand. "Your name is Welling?"

"Minox Welling, Inspector Third Class," he said. His eyes danced up and down her person, though Satrine saw it was some form of meticulous analysis of detail rather than any kind of lechery. "She has the same rank?"

"Provisionally," Cinellan said. "I'll have Miss Pyle bring you what you need, Missus Rainey."

"Thank you, Captain," she said. "I won't disappoint—"

"Right," Cinellan said, giving her a dismissive wave as he walked away.

She turned back to Welling. "So, Minox, was it?"

"Inspector Welling," he said. He went back around the slateboards to the desks. She followed him, noting that both desks were covered with papers, stacks of newssheets, used teacups, chalk, ink bottles, a smoking pipe, crusts of bread, and a leather belt with a crossbow holstered onto it. There was one relatively clear section of the desk with only a leather journal sitting open.

"Got comfortable working alone, did you, Inspector Welling?"

"I work better alone," he said, sitting down at the desk which had a clear view of the slateboards. He gave her another large-eyed glance. "You're lying to Captain Cinellan about something."

The frank and dispassionate way he announced it took Satrine by surprise. She recovered her composure, asking, "Why do you say that?"

"It was quite plain on your face in any moment he wasn't looking directly at you. When he turned back to you, there was a noticeable increase in the tension you held in your cheeks and neck. Yes, like you are doing right now."

"That doesn't mean that—"

"It usually does," Welling said. He focused his attention on one of the pages on his desk. "It scarcely matters to me, though. What matters is if you can do the job and function serviceably as my partner in our assigned investigations." He glanced up at her again. "Can you?"

"Absolutely."

Welling nodded. "That was the truth. Have a seat, Inspector Rainey."

The other chair had a strange device sitting on it, a small contraption of iron and glass. Not getting any prompt from Welling, Satrine took it off the chair and deposited it on his desk. "What are we working on currently?"

Welling took the device and moved it to one side. "Currently, I have one open case that I personally consider 'active.' And twenty-four that I consider 'unresolved.' My notes are . . . all here."

"Bring me up to speed, then."

"Wait." Welling held up a finger.

"What are we—"

"Shh."

Two inspectors walked around the slateboards, which Satrine now noticed were covered with scrawlings of names, locations, arrows, and question marks. The older inspector, his ruddy face scowling, spoke first. "All right, Jinx, what is it?" He had the Inemar accent, and the nose to go with it; it must have been broken half a dozen times.

Welling winced noticeably when the inspector addressed him, but responded politely. "I have made a breakthrough, Inspector Mirrell, on one of your cases, as it tied to one of my own. However, before discussing that, I must first address a matter of civility. Inspector Rainey, these are two of our colleagues, Inspectors Henfir Mirrell and Darreck Kellman. Gentlemen, my new partner, Inspector Satrine Rainey."

Satrine bit her lip to keep from bursting with laughter. Welling's introduction sounded forced, like he had learned phrases from an etiquette book, and was repeating what he read like a clockwork toy going through its set motions.

"Inspector, really?" Kellman asked, incredulity in his voice. He was a bull of a man, towering a good foot over his partner, with a thick accent that placed his origins out on the poor west side of Maradaine.

"As of ten minutes ago," Satrine said, taking his hand in a firm grip.

"Pleasure," Mirrell said, barely giving Satrine a glance. His attention was fully on Welling. "What case?"

"Your murders outside Oscana Park," Welling said. Now the forced formality was gone.

Mirrell made a spitting noise. "That case? There was no mystery to solve, Jinx."

Welling's eye twitched again at the address, which Satrine realized was not any form of endearment on Mirrell's part. He held up his finger in front of Mirrell's face, continuing with his thought. "Two dead horsepatrolmen, found with knives in their chests right on the south side of the park."

Kellman shook his head. "Yeah, and a noted assassin, infamous for his skill with knives, dead not twenty feet away."

"Done deal," Mirrell added.

"An incomplete picture!" Welling cried out. "A canvas with but a small corner painted."

Satrine was intrigued. "Who killed the assassin?"

"Precisely the key question that is being ignored by our good colleagues," Welling said. "Though hardly the only one."

Mirrell rubbed his hand over his face. "We're not ignoring it, Jinx. The man was smashed across the skull, from above. There was a broken staff right next to him."

"Used by who?"

"The assassin's partner!" Kellman said. He looked over to Satrine, clearly trying to appeal to her senses. "This guy was known to work with a partner who is almost seven feet tall and strong as an ox."

Welling nodded. "Pendall Gurond, I know."

Kellman threw up his hands. "One kills the horsepatrolmen, then his partner kills him." He slammed his hand down on the desk in a mime of the killing act.

"Why?" Satrine asked.

Mirrell answered with a shrug. "A bigger share of the fee, most likely."

Satrine wasn't satisfied with that. "The fee for what?"

"For killing two horsepatrolmen," Kellman said, as if it was the most obvious thing he had ever heard or said.

Satrine looked over at Welling. "That doesn't quite add up, does it?"

Welling glanced over at her, and for the briefest of moments, he smiled. "No, it most certainly does not. The two horsepatrolmen were, if you forgive my saying so, men of little import. Members of the MC in good standing, of no doubt, but not men who would inspire a price being put on their heads, certainly not in the range of several thousand crowns."

"Those two horsepatrolmen interrupted them doing something else."

"The question is what," Welling said, tapping his finger on the desk.

Kellman and Mirrell both stepped away from the desk in obvious frustration. "Does it matter?" Mirrell asked.

Kellman pointed to his partner in agreement. "The patrolmen probably interrupted the two assassins arguing, and got killed for their trouble."

"Interesting," Satrine said.

"What's that?" Kellman asked.

"You have a conclusion in your head, and you force the facts to fit it. I thought it was supposed to go the other way around."

Welling smiled broadly, which looked wholly unnatural on his face. "I am definitely not displeased with your way of thinking, Inspector Rainey."

"That's what he calls a compliment," Mirrell said. He stalked off, with Kellman right behind him.

"There were three," Welling called after them.

Mirrell came back around the slateboard. "Three what?"

"Three assassins who worked in partnership, not two. Which would not be significant, as your theory works just as well with two partners turning on the third, rather than a pair turning on each other."

"What is your point, Jinx?"

"You may recall I had a case assigned to me of four bodies found together in a refuse barge, found the day after your dead patrolmen."

"Saint Jasper, Jinx!" Kellman snapped. "Will you stop teasing around the point and just tell us!"

Welling appeared legitimately injured by this rebuke. He nodded, and continued. "One of those four I have identified as the third assassin. The other three were mages, all belonging to the same mystical circle, The Blue Hand."

"Mages," Kellman and Mirrell both grumbled in unison. Again Welling had the twitch of his eye, same as when they called him Jinx.

"Indeed, and the connecting thread between the assassins and the Circle is Willem Fenmere." The name was written in large letters on the slateboard.

Both Kellman and Mirrell went pale, their eyes wide.

"Who is Willem Fenmere?" Satrine asked. She could probably guess. The names may have changed over the years, but the stories didn't.

"Crime boss in Dentonhill neighborhood," Mirrell said. "He greases enough hands in that neighborhood that the Constabulary doesn't touch him, can't prove anything."

Welling searched through his papers. "But his ties to the Blue Hand are interesting, since I have it on good authority that it and his ties to the assassins lead to a string of—"

"No, Jinx," Mirrell said, slapping his hand down on the papers Welling was sorting through. "Quick question. Can you prove—not suspect, not ties to, not leading to any string of anything—can you *prove* that Fenmere was involved in the death of the two horsepatrolmen?"

"Well, no, but what *is* interesting—"

"Blazes, Jinx!" Kellman shouted. "What good is it?"

Satrine answered automatically, "Sometimes just knowing the truth is enough." Of course, in Intelligence, knowing the truth was enough cause to do something about it. There wasn't any interest in Proof of Guilt or Trial Rights.

Mirrell shook his head, chuckling. "Missus Rainey—excuse me, Inspector Rainey—don't let yourself get chained into his madness, or the Jinx will drag you down too." He actually looked at her for the first time, and sneered openly. "Maybe that's for the best, though." He and Kellman left.

Welling muttered, "Now one active, twenty-five unresolved." He took a pen out of an ink jar and jotted into the leather notebook.

Satrine started clearing off her own desk. "Why do they call you Jinx?"

"It's just a stupid thing they say."

"But there's a reason why," Satrine pressed.

"Everything has a reason."

"Is it because you're a mage?"

Welling dropped his pen. He looked at Satrine with an expression of both surprise and admiration. "That isn't why, no. What gave it away?"

"You winced when they called you 'Jinx,' ever so slightly. Little more than a tick of the cheek and eye. You did the same when they groused about mages. Plus your thin build."

"The facts were plain to the trained eye, if said eye was connected to a functioning brain." He pursed his lips. "You may have the skills of an inspector."

"I did say so," Satrine said. "But what Circle do you belong to? I didn't think any of them cooperated with the Constabulary."

"I'm not," Welling said quietly.

"But that would mean you're . . ." She let the sentence hang.

"You can say it," he said. "The word is *Uncircled*."

"But—"

Miss Pyle came around the slateboards before Satrine

had a chance to finish her thought. She was a bright smile of energy, carrying a small wooden crate that she placed on the empty space Satrine had cleared on the desk.

"Sorry it took me a while to bring you this, Miss—I'm sorry, Inspector Rainey," she said. "The matron in the supply room wouldn't believe me when I told her I needed a woman's inspector uniform. She said they didn't exist!"

Didn't exist. Like Uncircled Mages in Constabulary didn't exist.

Satrine removed her coat and draped it over her chair, then put the crate on the desk. She pulled out the vest, a rich, deep green accented with the dignified dark red, the same as Loren had worn for years. She held it reverently for a moment before putting it on. It fit loosely, but that could be fixed.

She next took out the belt, like the one Welling had carelessly left on his desk, and strapped it around her waist. It was far too big, so the crossbow holster hung down at her hip. She took it back off and put it on her desk.

The last item in the crate, a skirt like the one Miss Pyle wore, she pointedly ignored. Miss Pyle seemed expectant, however, so she took the crate off the desk and put it on the floor.

Miss Pyle turned to Inspector Welling. "Minox, you cannot keep used teacups piled up on your desk. I have told you this before, and I will *not* come back here twice a day to clean up after you."

Welling gave her a glance, which Satrine noted as having a hint of genuine warmth buried under it. "You know better than trying to clean this desk."

"Which means you need to take care of your own—"

A boy, one of the Constabulary pages from his coat, ran in. "Murder!" he shouted. "Over at Jent and Tannen!"

The familiar names of streets from Satrine's childhood jarred her senses. Her gut twisted. She knew she'd have to go back there, but she didn't think it would be right away.

Welling was on his feet, grabbing his belt off the desk and strapping it around his waist as he charged out. Satrine threw her own belt over her shoulder, grabbed her coat, and followed.

It was time to start earning those nineteen crowns five.

Chapter 2

SATRINE HADN'T BEEN ON the corner of Jent and Tannen in twenty years. That had been a different time; the city emaciated by a distant war, teetering on the edge of famine. Scores of fatherless children scraped and scrounged their way through, living in solitary squalor or rough clades. Satrine had been one for most of her young life. That corner had been her home, her family, her nightmare.

The corner of Jent and Tannen clashed with her memories. The bones of it were the same—the shape of the buildings, the cut of the alleys, the way the morning sun hung across the street. But where she recalled gray and drab, there was a vibrant, bustling commerce square. Fresh paint on the bakery sign on the southwest corner. The windows of the tenement she had flopped in were now intact. The cobblestone road no longer in a state of pitiful disrepair. The streets were still far too narrow, of course, as dozens of carriages and pedalcarts choked their way through.

Satrine surprised herself with the warm fondness she felt at seeing something familiar: Ushman's Hot Pot, where she had gotten the potatoes, butter, and salted pork that kept her marginally fed in those years, with the dented ironwork grate that Heckie Moss smashed with a stolen milk cart.

She refused to let her thoughts get mired in nostalgia.
A crowd surrounded the mouth of the alley between a
butcher shop—had that been the Empty Can Pub?—and
a barber. Three patrolmen—young regulars in shabby
coats of Green and Red—guarded the entrance, keeping
people from getting in.

"That where our body is?" Satrine asked Welling, who
had been focused in determined silence during his quick-
paced walk to the scene.

"The level of coincidence otherwise would be stag-
gering," Welling replied.

"I would have just said 'probably.'"

"Most people would." Welling pulled a whistle out of
his coat pocket. He gave a shrill blast, and the crowd
jumped and made a hole for them to pass. Obedience to a
stick's whistle was definitely a new trait in this neighborhood. The three men at the mouth of the alley stood their
ground, reminding Satrine of the giant bronze sculpture in
front of the stationhouse in North Maradaine: standing
vigilant, one with a crossbow, one with a lantern, one with
a handstick. The only part missing was the dog.

"Patrolmen," Welling said with a nod as he and Satrine approached them. "You have something for us?"

The three patrolmen, almost in unison, gave an uneasy glance to Satrine before the one in the center focused his attention back on Welling. "Yeah, there's a,
uh . . . Inspector, who is this?"

"This is Inspector Rainey, Patrolman," Welling said
flatly.

"She's an—" The patrolman looked confused, even
more so when Satrine flashed open her coat to show her
vest.

"There's been a murder, we understand," Satrine said.

"Well, yes, there has been, it's just . . ." He glanced
back into the alley, and then back at Welling. "This one,
sir. It's, if you pardon me saying so, particularly gruesome."

Satrine was not in the mood for this, and took the
lantern from the patrolman. "You think your stomach
can handle gruesome, Inspector Welling?"

"I haven't had lunch yet." He brushed the patrolman with the back of his hand, and the man got out of the way. He took the lead; Satrine held up the lantern as she entered behind him.

The patrolman had been accurate. The sight was particularly gruesome.

The body—a man—was missing its heart. That was the most prominent feature of the grotesque display, which was notable, given that there were several features that on their own would have stood out. But Satrine's eye unconsciously went to the most shocking element: the cavity in the man's chest where a heart should be.

The man had been stripped naked, all four limbs spread out. His hands had been nailed into the ground. Two extinguished candles, melted down to the base, on either side of the body's head. Blood pooled underneath, filling the cracks in the cobblestone, but the body itself was relatively neat.

"Tell me what you notice," Welling said.

"He was killed here, obviously," Satrine said, noting the blood. She crouched down, looking closely at the hands. "The spikes were driven in while he was still alive." She pointed to the blood underneath the wounds.

Welling nodded. "What else?"

"Ritual," she said. "The candles. The precise method of removing the heart." She pointed to the cuts in the chest: clean lines, sharp blade.

"Meticulous," Welling said. "Not a crime of passion or opportunity." He stood back up, looking around the rest of the alley. "So, Inspector Rainey, what questions does this raise?"

"Are you testing me, Welling?"

"Yes," he said plainly. "Same way I test every partner I have."

"Fair enough," she said. It was—he had known her for less than an hour. "Why kill him in the alley? It seems an unnecessary risk."

Welling glanced about the alley, barely more than eight feet wide. "Out of sight, but hardly private. One could easily be interrupted. He must have had a specific reason. Excellent question. What advantage is there in committing a ritual murder here?"

Satrine recognized this was a legitimate question from Welling, not a rhetorical exercise or test. "There's the advantage of being between a butcher and a barber. If blood seeps out to the street, no one will think too much. Blazes, you could walk out of here in a blood-covered smock, and no one would give you a second glance."

"Presuming legitimate purpose," Welling said, nodding. "What about the other end?"

"It dead-ends on the other side," she said, pointing off into the darkness. "At least, it used to."

"You know the alley?"

"Knew it," she said absently. She ventured deeper into the alley, where little direct sunlight reached.

Welling kept talking, "Even given that the killer could walk out of here, carrying a bloody heart, without drawing much notice, how did they arrive? Or the victim? Did the victim walk in, or was he forced?"

"Unconscious?" Satrine asked. "Drugged?" The alley still came to a dead end, the back of a brick tenement on the other side of the street. The windows on the building were all covered in iron grates and high off the ground.

"Carrying this man unconscious would have taken considerable strength."

"So would driving these spikes into the cobblestone."

"Fair enough," Welling said. "There are no bruises or injuries on the victim's head. What does that tell you?"

"He wasn't knocked out. So drugged. Poisoned, perhaps. Or . . ." The idea was silly, and she shook it off.

"Or—ah!" He cried out in shock.

"What is it?" Satrine hurried back to her partner. He was kneeling next to the body, but his attention was on his hand, which he was flexing open and shut slowly.

"I touched the spike and it . . . I'm not sure." He looked up at her. "It was like I lost all feeling and strength in my hand."

"Magic?" she asked. Cautiously she touched one of

the spikes with her bare finger, and then grasped it fully. "I'm not feeling anything."

Welling raised an eyebrow. "Perhaps it was just a co-incidence." He touched the spike again, and pulled his hand away. "No, definitely not. I don't think we need another test to establish a pattern."

"So it is magic," Satrine said. "Or it involves it."

"Probable," Welling said. "My knowledge on the subject is quite inadequate."

"But how can you—"

"As I told you, Inspector Rainey," he said testily, "I am Uncircled. Untrained. Ability but no skill or discipline."

"But even still—"

"Whatever you are about to say may be true in the general sense, but not in my specific case. And the details of my specific case are not up for discussion at this time." Welling lost his detached affectation. He didn't shout or rave, but filled each word with a deep ocean of long-standing, embittered anger.

"Very well." Satrine let it drop, despite the incredulity of Welling's claim. Even without training, it didn't make sense that someone with Welling's deductive powers would be ignorant of his own abilities. However, since Welling was already willfully ignoring her secrets, it was wise for her to do the same.

She turned back to the body. "You will agree, whatever the spikes are, they are uncommon."

"Certainly," Welling said. "To the point that they clearly have specific purpose."

Satrine, fighting back any urge to wince, touched the skin that had been folded back to remove the heart. "Very specific," she said, lifting the fold of skin. It revealed the remnants of a bright tattoo. Only a small piece was left, a flash of orange and yellow. "If I'm not mistaken, that is the mark of a Circle."

"That settles that point," Welling said. "The victim was a mage."

Chapter 3

MINOX EMERGED FROM THE ALLEY, the bright sunlight forcing him to blink. This wasn't the first time he had come across a dead mage in the course of his duties—there were the three found dumped on a trash barge just a few days before. Something about this one unsettled him, beyond the presence of a new partner.

Inspector Rainey came out into the street and stood uncomfortably close. "This was specifically about killing a mage, wasn't it?" she said in a low whisper. She had homed in on exactly the key point that was troubling him. His instinct told him that the specific identity of the victim mattered less to the murderer than what the victim represented.

There wasn't enough empirical information to match to that feeling, only the removal of the victim's clothing. There could be a host of reasons for a killer to do that.

"Indeed," he told her. He addressed the patrolmen, still waiting at the entrance. "One of you, return to the stationhouse, have them send the bodywagon. The rest, keep the alley clear until it's here." The patrolmen had a brief, unspoken moment of glances, where the implicit pecking order of rank, size, and seniority singled out one to run back to the stationhouse.

"We'll be across there at the teashop," he told the remaining patrolmen. "When the cart gets here, come fetch us." He left them and crossed to the shop—Madam Rosemont's Steeping Pot.

Inspector Rainey was again at his elbow. "Why are we going to the teashop?"

"Two reasons," he explained, though he wished he didn't need to. Nevertheless, Inspector Rainey was proving herself to be adequately capable, even pleasingly inquisitive in the proper ways. That was definitely an improvement over Inspector Kellman, who only wanted a quick resolution to any case that crossed his desk, and thus despised anything complicated, or Inspector Mirrell, who rarely let actual facts penetrate his skull if they didn't fit his initial notion. "The first is I want some literal distance from the scene of the crime from which we can observe the surrounding area with a small amount of discretion."

"And the second?" She asked an obvious question, but that still put her three rungs up from all the sods who never think to ask.

"I need to eat something."

Madam Rosemont's—a cramped wood and iron shack inartfully wedged between two brick tenements—served both reasons, though far from perfect in terms of the second. He found the fare tolerable at best, but the requirements of the first need had to take precedent over the preferences of the second. Minox took a seat at one of the iron tables that pushed outside the boundaries of the teashop proper and into the walkway. Inspector Rainey, looking less than pleased with his decision, took the opposite chair.

"What are we observing, exactly?"

"We are taking a chance on a quirk of human reaction," Minox offered. "Whoever committed the crime has a high degree of emotional connection to it, don't you agree?"

"A ritualized murder where they removed the victim's heart? Do you think?" She said this as if she were making a joke, and indeed the look in her eye was one of bemusement.

Minox failed to see what was funny, exactly. Though that was often the case.

He must have let his irritation show, as her expression sobered. "Sorry, yes, I see your point. You think they'll return now?"

"I think the crowd before was little more than common rabble turning their neck for the spectacle, though the killer may have been in there. But if my suspicions are correct, now that we have given the body its official due—the inspectors have inspected, if you will—now the real nibbles will be placed on the line cast."

"You're talking fishing, yes?"

"Fishing, yes," Minox said. Fish sounded good, though he recalled it rarely being an option at Madam Rosemont's, which was odd, given how they were a scant two blocks from the river. Not a matter of import. A young man, who Minox was reasonably certain was the nephew of the eponymous Madam Rosemont—herself a lifelong spinster—approached their table.

"What can I bring you both?"

"Tea and cresh rolls," Minox said.

"Same," Inspector Rainey told the young man. When he walked away, she shook her head with wry amusement. "I haven't had cresh rolls in a very long time."

"Since you lived in this neighborhood?" She hadn't specifically told him, but her knowledge of the alley, and the regular looks she would give to elements of the area—looks that marked they held deeply entrenched significance to her—gave her away.

"There's no keeping secrets around you, is there?"

"I'm sure some people succeed," he said. "By doing it so well I don't notice."

"You were talking about fishing."

"I was. The crime scene was filled with reverence and meticulous care, but it had another quality that stood out just as strongly."

Inspector Rainey nodded. "Daring."

That was the exact word. Her assessment of her own skills was well founded. "For whatever reason, our killer has chosen to commit a murder that is audacious, even foolhardy."

"Elaborate setup, no easy escape."

"I hypothesize that the reason for that was to prove that they could."

"Just to prove it to themselves? Or do you think it was aimed at the Constabulary?"

"Possibly. Following my theory, our killer wanted us baffled. There's no point in doing that unless you get to see it."

"But now they've seen it."

"At a distance! I would believe that such a person, having now baffled the inspectors, would take the next logical step."

"To observe the inspection closely to see how baffled we are."

Minox couldn't hide his own excitement. Previous partners would not have followed this conversation, nor have cared. Inspector Satrine Rainey possessed a unique mind. Minox dismissed that thought as meaningless— every person had a unique mind. But hers was one of outstanding clarity and character. "Yes, precisely. And what better way than at this moment, after the crowd has dispersed, for someone to show a casual interest in the affair?"

"Whoever walks up to the patrolmen is the killer?" Her voice had the necessary skepticism.

"Of course not," Minox said. "Given the care taken in the murder itself, such a method would be sloppy. And I think our killer is too smart for that."

"So you want to casually observe who, in the corner square, is casually observing?"

Teas and cresh rolls were delivered as Inspector Rainey asked this, so there was no time to adequately form a response. The faint hunger that had struck him when he touched the spike drove him to eat as quickly as possible in polite mixed company. He was used to hunger, the gnawing need that arrived with his magic ability, but the sudden onset of this bout was a new sensation.

The cresh rolls—fried pork sausage and potato wrapped with buckwheat griddlecakes—were serviceable satiation. Inspector Rainey ate her own rolls leisurely.

Inspector Rainey put her first cresh roll down and sipped at her tea. "You never did answer my question."

"You have asked several questions this morning. Do you mean your most recent?"

"Not at all. If it's not for being a mage, why do the other inspectors call you 'Jinx'?"

Minox grit his teeth. This was inevitable. He had made it clear to her that he would not be discussing his Uncircled status, so she would naturally gravitate to the other uncomfortable question. This one, however, had an answer she deserved to know.

"I've held the rank of Inspector Third Class for eight months now. In that time, you are my fifth partner."

"Fifth?" She chewed on her cresh roll deliberately, as if the act of eating helped her swallow the information as well. "I presume the other four weren't promoted out?"

"You presume correctly." Minox held his breath for a moment, building up the strength to continue the narrative. "The first died during an investigation. Not killed in the line of duty, but accidentally struck by a runaway horsecart. The random incident was ignored until my second partner—the morning after the first snow—slipped on ice and broke his neck."

"On the job?"

"Prisoner escort. However, for many of the others at the stationhouse, two points is enough to form a pattern. They told my next partner, during lunch, to be careful, as I was a 'jinx.' He laughed, and consequently choked on his meal."

Inspector Rainey's eyes went wide, and her face quavered in that nebulous expression where either laughter or tears could suddenly erupt.

"And from there it stuck."

"Indeed. My last partner was Inspector Kellman, who clearly did not have a fatal accident."

"A near fatal one?"

"We were arresting a group of smugglers when we were ambushed. Badly outnumbered, I . . . resorted to magic."

"You've said you're untrained." Inspector Rainey said it as a statement of fact, with no level of rebuke or confusion.

Minox lowered his voice to a whisper, involuntarily glancing to either side to see if anyone was listening. His status as a mage was not a secret among the Constabulary, but it wasn't explicitly spoken of, and it certainly was not something he talked of too openly in public. "My use of magic tends to be instinctual. Raw. In this case I released a wide blast of energy, knocking down everyone else in the room."

"Including Kellman."

"Who requested a new partner shortly after the incident." Magic made most people nervous, including Minox himself. He had heard, and even made, arguments against mages like the classic Unseen Knife justification. The apprehension Inspector Kellman displayed was not unexpected. The young horsepatrol officer Minox had been five years ago would have been as troubled by the man he was today.

Inspector Rainey sat quietly, taking further sips of her tea, her face for the first time completely inscrutable. Finally she said, "How much stock does the captain put in this?"

"He's never used the epithet, at least in my hearing. But he cannot ignore the record of my partnerships. And his demeanor was strangely gleeful when he introduced us."

Inspector Rainey gave a strangely wry smile. It was all too familiar—the kind his mother or sisters made at him far too often. A mixture of warm affection with mild, teasing condescension. "You clearly have one fan on the inspectors' floor. I think Miss Pyle might be sweet on you."

That was why. It was an obvious conclusion to make based on the short interaction she had witnessed, no doubt. Minox had to give Inspector Rainey that credit. But she missed the important details.

"Nyla is quite fond of me, as is only proper," he said. "She is, after all, my cousin."

"Oh!" Rainey's face flushed. Mild embarrassment. "Of course. I know all too well about Constabulary families." She bit at her lip for a moment. "How much family do you have in Green and Red?"

"A significant portion," Minox said. "However, at the Inemar station, there is only Nyla, and my sister Corrie, who is assigned to night shift duties." He had no urge to further elaborate his family history. It wasn't relevant to the situation.

"The rest are . . . all over the city?" A slight line of sweat formed at her brow. Whatever secret she was hiding from the captain, the idea that he had family at other stationhouses made her worry. Why would that trouble her? Unless she didn't want her duties as an inspector to be common knowledge in other parts of the city.

Across the river, where her husband had been Inspector. A simple way to test the theory.

"Mostly Keller Cove or East Maradaine. All south side houses."

The muscles in Inspector Rainey's neck relaxed. Clearly, that had been the issue.

There was no need to press it further, not at the moment. She was proving astute and intelligent. If Captain Cinellan insisted he have a partner, she was by far the most tolerable option he had had to date.

Inspector Rainey finished her cresh roll. "Pork sausage is too greasy."

"It usually is," Minox agreed, taking her statement as a cue to change the subject. "I've observed several people loitering in the square, but none have taken more than a passing interest in the alleyway."

"Any you want to take a closer look at?"

"Possibly," Minox said. "First, if you'll excuse the crudity, I need to make use of the water closet."

Inspector Rainey waved him off lightly, saying, "I'm amazed that there are water closets in this neighborhood." Right after she spoke, her face changed, some idea crashing across her thoughts. She leaped to her feet and dashed across the street back to the alley.

Minox had little choice but to follow, the call of nature needing to wait. He dropped a few coins on the table and went after her.

"What is it?" he called as she passed between the two guards, leaped over the body of the victim, and charged into the back of the alley. It wasn't until she stopped at the end that she turned back around and acknowledged that he was there.

"Years ago, this alley led to a few backhouses. No water closets back then."

"Right." Minox nodded.

"So the backhouses are gone." She focused her attention on the ground, which was covered with refuse and trash, most likely thrown out the windows above. She scraped some away with her foot, revealing metal grates in the ground. "But the way to the sewers isn't."

"Are you proposing the killer entered through the sewer, or escaped?"

"Either. Both." She pulled out the grate, which came up easily. So easily it added credence to her theory. She put the grate down and glanced down the hole, covering her face. "I'm not sure, exactly. It's something to consider."

A valid point, Minox had to acknowledge. In fact, Minox wished she hadn't pushed aside the covering refuse so carelessly. A close inspection might have revealed if it had been placed deliberately to hide the killer's method. "It may not currently bring us closer to solving the case, but it certainly could be crucial information." He realized he made that sound more condescending than he had intended. "Good thinking."

"How far down does that go?"

He bent down and peered into the darkness. "Ten feet, perhaps. Though I understand there is layer upon layer of underground, especially in this part of the city." Perhaps it was due to this particular section of sewer not receiving direct use anymore, but the scent was nowhere near as bad as he had feared.

"I heard some stories." She stood back up.

"That might be all they are," Minox conceded.

"What are you thinking?"

"I'm not sure. I want to do an experiment. Are you willing?"

They came out into the street.

Inspector Rainey looked wary. "What do we need to do?"

"Make a call, first," Minox said. He pulled out his whistle again, and gave it four short, shrill blasts. People on the street glanced their way, then went back to their business. The two footpatrol gave him annoyed glances.

A moment later, a Constabulary page came running up. An older one, with blond hair that was a bit longer than preferred. This one would have a hard time making senior page. "What's the word, specs?"

"The word is, we need some eyes, boy," Welling said. He led them over to the mouth of the alley. "Can you see the clock tower of Saint Limarre's from outside this alley?"

"Sure can!" the page said.

"I mean, really see it. See it to the minute."

"You bet!"

Minox was too familiar with overeager pages exaggerating their abilities. "What's the time?"

"Ten bells nineteen."

"Very good." He tapped the shoulder of one of the footpatrols. "I would prefer we not be disturbed. Eyes front, and if the wagon arrives, hold it here until we are finished. Now, if you will be so kind, Inspector Rainey, to join me in re-creating the event."

Rainey had the grace to look intrigued. Even excited. "Fair enough. But are we presuming the victim is grabbed here in the street, or brought in from the sewer, already incapacitated?"

"The latter," Welling said. "That strikes me as the more likely scenario, and what I want to know is how fast, under ideal circumstances, the killer could have done everything he needed to do."

Rainey nodded. "Then we should go to the end of the alley, and you carry me from there."

Minox couldn't hide his smile. Inspector Rainey could definitely be the most useful partner he had been assigned. "Boy, when you hear the whistle, I want you to start marking time. When I blow it again, then stop. If we're all clear, let's begin."

◄━━━◆━━◆━━━►

Minox went down to the end of the alley, Inspector Rainey right with him. "I'm working on the theory that the killer entered the alley from here, with the victim, carried him out to the mouth of the alley, performed the ritual killing, and exited again from here. Is this reasonable?"

Inspector Rainey nodded. "Reasonable enough."

"So we're clear, you will be playing the victim while I will be acting out the killer's part, save causing you actual harm." On a rough estimate of height and weight, Inspector Rainey was almost the same as the victim. For the purpose of this experiment, she was within acceptable tolerances.

"And your theory is that the victim was, at this stage, incapacitated somehow?"

"Yes, exactly."

"So I should be dead weight." Promptly she dropped to the ground in a heap.

Minox was quite pleased that she had reached this conclusion on her own. None of his previous partners had ever understood what he was doing when he tried to work through the physical reality of committing such a complicated crime.

"Wait," Rainey said from her collapsed position. "This isn't right."

"How so?"

"We need to start inside the sewer. The act of pulling an incapacitated body from there would take a significant amount of time."

Minox nodded, impressed. "Excellent point."

"Open the grate." Rainey got back on her feet. Minox had to admit, he was finding this early partnership far more satisfactory than he had imagined would have been possible. Rare was the officer who would willingly go into the sewer system even for the sake of pursuit, let alone for a mere deductive experiment. He pulled open the grate, revealing the dank, fetid tunnel beneath the street.

Inspector Rainey shucked off her boots, coat, and vest, putting them in a neat pile on an abandoned crate. Without any trace of hesitation she removed her blouse and slacks and placed them on her pile.

Minox turned to one side. "That is sufficient, Inspector," Minox said. Her linen underthings were sufficiently modest to maintain some propriety.

"I want to minimize what I ruin here," she said. She peered down the hole. "Once more in." She sat down and lowered herself underground.

Minox paused only briefly to remove his own coat and vest before dropping in after her.

"This is interesting," Rainey said mildly, pointing to the knotted rope that hung from the top of the tunnel. "Fairly sure that isn't typically installed here."

"You spend a lot of time inside the sewers?" Minox asked her.

"In my youth, Inspector," she muttered. "Come on." She went limp, and Minox had to rush to catch her before she fell into the fetid water at their feet.

"You could have given a little warning, Inspector."

"Keeping you on your toes," she whispered, not moving in any other way. "Give the signal."

Minox put the whistle in his mouth and blew. As soon as he did, he hiked Rainey's limp body over his shoulder. He grabbed the knotted rope and struggled to climb.

"Not . . . easy . . ." he choked out.

"I wouldn't imagine."

After a hard slog, he managed to get one hand over the lip of the sewer hole.

"This may be impossible," he said.

"What, exactly?"

"The aperture is too small for me to get out with you over my shoulder, but there's no way to get the necessary leverage to push you through ahead of me. Not with one hand. And I can't imagine a man being strong enough to be able to do so." Unable to hold himself up on the rope any longer, he dropped back to the bottom of the sewer. Rainey coughed hard at the impact, and he put her back on her feet.

"You could have warned me," she said.

"My apologies," he said.

"All right, then." She rubbed at her chest and looked back to the hole to the street. "Our killer could have attached the body to the rope, climbed up, and then pulled up the victim."

Minox agreed with that idea, and, after giving her a nod, quickly climbed the rope. The timing aspect of this experiment had been thrown off, but not so badly that he couldn't glean something useful out of the exercise. Trying to start everything over would just confuse the matter. Press forward when in doubt, that's what Fenner used to say.

Minox surprised himself so much with that thought he almost lost balance at the top of the hole. He hadn't thought about Fenner in some time. A gnawing twist hit him in the gut. He shouldn't be forgetting the old man. He should go see him when he had the chance.

This was not the time. Idle thoughts did nothing but delay what he needed to accomplish. He planted his feet over the hole, and grabbed on to the rope. Hauling up Inspector Rainey was significantly easier this way. In moments he had her at the top, and pulled her out onto the cobblestone.

"You all right?"

"Fine," she said. "Shall we?"

Minox threw her over his shoulder—the stench of the sewer was all over her feet—and hurried down to the mouth of the alley. He laid her down on the ground near the body.

"Next?" she asked.

"Driving the spikes into the hands," Minox said. "Which we will only mime."

"Thank you," she said with a slight smile.

Pretending to hold a spike and hammer in his hands, he played out the actions of striking the spikes into the ground. "Four hits each?" he asked her after he had done the first one.

"Reasonable as anything," she said. He feigned driving the other spike in.

"Now the heart," he said.

"How long does that take?" she asked.

Pretending to hold a blade over her chest, he narrated his actions. "From what I saw, the job was done with four cuts, done with strength and precision. Like so. Chest opened, four more cuts removed the heart itself. And so." He stood up, holding the imaginary heart in his hands.

"That quick?" Rainey asked.

"It would have to be. Then back out the sewer, or just walk out the alley?"

"We're presuming the killer is daring, yes?"

"So walk right out, heart wrapped like he just bought it at the butcher shop?"

"Perfect," Rainey said. Minox blew the whistle again. The page turned around.

"Sweet Saint Heprin!" the boy shouted, his eyes wide as he stared at Rainey.

"Eyes around, page," Rainey said flatly. The boy spun on his heels in fast compliance. Rainey returned to the end of the alley.

"What was that time, boy?"

"Oh, it was . . . twelve and a half minutes. Near as I could tell."

Minox considered this. Too long, too big a window for discovery.

"Twelve and half minutes," he called back to Rainey. "I think that's far too long."

She was at the end of the alley, getting her clothes back on. "I agree. Our theory is flawed."

"How is it fixed?"

Rainey pulled her boots on. "Several ways."

"Earlier you had a theory you didn't tell me."

Rainey had her coat on, and came back out the alley, carrying Minox's own coat. "It was nothing."

Minox clucked his tongue. This wouldn't do. "It is only nothing if it doesn't fit the facts at hand. Does it?"

Inspector Rainey hesitated. "It does, but it . . ." She shook her head.

"It is highly likely I've already considered your possibility," Minox said. "Nonetheless, I would be remiss in not pressing your opinion."

"This is a ritual killing involving a mage, yes? Involving magic." She was leading her idea, holding back. That wouldn't do.

"That's not all you were thinking."

"What if the victim participated willingly?"

Minox acknowledged that was an obvious solution. "It seems unlikely, but we would be remiss to ignore it."

"The other solution is two killers."

"Or three, for that matter."

"Or a small group. Perhaps a group united together in common cause."

"Such as?"

"I was thinking a Mage Circle."

Minox looked back to the space on the ground where the body had been. Ritualization. Dead mage. Circle tattoo desecrated in the process. "An ousting?"

Rainey handed over his things. "Or some sort of power ritual, with a willing sacrifice. Have you ever heard of such a thing?"

"My knowledge of magic rituals or Circle politics, either internal or external, is notably lacking." Minox didn't like having information gaps. He wasn't sold on the theories, not entirely. Something didn't fit, but he had to admit it had enough merit to keep looking into it. "We need to identify our victim to go any further along those lines."

The patrolmen at the mouth of the alley called out to them. The bodywagon from the stationhouse had arrived.

"Come on," he told her. "We've got work to do."

Chapter 4

THE BODYWAGON DRIVER was a small man, barely coming up to Satrine's chin. Her first impression was he was compensating for this by wearing big things: his leather gloves went past the elbows, and the smock he wore over his Constabulary coat covered most of his body. The strangest part of his outfit was his headgear, a skullcap with some lensed device hooked to the front.

"Oyah, Welling," he called out as they approached. Accent from northern Druthal, likely Archduchy of Acora. "You always pull the strange cases, don't you?"

"This could be one of the strangest, Leppin," Welling responded.

Leppin looked at the body, giving a low whistle. "Ain't that a whole piece of truth?" He turned his attention to Satrine. "So you're the new dress who got made inspector, eh?"

"You should be careful who you call a dress with that thing you're wearing, mister."

"Ha!" Leppin said out loud. "She's funny. Let's get this dead guy in the wagon."

Leppin went over to the body, running his fingers on the spikes. He grumbled something incoherent while pulling the device on his cap down over his eyes. He leaned in closer.

"Hammered in?" Welling asked.

"Mighty big hammer at that," Leppin said.

"Like a mining sledge?" Satrine asked.

Leppin ignored her. He flipped one of the lenses around and leaned in closer to the spikes. "I don't know what the blazes these are made of, but look at that. Look!"

Satrine knelt down, looking closer at the head of the spike. "I'm not seeing anything."

"Exactly!" Leppin shifted his weight so he was sitting on his haunches like a rabbit, and focused on Minox. "You take a regular iron spike and drive it into the cobblestone, it's going to take, let's say, at least eight to ten swings."

"Loud swings at that," Welling muttered. He wandered out of the alley over to the wagon.

Leppin pointed to the bright, shiny head of the spike. "Iron would be smudged, dented. A mark from each blow would show."

"There're no marks at all." Satrine almost sat on the ground in thought before she realized it was still covered in blood. She should have worn pants she didn't mind getting dirty. "So two things—either they weren't driven in, in a conventional way, or the metal is so strong it resists marking."

"Mystical," Welling said abstractly from outside the alley.

"Right," Satrine called back. Turning back to Leppin, she said, "The victim is likely a mage, and the spikes of a mystical nature."

"Mage killing." Leppin got to his feet, shaking his head. "End of the day, mage ain't nothing but a man. Dies just as easy."

Satrine got up close to Leppin. "Someone went through a whole lot of trouble killing this one!" She was already done with the sentence when she realized she was staring into his lens device, his eyes enormous. Something about this man's disaffected manner raised up the temperature of her blood.

Leppin calmly removed the device from his head. "We all got our work cut out for us on this one, for sure."

He sidestepped away from her, took a pair of pliers out of the pocket of his apron, and started prying the spikes out of the ground.

"Value," Welling said, still wandering back and forth in the mouth of the alley.

"What's that?" Satrine asked, coming out to him.

"Those spikes. Let's presume they are mystical, too strong to dent and capable of blocking a mage's power."

"What's something like that worth? Is that the question?" Satrine couldn't even imagine. "Who could even make such a thing? And why?"

"Why is easy enough," Welling said. "They were paid for the job. The big question that strikes me is, if our killer invested, presumably, quite a lot of money or effort in acquiring such spikes—"

"Why abandon them in the alley with the dead body?" Satrine finished.

"This case is generating a large number of questions, none of which are adding up to satisfying answers. And they are all, so far, only addressing questions of method. Save speculation, motive has remained untouched."

"We need to know who this mage is to even guess at that."

Welling nodded. "Leppin, do you have the spikes out?"

"Ayuh," Leppin said, emerging from the alley. "Came out damn easy. You want them?"

"Give them to Inspector Rainey. Given their nature, it is best that I have minimal contact with them."

Leppin wrapped the spikes in a cloth and handed them to Satrine. "I'll take him to the examinarium."

"Excellent," Welling said. "He has a tattoo close to the wound, which is likely a Circle Mark. The sooner you identify it, the sooner we can identify him."

"All right," Leppin said. "Anything else you need here?"

"Not that I am aware of," Welling said. "Load him and go."

Leppin and the patrolmen carried the body into the wagon. In moments Leppin was back in the driver's seat, and spurred the horse on.

"Now?" Satrine asked.

"Now, given our lack of further options until we know more about the victim, the best course to follow is the questioning of witnesses."

"Including whoever found the body."

"Yes, of course," Welling said. "Though I've often found those interviews to be unsatisfying."

"Unless finding the body inserts them into the narrative."

Welling's eyes brightened. "A very good point, Inspector. Patrolman, who found the body?"

The patrolman screwed his face in thought. "Who did find him? Oh, right, it was one of the Hoffer kids."

"Did you say Hoffer?" Satrine asked. A shiver went up her back.

"Yeah, you know," the patrolman said, though he clearly didn't know how well Satrine actually knew. "Old Idre herself reported it, but it was one of her brats that found him."

"Where do they live?" Welling asked.

"Up there in that one." The patrolman pointed to the tenement building across the street. That building, Satrine remembered all too well. That building, a crumbling blight on the square, looked like it hadn't changed a bit in twenty years. Not surprising that Idre Hoffer lived up there.

Idre Hoffer. There was a name Satrine had hoped to never hear again.

<hr/>

The last time Satrine had seen Idre Hoffer, the girl was being carted off in a Constab lockwagon, bound for a six-month stay at Quarrygate. At the time, Satrine couldn't think of any happier moment in her life. Idre was sixteen years old. Satrine was fourteen.

When Satrine was nine, Idre had taken a piece of broken glass and cut her until she agreed to give her all the coins she had hustled. She still had a scar along the left side of her back, thick and ugly.

When she was eleven, Satrine spent a winter night

locked in a backhouse. Idre had pegged it shut and threatened her wrath on any other kid who let Satrine out. In the middle of the night, barely able to feel her feet and fingers in the cold, Satrine crawled through the sewer to escape. Idre had thought that was a good laugh.

When she was thirteen, Idre's brother Pio decided he wanted her. Idre held Satrine down for him, her face smashed against the dusty floor of an empty flop. In the same building Satrine and Welling were going into.

Several coats of paint couldn't cover the rot in the walls, the cracks in the plaster. Money and influence may have come to Inemar, Jent and Tannen might be brighter and cleaner, but nothing could be done to heal this building short of tearing it down.

"Do we know which flop?" she asked Welling.

"Fifth floor, southwest."

She led the way up the stairs, every step spotting some place she could tell a story about, few of those stories happy.

The fifth floor stank of piss and rot, with a sting of vinegar mixed in that failed to do anything to wash out the rest of the scents. Graffiti and knife scratchings marked the walls. The doors of the flops were all shut, save one that had no door. Satrine was sure she heard a couple goats in there.

"It gets worse two more floors up," Welling said lightly.

"I imagine. 'Up and west,' as they say."

"This is it," Welling said, pointing to a door, carved and nicked. Satrine couldn't tell if that was the result of years of abuse, or a single, brutal incident, or some combination of both. Satrine imagined someone smashing at Idre's door with an ax.

She knocked twice, the first time too soft because her hand trembled more than she thought. If Welling noticed that, he gave no sign. Shouts of voices came through, mostly young ones, wild cries of excitement.

"What?" one of the more coherent voices from behind the door responded.

"Constabulary," Welling said. "We have some questions."

"Nobody did nothing, stick!"

Welling shrugged at Satrine, as if to say this was going as he expected. "Somebody found a dead body this morning."

The door flew open, and a piggish woman in a thread-bare nightdress came barreling out, her meaty finger targeting Welling's face. "Ain't none of you gonna come in here and hassle my kids!"

Twenty years older, hair more gray than brown, face marked with deep lines—but there was no mistaking Idre. The voice was the same throaty blare, scraped with a razor, and her Inemar accent had calcified into near incomprehensibility.

"Not here to hassle, Missus Hoffer," Welling said, not giving a hair of ground to Idre. "You and your children did the right thing in reporting what you found, and we just want some more details."

Idre's lip curled as she turned to Satrine, barely giving her more than a glance. "You even brought the secretary?"

"This is Inspector Rainey," Welling said. A name, Satrine knew, that would mean absolutely nothing to Idre.

"Inspector?" Idre made a noise of disbelief. "Good on you, skirt."

"We—" Satrine started. Her voice was not there for her. She coughed and tried again. "We need to talk to whoever found the body."

"Oy!" Idre shouted back into the flop. "Who found the corpse?"

"Banky!" someone shouted back.

"Banky did!" A few more joined the chorus.

"Banky!" Idre snapped. "Bring my pipe and get out here!" She wiped her nose with the back of her hand. "Don't suppose either of you carry any *hass* or *phat*?"

Hassper was illegal, and *phatchamsdal* might as well have been. Asking the question itself was almost a crime. Satrine was surprised by the calm stride Welling took it in.

"I'm afraid I only carry Fuergan tobacco," he said, pulling a small pouch out of his pocket. He held it open to Idre. A child, no more than five, presumably Banky, came out of the flop, giving a pipe to his mother. She took a pinch out of Welling's pouch and stuffed the pipe.

"There he is," Idre said, lighting a taper off a candle in her flop. She leaned against the doorframe and took a deep pull of her pipe.

The boy was dark, like his father was Ch'omik or Imach. Satrine glanced in the flop, taking note of the other children. At least six, and to her eye each one had a different father. All of them, including Banky, were dirty and half-dressed. Still, Idre was doing better than Satrine's mother had done. She was still here.

Satrine crouched down to get eye to eye with the boy. "My name's—Inspector Rainey." She stumbled, almost using her given name. "You found that body across the street in the alley."

Banky nodded. "He was naked!" he said with manic glee.

Satrine smiled back. "Yes, he was." The boy clearly thought that was more interesting than that the man was dead. Satrine didn't want to think about what that said about the boy, other than she could easily imagine Idre at the same age saying the same thing. "What time was it? When you found him?"

Banky screwed his face in thought. "Musta been about eight bells or so. Ma sent me to get the milk, and I had to piss so I went in there, and there he was. Dead and naked!"

Welling crouched down next to the boy, put a hand on his shoulder and looked at him with firm, hard eyes. "This is an important thing, Banky. When you found him, was he still bleeding?"

"Oy, stick!" Idre snapped. "What're you asking that for?" Her hand lashed out toward Welling.

Satrine felt no small amount of pleasure grabbing Idre's wrist mid-swing. "Watch your hand, Miss Hoffer." Idre still had plenty of muscle on her meaty arm, but she wasn't stronger than Satrine, not anymore. Idre struggled briefly, but Satrine didn't yield, pushing the offending arm away from Welling. Idre scowled, but didn't say or do anything else.

"Well, son?" Welling asked.

"Oh, and how!" Banky said. "Blood was creeping out from under him and down the alley. It was neat!"

"That's very helpful, Banky." Welling slipped a coin into the boy's hand. "I don't suppose you saw anyone around the body who looked suspicious?"

"Naw," the boy said.

"That whole lot in the butcher shop is dodgy," Idre said.

"What's dodgy about them?" Satrine asked. As soon as she said it, she knew it sounded far more aggressive than she had intended.

"No reason a high-chin skirt like you should care," Idre said. "They're all hands and fingers when you try and buy anything."

"Real shame," Satrine said. "You'd think they'd see you as a pillar of decency."

"The blazes you think you are, stick?" Idre's face was flushed with anger, her beady eyes narrowed.

"Think I'm the new inspector on this block, Hoffer," Satrine said. "And I'm watching you."

Satrine stalked back to the stairs. Welling muttered a quick thanks and farewell and chased after her. He didn't catch up until the third floor. Satrine had pounded down the stairs, heart like a stampede in her chest. She heard nothing from him until he grabbed her shoulder.

"What was that about?"

"Nothing, Welling." She started to go back down the stairs.

"It's not nothing if it impairs our investigations, Inspector Rainey."

"It's nothing, get it?" Satrine said. "Like you being Uncircled. Not up for discussion."

Welling gave a nod of acquiescence. "The murder must have happened just before the boy found the body."

Satrine accepted his immediate change in subject. He was right, she needed to keep her feelings about Idre from affecting her job, in any way. "Streets are usually crowded with the morning business then, right? Hard to sneak about unseen in that."

"Or easy," Welling said. "Crowds so huge, no one notices anything."

"Loud, too," Satrine said. "The pounding of a hammer might not stand out."

Welling scratched at his chin, and started going down the stairs. "Blood was freshly flowing, but the killer had cleaned the body. So the killer might have only left the scene minutes, if not moments before."

"You think he saw the killer? Or killers?"

"I'd be surprised if he didn't, but likely he didn't realize the significance. That doesn't help us find a suspect, but it may be useful. Of course, speculating on a suspect is, at best, highly challenging without identifying the victim."

"Back to the station? Leppin might have figured it out."

"My thoughts exactly, Inspector Rainey."

Minox often found the inspectors' floor to be a far too boisterous atmosphere to engage in serious thought, let alone to give proper contemplation to the cases he was expected to solve. True to form, Mirrell and Kellman were sitting atop their desks, drinking tea and laughing.

"Jinx and Tricky!" Inspector Mirrell called out when he spotted them. "Heard you got a real crazy one."

"Tricky?" Minox asked her.

Rainey shook her head and whispered, "That didn't take long."

"Usually it takes them a few days to come up with a new nickname for someone," Welling said.

"Isn't new," Rainey said. She called back to Mirrell, "What did you hear?"

Mirrell and Kellman both crossed over from their desks. "What did we hear, Kellman?" Mirrell asked.

Kellman laughed and looked at Minox. "We heard that you finally got someone who'll play along with your games, Jinx."

"They are not games, Inspector Kellman." Minox tightened his jaw. "They are a valuable tool of analysis."

Mirrell gave a mirthless laugh. "Which part of that involves your partner running around in her skivs?"

"The pages are fast," Rainey said. "I was counting on getting another hour before that one got out."

"Stories of constablewomen in states of undress travel quickly among young boys." Mirrell didn't look her in the eye.

Her face changed. The hints of roiling anger buried, replaced by a sweet smile. It was utter performance, Minox could see, but it was a well-crafted one.

"Hey, Mirrell, you shouldn't be jealous of Minox here." She leaned in close, casting her eyes to the ground. The very picture of appearing demure, submissive. She whispered, "You know why they called me 'Tricky'?"

His breath quickened, and his face flushed. The man was actually taken in by her performance. "Why?"

She smashed her forehead against his nose. As he was dazed from the blow, she grabbed him by the front of his vest. Before he could react, she kicked out his leg and picked him up off his feet, then slammed his body hard on the floor.

No one else on the inspectors' floor had moved by the time she had sprung back up onto her feet, wiping his blood from her face. "That's why."

"Blazes," Kellman whispered.

Minox didn't appreciate Kellman's coarse language, but he agreed with the sentiment behind it.

"You crazy skirt!" Mirrell shouted, holding one hand over his nose. The other went for his handstick. "I should knock your teeth—"

"Let's not knock any teeth in here," Captain Cinellan said from his office door. "Stand up, Hennie."

"Did you see what she did, Captain?" Mirrell said.

"I see you got your nose cracked, thrown off your feet. Shouldn't let that happen, hmm?" The captain crossed over to Mirrell's desk. "Nice moves, Inspector Rainey. Not on the floor again, eh?"

"As you say, sir," Rainey said.

"So," Cinellan said. "Welling, Rainey. You've got a story to tell me?"

Rainey stepped forward. "Dead body, back in an alley off of Jent and Tannen. Heart cut out, ritual with candles."

"That sounds interesting," Cinellan said.

"Sounds like a freak case," Mirrell added. He was rubbing his face. "Pyle, there any ice in the house?"

"No," Nyla said, crossing past the desk. "Tea, all around? Just cream, Inspector Rainey?"

"Right," Rainey said. "Tattoo on the victim's body indicates he might be a mage. Otherwise unidentified at the moment."

"Real freak case," Kellman said. "Glad you pulled it."

"What's on your boards, boys?" Cinellan asked.

"Closed up the two horsemen in Dentonhill," Mirrell said.

"Closed it wrong," Minox muttered.

"Stow it, Jinx," Mirrell said. "We're still working that thing on the docks. Warrant would be nice."

"Give the Protector something to base a warrant on, and we'll get on it. What's the story on your other case, Welling?"

"I have twenty-five cases, Captain."

"Your actual open case, not the ones you think are—"

"Unresolved?" Rainey offered.

"Exactly," Cinellan said. "As far as I'm concerned, you closed every one of those. And blazing well at that."

Minox knew better than to argue with the captain on this point. "Well, I fear I may be at a loss on that one." The pieces didn't add up on that particular case.

"Can you narrow it down at all?" Cinellan asked. "Was she murder or suicide?"

Minox went with what his instinct told him, even though he couldn't prove it. "I believe it's murder. But I can't prove that."

"Well, you've got a new partner now," Cinellan said. "Go over it with her."

Nyla came over rolling the teacart. "Word came up from the examinarium. Mister Leppin wants to see the two of you as soon as possible."

"Maybe he's identified the body for you," Kellman said. He laughed, in the cruel, derisive way he was prone to. "You didn't figure him out by the dirt of his boots, Jinx?"

"No boots this time, Inspector Kellman," Minox said.

"The man was naked," Rainey added.

"You've got the extra freak case your first time out, Trick," Kellman said. "Aren't you the lucky one?"

Inspector Rainey stepped up to him, but his height made it impossible for her to glower down on him like she had to Mirrell. "You got something to say to me, Kellman?"

"Don't think your head will reach my nose, Tricky."

"Leave it, Rainey," Cinellan said, resigned and tired. "Everyone, get to work. Make the streets a little safer." He went back to his office.

Rainey backed away from Kellman. "I'm not out of tricks, you know."

"I'm sure you're not," Kellman said. Mirrell grumbled something and pulled his partner away to the teacart.

A page bolted out of the stairwell. "Murder! Two dead workers in the sewers! Silver and Dockview!"

"Same old Inemar," Rainey muttered.

Cinellan waved the boy over. "Mirrell, Kellman. You've got this one."

"Saints, Captain." Mirrell still rubbed at his nose. The bleeding had stopped, but it was turning purple. "We shouldn't have to—"

"Get on it!" Cinellan barked. "And you two, get back on your case. And try to close up your old business, Welling."

"As you say, Captain," Minox said. Kellman and Mirrell left, both sneering at Rainey as they passed. She held her ground until they were out of sight.

"So," she said, turning to Minox, all the confrontation in her face melted away. "Where is the examinarium?"

❖ ━━◆◆━━ ❖

The examinarium sat at the bottom floor of the stationhouse, almost as cold as an icehouse. The room was full of tools, instruments, and lenses, not one of which made the slightest bit of sense to Satrine's eye. Her nose was assaulted with the scent of decay, slightly masked by astringent chemicals. Leppin seemed utterly in his element here, grinning like an excited schoolboy as he stood next to the body laid out on his examination table. Behind Leppin, wearing an oversize apron and carrying tongs in both hands, was an actual excited schoolboy.

"What have you learned, Leppin?" Welling asked him.

"About the victim, or the killer?"

"Killer first, since you've got it," Welling said.

"Cuts are surgical. Very sharp instruments."

"We already knew that," Satrine said.

Leppin sneered. "You suspected it. But now you *know*. The point is, the killer knew exactly what to do, where to cut. Look at that." He pointed to the hole in the dead man's chest.

Satrine moved closer so she could see what Leppin was showing them. "What is it that I should be seeing?" The wound was nothing but a mess of blood and cut flesh to Satrine's eye.

"Not a single wasted stroke. It's clean and perfect. That said, I think this is the first time he actually did this."

"That doesn't make any sense," Satrine said.

"You might think so." Leppin snapped his fingers, and the boy grabbed a heavy lens and a lamp. He placed it over the wound and waved Welling over. "Look at that, Minox. The beginning stroke of the first cut." Leppin pointed out the specific location.

"Indeed," Welling said, looking through the lens.

Satrine turned to the other two. "Gentlemen, I haven't made a practice of studying bodies, so I have no idea the significance of this is."

Leppin sighed, giving Satrine the distinct impression he was disappointed in her. "Here. The first incision has more bruising around it, and starts thicker than any other."

"Meaning?"

Welling answered. "Meaning the killer held the blade in place, pressed against the flesh, for a short time before he began the incision."

"Hesitation?" Satrine asked.

"That was my thought," Leppin said. "So you just have to ask yourself, who would know how to make the precise cuts to remove a heart, and have the steady and practiced hand to do it perfectly . . . but might still hesitate with a live human being? You're looking for a doctor."

Two other answers leaped to Satrine's mind. "Or a butcher. Or a barber. The very shops on either side of the alley."

Welling nodded. "Valid points, but what's the motive? Who is the victim?"

"We still don't know," Satrine said.

Leppin coughed to get their attention. "But we have that Circle tattoo. I don't have a complete listing of all Circles and their marks, but—"

"You don't?" Welling asked. "That strikes me as the exact sort of record we should have."

"Should, won't get any argument from me," Leppin said.

Satrine couldn't help herself. "Welling, do you know how many Circles there are in just the city, let alone all of Druthal?"

Welling shrugged. "I'd imagine twenty, perhaps thirty."

So he did have significant holes in his knowledge, especially in this subject. "More like a hundred twenty," Satrine said. "Am I right, Leppin?"

"Ayup. And most of those don't have more than a handful of members."

"There are that many mages in the city?" Welling asked, shaking his head. This was information he clearly had never considered.

Leppin went on. "You got your bigger ones: Lord Preston's Circle, The Grand Chalice Circle, Brave Sun."

"Red Wolf Circle," Satrine said. Any mage or telepath she had met in Intelligence were Red Wolf, the only

Circle she was aware of that worked directly with the government.

"So those I know, and a few others that have major presence in the city, especially this neighborhood." He folded back the skin showing what remained of the tattoo. "Flaming eagle, it looks to me. So if I were to hazard a guess, I'd say the Firewings."

"Then they're who we need to look at first," Satrine said. "They're our best suspects."

"If your theory holds," Welling said.

"We have a theory?" Leppin asked.

"Several at this point," Welling said. "Inspector Rainey has one that this was a magic ritual performed by the victim's own Circle."

"Do you have a problem with that, Welling?" Satrine asked. "If anything, Leppin's information supports it. That moment of hesitation may be because the victim was a close friend."

Welling gave a slight nod of his head. "I'm skeptical of any theory that has the victim as a willing participant."

"Blazes, Welling, if you're not—"

He held up his hand. "But I acknowledge that nothing contradicts your theory so far."

"Too kind," Satrine said coldly. But she had to admit, from what she had seen of Welling, this was almost high praise.

"Of course, without identifying the victim, anything regarding motive is rampant speculation." He turned to Leppin. "We're going to need—"

"Charcoal sketches," Leppin said. He snapped at his boy again, who ran to a cluttered desk in the corner of the room. "I had them done already." The boy grabbed a few paper sheets and scurried over to Satrine. Satrine took them.

"Your work?" she asked the boy. They were all decent representations of the dead man's face.

"Yeah," the boy said. "Is it true you took your clothes off?"

"That's enough," Leppin said, grabbing the boy's head and shoving him back toward the desk.

Welling coughed uncomfortably. "Well, plenty of work for us, then. Which first, butcher and barber, or Firewings?"

"Firewings," Satrine answered, surprised that it was even a question. "If we can learn who the victim is, then we have a better sense of what we're looking for in the butcher shop."

"Well-reasoned," Welling said through tight lips.

"Do they have a house or something in the neighborhood?" Satrine asked.

"They do," Welling said. "About five blocks from the crime scene, I believe. Boy, have a clerk pull the Firewing file. They can brief a page and send him to us at Missus Wolman's stand out front."

"Missus who?" Satrine asked.

"A necessary stop."

Leppin spoke up. "Do you still have those spikes used to pin the victim down?"

"Here," Satrine said, taking them out of her coat pocket. "You think you might figure something out about them?"

"Worth looking into. Give me one," Leppin said. "You might learn something out there with the other one." Satrine did as he asked, pocketing the one she was keeping.

"All right, Inspector," she said to Welling. "Let's go meet the Firewings."

The look on her partner's face was one of distinct nausea.

Chapter 5

SATRINE SIMPLY WASN'T GOING to be able to eat every time Welling did, if this was the way he ate every day. As soon as they walked out of the stationhouse he crossed the street over to the cookstand.

"Fast wrap if you please, Missus Wolman," he said to the woman in the stand. He turned to Satrine. "You want one?"

"Saints, no," Satrine said. "We just had cresh rolls."

"Did we? I'm famished."

Satrine watched the woman toss a flat strip of dough on her grill. She reached into a bowl filled with cooked meat, cold with congealed fat, and threw it next to the dough.

"What is that?" Satrine asked.

"It's meat," the woman said indignantly.

Satrine wasn't going to let that suffice. "Lamb? Beef? Pork?"

"That's right," she said, glaring at Satrine. She flipped the dough and stirred the meat around, letting the grease render down. She focused her eye at Welling. "You getting to bad ones today, Inspector?"

"Trying, Missus Wolman."

"That's one of the bad ones," Satrine indicated the simmering meat. "You don't even know what it is."

"It's meat," Welling said. That seemed to be answer enough for him.

"Aren't you curious?" She sniffed at it. "That is rancid. Or kidneys. Or both."

"I have enough to think about," Welling said.

The woman scooped the pile of meat into the dough—now a finished flatbread—and rolled the whole thing off the grill. "Here you are, Inspector."

Welling dropped a few ticks on the counter. "Very obliged. Inspector Rainey, after you." He bit greedily into the wrap.

Watching him eat it made Satrine's stomach turn. "Did you know that in Poasia eating in public is a crime on the same level as murder?"

"I did," Welling said. "One of many reasons not to live there." He took another bite, juice dripping down his chin.

"Lovely," Satrine said.

A page ran over to the cookstand, fortunately not the same one who had counted the time in the alley. This one was tall and muscular; he looked almost ready to become a cadet.

"Inspectors?" he said, crisp and serious. "Senior Page Henterly reporting." This boy certainly was running for cadet.

"Go ahead, Page," Welling said. "What's your report?"

"I've been briefed on the contents of the file regarding the Mage Circle dubbed 'Firewings.'"

Forget cadet, this one was going for station captain.

"The Circle is fully acknowledged by the Royal Registry of Guilds and Associations, founded in 1045. Their founding chapter is located in Kyst, but they have chapterhouses of acceptable standing in several cities, including Maradaine—"

"Henterly," Welling said curtly, "first, where is their chapterhouse?"

"They have three within the bounds of the city, but the address of the most local one is Jewel 817. I can provide directions or lead you personally."

"I know Jewel Street, Henterly," Welling said. "Brief us on what we can expect from them. Members, goals, charter, and so forth."

Henterly nodded, though he looked slightly uncomfortable. "The Firewings have exercised their various rights of privacy, in full accordance with the rules of the Royal Registry of—"

"Yes," Satrine snapped. "What can you actually tell us?"

Anger flashed in Henterly's eyes, white hot at Satrine, and he focused back on Welling. "In full accordance with the rules of the Royal Registry. Member names are not disclosed. Charter is not disclosed. We have no record of associations with the Firewing Circle, nor do we have record of arrests or altercations involving a known current member."

"That's a lot not disclosed," Satrine said.

"They have a right to privacy," Welling said. Satrine shrugged, certain that there was a records room over at Druth Intelligence that had a file on every Circle in Druthal with every bit of information not disclosed. Right to privacy was a very different matter over there.

Welling took another bite of his wrap. "Is that all?"

"There were some notes regarding deceased members. The only ones of note involved the Circle Feuds of 1212. I have memorized—"

"Not necessary right now," Welling said. "Write the salient points down and deliver it to Miss Pyle on the inspectors' floor for my attention. Dismissed."

Henterly gave a sharp salute and went back inside the stationhouse.

"That was useless," Satrine said. "Except we have the address now."

"Which is perfectly useful," Welling said. "But the rest, not entirely useless. They have invoked full rights of privacy, for one."

"Most Mage Circles do." Though she had only tangential experience—a few Red Wolf associates, mostly.

"To some degree, but even to the extent of charter and roster is, I believe, uncommon. And they have maintained a clean face, at least as far as our stationhouse is concerned. Given that their chapterhouse is in our district, it is unlikely they could maintain a clandestine, illegal agenda without us getting wind of it." He signaled for them to start walking.

"What about the Feuds?" Satrine had read some news of the Circle Feuds when it happened three years ago, but as it had stayed confined to the south side of Maradaine, she didn't pay it much mind. A handful of Circles were involved in some sort of feud that boiled into the streets.

"I did not investigate any specific aspect of that at the time. I know that mages of several Circles—I presume the smaller ones—were killed in it. That Firewings had members involved is not distinctive, nor does it give us much insight."

"Unless this is connected to the Feuds somehow."

Welling shrugged, as if considering it. "It's not a theory I've dismissed."

"That sounds dismissive."

"Perhaps so."

"Are you trying to be deliberately ignorant of Circles and mage matters?"

Welling was taken aback. "Absolutely not. However, I've reached the conclusion that our killer—or killers—is most likely not a mage of any sort."

"And how did you decide that?"

"Consider the nature of the spike used in the murder."

"It seems magical in nature."

Welling's eyes lit up as he snapped a finger. "Not so. Just the opposite, in truth. It is anti-magical."

"Is that a real word?"

"If not, it needs to be. Consider the fact that the most brushing contact with it left me weak and dizzy. The prolonged contact necessary to subdue and bind our victim would be intolerable. Therefore, our killer cannot be a mage. The Firewings are therefore not going to prove a useful avenue of investigation."

"You don't want to do this, do you?" she asked.

Welling stopped walking and chewing, and gave Satrine a strange regard. "Why do you think that, Inspector Rainey?"

"You've been noticeably out of sorts since we first decided to come here."

"We have only been in acquaintance for three hours, Inspector Rainey. I would be surprised if you could determine that in so short a time."

"Aren't we supposed to make quick assessments of people, Inspector?" she asked.

"And what is your assessment?"

"Would you agree that the most logical action right now is to go to the Firewings chapterhouse? If for no other reason than to help identify our victim?"

Welling made a face that reminded Satrine of pulling out her daughter's tooth years ago. "Granted."

"Yet you seem to be deliberately delaying going."

Welling nodded in acquiescence, taking another bite of his wrap. "Another block to Jewel, and then we turn west."

"You don't want to see any Circled mages, do you?"

His voice dropped low. "It's me they won't see." He quickened his pace, eating the last of the wrap.

"Of course they'll be uncooperative, Welling. Most Circles want nothing to do with Constabulary." Since protecting member mages from spurious legal action was a primary function of Circles, not cooperating with law enforcement was standard business.

"Me, especially." He pressed his lead, and Satrine hurried up to catch him.

"Trust me, Welling," Satrine said. "They won't be any nicer to me. I'm sure — " She crashed into a man carrying a pile of books. The man hit the ground, books scattered all over the walkway. "Sweet saints, I'm so sorry, sir."

The man, a narrow-faced young man with short hair and spectacles, stood up quickly, brushing himself off. "Not at all, lady, not at all. I was carrying far too much, as you can see." He started collecting the books on the ground.

"Let me help you." Satrine started picking up the books closest to her. The title of one of them caught her eye. "My goodness. *Lost Poems of the Sarani*?"

"You know it?" the man asked.

"Know it?" Satrine smiled warmly. "This book saved my life."

The man's eyes went wide with surprise. He looked delighted to hear that. "Really? Tell me!"

"This book—it's a long story, you don't—"

"No, I do!" The man was breathing heavily with excitement. Welling had slowly returned to the vicinity, but he kept a wary distance.

"Well, I—I was a street girl, just a few blocks from here. And I was sitting on the corner when Old Man Plum threw it at me—I mean that, he threw it at me."

"Old Man—that was my grandfather!" He shuffled the books in his hands to be able to offer one to her. "Nerrish Plum."

"Satrine Rainey. So do you still run his bookshop down there?"

"I've just recently taken it over. But tell me, then what happened?"

"He yelled at me. He said, 'You stop wasting your time sitting and causing a nuisance. You read that instead!'"

Plum laughed. "Sounds like him. But it saved you?"

"Well, I had the book, then. I couldn't read it at first, of course. But I kept it, and used it to teach myself to read."

Plum nodded, his tone now more muted. "Of course. That would have saved your life."

"I still have the book."

"That's excellent." He took the books from her, completing his pile. "He would have been very pleased to know he had that effect on someone's life."

Welling edged closer. "Inspector Rainey? We really should continue."

"Of course, Inspector," she said. "A real pleasure, Mister Plum." She shook his hand again, and continued down the street with Welling.

"You're smiling quite broadly, Inspector," Welling said. "It's a bit disturbing."

"A rare happy memory of this neighborhood, Welling," she told him. "Don't worry, they're unlikely to come up often."

"It is odd, though," Welling said. "He seemed to be excited to hear your story about the book, but almost disappointed in the actual story."

She shrugged. "An old man throwing books at a child is more or less the climax."

Welling nodded. "So correct me if I make any mistakes."

"All right," Satrine said, not sure where he was going with this.

"You grew up in this neighborhood, but haven't been here since adolescence. Self-taught street girl, and this was in the 1190s, so at the height of wartime scarcity. A fair amount of scrapping and scraping to stay alive. Probably more than one altercation with Miss Hoffer."

"You've been paying attention," Satrine said.

He took this as a sign to continue. "At around the age of fifteen, you left Inemar, in an atypical way. I couldn't possibly ascertain the specifics at this point, but I'm willing to wager that it was some form of recruitment into Druth Intelligence."

"Fourteen," Satrine said, trying to keep a straight face. She wondered how much else he had figured out.

"Of course, that is not the secret you are keeping from Captain Cinellan," Welling said. "But it does explain your skillset, and his interest in taking you on at this rank without previous Constabulary experience."

"If it concerns you so much, Welling—"

"It doesn't," Welling said. "I am reasonably certain that your secret does not present a danger to the Constabulary or myself, and I've already observed sufficient competence on your part that I have no desire to root it out."

Satrine took that as a cue to let the subject drop and walk in silence.

Jewel 817 was an unremarkable brick row house, nearly identical to the rest of the ones along the block: three stories high, iron-grated windows, gabled roof. The only thing making it stand out was the small flaming hawk painted onto the front stoop—easy enough to notice, so someone looking to hire one of their mages could find it easily, but not so ostentatious that the locals on the block would get too riled.

Satrine couldn't remember if there had been any Mage Circle chapterhouses around her blocks when she was a child. If there had been, it simply wasn't part of her world at the time.

"This is the place," Satrine said.

"So it is," Welling said. He stood still at the bottom of the steps. Satrine gave him a moment, but realized he wasn't going to move without action on her part. She went up to the door and pounded on it.

Silence from within.

Welling pulled his pipe out from his pocket, not moving from his spot on the street.

Satrine pounded on the door again. "Constabulary!"

"Now they'll never answer," Welling said. He pinched some tobacco from his pouch and put it into the bowl.

A small panel in the door opened up, just enough for Satrine to see a hint of a man's face.

"What?" the man asked.

"We're inspectors from the Constabulary House, investigating the death of—"

"Do you have a warrant?"

"No, we just have—"

"Go away." The panel slammed shut.

Satrine pounded on the door. "We just have a few questions for you!"

No answer.

"If you just talk to us—"

"They don't want to talk to us," Welling said.

"You have a better idea?"

"I do," Welling said. "But I don't like it."

"Let's hear it."

Leaning against the wall, Welling put the pipe in his mouth and held his finger over the bowl. He closed his eyes for a moment, and then a burst of flame came out of his finger. He took a slow toke from the pipe, and blew it out in rings.

"That's your idea?"

"Wait," Welling said.

The door flew open, and three people—two men and one woman—came out onto the front steps, nearly barreling into Satrine. They barely glanced at her, then pounded down the stairs to Welling.

"What the blazes do you think you're doing?" one of the men said. He was much older than the other two, and was definitely not the one who answered the door before.

"Getting your attention," Welling said. He took another puff of smoke. "We need to speak with you about a Constabulary matter."

"We will do no such thing," the old man said. "And why are you—"

"He's in a constab uniform!" the woman said. Her eyes were wide, but Satrine couldn't read her face beyond that. Dark eyes, dark hair, long and elaborately braided. She wore a blue corset, and a sheer shawl over her bare shoulders—typical for the southern archduchies, matching her accent, but near scandalous in the streets of Maradaine—so her Firewing tattoo was boldly visible over her heart.

Satrine came down the steps. "I'm Inspector Satrine Rainey, this is my partner, Inspector Minox Welling. We're investigating."

"Partner? Inspector?" The old man's face filled with rage, his teeth grinding. He turned back to Welling, almost spitting in the inspector's face. "How could you be one of them? Who would allow that?"

"No one tells me what I can't do," Welling said calmly, but there was a stern undercurrent of anger that Satrine heard in his voice.

"He's Uncircled!" the young man said with a laugh. He wore just a vest and cotton pants, also showing off his Firewing tattoo. "That's why he made such a messy noise."

Welling's face twitched, and Satrine also saw her partner's hand inch toward his handstick. She moved closer to the group of mages. "We just have a few questions for you. This morning a man was—"

"Questions?" the old man said. He spun to face Satrine, and she swore the light around him dimmed as he did so. "Why should we help you with anything?"

Several people on the street were marking them all now, some coming out of shops to see what the commotion was.

"A man was murdered," Satrine said flatly.

"And?" the young man said. "You have no arrest warrant, so why are you bothering us about it?"

"Because the dead man may be one of your Circle," Welling said.

All three mages turned back to Welling. "What do you mean?" asked the woman.

"The body was found this morning, over at the corner of Jent and Tannen. We believe he may have been a member of your Circle."

The old man lowered his voice, a growling whisper. "Why do you think that?"

"A partial tattoo over his chest," Satrine said.

"Why partial?" The woman asked the question, her voice quavering. As much as Satrine hated to acknowledge it, she could read this woman was the weak link of the three, the one most likely to be of any help to them.

"Because his heart was cut out," Satrine said. She pulled the charcoal sketch out of her pocket and handed it to the woman. The woman needed only a glance at the picture before her face melted in grief and rage, a guttural scream releasing from her throat. A wave of force came with her voice, knocking Satrine off her feet, shattering glass down the street.

"Jaelia!" the old man shouted. He grabbed her, holding her tightly. Her scream dampened to muffled tears.

"So you know the victim," Satrine said, getting back on her feet. She felt like she had just been hit by a horse. A glance around the street showed her that most of the rest of the crowd around them were similarly affected, some of them further injured by falling or broken glass.

"His name is Hessen Tomar," the young man said. "He was her husband."

"Is that all you needed?" the old man asked harshly.

"No, that's not all—" Welling started.

"Well, that's all there will be," the young man said.

"We need to know more about Mister Tomar," Welling said. "Enemies he had. Who might have wanted to—"

"No!" the woman—Jaelia—shouted. "Don't you dare talk of him."

"Missus Tomar," Satrine said, "I know what you must be feeling, so . . ."

"You tell me my husband's heart has been cut out and you think you know what I'm feeling?" she shouted. "Both of you get out of here." She sneered at Welling. "Especially that one."

Jaelia Tomar went up the steps of the house, the other two behind her.

"Oy!" someone shouted from across the street. "You sticks gonna let her walk away?"

People were forming a crowd around the house. Some of them were holding brooms or other heavy items.

"She just wrecked the street!"

"Who's gonna pay for my window?"

"She's not going anywhere!"

This was getting ugly quickly. Satrine saw out the corner of her eye that the other Firewings were about to react with anger. If they did more magic on the street, the whole situation would explode into a riot.

"Back off!" she shouted. "This is a Constabulary matter."

"Then do your blasted jobs!" someone in the crowd shouted. "Arrest her!"

Welling was at Satrine's shoulder, his handstick out. "We'll do our duty, people. Go about your own."

The mages continued to go into the house, ignoring the situation behind them. Something flew out from the crowd—a rock, a beet, Satrine couldn't tell—striking Jaelia Tomar in the head. She spun around, her hands splayed out. Green light formed around her hands, burning in a hot flash.

Satrine sprung up the steps, her handstick out, charging at the woman. Before she was able to close the distance, the light burst out of the mage's hands.

Satrine was hit, full in the chest. It didn't hurt her, didn't slow her down. Two more steps and she was on Jaelia, handstick pressed against the woman's neck. She pushed Jaelia up against the doorframe. The other two mages stood in shocked silence, staring at Satrine in amazement.

"Rainey?" Welling asked from the bottom of the steps. "Are you all right?"

"Fine," she said. She turned back to Jaelia, stick hard at her throat. The woman's face was a shifting mix of fear, shock, grief, and anger.

The crowd all cheered. They wanted to exact vengeance on Jaelia, and they were getting that through Satrine. She wasn't happy about giving an angry mob what they wanted, but she had no other choice. "Get rid of them, Inspector."

"You heard her, people," Welling said to the crowd. "Disperse and be about your business."

The crowd grumbled. Satrine heard some disturbing snippets. "Blazing mages." "Nothing but trouble." "Should burn the lot of them out."

"What are you?" Jaelia asked Satrine.

Satrine didn't know what to make of that question. "I'm arresting you, Missus Tomar. Consider yourself bound by law as of this moment," Satrine said. "I'm very sorry for your loss, but that's no excuse for your actions."

Jaelia shook her head. "No, no . . . you . . . you should have been . . . you just kept coming. How?"

Satrine realized there was a warm sensation in her pocket. The spike. It must have protected her from Jaelia's magic. She lowered her handstick and stepped away from the woman. "That's none of your concern. Inspector, if you would be so kind as to call the lockwagon." Welling took out his whistle and gave a series of sharp blows.

"You're not taking her away!" the old man said.

"She's under arrest," Satrine said. She took Jaelia by the elbow, who made no attempt to resist. "And you better not try and stop us, sir, or we'll have to take you in as well."

"But if you take her from here, she . . ." The old man trailed off.

"She'll what?" Welling asked. He came up the steps. "If you have something to tell us about all this, now is the time!"

"We have nothing to say to you," the young man said. "But you will regret it if you take her from here."

"Damn it!" Welling snapped. "One dead, one arrested, and you won't help us?"

"This is our own matter," the young man said.

"Tell us something! We're trying to help you," Satrine said. These mages seemed addicted to their secrets.

The young mage looked at Jaelia, and then at the two of them and sneered. "Some help." He stormed back into the house.

The old man still stared at Satrine, shaking his head. "Please do not do this."

"We've no choice," Satrine said.

"If you find you have something to share," Welling said, producing a small printed card from his pocket, "we can be reached at the stationhouse."

The old man growled, and the card turned into ash in Welling's hand. He then turned to Missus Tomar, "Jaelia, go along and give them no further reason to harry you. We'll contact counsel and have you home in short order." He went into the house, slamming the door behind him.

"This actually went better than I had hoped," Welling said. He walked down to the street, calmly smoking his pipe again.

"You'll have to explain to me how you thought this would have gone."

"We have a name for our victim. We're bringing in a clean arrest, even if not for our case. And neither of us is dead."

"A clean arrest?" Satrine asked. "This is anything but—I'm really very sorry, Missus Tomar. I wish this wasn't necessary, but you did force our hands here."

"It's all fair," Jaelia whispered. "I'm sorry I tried to kill you."

Welling gave Satrine a quizzical look. "How did she not—" He stopped, realization dawning on his face. He nodded, not saying another word.

Satrine sat Jaelia on the stoop. "Welling, go see if the lockwagon is coming."

He glanced down the street. "I think I can see it."

"Go meet up with it, would you?"

Welling hesitated. He opened his mouth to speak, then closed it. He gave Satrine a crisp nod and jogged off.

"My husband is also Constabulary," Satrine told Jaelia.

"How wonderful for you," Jaelia said, her voice dull and empty.

"Two weeks ago he was ambushed on the job," Satrine said. "Beaten within an inch of his life, and thrown in the river. By the grace of whatever saints were looking over him that night, he managed to survive, but . . ." Her voice caught. Jaelia Tomar was now focused fully on her. "He's not the man he was. I don't think he ever will be again."

"But he's not dead."

"No," Satrine said. "Though to be honest with you, had he just died, that would have been cleaner, you know? I'd know he was dead, and that was it. The man that my husband was is dead, but his body is still alive."

"I'd rather have my husband alive than this, Inspector."

"I know, Missus Tomar," Satrine said. "I keep telling myself I should be grateful. But every day, I have to tell myself."

Jaelia Tomar scoffed, but said nothing more.

"Anything you could tell us, Missus Tomar, about enemies your husband may have had. People he was dealing with. Anything that could lead us to his killers."

"Killers?" Tomar asked. "More than one?"

"It's possible. Do you know anything?"

"There had been some heated letters exchanged with a member of another Circle. I don't know who or from where, but—"

"Oy!" A shout pierced across the street. The lock-wagon was pulling up, and a few members of the earlier crowd were gathering back around. Satrine figured they wanted to make sure they were getting their full measure of justice. Or that they enjoyed seeing someone get hauled away.

"We're ready," Welling said, walking back over.

The wagon driver came down off the wagon, shackles in hand. "This the one?" he asked, looking at Tomar.

"That's right," Welling said. "Take her down to the station. We'll meet up with you there."

"No ride along, Jinx?" the driver asked. He shook his head. "Bad procedure, mate." He stepped over and lowered his voice. "I'm not carrying mage shackles, just so you know."

"Can't be helped," Welling said, not looking at the driver. "We've got further business. Isn't that right, Inspector?"

"Right," Satrine said. The driver came over and shackled Tomar. "We'll be back by later to follow up on this one."

"You're going to have to tell me the charges at least," the driver said.

"Assault on a Constabulary officer," Welling said. "And disruption of the peace."

"Disruption?" the driver asked, glancing over to the Firewing chapterhouse. "You really gonna go with that, Jinx?"

Minox gave a nod of his head over to the annoyed crowd. "It's actually quite apt."

"Take her out of here!" someone in the street yelled.

"Take the whole lot!"

"That's enough!" Welling snapped back at the crowd. "She's arrested, shackles on. Go about your business."

The shackles were on, and the driver was taking her up into the wagon. The woman looked defeated, broken, staring at the street while shuffling to take her seat. Satrine felt she should say something, that this was her fault. Jaelia Tomar didn't seem to be too interested in any comfort or connection Satrine had to offer, though.

"Best be quick about your business, Jinx," the driver said as he locked Tomar inside the wagon. "You know the boys in the pens don't like to wait around."

"That's their problem," Welling said. "Ride off."

"Hmph," was all the driver offered in response. He got back up on the wagon. A few people in the crowd cheered, but for the most part they had lost interest.

"Do you still think the Circle killed their own man?" Welling asked.

"I'm not sure what to think," Satrine said. "There's more going on than they're admitting."

"That is quite obvious."

Satrine scowled at him. "I don't suppose you observed anything more useful you'd like to share?"

Welling screwed his face. "They were not directly responsible for Tomar's death, they were all surprised by the news. The old man had already suspected something had happened to Tomar. They're all afraid of something, and were before we arrived."

"Not hard to imagine what," Satrine said. "All their neighbors probably want to burn them out."

"No," Welling said. "They showed no concern over the crowd at all." He closed his eyes. "I think they're afraid for Missus Tomar's safety."

"Do they think we'll torture her or something?"

"No," Welling said. "If I were to hazard a guess . . ."

"Hazard, by all means."

"They're afraid of something we can't protect her from."

A thought crossed Satrine's mind. "Mage shackles?"

"They keep a mage from using their magic. Uncommon, but the station has a couple pairs."

"Like the spikes?"

Welling's eyebrow went up. "No. I've . . . I don't think they are the same." His face screwed in thought, but then he shook his head, like he was dismissing the idea. "Come on, the butcher shop awaits."

Chapter 6

MINOX FELT NO SMALL annoyance at his earlier dismissal of the butcher shop as a source of information. It was even a strong source for a suspect. He realized he had based that decision entirely on its overt obviousness. He had already made the presumption that the alley had been chosen out of significance to the killer that was either magical or ritualistic, and had chosen to ignore the more mundane reason of proximity.

He contemplated this amateurish error on the walk over to the butcher shop, chewing on roasted nuts he had bought from a pedalcart vendor. Inspector Rainey had made an idle comment about how much of his weekly salary he must spend on food. He ignored it—he knew full well sustenance was his single greatest expense.

"It does seem too convenient, doesn't it?" Inspector Rainey asked.

"The butcher shop?" he replied.

"Exactly."

"I think so, but the points match a bit too well to ignore." He didn't say this with conviction. He wasn't very convinced at all this was worth pursuing. The truth was there was nowhere near enough information to make anything more than educated stabs in the dark. That was not the kind of investigation he liked to run.

"Our victim seemed to have rivals in another circle. I think that's what we need to look at."

That was interesting. "She told you that when I stepped away?"

"She said there were letters, but she didn't know from whom, though."

"Unlikely." He could explain to her how, since both Tomars were in the Firewing Circle together, the likelihood of Jaelia Tomar knowing of an enmity between her husband and another Circle, but not knowing which Circle, was so low it was not worth considering. But he had grasped enough of how Inspector Rainey thought to know she had already made the same assessment. She nodded in agreement, solidifying his deduction.

It did all line up with the theory he was formulating: this was not just a murder, but an opening volley to a larger action. Possibly not as large as a full Circle Feud, but he couldn't dismiss it. Another amateurish error on his part. Inspector Rainey was correct. He was deliberately avoiding such obvious points of investigation, especially involving Circles. He couldn't let that happen anymore.

The butcher shop, Minox noted upon this approach, was Brondar & Sons Meats and Chops. "Meats and Chops," Minox thought, was a redundant statement. Not that it was surprising. Most signage in this part of town barely used words at all, let alone correctly.

"Hey, hey!" an older man called out as soon as they walked in the door. He stood, a huge, muscular figure at the main chopping block counter. His gray hair and long mustache drew Minox's eye, overshadowing any other feature of the man's face. "We got some sticks coming in here!" His tone was jovial, but it held an undercurrent of hostility Minox could easily read.

Inspector Rainey stepped forward, her arms wide, giving the man a broad smile with bared teeth. "You never get any sticks in here before or something?"

"Doesn't happen very often," the old man—presumably the Brondar of the signage—said with a scowl.

"Sure it doesn't," Rainey said. "But it's not every day you get a dead body right next door to you."

"Boys!" Brondar called to a back room. "Which one of you is bringing out that pork?"

"Gunther is!" a voice yelled from the back.

"Joshea is!" another yelled.

"Joshea!" the old Brondar yelled back. "Bring the blasted pork!"

"Sir," Minox said, stepping closer to the counter. "We do have a few things to ask you."

Mister Brondar picked up a large cleaver. "I'm sure you do. You ever serve?"

"Excuse me?"

Mister Brondar held up one of his muscled arms for the two of them to see. He had a crossed sword tattoo on his bicep, with nine hash marks underneath it. "Nine years I wore the Gray." Druth Army colors. "Served in the war in the Islands. You look too young to have made that."

"I was," Minox said. "I've served in the streets, though."

"Constabulary." Mister Brondar snorted. "That's not service." He gave a scornful look at Rainey. "You did nothing either."

"Four years in Gray and Green," Rainey said. "They don't ink us for that." She used the uniform colors—even though she likely never actually wore an Intelligence uniform—since he would probably respect it more. Army men tended to think "service" meant to country, to Druthal. Serving the city of Maradaine didn't mean much to them. A mindset Minox couldn't understand, especially since it was everything to his family, serving in Constabulary, Fire Brigade, Yellowshields, River Patrol, and Hospital Wards.

The man released a huge laugh. "That's very good, stick woman." He slammed the cleaver onto his cutting board. "I do my time for Druthal. My boys, all of them, they do their time in the Gray. Joshea!" So it was one of those families. In some ways, just like Minox's.

A young man—only a few years younger than Minox himself—came out from the back carrying a large side of meat. "Got the meat here, Pop. Don't have to yell." Dark hair, cropped short in military style. He didn't mimic his father's style in facial hair, so in comparison his face was narrow and drawn.

"Always have to yell, Joshea," the old man said. "Show these sticks your arm."

"Constabulary?" Joshea asked, looking at the two of them for the first time. His voice cracked slightly, Minox noted, likely out of fear. The only question was, was Joshea Brondar afraid for a real reason? Minox found that a Constabulary uniform solicited far too much unfounded fear.

The old man took the meat from his son and tossed it on his block. "Yes, yes, the sticks are here to give us trouble over the dead whoever in the alley. Show them your arm."

"Pop, I don't think . . ."

"Sir, it isn't necessary for him to—" Inspector Rainey started.

"Damn and blazes, boy!" the old man shouted, cutting her off. "Pull up your blasted sleeve and show the sticks you served!"

"That doesn't matter," Minox said, even though Joshea was rolling up his sleeve. His muscular, scarred arm had the same tattoo as his father, though only three hash marks underneath it.

"Doesn't matter?" the old Brondar asked, picking up the cleaver and slamming it down on the cutting block again. He glowered at Minox as he positioned the meat on the block. "You stand on a blasted beach with Poasians charging at you, and then tell me it doesn't matter."

"Pop!" Joshea shouted. Minox felt a wave of anger come off the young man, hot and passionate.

"Don't you snap at me, Joshea." The old man cut a hunk of meat off—a clean, perfect cut, despite his attention being entirely on his son. Minox noted the man's mastery with the cleaver. Another cut, and then the cleaver was being pointed at Minox and Inspector Rainey. "We Brondars have given, sticks. Given plenty. I had five sons, and three stand here with me now."

"That's a very pretty speech, Mister Brondar," Inspector Rainey said. She moved in closer while he pounded out perfect chop after perfect chop. "We still have a dead body next to your shop to ask you about."

"I've got nothing to say," the old man said.

Inspector Rainey's hand shot out, under the old man's falling cleaver. It was already coming down hard and fast, a clean cut through her fingers. The blade stopped, though, just a breath above Rainey's knuckles.

The old man looked at Rainey, horror in his eyes. The muscles in his arm were stiff and still, sweat dripping from his face. Minox sensed something else, though. He wasn't sure what. "Why the blazes you do that, stick woman?"

"Get your attention," Rainey said calmly. "Now I have it. You will answer our questions."

"You're crazy!" His arm was still held in the exact position, blade hovering right over her hand.

"There's a door that goes out here into the alley, isn't there?"

The old man moved away, his arm yanked away from its position. Minox definitely felt something. A snap, like a whip cracking. It was . . . coming from something. Someone.

"Of course there is," the old man told Satrine. Minox wasn't paying attention. He was looking right at the source of the feeling. The energy.

Joshea Brondar was a mage. And if he served in the army, then he was also Uncircled.

"We should question all the Brondars, Inspector Rainey," he told Satrine. "I'll start with young Joshea here."

"All right," Inspector Rainey said cautiously. "That leaves me with the old man."

"Joshea," Minox said as calmly as he could manage, "Why don't we go out to the alley to talk?"

❦

Out in the sunlight, out in the alley, Minox got a good look at Joshea Brondar. Now it was obvious, his magical affinity. Not only in his physique, though the signs were all there. Despite his muscular build, he was very lean, especially in his face. His cheeks were sunken, his face drawn, gray circles under his eyes.

But beyond the pure visual evidence, Minox could sense it. It was a sensation that Minox couldn't quite describe—more taste than touch. Energy bent toward Joshea Brondar. Minox realized he had felt the same sensation around Jaelia Tomar and the other Firewings, but at the time he had dismissed those feelings as irrational emotion, his own nerves playing tricks with him due to his discomfort. Now he understood what he had sensed, it was a revelation. It was not unlike when water drains out of one's ears, and clear hearing is suddenly restored.

"What are you looking at, Inspector?" Joshea Brondar asked,

"What do you mean, Mister Brondar?"

"No offense, sir," Brondar said with the courtesy Minox had always connected with military discipline. "But you're looking at me like most of the customers look at the meat."

Minox stepped back. He had gotten excited, and was standing closer than most people preferred for comfort. "My apologies, Mister Brondar. I've just had something of an epiphany, thanks to you."

"A what?"

"A moment of clarity, Mister Brondar. However, I will table that for the moment. Would you look over there?" Minox pointed into the alley, to the lingering bloodstains still clearly visible on the cobblestones.

"That's where the body was?" Brondar asked.

"Indeed," Minox said. "As you can imagine, given the visibility of the spot just from our vantage point a few feet inside, the body hadn't been here very long when it was discovered, nor could the act of killing have taken very long."

"I suppose not," Brondar said, his eyes still on the stain of blood. "Not that it takes that long."

"You are familiar with how long it takes to kill a man?" Brondar glanced back up at Minox. "You did understand my father's whole show back there? Three years in the army?"

"When were those three years?"

"The past three, really. I . . . I came back home just last month."

"I wasn't aware of a war in the past three years."

"Neither was I," Brondar said. "They still found places to send us." His voice was empty, hollow.

"So you chose to leave after three years?"

"Time to come back home," Brondar said quietly. He turned away, taking a few idle steps down the alley. "Figure out what I was doing with myself."

"So you weren't kicked out of the army?"

Brondar's eyes flashed hot as he looked back. "Of course not! Why would I be?"

"For being a mage, of course."

Minox immediately regretted saying that. It was a calculated risk, he had thought, to throw Joshea off balance so he could then get at questions about the murder. Joshea Brondar, instead, reacted with a quick and fell rage. He closed the distance between the two of them in a flash, and his hand was around Minox's throat. Brondar picked him up off the ground and slammed him into the brick wall.

"How do you know that?" he hissed.

Minox reacted without thinking, blasting out with magic and knocking Brondar away. He put too much into it, throwing Brondar into the opposite wall. Brondar cried out; the plaster cracked. He landed on his feet, a fighting crouch, ready to strike.

"Wait, wait!" Minox said, drawing out his handstick. He didn't want a fight, but he had to be ready to defend himself. The energy around him crackled—magic energy, now he could feel it, he knew what it was—and the energy fell into Brondar. No, more like it was pulled out of Minox, forced from him. Minox tore at the energy, yanking it like it was a tether. Brondar's reaction was purely physical, a wild punch at Minox's face. Minox blocked with the handstick, sweetening it with more magic.

"Stop!" Minox said again. He grabbed Brondar's arm

and twisted it behind the man's back. The man was strong, almost impossible to hold. Magic crackled around them both, Brondar lashing out, Minox having to respond in kind to hold him fast.

"Please!" Minox said. He pushed Brondar to the ground, pinning him with his knee. Brondar still fought, bucking like an unbroken horse. Minox hissed in the man's ear, "I'm the same as you are."

Brondar stopped. His face on the ground, he turned his head and looked up at Minox. "Mage?"

"Yes."

The next word was a hoarse whisper, so low Minox barely heard it. "Uncircled?"

"Yes."

Minox let go, stepping away from Brondar and letting him get up. Brondar kept his head down as he stood, not looking at Minox at all. "Am I going to be arrested now?"

Minox considered his options. He knew he was at fault here, or at least had some culpability. He could have handled things better. "Assaulting an inspector is a crime, but I don't see any witnesses here." He tried to smile, to put Brondar at ease. It didn't seem to work.

"So now what?" Brondar asked.

Minox wasn't sure. He had lost the sense of what he was supposed to be accomplishing: questioning Brondar about the dead mage. "We don't have to discuss it right now."

"So I can go back in?" Brondar said.

"No, not yet," Minox said. "Did you see the dead man earlier?"

"No," Brondar said. "There was a commotion outside the shop, but we stayed in and kept working."

"Did you know he was a mage?"

Brondar looked up, finally making eye contact. There was fear in his eyes. He stammered and looked around. "Uncircled?"

"No," Minox said. "He was a Firewing, named Tomar. Had you ever met him?"

"A mage named Tomar?" Brondar asked. "No, not that I'm aware of. Mages don't usually come into our shop. Or, at least, they don't announce themselves."

"And no one ever mentioned the name that you know?"

"No."

"And you saw nothing suspicious? Nothing at all?"

"Not that I can think of, Inspector." Brondar paced back and forth in the alley.

"All right. Now, where were you at seven bells this morning?"

"Seven bells? Making sausages with my brothers."

"They can corroborate?"

"Of course!" Joshea's voice cracked as he dropped it low midway, giving a glance back to the door. "Is this all?"

Minox bit his tongue. He needed to think some more about this case. His thoughts were far too disorganized right now. He needed to calm down, sit at his desk, and contemplate in silence. But he felt there was something here, something he had to explore.

Something that had nothing to do with the case.

Minox rarely had trouble finding the words for what he wanted to say, never lacked clarity of thought. But this was something he could not seem to put into words. Finally he managed to say, "Do they know?"

"Who?"

Minox gave a nod over to the butcher shop. "Your family."

Joshea shook his head, his face going dark.

"You've never wanted to tell them?"

Joshea's face dropped, his angry expression melting away. "Every blasted day."

"And you know you can't."

Joshea looked out of the alley, and then sat in the front of the butcher shop door, shaking his head. "There's rarely a word out of that man's mouth that isn't about meat or serving in the army. But if the subject of magic ever comes up, he'll spit on the floor, and say something about how we should string up all the damned mages."

Minox took that in. "My father was the same way." Fenner as well, and most of Minox's uncles and cousins.

"Stick?"

"Horsepatrol in Keller Cove. Wellings have been in

Constabulary for eight generations," Minox said. "Going back to the city first establishing the organization."

Joshea gave a small, mirthless laugh. "My father could name six generations of Brondars in the Druth Army, and for most of them, tell you the battle they died at."

"Legacy," Minox said.

"And mages aren't part of that legacy."

"Not at all." Minox knew he needed to get back on track of his case. But Joshea Brondar was the first person he had ever met who might understand the choices he had made. "I'm afraid I must continue my investigation. But I would—"

"Like to talk again later?" Joshea nodded. "But not around here."

"Of course," Minox said. "I live on Escaraine, in Keller Cove. And there's a Fuergan tobacco shop I frequent right near. We can talk there later. But for now I need to attend to this case."

"I'll look you up."

"Very good," Minox said. He extended his hand to Joshea, who cautiously took it and shook it.

"I can go, then?"

"Yes, of course."

Brondar went to the alley door, and then turned back. "Could we . . . could you, that is, not mention to your partner what happened?"

"It's a private matter," Minox said. "As of right now, I don't see a need for it to be anything else."

Chapter 7

SATRINE COULD TELL Welling had been out of sorts since the butcher shop. More correctly, he had been showing different mannerisms than he had before. When they went to the Firewings, he had been nervous, apprehensive. What he was showing now wasn't nerves. This was a burden, weight on his shoulders.

He had barely spoken when they went into the barbershop. The barbers, though, were pleasant and helpful and gave Satrine no indication that they had anything to do with the murder.

Welling had been surly when he insisted on going to Ushman's Hot Pot for potatoes and pork. Satrine joined him, now actually hungry. Hunger—daily, pervasive hunger—had been a constant companion during her childhood, and Ushman's was the easiest alleviation. Three ticks a bowl, it had often been the only hot meal she had just about every day. Boring, but it had kept her alive. They sat at the street counter to eat, Welling silently shoveling the potatoes into his mouth.

The quiet unnerved Satrine. "Good?"

"Hmm?"

"Your lunch, or whatever you call this meal."

"Fine," he said.

Satrine realized he wasn't going to discuss the case, or

the recent events, any further without provocation. "What happened in the alley?"

"Nothing." Jaw set, eyes down and to the left. Clear sign.

"That's a lie."

Welling considered this, and then gave Satrine a hard glare. "Nothing that holds relevance to our case."

Satrine wasn't convinced of the honesty of that statement. "You're certain of that, Inspector?"

He put his fork and bowl down. "It's not . . . a Constabulary matter, Inspector Rainey."

That was a hook. Something had happened, something important. "Are you being objective about that?"

"Here's what I'm being objective about, Inspector Rainey. I know that you are being untruthful to Captain Cinellan, and by extension the whole of the Constabulary Inspectors Unit. Despite not knowing the nature of these untruths, I have your assurances, which I have taken as honest, that they will not affect your job performance."

Satrine wasn't sure what to say to that, and kept her face clear of reaction.

"So my objective perspective is, based on my observation, you have the skills, drive, and imagination to do this job in a way that is not only effective, but compatible with my own style. I find this quite agreeable, and therefore have not delved into your secrets."

"Point made," Satrine said. Let it lie, change the subject. "So explain to me your twenty-odd 'unresolved' cases."

"They are cases which I haven't resolved to my satisfaction."

"Then why doesn't Cinellan care about their resolution?"

"My satisfaction, Inspector Rainey. That is a very different thing from how the captain sees it."

"Ah. You mean he thinks the case is closed, but you think there's more to it."

Welling shrugged. "Apt enough."

"Like with the two horsepatrolmen this morning." Satrine put down her bowl. "But that's not your case."

"Many of my unresolved cases were not, strictly, my case." Welling ate the last few bites of his meal. "Are we done?"

"Eating or something else?"

"Eating." Welling got to his feet. "I think we need to return to the stationhouse."

"Why do you think that?"

"Because that page is standing across the street, his eyes on us, with an apprehensive look on his face that typically indicates a mild internal struggle. Likely he has been sent to fetch us, but doesn't wish to interrupt our meal."

Satrine looked over her shoulder. He looked familiar: flat, blond hair and wide nose. "Isn't that the same page who counted time for us this morning?"

"Yes, I think so."

"And told the stationhouse about our experiment?"

"Are you suggesting that his presence and apprehension are not work-related?"

"I'm saying it's worth considering."

"True enough. However, further speculation is not necessary." He pushed his empty bowl across the counter back at the cook—not an Ushman, Satrine had noted, but someone with a familiar face—and walked over to the page. Satrine ate a final bite and followed after him.

"What's the word, Page?" Welling asked.

The page glanced about the street nervously, his eyes only briefly landing on Satrine before he'd look away again. He finally settled his gaze on Welling. "Yes, Inspector, I was supposed to tell you—you both, of course—to return to the inspectors' floor once you have the opportunity."

Welling gave a sidelong glance at Satrine. "My theory was correct."

"Doesn't mean mine wasn't," Satrine muttered back.

Welling seemed to think on this for a moment, his focus switching between her and the page. The page, under Welling's scrutiny, paled visibly. Finally Welling gave a small nod. "A valid observation." He walked off toward the stationhouse.

Satrine noticed every eye on her when they entered

the stationhouse. The main floor, filled with clerks and patrolmen, had a sudden lull in activity and chatter as she and Welling came through to the stairs. Definite disapproval from many of the patrolmen, some of them showing outright hostility. She did notice, though, two or three of the clerks—the women—giving her the slightest of smiles.

At the top of the stairs, Miss Pyle was also giving Satrine a warm look. Satrine knew this was about how things were going to go, though she thought she would get a few days of grace—out of respect for Loren, if nothing else.

"Exciting day, isn't it?" Miss Pyle asked her.

"So far," Satrine said.

"Is there anything you need from me, Inspector?" Miss Pyle asked. At the same time she asked this, she passed a folded paper to Welling.

"Not at the moment," Satrine said. Was Miss Pyle trying to smokescreen her, or just do multiple things at once? The warm smile seemed genuine, and there did not seem to be any attempt at subterfuge in passing her note.

"Well, please let me know," Pyle said. She went back to her desk.

Welling read his note, a sour look passing on his face. "I'll catch up with you." He went back down the stairs.

"Something up?"

"Old business. I'll meet you at the desk." He hurried off. Satrine was tempted to follow after him, but then decided she could use a few minutes at her desk to actually clear it off and make it her own.

———◆———

Nyla's note sent Minox down to the back alley entrance, by the horsepatrol and wagon barn doors. "Rencir is waiting for you" was all he needed to know. Rencir would wait in only one place, out of sight. For more than one reason, if Captain Cinellan spotted the man, there would be trouble.

Rencir leaned against the brick wall, beady eyes on the door. "Inspector." Despite his unkempt hair and beard, Rencir was of good character.

"It's a busy day, Mister Rencir," Minox said. "I can't spare you much time."

"Busy day, indeed." He pulled a notebook and a charcoal pencil out of his pocket. "Dead body at Jent and Tannen. Your case?"

"Mine," Minox said.

"Victim is a mage, can you confirm?"

"Confirmed."

"Don't suppose you could give me a name, or at least an affiliation?"

Minox considered it. There was value in letting Rencir publish privileged information in the *South Maradaine Gazette*. More than one killer had been smoked out using the *Gazette*. "Not at this time."

Rencir nodded. "Fair enough. How about the sewer murders?"

"Inspectors Kellman and Mirrell are handling that."

"Pff. No fun. I hear it's salacious though. Two old hands in the business, working together for fifteen years. Hints of one of them rolling the other's wife."

"Not my case, Mister Rencir," Minox reminded him.

Rencir held up his hands. "Fair enough. Thought you might like to know. Now what I really need to know is about the new set of hair that's been spotted next to you. Hear she's quite a stir."

"My new partner is Inspector Satrine Rainey," Minox said.

"Rainey? Connected to the spec who ended up knocked out of his senses across the swim?"

"She's his—" He paused. "Let's keep her details out of the *Gazette*, at least for a while."

"How do you mean, Inspector?"

"I would appreciate it, Rencir, if you didn't make news of her or her name."

Rencir's eyes narrowed. "If anyone else was asking, I wouldn't even consider it."

"I understand. I won't ask you to lie or omit. Simply do not make her a subject you focus on."

Rencir nodded. "I can do that. Until she really becomes news."

That should help. The *South Maradaine Gazette* was the larger newsprint on the south side, and certainly in Inemar. If the lesser papers made noise about Inspector Rainey, it wouldn't be taken as seriously. "What else?"

"I haven't asked you about the case with my son in some time," Rencir added.

"And I have not forgotten it," Minox said. "I consider it among the most crucial of my unresolved cases." The boy's mysterious and sudden death was perplexing, and Minox was convinced it was part of something greater. "There have been several disappearances of boys of a similar age in Dentonhill in the past two months."

"Connected to my son?"

"I think it's worth further consideration. I have a lead that will, I hope, bear some fruit regarding poisons that leave more subtle signs on their victims."

"If you need anything, Inspector . . ."

"For now, only my issue."

Rencir reached into his coat and pulled out a copy of the *South Maradaine Gazette*. "Always appreciate your time, Inspector."

"And I your discretion, Mister Rencir."

Rencir went off down the alley. Minox scanned through the day's news. Nothing leaped out at him as being of interest, but it deserved deeper study. Inspector Rainey was surely waiting for him, and further delay would only bring about more questions.

———◆———

Satrine found her chair occupied by a sneering man with long fingers and salt-and-pepper hair. He was bent over the desk, digging through papers and scribbling notes. The oddest thing about him was his suit—it looked expensive and well cared for, but it didn't fit him right, and with its large brass buttons and high-necked collar, it was several years out of style.

"You're at my desk, sir," she said.

He glanced up at her, his eyes dark and beady. "Then they have given the Jinx a new partner." He shook his head, clicking as if the idea was distasteful. "And a woman at that." Educated accent. Private schools and Royal College of Maradaine, most likely.

"Is that a problem?"

"Far as I know, you might be the first woman to get an inspector rank. To get killed right away would be a horrible shame." He bent back down to his notes.

"Who the blazes are you?"

"Language, Madam Inspector," he said, putting down his pen. He extended his hand to her. "Zebram Hilsom, with the City Protector's Office."

A lawyer.

Satrine took the offered hand. "Satrine Rainey. Inspector."

"Related to . . ." He let it hang.

"Loren Rainey, yes. His wife."

"Condolences," he said with a crisp nod.

"Why are you at my desk?"

"Because it's the best way to force the Jinx to actually have a conversation, which really must happen. Though I suppose I must force the same thing upon you as well, mustn't I?"

"I'm not sure," Satrine said.

He shuffled through some papers. "Did you or did you not arrest one Missus Jaelia Tomar? For assault and disruption of the peace?"

"Inspector Welling and I both did, yes."

"Excellent. I've already had several petitions to expedite this case in court, which is always tricky when magic is involved. Can you answer a few questions?"

"Of course," Satrine said.

"Was this 'disruption of the peace' involving the applied use of magic?"

"Yes, I suppose it was."

Hilsom shook his head. "Trouble, trouble. We may not be able to prosecute that charge with any success."

"The woman let out a blast of magic that shattered every window on the street," Satrine said.

"So there were tangible effects of disruption of peace?"

"Absolutely." Satrine wasn't sure what to make of the question. Her confusion must have been apparent.

"You see, Inspector Rainey—you're new to this, else you would understand." He shook his head with a look one would use with a poor student who hadn't learned their lessons. "There is a long-established habit of filing a complaint of 'disruption of peace' against a mage for doing little more than being a mage. The complaint has been so misused, and therefore challenged by Circles in courts, that the legal standard for the charge is almost impossible to meet. If the Justice Advocate doesn't tear it to pieces, the Circle's lawyer certainly will."

"What other charge should we use?"

"That's immaterial, Inspector Rainey. The prudent thing to do would be to focus on the assault charge. Whom did she assault?"

"Me."

Hilsom's face brightened. "Now that is something we can have better luck prosecuting." He dug through the papers on Welling's desk until he came up with a blank sheet. He sat and took Welling's pen out of the inkpot. "Please tell me how she assaulted you."

"She struck me with a magic blast."

Hilsom put the pen back in the inkpot. "A 'magic blast'?"

"I'm really not versed on a more technical term, Mister Hilsom."

"Surely," Hilsom said, giving her a withering look. "Please, elucidate for me, Inspector Rainey. What injuries did you suffer as a result of this . . . 'magic blast'?"

"Well, none, but that wasn't from a lack of trying on—"

"No injuries." He shook his head and scribbled a note on the sheet. "So we're clear, you are attesting that she attacked you, magically, but through some sort of miracle, you escaped unscathed."

"I wouldn't say a miracle."

"Then what would you say, Inspector? How did you survive?"

Satrine pulled the spike out of her coat pocket. "I think because of this."

Hilsom raised an eyebrow. "Really? Is that your good luck charm? One of those trinkets that the swindlers by the bridge sell?"

"No, it—" Satrine stopped herself. Hilsom was already predisposed against everything she was going to say, there was no need to sound crazier than necessary. "The murder case that Inspector Welling and I are working involves a mage."

"Oh, so the mage is a murderer."

"No," Satrine said. She was getting very tired of Hilsom's attitude and the condescending smirk on his face. "The mage was the victim. He was pinned to the ground with this spike. We believe that the spike has the ability to disable magic."

Hilsom's smirk melted off his face. "You're serious."

"It's a theory."

"A strangely convenient theory," he said.

"How is it convenient?"

"Do you know what is the biggest cause of headaches in the Protector's Office?"

"Is 'your voice' too obvious a choice?"

Hilsom's jaw hardened. He was not amused. "Unsubstantiated claims of magic attacks."

"You've already said, Mister Hilsom. The charge has proven near useless."

"Disruption of the peace is the charge that is nigh impossible to prove. Perhaps I might be able to get some traction on property damage, but I can assure you that the Circle will have a lawyer who will do their damnedest to cast doubt on the fact that Miss Tomar was the source."

"She screamed and glass shattered."

"Coincidence. How many other mages were present?"

Satrine considered. "At least three. Maybe more in the house."

"So that's out. It'll be argued it might be any one of them, so I can't prove which one it was."

"But—"

"Brush up on the particulars of laws regarding Circles, Orders, Guilds, and Leagues. They are ridiculously complex, especially when it comes to proof regarding application of magic and its origin."

Satrine nodded. "To make—let me see if I have the

language right—'spurious' arrests of mages more challenging."

"Exactly," Hilsom said. "You know that from your husband?"

"Something like that," Satrine said. She had worked with a couple mages in the service, and her husband had had a few challenges that he had griped about at home.

"But let's allow that I pursue your 'assault.' Given your status as an officer and inspector, your testimony has weight, and your description of her actions would make it challenging for an advocate to argue it came from any other mage."

"I would hope so."

"And I am presuming that the Jinx would back up your claim."

"I don't know why he wouldn't."

"I can easily see why it's in his interest not to. You don't see it?"

Satrine shook her head warily.

"Of course you don't. Then let me break it into simple ideas for you. Let us presume this spike does what you say. And you testify at trial to that effect. Are you following me?"

Satrine's fist was about to follow its way into his nose, but she held back the bile and nodded.

"Then, if we convict Missus Tomar, we have established a legal precedent. A mage could be charged with assault with no actual injuries. Do you see how that would let sheep out of the yard yet?"

"You think these unsubstantiated claims would increase?"

"Yes!" Hilsom said, apparently jubilant at getting through to her. "Anyone could claim they had a protective device in their pocket when they were attacked. 'Oh, thank the Saints I wasn't hurt when that mage blasted at me, but I had my sacred spoon behind my ear!'"

"I get your point."

"It would do wonders for the charlatans and junk peddlers, though."

"So you're not going to pursue the complaints, Zebram?"

Captain Cinellan asked the question, having come around the slateboards to the desks.

"Of course I'll pursue them. I've got a dozen people swearing about the broken windows, I can't ignore that. But I can tell you now that the Firewings will bring in their counsel and Circle Law will get cited and in the end the Circle itself will pay a fine — admitting to no actual culpability — that won't even cover the expense of keeping her here overnight."

"Hmm," Cinellan said. "So what should we do? The boys down in the holding pen aren't too keen on keeping her overnight."

"I can imagine. We might have a solid case here, but to pursue it, we're going to have trouble with Circle Law." He sighed. "As much as it frustrates me, the laws regarding mages, magic, and Circles have a purpose. There are plenty of towns out in the country where a tolerant attitude about a mage would be 'Let's only throw *just enough* rocks at him to chase him out of town.'"

Cinellan shrugged. "Everyone's afraid of being stabbed by the Unseen Knife."

Hilsom groaned but didn't say anything else.

"So what do we need to do?" Satrine asked. Cinellan gave her a questioning look. "It's my first arrest. I can't let it fall."

Cinellan grinned. "That's good. I'll tell you what you need to do, Hilsom. Kick it up."

Hilsom winced slightly. "You're asking me to give up my claim."

"Does it really matter if your name is on the case, as long as the conviction holds?"

"Especially if the conviction holds," Hilsom said.

"Sounds like you can't get it to hold," Satrine said. Hilsom's eyes narrowed on her, but Cinellan put a hand on his shoulder.

"Justice, Zebram, not glory. Kick it up to the Archduchy Court."

Satrine remembered her husband talking about this sort of thing. The archdukes — and by extension their courts — had the authority to lay a charge against the Circle as a whole entity. Doing that meant handing the claim over, which any city official worth their ink would hate doing. More than once she had heard Loren rant about Archduchy Sheriffs or King's Marshals trampling over his investigations.

Hilsom didn't look pleased, but he nodded. "I'll have it done. But that means you'll have to transfer Missus Tomar over to Eastwood tonight."

"Fair enough."

Hilsom picked up his papers and gave a glance over to Satrine. "You're picking up a cinder with this one, Brace."

"I got tough hands," Cinellan said. "Send a page over with the transfer orders."

Hilsom nodded and stalked off.

"Thanks for that," Satrine said.

"Eh," Cinellan said. "He knows it's right." He turned and looked straight at her for the first time. "That vest works pretty well on you."

"Thank you, sir." That was more compliment than she was expecting to get from the captain today.

"One murder, one arrest, and one bloody nose on the inspectors' floor. Blazes of a first day."

Satrine couldn't get a read on the captain, if he admired or admonished her for knocking Mirrell down. "Just doing what I can."

"Let's try more arrests and less bloody noses tomorrow, hmm?"

"Right," Satrine said. She couldn't keep herself from smiling.

Cinellan looked over Welling's desk, running his fingers over a few of the pages. "I hate the nickname, by the way."

"Mine or Welling's?"

"Welling's." Cinellan gave her a quick wink. "Yours is almost a badge of honor. But Minox, he . . . he doesn't deserve that."

"Good to know," Satrine said. That made one thing clear: Cinellan hadn't stuck her with Welling as some form of hazing. "I'm still trying to figure out how an Uncircled mage ended up in the Constabulary."

"He told you already?"

"I deduced it."

Cinellan gave an approving nod. "It's one of those things that's not exactly a secret, but not exactly public. Most people are more comfortable not talking about it at all. Including Minox."

"I gathered that."

"The question is, Rainey, do you have a problem with it?"

Satrine sat down at the desk. "I'd be lying if I didn't admit that the idea of an untrained mage didn't make me nervous. There is a reason why Circles were established in the first place." The mages she had known often spoke of training and Circling as an absolute necessity.

"True," Cinellan said, his tone completely neutral.

"But as for Welling himself, he's clearly a brilliant investigator. And with this case in particular, we wouldn't have accomplished what we did without all of his unique gifts."

"Good," Cinellan said. His shoulders relaxed, and he sat on the edge of her desk. "If you don't mind me asking, where is your husband now? Ward of Saint Alexis?"

"Blazes, no," Satrine said. "He's at our home, where he belongs."

"I had gotten the—well, we had all heard that he's . . ."

"He's awake," Satrine said. "But he doesn't speak. He doesn't move, except his eyes. He'll eat if you put food in his mouth, but . . ." She trailed off. There wasn't much need to say anything else.

"So he's like an infant?" Cinellan asked. His face blanched. "I'm sorry, Satr—Rainey. That was—"

"Pretty accurate, actually," Satrine said. "And there's nothing to be done for him at the ward that couldn't be done at home."

Cinellan raised an eyebrow. "You've got people, right?"

"Our landlady. Her own husband was sick for years before he passed, so she knows what to do here."

Cinellan shook his head, eyes on the desk. "It's just . . . I can't imagine what that's like for him."

"Had you ever met him?"

"Never had the pleasure," Cinellan said. "Not a lot of our business crosses the river, after all."

That was a point Satrine was counting on.

"He was brilliant, you know. I want to believe that his mind is still alive in there, some spark of it. But then I think, if it was, if he was aware, then . . . that would be even more horrible." She felt tears welling up at the corner of her eyes, and she be damned if she was going to let herself cry in front of the captain.

"Well," Cinellan said, standing up. "Shift is just about up. You'll be able to head back to him soon."

That was good. She had told Missus Abernand that she'd probably be back home before four bells. That estimate had been based on the idea that her whole plan would fail and she'd spend the rest of the day scrounging up money however she could.

Welling came around to the desks. "Any news?"

Cinellan's face went back to all business. "You missed Hilsom."

"Shame," Welling said, sitting down and pulling his journal out of his pocket. "Did he say anything worthwhile?"

"Your arrest is getting kicked up to the Archduchy Court," Cinellan said.

"Missus Tomar? What for?"

"Hilsom thinks the assault charge will hold better if it's brought at that level," Satrine said.

Welling's face screwed up. "The assault charge hardly matters. Not that assaulting an inspector is immaterial, but you weren't even injured. Her value as a source of information on our current case is far greater than that conviction."

"She hasn't said a word since she was brought in," Cinellan said. "On that, Welling, you know better than to send in a charge with the lockwagon unaccompanied."

"We had pressing matters," Welling said. "Further people to question for our investigation."

"And how did that pan out?" Cinellan asked.

"Less than ideal."

"Do you mean it got you no further?"

"The case is not yet resolved," Welling said.

"Fair enough," Cinellan said. "Well, you better go question her, since in about two hours, you and Mirrell will be doing a transfer escort over to Eastwood."

Satrine didn't like the sound of that. "Welling and Mirrell, sir? Shouldn't I be doing that with him?"

"Against protocol, Rainey."

"What protocol?" she asked, though she had no hard time believing that there was a rule against women doing escort duty.

"She's charged with assault of a Constabulary officer, Inspector," Welling said. "With such charges, the assaulted officer is forbidden from escort, guard, or interrogation duty."

"Ah," Satrine said. "So I can't go question her either?"

"No," Cinellan said. "It'll have to be Welling. You'll have to listen in from the transcription gallery."

Welling frowned. "I don't think I'd get much from her."

Cinellan shrugged. "The clock is clicking away, Inspectors." He rapped his knuckles against Welling's slateboards. "This isn't going to solve anything this time. I'll have her sent to Interrogation. And I want a report on your other case, Welling." He left their desks. Welling opened his leather notebook and started writing.

"Where did you go?" Satrine asked once Cinellan was out of hearing. "Miss Pyle gave you a note?"

"Something that involved one of my unresolved cases," Welling said. His attention was almost completely in his notebook.

"What about it? A new lead?"

Welling looked up, annoyance flashing on his face. "No, it remains unresolved."

"Then what—"

"Inspe—" he spat out, then stopped. He put his pen down. "I apologize. The case in question involved a young boy who died a few months ago."

"Murdered?"

"Not that we could discern," Welling said. "No injuries, no signs of sickness or poison. As far as Leppin could determine, the boy just fell over and died. The captain decided it bore no further investigation."

"So then . . ."

"I did not find it plausible that a healthy boy would simply drop down dead in the middle of the street for no reason. Nor did his father."

Satrine understood. "His father was here to talk to you. And since the captain considers the case closed, Nyla—Miss Pyle kept the matter discreet."

Welling closed his journal. "As I said this morning, I have twenty-five cases which I consider to be unresolved. And if I wasn't clear earlier, most of these cases are, as a matter of official record, closed to further investigation. My cousin has extended a fair degree of courtesy in assisting me when matters like this arise."

"That's probably not a courtesy she extends to everyone."

"I could hardly say what she does for every person on the inspector floor. She is a highly efficient woman, however."

Satrine turned that over in her head. "Hilsom said something that surprised me. I'm not the first woman to be made inspector, am I?" The last thing she needed was publicity or special notice.

Welling smirked. "Hardly. Hilsom has no sense of history. It's true they are uncommon, but . . . look over there."

He pointed to a framed sketch on the wall near his desk. A dozen men and seven women in old-style inspectors' uniforms, from the last century. Scrawled on the bottom it said, "Inemar Inspectors, 1164."

"Height of the war," Satrine said. "A lot of able-bodied men across in the islands."

"And therefore many women rose up in the ranks." He pointed to two of the faces, a man and woman standing together. "Fenner Welling and Jillian Timmsen. Later Jillian Welling."

"Your grandmother?" She looked closer at the sketch. There was something of Welling's eyes in his grandfather's face. And now that she was looking carefully, she could see a lot of Miss Pyle in Jillian. They had the same smirk. "That's amazing."

"They were both—" He stopped himself. "They are both quite brilliant. I have to admit, I've gone down to the archives and read through every file they wrote."

In the distance, the bells of Saint Limarre rang out. Three bells already.

"Come on," Satrine said. "Like the captain said, the clock is clicking. You need to question Missus Tomar."

Chapter 8

TWO MEN STOOD in quiet argument outside the interrogation room. One of them was Zebram Hilsom. The other was a thin man in a rich green vest with a half cape and rings on almost every finger. Satrine noticed a hint of rouge applied to his pallid cheeks. His shirtsleeves ended just below the elbow, showing a tattoo on his left arm: two letters surrounded in flame.

"Miss Tomar's Circle counsel?" she asked Welling in a low voice as they approached the two lawyers.

"One would gather," he replied. "Mage?"

"Lord Preston's Circle if I recall correctly," she said.

"You're familiar with them?"

"They dominate the University system. Tend to be well educated, cooperative, and relatively neutral in Inter-Circle affairs."

"And moneyed," Welling added. "Or at least he is."

"And very good ears," the mage lawyer said. "Quentin Olivant. And you must be Inspectors Welling and Rainey, arresting officer and victim. I was offering my dear colleague here the opportunity to release Madam Tomar now and save himself the embarrassment and expense of a failed trial."

Hilsom scoffed. "A solid case with a Constabulary officer as witness and victim? You're chasing an empty wagon, Quentin."

Olivant shrugged. "It's your trouble. I, for one, would enjoy a trial. I so rarely need to go to court."

"Is Missus Tomar in the interrogation room?" Welling asked. "We have some questions for her."

"Not the both of you." Olivant pointed a slender finger at Satrine. "The lovely Madam Inspector is prohibited."

"We know that," Satrine said. "It'll just be her and Inspector Welling."

"And me," Olivant said.

"This isn't regarding her arrest," Welling said.

"Oh, it isn't?" Olivant asked, pressing his bejeweled hand to his chest in grand dramatic gesture. "Then that's a perfectly good reason to trample on her right to counsel."

"It's fine," Hilsom said. "You two go in there. Inspector Rainey and I will be listening in transcription."

"Then by all means," Olivant said, opening the door to the interrogation room. "I'll still have Madam Tomar in her own bed by tomorrow night."

"We'll see," Hilsom said. He walked between Satrine and Welling, and grabbed Welling at the elbow. "No deals here, Jinx," he whispered. "She's going to Eastwood tonight, no matter what."

Welling pulled his arm away. "Understood."

"I suppose we're lucky she doesn't also have someone from the Advocate's Office," Hilsom muttered. "Come along, Inspector Rainey." Hilsom entered the door next to the interrogation room. Welling gave Satrine a polite nod and went in with Olivant. Satrine followed after Hilsom.

There were a few short steps up into the transcription gallery, though Satrine felt that *gallery* was a generous word to describe the room. It was barely more than a closet, with several lamps burning low over a bench and two desks. Women sat at the two desks, one in Constabulary coat and skirt, the other in a modest gray wool dress. Hilsom was whispering something to her, so Satrine presumed she was the secretary from his office.

Several earhorns were mounted on the front wall, surrounding a thick glass window. Through the window, the interrogation room was visible. Many lamps hung on the ceiling in there, burning hot and bright. Jaelia Tomar sat at a simple wooden table, hands shackled. Olivant went around the table and stood behind her, as Welling took the chair opposite her.

"Jaelia," Olivant was saying, his voice tinny through the earhorn. "You've already met Inspector Welling, I presume."

The two secretaries started scribbling furiously. Hilsom silently beckoned Satrine to sit on the bench beside him. Grudgingly, she took her place. She figured she should be grateful that she wasn't expected to transcribe.

Jaelia gave little more than a grunt in response.

Welling took out his journal. "Missus Tomar, I'm not here to discuss your arrest earlier today. I need—"

"Shut it," Jaelia whispered.

Welling wasn't fazed. "I need to ask you a few questions regarding your husband."

She spoke louder this time. "Shut it."

"I think Madam Tomar has made herself clear, Inspector," Olivant said.

"I've not asked my questions," Welling said.

"I've got nothing to say to this Uncircled trash," Jaelia said.

"Uncircled?" Olivant asked, his eyes going wide.

Hilsom turned to Satrine and raised an eyebrow. "She knows?" he whispered. Satrine gave him the barest of nods.

"I am not the issue," Welling said calmly. "The issue is the murder of your husband."

"No, no," Olivant said. "This is most irregular." He started fanning his face, as if just being in the room with an Uncircled mage was making it hard to breathe.

"When did you last see your husband?" Welling asked, ignoring Olivant's dramatics.

"Not your business," Jaelia said.

"I'm investigating his murder," Welling said. "It most definitely is my business."

"You have no business in these matters, blank," Olivant said. "You have no business at all."

Welling's eyes narrowed. Satrine thought she saw all the lamps in the interrogation room flicker brighter. "That's not for you to decide, Counselor."

"But it is for Missus Tomar," Olivant said. "And I believe we are finished now." His hands were shaking. To Satrine's eye it could have been with either fear or rage.

"When did you last see him alive, Missus Tomar?" Welling's voice had risen. The lamps were definitely burning brighter now.

"Shut it!" she shouted.

"Who was he with, Missus Tomar? Where was he going?"

"This is enough!" Olivant snapped.

The lamps were now blue. Hilsom turned to Satrine, "Is Jinx doing that?"

"Could be any one of them," Satrine said.

Welling locked his eyes with Jaelia's. "Did you even see him leave your chapterhouse? Or did you all leave together?"

"Don't say a word, Jaelia," Olivant said, taking her by the arm and bringing her to her feet.

"Sit down!" Minox snapped. "Is that it, Missus Tomar? Did your whole Circle go to that alley together?"

Jaelia looked up at Welling for the first time. "Is that what you think?"

"What else can I think if you tell me nothing?"

"No," Olivant said. "Not to him."

"Never," Jaelia whispered. "He was—we would never—"

"Then who?"

The lamps were white hot now, forcing Satrine to squint. Hilsom had a hand up over his eyes.

"Who, Missus Tomar?"

Olivant was by the window. "Zebram! This is over! Pull him out!"

"Damn it, Missus Tomar." Welling's stare was intense, but his voice stayed even. "For his sake."

Tears were streaming down Jaelia's face. She was barely able to speak through her sobs. "Hessen, he said he was going to . . ."

Olivant turned back to Welling and grabbed him by the shoulder. The lamps all flared, too bright for Satrine to bear.

Then it was dark.

Satrine was on her feet, handstick drawn, and raced out the door. Hilsom shouted something, but Satrine didn't listen. She tore down the hall to the interrogation room. Before she reached it, it burst open. Welling had his arm locked around Olivant's shoulder, dragging him into the hallway.

"You see?" Olivant shouted. "You see what he did?"

Welling released the man, dropping him to the ground. "Your authority as a counselor does not extend to touching my person, Mister Olivant."

"He's uncontrollable!" Olivant said. "You saw what he did in there!"

Satrine glanced into the interrogation room, the light from the hallway casting dimly. Jaelia Tomar still sat weeping at the table, but otherwise seemed unharmed.

"What did Welling do?" Satrine asked.

"The lamps!" Olivant said. "Just like an Uncircled mage! Out of control!"

Welling gave Satrine the slightest shake of his head. "There were three mages in that room, Mister Olivant."

"Only one Uncircled!"

Hilsom stepped out into the hallway. "What happened in there is unclear, Quentin."

"He's—"

Hilsom cut him off. "Inspector Welling was the most stable person in there. Missus Tomar is a weeping, angry widow, and you were a screaming ninny on the verge of foaming at the mouth. Don't try and sell to me that he was responsible for the lamps."

"He's Uncircled!"

"And you and Missus Tomar are very well trained."

"And he assaulted me!"

"After you grabbed an officer," Satrine said. "We all saw that." Several patrolmen came running into the hallway. They took hold of their handsticks, but looked to Satrine and Welling before moving any closer.

Hilsom brushed dust off Olivant's vest. "Emotions are high right now, Quentin. You go home. Missus Tomar will be transferred to Eastwood. Tomorrow we'll all start fresh, without this . . . incident to muddle the issue."

Olivant snorted, but didn't say anything else. He went into the interrogation room, and came back out, leading Jaelia.

Welling looked to the patrolmen. "Take her back to holding, and prepare her for the transfer wagon." They escorted both Jaelia and Olivant off.

Once it was just the three of them, Hilsom cleared his throat. "That was quite a performance, Jinx. I hope it was helpful."

"Enlightening," Welling said. Satrine wasn't sure if it was a joke or not, but Hilsom gave it a dry laugh.

"I must return to my office before four bells. I trust you and yours can handle the transfer process without incident?" He left before receiving any answer.

"Nearly four bells," Welling said. "We still need to go over my open case. Would you prefer I brief you on the salient details while we go to the scene of the incident?"

"I would," Satrine said. "We shouldn't waste time."

"Excellent," said Welling. "However, on the way . . ."

"I can guess," Satrine said. "Something to eat?"

"Open case," Satrine said as Welling consumed two more of the fast wraps. He was pale and sweaty, and looked like he needed the food more than ever before. "Dead woman. Could be murder, could be suicide. Have I got that right?"

"You've paid rudimentary attention earlier," Welling said between bites. "The body was found in the root cellar of a pub on Jent, called the Red Hatchet."

"Lovely," Satrine said. New place, or at least a new name. "So what's the mystery?"

Welling led her down Easting. "The woman, identified as Jeyanne Holcomb—"

"Juicy," Satrine interrupted. Welling looked in askance,

so she clarified. "Juicy Holcomb, girl a little older than me, back in the neighborhood here."

"Friend?"

Satrine shrugged. "Someone whose existence I had been aware of. Little more."

Welling pointed around the corner of Silver and Easting. "So you could hardly guess if she was prone to suicide?"

"Back then? Any of us might have been called that. We were crazy. Fighting each other. Fighting sticks. Fighting anyone." She laughed, despite herself. "Frankly, it's probably a miracle that someone like Juicy lived this long, you know?"

He cleared his throat. "Well, Miss Holcomb was last seen alive at the closing of the pub on the night of the sixteenth. Three individuals saw her as they left the pub, as she was cleaning up and locking down."

"They all left together?"

"They did. Lorr Kimmen, Westley Earn, and Stand Overman. Any names familiar at all?"

She shook her head. "I presume you consider them potential suspects anyway?"

"None of them back each other up beyond leaving at the same time. They all claim to have gone their separate ways, and they agree upon that. They each went to their respective homes, where each of them have a spouse or family member who backs their claim of a timely return."

"Do you believe those claims?"

"I find them all dubious."

"This doesn't clear up the 'murder or suicide' question, Inspector."

"Indeed, and I will clarify. The pub was closed the following day for Saint Ilmer Day. Two employees came in yesterday morning to start business up. Together they found that the cleaning had not been handled, and could smell something horrible in the root cellar. But they couldn't open it."

"Why?"

"It was latched from the inside. Footpatrol and I had to break our way in. She was dead on the floor, throat slit, knife in her right hand."

They turned down Jent. The creepy familiar feeling of the street crawled up Satrine's spine. She didn't like being here. "Seems like she killed herself. So why the doubt?"

"First, the three witnesses: Kimmen, Earn, and Overman. They were consistent in their description of her behavior that night. Jovial, carefree. Even flirtatious. They all displayed shock at the idea she might have killed herself."

"That can't be all," Satrine said. She could hardly believe that Welling would let the emotional read of three laymen affect his judgment that much.

"It's her hands. The knife was in her right hand, and the cut across her throat is consistent with performing the action with that hand. Her hands, however, had the scars and calluses one would expect for a woman working in a pub and kitchen. Far more calluses on the left hand."

"Indicating that was her preferred hand to use," Satrine said. She tried to dig deep in her memory of Juicy Holcomb. She could barely remember the girl's face, let alone which hand she'd hold a jackstick or knife in.

"It's hardly anything I can hang a murder on, though," Welling said. "Especially given that I can't see how a killer could get out of the root cellar afterward."

"Magic?" Satrine offered.

"Granted," Welling said. "I may have to concede that would solve the mystery of how it was done. But I do not believe that is the case. I have nothing solid on which to base that belief."

Satrine had had enough experience with magic to know that it would leave traces that a skilled mage would notice. Welling was not a skilled mage, or at least not a trained one. And he refused to discuss the subject with her. It was possible he could sense the lack of magical traces but wouldn't consider it solid evidence. There were some devices and trinkets that could give a rough idea if magic had been used. "I don't suppose anyone brought in a mage balance to check."

Welling's eyes flashed hot, and then he turned back to focus on their walk down Jent. "Our house does make use of one, when magic is considered a possibility. Unfortunately, my presence renders the readings meaningless."

"Never mind, then."

"This is it," Welling said, pointing to the squat ugly building that was the Red Hatchet. A slateboard sign on the door read in rough scrawl CLOSED FOR MURDER, with the Constabulary seal in wax at the bottom. The pub was wedged in between two brick tenements, where in Satrine's memory there had once been an alley. The tenement to the right of it was more familiar. She and her mother had lived in it, for at least a little while.

"Root cellar, latched from the inside?" she said. "I wonder." She went inside, where it smelled dank and awful. "They haven't cleaned."

"Instructed not to, with the writ of investigation to back it up. That writ will expire tonight, though, which is probably why the captain was intent on my making progress quickly."

"I may have progress for you." She went into the back, where she figured the root cellar must be. "This building didn't exist before, you see. But the two on either side have been there for many decades."

"Obviously," Welling said. He pointed out the hatch to the root cellar, and she went down. It was dark, damp, and narrow. Welling followed her down with a lamp.

"What might not be obvious is that both buildings shared a basement back in the day." She took the lamp and held it up to one wall. Ugly masonry, mismatched stones. She gave it a tap. Not very thick. "I would imagine it wouldn't be too challenging to knock through that, get into the next building."

Welling came closer. "Possibly not, but that would leave some obvious signs. Not the least of which is the hole in the wall."

Satrine scanned the wall, looking along the floor. Near

some barrels, there was a hint of dust on the ground. She crouched by it, ran her finger through it. "There's this."

"Hardly damning."

She looked closer at the wall by the barrels. "The grouting is a very different color here. The rest of the wall is dark gray. This is chalk white." She scratched at it. "And it's a bit on the soft side."

Welling leaned, examining the wall. "Quite intriguing." He stood up fully, stepped back, and gave a sharp kick at the chalk-white patch.

It knocked through with surprising ease.

"Freshly made, covering a previously unknown exit for our killer," he said. "Quite ingenious, Inspector Rainey."

"And he would have had a whole day to do it," Satrine said. "Since the pub was closed on Saint Ilmer's."

"This revelation clarifies things immensely." He smirked at her, triumphantly. "Westley Earn is a stonemason. Furthermore, his alibi is a sister whose honesty I found dubious. Her demeanor was mousy and subjugated, and she repeated her story to me verbatim several times."

"A practiced speech," Satrine said. She remembered back in the day, someone like Idre would make the other kids repeat their stories over and over until they got them right. She never believed that would fool the sticks. "Motive?"

"Were I to hazard a guess, Earn was the only one who insisted Holcomb's demeanor was 'flirtatious.' Perhaps he returned to the pub with amorous intentions, and when denied, reacted with violence."

A little too clinical for Satrine's taste. Her hand instinctively went to her face, remembering a few too many moments of "amorous intentions" that ended with a violent reaction.

Welling was already climbing his way out of the root cellar. By the time Satrine caught up with him, he was back in the street, blowing his whistle to call a page. He took the slateboard off the door and wiped it clean with his sleeve. "Inspector Rainey, I am quite pleased with your investigative eye, and your unique perspective on the neighborhood."

"Glad to be of service."

Welling had produced a piece of chalk from a pocket and scrawled some notes on the slateboard. A page had arrived as he wrote. "Page, deliver this to Captain Cinellan, with instructions that he should send footpatrol and lockwagon to the home of Westley Earn—I have indicated the address here—and have him ironed and brought in for the murder of Jeyanne Holcomb. I will be along shortly to clarify points."

The page took the slate and ran off.

"All done quite nicely," Welling said. "Now we have only one officially open case. However, we will not make further progress on it now."

"Why not?"

He pointed over to the clock tower of Saint Limarre's. "It is nearly five bells," Welling said. "End of shift."

"Not for you," Satrine said. "I'm sorry you got stuck with transfer duty."

Welling shrugged. "Given the circumstances, my presence is logical. Should Missus Tomar, or her Circle brethren, make some sort of escape attempt, I'm the best suited to defend the lockwagon."

"What did happen in the questioning room, Welling?" Satrine asked. "I'm pretty sure it wasn't you."

"As am I," Welling said. "Though I am not entirely certain what did happen." He shook his head. With a clipped tone, he said, "It is of no moment. For now, you should return home. We will continue fresh in the morning."

He turned and walked off toward the stationhouse before Satrine could respond.

Satrine walked toward the bridges. She could hardly believe this had been only one day.

Chapter 9

SATRINE'S LEGS ACHED MORE than she could ever remember on the walk across the bridges back to the northern bank. She wanted to flag a cab, or at least hop on a tick-wagon, but she couldn't afford to waste a tick, even a pence, at this point. If that meant walking back and forth over the bridge each day, her feet bloody and callused, that would be what she would do.

The sun was nearly set by the time she reached the north bank. The streets and walkways widened here, and pedestrians and carriages moved around each other at a relaxed pace. Cottonwood and poplar trees cast long shadows down Upper Bank Road. Several shopkeepers were pulling their shutters down, exchanging pleasantries with their neighbors. The streetside tables of the High River Wine Club were overflowing with well-dressed students from the Royal College of Maradaine, drinking and arguing over politics or philosophy. Lightboys ran along, burning tapers in hand, lighting each streetlamp. Several people noted her as she walked past, smiles faded to respectful nods, stepping to the side of the walkway to let her pass. She was almost home before she realized why: she wore the coat and vest of a Constable Inspector. In this neighborhood, people gave that some respect.

The sight of the warm red bricks of Beltner Street—

both the buildings and the road itself—filled Satrine with warmth. Home. She went down the side steps of number 14 to the basement apartment. She knocked on the door sharply—it would be locked, of course. She needed to get back in the habit of carrying the key on her person.

"Who's there?"

"It's Satrine, Missus Abernand."

The door unlatched and opened, revealing the lean old face of Missus Abernand, lit by the flickering candle in her hand. "Got here later than you said."

"It's been quite a day, Missus Abernand," Satrine said, entering her home.

"This going to be regular?" The woman coughed out as she latched the door back behind her.

"Most likely, saints willing." Satrine hung her coat and vest by the door. "How is he?"

Missus Abernand shrugged. "He is. Ate some soup. Messed himself. Same as yesterday."

"Thank you, Missus Abernand." Satrine reached out to the old woman, who brushed her hand away and walked into the kitchen, the cramped centerpiece of the Rainey apartment.

"I made a stew," Missus Abernand said. "Beets and parsnips."

"Fine, thank you," Satrine said. "The girls?"

"I sent them to get bread," Missus Abernand said. "Heckman usually knocks it down a tick around six bells, you know." She slid the pile of schoolbooks off the table onto one of the chairs.

"Yes, I know." Missus Abernand made that comment three or four times a week.

The old woman narrowed her eyes at Satrine and pointed a bony finger at her. "You need to know that. More than ever." Her voice was a sharp rasp.

"I know, Missus Abernand."

"Hmph." The old woman looked about the kitchen. "I also swept. I'm going up now." She made her way to the inside stairway that led to her own home upstairs.

"Thank you for everything," Satrine called after her.

"It's nothing. See you in the morning." Missus Abernand gave a dismissive wave without turning around as she went up the steps.

Satrine crept over to the bedroom, opening the door enough to look in. Loren lay there asleep, a dim oil lamp burning low next to the bed. In moments like this, Satrine swore he looked like everything was fine, that he would wake up and get out of bed and be exactly how he was.

The front door opened. "We got it, Missus Abernand!" a girl's voice called out.

"She's gone up, Caribet," Satrine responded, closing the bedroom door.

"Mama!" Satrine's daughter ran over, grabbing her in a tight embrace. "Did you really work today?" Caribet's bright face was wide with joy and excitement.

"I did," Satrine said.

"As an inspector?" Rian, the elder daughter, had latched the door shut and was regarding the vest hanging on the hook. Rian took after Satrine, in coloring as well as her sharp eye. She had the same red hair and knowing smirk Satrine had always worn at that age. Caribet, of course, was her father's daughter. She had Loren's brown hair and caring eyes.

"That's right," Satrine said.

Rian brought the loaf of dark bread over to the table. "Did you see any dead bodies?"

"Rian!" Caribet squealed. "Don't be grotesque!"

"It's her job, Cari."

Caribet turned back to her mother, her eyes wide with horror. "Is it really?"

"It—" Satrine hesitated. The day had been filled with such lies and hidden truths, she couldn't bring herself to hide anything from her daughters. "It is an aspect. And yes, we did."

"We?" Rian's eyebrow went up.

"I have a partner, young lady. Do you think I'd manage better than Inspector Third Class?"

"I really can't believe you managed that, Mother," Rian said. She started ladling out bowls of stew. "I don't suppose you got your salary already."

"Not yet," Satrine said. She dug into her pocket and took out some coins. "But the sticks there had, you know—" She faltered.

"Passed the hat around for Father's sake?" Rian asked.

"Yes, that's right." Satrine glanced involuntarily back at the bedroom door.

"Good." Rian scooped up the coins and put them into a clay jar on the counter. "Wash your face, Caribet."

"Don't give me orders."

"Do it," Satrine added.

Caribet sighed and went off to the water closet.

Rian put bowls of stew on the table, glancing down to the door of the water closet. "I said before, Mother, I can stop school, go apprentice."

"Not a chance, Rian." Satrine was both proud and annoyed at how readily her eldest daughter was willing to sacrifice her education for the good of the family. Rian was her mother's daughter, no doubt. "Only one person is going to break her fingers over this business, and it's my job."

"We're together in this, Mother."

"Good," Satrine said. "Finish school, then go to university. Then you can take over working."

"You never did university. Or school."

Caribet came back to the kitchen, going straight to the teapot on the stove. "Can you stop it, Rian? Mother knows what she's doing."

Rian put a bowl of stew on the table in front of Satrine. "Do you, Mother?"

"Of course I do," she lied. She didn't need her daughters to hear otherwise.

Chapter 10

MINOX LIT HIS PIPE while waiting outside the stationhouse barn doors. The sun had set, the cool night wind whipped through the back alley. It was a dark night; both moons were only slivers.

"What's this I heard about a blasted skirt walking in the blazing door and being made a goddamned inspector?"

Minox didn't have to turn around. He knew the profane voice of his sister well enough, and knew that she would be at his side in seconds. "That's simplifying things to a degree."

Sure enough, Corrie came over to him. Her horsepatrol uniform was impeccably neat, long brown hair tied in a tight tail, covered partially by her riding cap. "Don't feed me sewage, Mine."

Minox winced slightly. He hated his sister's habit of shortening his name almost as much as the "Jinx" nickname. "That wouldn't be healthy."

Corrie gave a playful punch to his shoulder. "Blazing well right it wouldn't. So what's the rutting story? Did this skirt walk in the door and become inspector?"

"You have a correct order of events, but you're short on details. Missus Rainey came in with a letter from the commissioner, orders to hire her at the rank of Inspector Third Class." Saying it out loud, Inspector Rainey's unnamed subterfuge was suddenly clear. He tried not to let it show on his face. "While she may have not taken a traditional path to the rank, she has skill and clarity of thought."

Corrie's eyes went wide. "She's your blazing partner, isn't she?"

"And has proven herself to be the most suitable one I've been assigned to date."

"I bet she's suitable," Corrie said. "You heading to the house?"

"Not yet," Minox said. "Wagon escort out to East-wood."

"That's a wash of blazing sewage," Corrie said. "You going to need a ride along?"

Despite a twinge in his gut telling him otherwise, Minox shook his head. "No need to make this bigger than it needs to be."

"Well, get it done and get home, hear? Everyone will probably want to ask you about your rutting skirt part-ner." She clapped him on the shoulder once more and headed to the stables.

Minox looked out into the alley. Something wasn't right, but he couldn't put a name to it.

"Bad night for a wagon escort, eh?" The voice from inside the barn echoed his own thoughts. Minox turned to see the craggy features of Inspector Mirrell.

"How's your nose?" Minox asked, noting it was still purple and swollen.

"Been worse," Mirrell said. He stepped out of the barn, taking out his own pipe. "Heard the City Protector was making a lot of hay out of this one."

"I don't know much about that," Minox said. "He's kicking it up to the Archduchy Court."

"Feh," Mirrell said. He puffed on his pipe. "She doesn't deserve this." He glanced over at the lockwagon, where two footmen were chaining Jaelia Tomar into the seat.

"I agree," Minox said cautiously. He wasn't sure what Mirrell was up to. "I'm surprised you care."

Mirrell turned quick on Minox, his eyes hard. "What

kind of stick you take me for, Jinx? I know what justice is supposed to be, and this ain't it. Woman's husband was killed, you should be dragging in the man who did it, not making her life worse."

"Is there some evidence I haven't seen, Inspector Mirrell?" Minox asked. "Some bit of diligence I haven't done?"

"That's not what I'm saying, Jinx." Mirrell scowled as he took another puff from his pipe.

"Then what are you saying?"

"Just . . . something stinks here. I don't know what." He glanced over to the lockwagon, where Jaelia Tomar was being loaded and locked in. Minox knew there was something out of sorts about Mirrell, but he also knew well enough that he wasn't going to get anything out of the laconic man that he didn't want to share. Normally, he wouldn't even engage the man, but he was curious about other matters.

"Your sewer worker case, what happened?"

"Nothing worth noting. Two men dead, each of them with a knife in their hand. Looked to us like they killed each other, and Leppin thinks it's likely."

"Possibly over jealousy?" Minox asked. "Or an unfaithful wife?"

"Blazes if I know." He turned back to Jaelia in the lockwagon, scowling. "Hardly matters. Both dead by each other's hand. Closed book."

"You aren't curious, though?"

Mirrell opened his mouth, but anything he was about to say was interrupted by the wagonmaster calling out that he was ready to drive. Mirrell snuffed his pipe and went to the far side of the wagon, and took his place on the runner.

"Eastwood facility, gents?" the driver asked.

"That's right," Minox said.

The driver nodded. "All right. Easting to Lowbridge, then Waterpath out to Eastwood."

Mirrell offered his own navigation advice. "Fannen cuts you through East Maradaine straight across."

"Narrows in that neighborhood, Inspector. Blazing hard on a two-horse wagon. Would take half a bell longer."

Mirrell grumbled but said nothing audible. Minox understood Mirrell's annoyance. At earliest, Minox could hope to be at his home by half-past seven bells. Mirrell lived out west in Gelmoor, so it might be as late as nine bells before he was home.

The lockwagon rolled out of the barn. Minox snuffed out his pipe and took his place on the side. It turned out of the alley onto Easting.

"Clear," Minox called out, following the escort protocol.

"Clear," Mirrell called back halfheartedly.

Most people on the street avoided looking at the lockwagon. Most of them, living or working near the stationhouse, knew how to recognize a transfer run, and also knew well enough not to cause any trouble. The few pedalcarts and wheelstands in the street were quickly scurried out of the way so the wagon could pass unobstructed.

"Easting and Silver," Minox called as they approached the intersection. There was a small crowd to the left, in front of Saint Limarre's. Most likely going to sunset services. Nothing to be concerned about. "Clear."

No return call from Mirrell. This was typical of the man, if annoying. The protocol was supposed to be followed, but many officers, including Mirrell, didn't bother.

"Inspector Mirrell," Minox said pointedly. "Left side clear." That should be enough to shame Mirrell into responding.

Nothing.

Minox glanced back down the street. A small crowd had formed around something lying on the ground. Something wearing Inspector Mirrell's coat.

"Driver!" Minox shouted. He drew out his handstick and crossbow and dropped off the runner. He ran around the front of wagon, crossbow aimed ahead of him. The lockwagon door was open on the right side. Minox took two steps closer so he could see inside. Jaelia Tomar was still there, still shackled into her seat. Her head drooped to one side, eyes closed. Welt across her temple.

Dead?

Still breathing, if shallowly.

Minox turned back toward the driver. "Did you see—"

The driver fell from the seat, his body hitting the cobblestone.

Minox leaped up onto the runner, and scrambled up to the seat. Before he got his footing, someone grabbed his right wrist.

The attacker was fast, yanking Minox's arm out in a wide arc and forcing the crossbow to go flying out of his hand. Minox responded with his handstick, off-balance as he was, knocking his assailant in the ribs with a hard jab.

He hadn't even gotten a good look at the man attacking him. Dark clothes, hood over his face. Nothing else before a fist cracked Minox in the face. Minox stumbled back, almost falling off the wagon. He forced himself to lurch forward at the hooded figure, use his imbalance to his advantage.

The figure grabbed Minox by the front of his coat and rolled back, hurling Minox off the front of the wagon, crashing through the yoke.

Minox was dazed, head spinning, barely able to get his eyes to focus on the figure as it dropped down off the wagon. The figure leaned into the open door. Minox tried to pull himself up on his feet, focus his thoughts. Push through the pain.

The figure pulled the limp form of Jaelia Tomar out of the wagon, slung her over his shoulder. Minox was up now. In the distance, people were screaming or running away. Never any help. Minox charged at the figure to tackle him. Missus Tomar would undoubtedly be injured in the process, but that was a necessary risk. The figure reacted before Minox reached him, throwing two darts that sunk into Minox's shoulder. Minox cried out, but he still had momentum working for him. He piled into the figure and Jaelia Tomar, and all three of them hit the ground in a hard crunch.

A fist hit Minox again and again in the sides. Woozy and dizzy, Minox was unable to block the attacks or respond. The figure pushed Minox off from on top of him, then kicked him hard in the face. Minox lost a few moments in a red, blurry haze, and when he had his senses back the figure had run to a waiting horse, hurling Jaelia's body over the animal before mounting it himself.

Minox's hand found his whistle, getting it to his mouth as he struggled to draw enough breath to blow it. He managed a weak trill, followed by a sharper one. He gave a glance down the road. Mirrell was stirring, but not on his feet yet.

The man spurred his horse and was charging down Silver.

Minox pulled the darts out of his shoulder. Fortunately they had barely penetrated his coat and vest. They were the least of his worries. "You won't outrace me," he muttered, forcing his screaming body over to the wagon horses.

The yoke was in pieces already, and Minox summoned a burst of raw magic to crack the rest of it off one horse. Despite the aching protest every joint and muscle gave him, Minox forced himself to mount the beast.

This was not a riding horse, definitely not a racing horse, but it would do. Minox blew the whistle again, the signal to summon any regulars or officers who could hear, and kicked his horse to a gallop. He hadn't ridden horse-patrol for five years for nothing.

Crowds had formed on the walkways along the street. People were cheering and jeering both. A part of Minox's mind analyzed that the people really didn't care what was happening, nor were they invested in his capturing the man, or in the man escaping from him. They just wanted the spectacle.

His horse pounded down the cobblestone. It was giving good chase, he had to credit the beast. The man's horse was a stronger, faster breed, but it carried two people. In a few seconds, Minox had closed the distance. He had to take out the figure, and quickly, though, as his horse could not maintain this pace for long. No crossbow. He'd have to use magic.

He gave a quick, hard blast at the figure. To his surprise, the green energy bounced off the man's back, no apparent effect.

Another blast. Nothing.

Minox's vision blurred. He could barely breathe. He wasn't going to last much longer.

Last chance. Last shot, poorly aimed. The magic was as weak as he was, splashing over the limp body of Jaelia Tomar like water.

That was too much for Minox. His head spun, his whole body went limp. He nearly fainted, barely managing to pull his horse to a stop before falling off it. His whole world went dark before he hit the ground.

⬦

"Minox!"

His face was being slapped. Consciousness came back into sharp focus.

He put up his hand to block another slap before it connected with his face. "I'm awake, Inspector Mirrell."

Mirrell hovered over Minox, his face a mix of anger and concern. "The blazes happened, Jinx?" Minox noted the switch that Inspector Mirrell made from his given name to his assigned epithet, as soon as he realized he wasn't dead.

"Our wagon was attacked, clearly." Minox extended a hand to Mirrell, hoping the other inspector would help him to his feet. Mirrell took his hand and pulled him up abruptly. Minox's whole body was hurting, especially the sharp pains in his right shoulder and hip. He must have landed on them when he fell off the horse.

"A breakout of the prisoner?" Mirrell asked.

"That's one possibility," Minox said. He glanced around the street. He had given chase almost to the corner of Silver and Nole. The horse stood a half a block away. It was too well trained to run off on its own. Minox started limping over to it.

Mirrell kept up with him, though it was clear by how he walked that his leg was injured. "One possibility? A constable lockwagon is attacked, and the prisoner is taken!"

Minox grabbed the horse's rein. "'Taken' being the important word here, Inspector."

"Oh, blasted saints, Jinx, what are you on about?"

"What did you see happen, Inspector?"

"Not much. We were rolling along, and next thing I knew, I was yanked off the carriage, and lying on the street."

"Hmm." Minox noted the streets were now empty of people to serve as potential witnesses of the event. "We should be making pursuit. I blew for footpatrol, and they clearly haven't arrived. Have you tried yet?"

"Not yet," Mirrell said. "I was still dazed, and then saw you on the ground." He glanced down Silver, to the clock tower over Saint Limarre's. "Six bells eighteen. How much lead do you figure he's gotten since we've been out?"

Minox reached into his pocket. No whistle. He must have dropped it earlier. "Seven minutes. Have you seen my whistle?"

"No." Mirrell took out his own and blew a call signal.

"At this point, it's only procedure," Minox said. He didn't think anything useful would be gained from calling in regulars, other than getting the lockwagon back to the barn. "Our attacker was well prepared, and with seven minutes to get away, I'm sure he has enacted a spectacular escape. Have you checked on the driver?"

"Not yet," Mirrell said. "Was he hurt?"

"I think so," Minox said, leading the horse back toward the wagon. "The attacker was cleanly methodical. He attacked you first, quickly and efficiently."

"Quite," Mirrell said harshly.

"Then he . . ." Minox trailed off, thoughts racing.

"He what?" Mirrell asked.

"Incapacitated Missus Tomar," Minox said. That was important.

"How do you mean?" They had reached the intersection, where the lockwagon sat, half broken. The driver was awake and kneeling, but clearly not in his full senses yet.

"Driver, are you well?"

"Do I look blazing well, tosser?" the driver snapped back.

"As well as any of us," Minox replied. His own body

was battered, he may have even broken a rib, and his thoughts were clouded with pain pounding against his skull. It was nearly impossible to concentrate on the idea that was trying to form through the haze.

Minox walked around the wagon, checking the door. "The attacker made a point of removing any conscious choice from Missus Tomar as soon as he possibly could. If he considered her an ally, surely he would want to keep a capable mage in play, able to assist him, wouldn't he?"

"Unless the plan is to give her deniability," Mirrell said.

"Impressive line of thought, Inspector Mirrell," Minox said. "You raise a valid point. But she had been knocked across the head. Hardly something to do to an ally."

"Except to drive home that deception," Mirrell said. "I've seen people do plenty worse."

Minox nodded. "Indeed. However, I still have the distinct impression that our assailant's purpose was not to rescue Missus Tomar from us, but to take her away."

"Why?"

"That's what I'm not sure of," Minox said. He turned to look back down Silver. His head was still pounding, but there a curious sensation drawing him in that direction. It was a singular thing, but it danced frustratingly along the outside of his senses. Almost a light mist in the corner of his eye. Almost a buzz in his ear. Almost the scent of a storm about to break. Almost a cord tied to his chest, pulling him forward. "What is that?"

"What?" Mirrell asked.

"I . . . I'm not sure."

"Jinx, you got walloped pretty good," Mirrell said. "We should take you over to the ward and have a splint check you out."

"I'm fine," Minox said. He stepped in the direction he was being drawn. "There is definitely something happening in this direction."

"Nothing is happening there, Jinx." Mirrell's voice was fuzzy and distant.

"I'm certain that there is." Minox took another step. His foot didn't touch the road. It felt like it sank into sand. His head filled with mud. Fog and buzz and storm and cord. Mirrell's voice shouting his full name. Darkness.

Chapter 11

SOUND RETURNED FIRST, just murmured voices in the background. Then taste—honeyed cider being poured in his mouth. Minox found the strength to open his eyes, to see Leppin's face hovering over him.

"There you are," Leppin said. "Welcome back."

Minox tried to sit up, and found it incredibly difficult.

"Give yourself a few minutes, Minox," Leppin said.

Minox coughed and found his voice. "What happened?"

"You dropped dead away in the middle of the street," Leppin said.

"Dead away?" Minox repeated. "Was my condition that grave that I ended up in your care?"

"Not really," Leppin said, stepping away. "Though Mirrell and Vince nearly believed it was."

"Vince would be?"

"The wagon driver, Minox," Leppin said. He shook his head. "Those two needed the splint to patch them up. But they were right shaken with your state. Pale, sweaty. Shaking in fit one minute, almost no pulse the next. So, of course, they call a specialist." He brushed off his vest, looking all too proud of himself.

Minox managed to push himself up on his elbows. "How are you a specialist?"

Leppin shrugged. "Fairly, they thought you might have been poisoned or such, which is why they called me over."

"Over where?" Minox was on a small cot, curtains blocking any other view.

"Ironheart Ward." Leppin sat down on the cot. "Anyhow, luckily for you, my studies were always somewhat eccentric, so I was able to recognize the symptoms of Magic Depletion Fatigue." He lowered his voice. "Plus the splints and Yellowshields didn't really know you were a mage, so they wouldn't have figured it."

"What is Magic Depletion Fatigue?" Minox tried to tune his ear for any voices past the curtain. Aunt Beliah was a nurse at Ironheart, and he didn't need her finding him here and fussing over him.

Leppin reached under the cot and pulled out Minox's belt. "How many bolts for your crossbow do you carry?"

"Six, typically," Minx answered.

"Right, so what happens when you shoot all six?"

"Out of bolts," Minox said. "Is that what I did? Used all my magic? Forever?" Was that it? He had no idea that it would just be gone like that.

"Not for life, idiot," Leppin said. "Just for . . . I'm explaining it badly. It's more like a water well, you see. You draw a lot out at once, it goes dry. Takes a while to replenish."

"How long is a while?"

"Blazes if I know," Leppin said.

Minox struggled to pull himself up to a sitting position. "That is my problem as well."

"You shouldn't be getting up, you know."

"I need to know the status of the situation with Missus Tomar. Has she been located? Or her abductor?"

"I thought she had been broken out," Leppin said. "That's what Mirrell reported."

"Fool," Minox muttered. "Are my clothes under the cot, Leppin?"

"What are you planning to do?" Leppin asked.

"I have to go to the stationhouse, report what happened."

"Oh, no," Leppin said. "You've got two choices, Minox. Stay here or go home."

Minox was not interested in staying in the ward. "Home it is. Give me my clothes."

Leppin pulled a crate out from under the cot. "I'm serious, Minox. Go home, eat something, and get some sleep. Do not come to the stationhouse until tomorrow. Promise that."

Minox took out his clothes and started to dress. "Fair enough. What is the time?"

"Half-past seven bells. More or less."

Minox nodded. "As you wish, Leppin." In just four and a half hours it would be after midnight, and then he'd return to the stationhouse.

"Tomorrow morning, Mine." Corrie came through the curtain, her face flushed. "You have to nail him down to blazing specifics, bodyman, or he'll pull a blasted trick on you. Sinner would sneak back in at a click after midnight, I'd rutting well bet you."

Leppin let loose a nervous cackle. "You've probably . . . um, you've surely got his number, Miss, um, Officer . . ." He trailed off, his hands fumbled on the lapels of his coat as he went through the curtain, his eyes fixed on the floor as he brushed past Corrie.

"Strange little rutter," Corrie muttered. "Come on, Mine. I'm gonna put you on my horse and take you back home. Don't you dare argue with me."

"Of course not," Minox said. "Aunt Beliah isn't working here tonight, is she?"

"She's off, and back at the house. Where we'll tell everyone you got clocked in the head and knocked out. I don't need to understand anything else the bodyman was rutting on about."

"Fine," Minox said. He felt no need to discuss specifics with Corrie or anyone else. "Let's go."

He noted, as they walked out of the ward, that Corrie did not extract any promise from him as to when he'd return. He certainly wasn't going to remind her otherwise.

Satrine and the girls had eaten, the dishes were washed, the last of the soup left covered on the back of the stove. Caribet had taken soup in to her father, and Satrine was more than willing to leave that to her daughter. She knew it was a horrible attitude to take, but feeding her husband was a task that filled her with dread. Caribet genuinely enjoyed it, and she was welcome to it.

Rian sat in the kitchen, reading a school text. Satrine asked her about what she was reading; Rian had sullenly responded it was history, the Druth Reunification. Satrine nodded, grateful that Rian was receiving a far more traditional education than she ever had.

Satrine went up the back stairs and knocked on Missus Abernand's door. The old woman was clearly still awake; Satrine could hear her clomping around in there. After a moment, Missus Abernand opened the door and walked back into her parlor wordlessly. Satrine took it for an invitation and joined her on the couch.

"I suppose that door will have to be open more often now?" Missus Abernand asked, pouring out a glass of apple brandy.

Satrine took the drink and sipped. "I don't want to have to impose—"

"You don't have people, Satrine," Missus Abernand said. "You don't and Loren doesn't."

"Loren has the Constabulary . . ."

"And where have they been, hmm?"

"Gave me a job."

Missus Abernand scoffed. "You gave yourself that job, and don't pretend otherwise."

Satrine took another swig of the apple brandy. Missus Abernand had no idea how true that really was. "Even still, they have been his family."

"Family steps up in times like this. They take you in, they do what's right. I know you don't get what it means."

Satrine poured a second glass of brandy. "Commissioner Enbrain did what he could." That wasn't true, and Missus Abernand jumped right on it.

"You should have had your widow fund. Not giving it to you was an insult."

"I'm not a widow." That was the story Enbrain had given her, it was the official ruling from the brass in the head office. Loren hadn't died in the line of duty. Even if he died now, she wouldn't see a tick of her fund.

"It's sewage," Missus Abernand said. She put down her glass. "Excuse my crudity. I just can't stand it when excuses are made not to do the decent thing."

"That's because you're extraordinary," Satrine said. "I don't think I could do this without your help."

"You couldn't." Missus Abernand finished her drink. "I'm to bed. You should do the same. When do you need to leave here?"

"Seven bells. But the girls will probably be around until eight."

A bony finger pointed to the stairs. "Rian was giving some mouth to me, you know. Be on her."

"Yes, ma'am," Satrine said.

"Sleep well," Missus Abernand said. "Get the lamps and close the door behind you." She went into her bedroom and shut herself in.

Satrine went around the parlor and snuffed the lamps. With only one left burning, she finished her brandy. Glancing at Missus Abernand's door, she poured a third glass and threw the contents down her throat. She poured herself one more, stoppered the bottle, and went down.

The Welling household was a three-story whitestone on the Keller Cove side of Escaraine, just half a block from Escaraine Square, where the neighborhoods of Inemar, Dentonhill, and Keller Cove met. Despite Corrie and him working in Inemar, the family had always been a Keller Cove family. Much of the family—that is, the children and grandchildren of Fenner and Jillian Welling— lived in the house. Not Fenner himself, of course. He hadn't lived here for years.

Corrie had blathered on profanely the entire ride over. She kept coming back to the subject of Inspector Rainey's appointment, which was a thorn she clearly couldn't pull from her foot. "I was running streets as a page, cadet years, footpatrol for how rutting long? And as a blazing lamplighter half that time. I had to rutting well knock some blasted teeth out of a few wastrels before they let me get a horse under me. And only in the goddamned night shift at that! But she walks in the blazing door—"

Jace and Ossen sat on the front stoop, the two youngest of the grandchildren, save for Minox's sister Alma. Jace—Minox and Corrie's eighteen-year-old brother—was in his cadet uniform. He had just come from his shift at the Aventil stationhouse. Ossen—their cousin, Nyla's brother—was two years younger, only a senior page at Keller Cove. They both perked up at their approach.

"What ya doing riding home, Cor?" Jace asked. "You ditching the night shift?"

"You wish, rutter," Corrie said. She thumbed to Minox, who dismounted uneasily. He still wasn't up to strength. "Giving the inspector a ride home after he took a hard knock."

"Saints, Minox," Ossen said. "Quite the bruise you got there."

"Took quite the knock."

"Some rutter busting on a prisoner escort," Corrie said. "Took out Mine here, as well as the driver and another inspector."

"Saints!" Jace said.

"Don't you need to get back to Inemar?" Minox asked. He didn't need any more of Corrie's commentary.

"Right." She turned her horse around. "Get some rest, hmm? See you all at breakfast." She spurred her horse and went off.

"How bad is it?" Jace asked.

"Looks worse than it is," Minox said.

"You should let Aunt Beliah look at it," Jace said. Minox gave him a withering look. "Or Ferah. She's home, too." Their cousin Ferah was a Yellowshield, and her ministrations would be less annoying than her mother's.

"I just came from Ironheart, I don't need anything more." Minox knew Jace and Ossen would let it rest at that. "Is supper ready?"

Ossen shrugged, as did Jace. "Let's find out."

Jace led the way in. The front sitting room was crowded: Uncle Timmothen and his three sons were drinking beers and talking with Cole Pyle—Nyla and Ossen's father—and Oren, Minox's other brother. All were still in Constabulary uniform: Timmothen a captain, Oren a lieutenant, Cole a horsepatrol commander. Only Timm's youngest son, Davis, stood out in this crowd, with his spectacles and slight build. He was an examinarium assistant, but he did his best to laugh and drink with his brothers.

"Hey, Inspector!" Oren called out. "You get knocked down good there?"

"Took it and got back up," Minox said, mimicking the phrase their father had always said.

"That's how you do it," Cole said, his South Maradaine accent thick. He raised up his beer and drank. Back in the day, Cole had been the horsepatrol partner with Minox's father.

"Supper on, Pop?" Ossen asked, coming over to Cole. He made a grab for his father's drink, which Cole easily dodged, grabbing Ossen in a headlock with his other arm.

"Nice try, boy," Cole said. "I think it'll be on in a click or two." He let Ossen go and pushed him away playfully.

"If you'll excuse me," Minox said, passing through the sitting room. Oren clapped him on the shoulder as he passed through, as did Timmothen, but they let him through without any further comment.

In the dining room, the table was set, though no food had been placed out. Despite that, Uncle Tal—Beliah's husband—sat with two of his three children. Ferah had changed out of her Yellowshield uniform into a simple dress and coat. Colm wore his Fire Brigade uniform, as did his father. The two of them were eating stew and rolls, the only food on the table.

"Eating without us, Tal?" Minox asked. "Or just couldn't wait?"

"Colm and I have to head out," Tal said, taking another bite. "Chief Yenner keeps switching schedules around. Not making a lick of sense, but he's not listening."

"He's trying to scrape every tick together or something," Colm said.

"I'm telling you, son, the way it looks, there will be nights where there's no Brigade at all in Seleth."

"I'm sure it's covered somehow," Colm said.

"Hmm," Minox said. "I might need to join you with the early eating."

"Never enough with you, Minox," Tal said. "You can chance asking. Dark ones will probably chase you out."

Ferah stood up and put an arm around Minox. "Don't pay them any mind. Let's go see what we can do for you." Scowling at her father, she led Minox into the kitchen.

The "dark ones" Tal referred to were Minox's mother and Aunt Zura, Timmothen's wife. Zura was Acserian, had dusky brown skin and black hair. Minox's mother was half Racquin—her father was Minox's namesake—and she had a rich olive complexion. The two of them ran the kitchen in the Welling house, and they were cooking up a storm as usual. Aunt Beliah sat at the table, shelling peas, while Minox's youngest sister Alma studied next to her.

"What happened to you?" Beliah said, dropping the peas and coming over to Minox. "You had this looked at?"

"Yes, Beliah," Minox said. "I'm fine."

Mother came over from the stove. "Are you sure, Minox?"

"I could use a bite, though," Minox said in a lowered voice. Mother understood. Minox's magical ability was not spoken of, not openly, in the household. The consequences of it, however, were obvious and dealt with discreetly.

"Of course," Mother said. She went back over to the stove.

"You were treated, yes?" Beliah asked. "Where?"

"At Ironheart."

"Who treated you? Was it Doctor Westron?"

"I'm not sure. I woke in the care of Mister Leppin from our stationhouse."

"Leppin? I don't know him," Beliah said. She looked up at Ferah. "Do you know him?"

"He's—" Minox paused. He didn't feel he should have to answer this, but he knew well enough that Beliah was not about to let things go unless he gave her a full report. She was a Welling, and Wellings do not give up. "He's the bodyman at our stationhouse."

"Were you dead?" Beliah screeched.

"Of course not, don't be absurd." Minox wished he could take his food and retreat to his room. "The doctors did think he might have insight to my condition, however. And he is a—" Minox stumbled on the word for a moment. "Close associate."

Minox's mother came over with a plate piled high with sausages, white beans, roasted beets, flatbreads, and spiced cracked wheat. Classic Druth cooking with Racquin and Acserian accents.

"Blessings of each saint," his mother said quietly as she put the plate down.

"May we be blessed," Minox said, which Beliah and Ferah repeated with him. Zura, back by the stoves, said nothing, but pressed a knuckle to her forehead. Minox sat down next to Alma and started eating.

Mother stood over him. "Rough day?"

"Aren't they all?" he asked.

Zura came over with a tray with another plate, more modestly portioned. "Ferah, dear, bring this up to Mother Jillian. Then come back for another one for your brother."

Minox perked up at that. As Ferah left with the tray, he looked over at his aunts. "Is Evoy still—out in the stable?" For the past months, Evoy had been spending more and more time in the old stable, often locking himself in there for days at a time, refusing to come in, refusing almost any contact except delivery of food.

"He doesn't want to come out," Beliah said, her voice cracking slightly. "You're the only one he really listens to, Minox. Could you have a word with him?"

Minox sighed, taking another bite. "I'll try, Aunt Beliah. But I can't make him do anything . . ." He trailed off.

Zura nodded and kissed her knuckle, touching it to her forehead. "God and Acser willing, he'll get through this. I'm sure he will. Not like—" She stopped, staring at Beliah, and then scurried back over to the stoves.

It didn't need saying, they all knew. Twelve years ago, Fenner had started the same way. Locking himself in his room, obsessively writing in his journals, collecting newsprint articles. He grew more agitated and reclusive, periodically screaming at family members. It eventually reached the point where they had to put him in Haltom Asylum, where he'd been ever since.

The last thing anyone wanted was to see the same thing happen to Evoy. They were all afraid he had inherited his grandfather's madness.

Especially Minox. Not just because Evoy was his favorite cousin.

Because every day Minox fought the urge to lock himself out there with him.

Aunt Beliah continued to talk while Minox ate, switching to mundane topics. Nyla and Aunt Emma—her mother—had gone to the dressmaker shop for the evening. She harped on not seeing Terrent—"Poor Terrent" she always called him, as he was widowed—in over a month. Terrent was the only one of his father's siblings who didn't live in the big house, instead living with his twin daughters out in East Maradaine, where they all worked for the Constabulary. There had been the occasional whispers among the aunts that Terrent might be facing the same sort of affliction as Fenner and Evoy.

Minox wasn't worried about Terrent, though. Terrent was sometimes eccentric, but never coming close to madness. Minox had it on good authority, through contacts in East Maradaine, that Terrent and the twins were doing just fine. At times he envied them. More than once the idea of taking a room at one of the boardinghouses in Inemar crossed his mind. Things would be easier if he could stay in Inemar.

"Minox?" Beliah said, her tone indicating she had said his name more than once. "Are you still hungry?"

He looked down at the plate, which was empty. He had been lost in thought, scraping at nothing for some time.

"No, I—"

"You're awfully distracted," Beliah said. "That's not like you."

"True," Minox said. "Perhaps I've been more affected than I thought." He looked down at himself. There were drops of blood all over his shirt and vest. "I should go clean up, I think. If you'll all excuse me."

Without waiting for permission or acceptance from any of his family, Minox made for the back stairwell to the second floor water closet. He stripped off the offending clothes and scrubbed his face and arms clean. He checked his face in the mirror. Some degree of stubble had grown on his cheeks and chin.

That wouldn't do.

He dug through his sack of personal items until he found his straight razor. Of course, it would be ill advised to continue without—

"Hot water?" Alma was at the door carrying a pitcher. "Mother thought you might need some."

"Indeed," Minox said. He took the pitcher and filled his basin. "What was today's study?"

"History. Eighth century."

"The mad kings of the Cedidore line?" Minox took the razor to his face.

"Exactly." Alma looked distinctly unhappy with the reading.

"Do yourself a favor, skip ahead to the ninth century. There's some good stuff in there."

She smiled weakly. "You really all right?"

"I'll be fine," Minox said.

"Then why are you pointing the razor at the window?" Alma asked.

Minox hadn't even realized his arm was outstretched. But he was pointing, his arm responding to something other than his own conscious directive. Pointing to the southeast.

Toward Inemar.

Minox put down the razor and wiped off his face. "Alma, you will have to forgive and excuse me. Something . . . something is afoot that I cannot explain. But I believe I must take action."

He went into his room and put on a fresh shirt and vest. Alma still stood in the hallway, carrying the pitcher and looking stupefied.

"What's happening? Are you leaving?"

"I must," Minox said. "Please extend my apologies to . . . everyone."

"You're scaring me a little, Minox."

Minox knelt down in front of her. "To be honest, Alma, I'm a little frightened myself. Keep this our secret."

She looked dubious, but nodded in agreement.

Minox nodded back, and went off down the front stairs and out the door before anyone could catch a word with him.

Chapter 12

THE STREETS WERE QUIETER NOW, only a few people bustling about by the light of the oil lamps. The lockwagon had been cleared out of the way; street sweepers had brushed away the splintered wood from the shattered yoke. There were no signs of the earlier excitement.

And nothing in the way of clues that could lead him to the current location of Jaelia Tomar, be she fugitive or victim.

But there was something. A compulsion drew him here, beyond the usual compulsion he had to solve every mystery to a satisfactory conclusion. This was something external. Something he could feel. Something he had felt when he was here before.

Tether. The word crossed his mind again.

He turned to look down Silver. Was what he had sensed there before just a figment, half imagined before losing consciousness?

No.

Whatever it was, it was still there. Fainter than earlier, but still there.

It felt like a pull, west down Silver. The path he had chased Missus Tomar's abductor down. He took a few steps along with the pull.

Then he stepped fully into it, like a current in the river.

He walked down the street with the current, letting it guide him.

This was clearly magic, there was no point in denying that. Was it Jaelia Tomar's magic? His own? Some conjunction of the two? Was that even possible? He had to admit, he had no idea. Still, the best possible lead he had was to follow it.

It led him down several blocks. In the back of his mind, he chided himself for even giving credence to the idea of following an ill-defined feeling instead of relying on solid observation, investigation, and deduction.

A block past Fannen, the current curved into an alley. The feeling, the shift in direction, was too powerful to ignore or dismiss. Minox was convinced that, if nothing else, the sensation was real and worth following. The only question remaining was if it would lead to anything of significance for his case.

He took two steps down the alley, letting the sensation guide him. The alley was nearly pitch dark, and Minox had no reason to believe it uninhabited. There was also no reason to be foolhardy, especially given his condition. He went back out to the street and reached for his whistle.

Not in his pocket. He had lost it in the scuffle earlier.

He briefly considered the possibility that, since he had lost it a block from here, he might find it in the street nearby. He then dismissed it as absurd to count on such serendipity.

A glance around the vicinity showed no patrolmen in sight.

He didn't want to go back to the stationhouse, or even search nearby for a patrolman. The idea that he might lose the current crossed his mind, and he could not shake the belief, irrational though it was, that this current was leading him in the direction of Jaelia Tomar.

If he could find no backup to pursue this possibility, he'd at least need light. He dismissed the idea of making some light magically. He had never had any success in the past with that, and he felt that any attempt to use magic right now could be catastrophic to his health.

A lantern hung over the door of a pub right next to the alley. Minox couldn't bring himself to justify theft, even in the name of pursuing justice. He called out to a young man exiting the pub.

"You there," he said. "Tell the pub owner that I would buy his lantern hanging there."

The young man raised an eyebrow. "You been taking the *'fitte*, friend?"

"I'm well in my right mind, sir, though it is good of you to express such concern, given my unusual request. But I'm in need of light, and I am in some haste."

The man opened the door. "Hey, Garren. There's a stick who wants to buy your lamp."

A beefy, sweaty man came out of the pub, wiping his hands on his apron. "What's the word, stick?"

Minox took a few coins from his pocket. "Your lamp there, good sir. A crown and twelve is more than fair."

The pub owner screwed his face. "I ain't seen you before, stick."

Minox held open his coat. "Inspector, sir. I don't do walking patrol."

The man nodded. "Right, I get it. I just . . . it's usually not the sticks offering money to me, if you get my meaning. Little confused."

Minox knew, from his own walking days, many patrol took bribes, or worse, shook citizens for "donations." He found such acts loathsome. "I assure you, I simply have urgent need of a lamp and I would find it distasteful to take it from you without fair recompense."

"All right," the man said, taking the lamp down. "Crown and twelve." He gave it to Minox and took the money. He gave Minox an appraising look. "Though, if you don't mind, Inspector, come back when you have the chance. I wouldn't mind talking to you about your fellows who have a different opinion of 'fair recompense.'"

"Absolutely. Though it may take me a day or two."

Minox paused. "Quickly, though. These fellows. Night or day? Foot or horse?"

"It varies. But mostly night. And horsepatrol."

"I'll look into it." He handed the man a calling card. "If you don't hear from me in reasonable time, ask for me at the stationhouse."

"I understand," said the man, and he went back in the pub. Minox held up the lamp, drew out his handstick, and went into the alley.

Satrine sipped at the brandy in the dull lamplight. Caribet had gone to bed. Rian continued to study, pointedly ignoring her mother. She seemed to turn each page in annoyance, as if Satrine's mere presence in her own sitting room was disturbing her.

She was welcome to feel that way. Satrine wasn't in any hurry to go into the bedroom.

She sipped again. Glass was empty. She tilted it back as far as she could, trying to drain those few stubborn drops at the bottom.

That was it. No more left.

Was there any wine in the pantry? There might be some. Or some cider.

No, she finished the cider last night.

"Blazes."

"What, Mother?"

Blazes, Rian was still in here.

"Nothing," Satrine said. "What time is it?"

"Nearly ten bells, I figure," Rian said. "Don't you have to work in the morning?"

"Don't you have school?"

Rian came over to the couch and picked up the brandy glass. She gave it a light sniff and took it into the kitchen. "You barely slept last night. If you're going to work this job, you need to rest."

"I know, I know," Satrine said, getting to her feet.

"I can do my part, you know."

"Rian, I told you—"

"When you were my age—"

"My mother had already run off. That isn't something you have to worry about, is it?"

"But—"

"I don't even want to talk about it."

Truth was, when she was Rian's age, she was hidden in a secret room on a slow ship to Waisholm, getting etiquette, accent, and manners crammed into her skull. Learning to become a Waish *quia,* turning a street rat into a noblewoman.

Had she really been the same age as Rian when that happened? It seemed impossible. Satrine couldn't even contemplate Rian being able to handle anything like that. Being able to handle any of the things she had had to do.

But Rian hadn't had to grow up on the streets of Inemar. Things were harder then. Children were harder then. Her mother had vanished, probably presuming that Satrine could take care of herself.

Rian would never have to worry about things like that.

"Focus on your studies," Satrine said, after she realized she had been in silent reverie for several seconds.

"That's what I'm doing."

"Fine." Satrine got off the couch and went to the bedroom door. "Go to bed soon, all right?"

"Yes, Mother." Rian sounded hostile, Satrine thought. Then she mused that when she was the same age, she would have broken the teeth of anyone who told her the same thing. In comparison, Rian was a diplomat.

Satrine put her hand on the knob. Nothing left to drink to steel herself with. Time to face it.

She opened the door.

———— ◆▶ ————

There were no signs of life in the alley, at least none that stepped out when an armed constable came down. If anyone other than Missus Tomar and her abductor were hiding back here, Minox was not concerned with them unless they interrupted him.

The current led him all the way to the end of the alley. The abductor had come this way with Missus Tomar. The signs were so obvious that Minox was overwhelmed with excitement. Hoof prints in the dirt. Boot prints as well, leading to the sewer grate leftover from the abandoned backhouses. The grate itself sat slightly askew. Minox would have preferred to have an obvious explanation as to where the horse went, or something tangible like Missus Tomar's shackles, but there was more than enough here to justify continuing along the path.

Minox pulled off the grate, as the current beckoned him to descend. There was a rope hanging from the edge of the grate. That increased the likelihood that the abductor and the killer were the same person, and the killer used underground passages to move about the city.

The main question left unresolved was whether Jaelia Tomar was the killer's next victim or his accomplice. Minox's inclination was it was the former, but he couldn't dismiss the possibility of the latter. It was not impossible that this entire business was an extraordinarily elaborate marital dispute.

Minox holstered his handstick, hung the lantern in the crook of his arm, and lowered himself into the sewer. Here the odor was atrocious, but not unbearable. He reached the stone floor with a half inch of fetid water flowing along. That wasn't the current he was following, though.

Walking through the sewer tunnel was fascinating, as it was far more elaborate than Minox had expected it to be. The construction was solid, and as Minox followed along the magic current's path, he saw several side passages, large chambers, and even doors. Minox made a mental note to give the area under the city further research. He wondered if there were maps anywhere, or if its cartography was long lost.

Eventually, after tracing through what must have been several blocks, the path led to another rope leading back up to street level. As Minox climbed up, he sensed something familiar about the area, which was confirmed when he emerged: he was in the same alley that Hessen Tomar was killed in that morning. Minox drew out his handstick again, prepared to find the worst at the mouth of the alley.

There was nothing. No one. That was the good news.

The bad news was the current had vanished. Minox walked back down, trying to find it again. It still existed at the sewer grate, but as he went out toward the street, it dissipated. He took each step meticulously, trying to sense where he lost it, where it fell apart. It was no use. He couldn't figure it out.

"Blast it!" he shouted to no one in particular. "Blast it to blazes!"

The back door of the butcher shop opened. "Who's there? I'm armed."

"Constabulary," Minox responded. "No need to be alarmed."

The door opened further, and the elder Brondar stepped out. "You again, stick? Why are you swearing in our alley?"

"I was . . . I was following a lead on something, and . . . it doesn't matter. I'm sorry if I disturbed you."

"You aren't here to hassle me again?"

"No, sir," Minox said. An idea crossed his mind. "But, if possible, I would like to speak to your youngest son."

"Youngest living son," the old man said. "Why you need to talk to him, eh?"

"Is there a problem?" Minox asked. "Is he not here?"

"I asked you a question, stick. Why you need to talk to him?"

"You are aware there was a murder right over there just this morning, sir? You should know I have more than enough cause to have the City Protector's Office issue a Writ of Justice to give us warrant to enter and search this home, as well as detain you and your whole family."

"So why don't you do that?"

"Simply put, Mister Brondar, that would be a lot of work and hassle—which I'm willing to do, mind you—when an easier solution would be to let me come in and have a few words with Joshea. That way no one's life gets disrupted."

"No one gets disrupted." Old Mister Brondar chuckled. "That is a good joke, stick. Yes, come in. But you will eat some meat, yes?"

This surprised Minox, but after what he went through, eating some meat, any kind of food at all, would be quite agreeable. "Yes, of course."

Brondar stepped back, allowing Minox to enter. He led Minox up through the back stairway. The apartment upstairs was cramped, with low ceilings and a larger table in the center of the room than there was adequate space for. The three Brondar sons sat around the table, in shirtsleeves and suspenders. The table was overcrowded with plates of meats, as well as bread, bottles of wine, and various other foods.

"Hey!" the eldest son—Jonner, if Minox remembered correctly—yelled when Minox walked in. "The stick came back!"

Joshea Brondar looked at Minox with surprise, suspicion. His eyes darted to his brothers, his father, and back to Minox. Minox had to admit, Joshea looked like a guilty man hiding a secret—but the secret he carried wasn't a crime. Not unless he had another one. The fact that the trail died right outside the butcher shop's back door was something Minox couldn't ignore.

"The stick wants to talk to Joshea!" the father announced, squeezing into the room and taking a chair at the table. "Sit, stick, and talk!"

"You're eating supper at ten bells?" Minox asked. "I didn't realize."

"It's when we eat, stick," Jonner said. "This meat needs a long time to cook properly."

"Very long, or very quick," Old Mister Brondar said. "Never in between. Sit!"

Minox took the chair closest to the door. The middle Brondar son—Gunther—reached out for a piece of meat, but his father's hand swatted it away. "New man at the table!"

"But, Pop!"

"We do it right, boy." He lit a taper off one of the candles on the table, and then snuffed all of the candles with his fingers.

"Blessings of each saint rain down on this table," he said, lighting one candle. "Bring warmth and joy and prosperity to all who sit and enjoy our bounty."

"May we be blessed," all three Brondar sons said in unison.

The father lit the second candle. "Blessings of Saint Jaspar, bless these men and this meat. May we eat knowing you watch over us, and our safety is in your hands."

"May we be blessed." The elder Brondar boys said it rotely, eyes hot on the food. Joshea's eyes were closed, reverent.

The father lit the third candle. "Blessings of Saint Ilmer, whose day just passed. We honor and respect you with this bountiful meal."

"May we be blessed."

The father sat down. "Now we can eat."

The Brondars—save for Joshea—smiled while grabbing chops or ribs and savagely biting into them. Joshea refilled his wineglass and poured another for Minox. "So what is it, Inspector?"

Minox studied Joshea's face, arms, and hands. No sign that he had been in a fight of any sort this evening. Boots clean, no appearance of having trudged through the sewers. Finally, Minox realized upon this inspection that Joshea Brondar did not have the right body type to have been the assailant at the lockwagon—he was a good six inches taller, and broader in the shoulder.

Plus there was an energy coming off of Joshea, but it had none of the flavor of the current that had led Minox here.

Minox picked up the cup of wine and sipped. "An incident occurred earlier tonight, connected to the murder from this morning."

"An incident!" the father said. "You mean someone beat you, hmm?" He pointed to Minox's face. "You've been hit pretty hard there, stick. Eat!"

The only thing holding Minox back had been a sense of Constabulary etiquette that needed to be maintained. "As with the murder, it had been suggested that Joshea had some connection. I came to ascertain that possibility."

"And?" Joshea asked.

"Have you all been here together all evening?"

"Yes," Joshea said.

"Anyone else here?"

"Just the four of us," Jonner said.

Minox picked up a roast rib of beef. "Then I believe that it is highly improbable Joshea was involved." He took a bite of the meat. It was succulent, perfectly prepared, with a sweet spiciness he was unprepared for.

"Good, yes?" the father said, watching Minox's face. "This stick is a good man, I think. I like you, Inspector. Eat more!"

Minox took another bite. The style of seasoning was from eastern Druthal. All the pieces fit: the late hour for supper, the specific prayer to Saint Jaspar, the hint of an accent from the old man. Minox asked the question to confirm, "Are you originally from Monim?"

"Born there, yes," the old man said. "After my tour, I stayed here in Maradaine. We go back from time to time. The boys visit their cousins, who then drive good Monic beef back to Maradaine. Best beef you can buy, no one else brings it all the way out here."

"It's very good," Minox said, helping himself to more.

"You have a big appetite, Inspector," Gunther said.

"Just like Joshea," Jonner said. "He eats and eats and is still a runt!" Jonner grabbed Joshea by the arm and twisted it behind him. Minox noted that Joshea would be a runt only in the context of his two brothers, who were ox-like men.

"Saints, Jonner!" Joshea shouted. "Grow up, would you?"

The large hand of the father swung out and cuffed Joshea on the back of the head. "Don't blaspheme."

"You all served in the army, eh?" Minox asked, doing his best to give an impression of convivial joviality. He was surprised, though, at how the three Brondar sons, especially the elder two, acted more like boys just out of school instead of men of nearly thirty years. They also acted like his cousins. In a way, Joshea reminded him specifically of his cousin Davis.

"Blazes, yes," Jonner said. He put Joshea in a headlock, though the younger Brondar didn't really resist. In the process Jonner showed his muscular arm to Joshea, including his army tattoo. "Five years."

"You five as well?" Minox asked Gunther.

"Absolutely." Gunther showed his tattoo with the five hash marks. "Jonner and I did a Kellirac border skirmish together four years back."

Joshea had served only three years. Minox made a note of that aberration, but didn't vocalize it. He suspected that it might, at least, be a point of soreness between Joshea and his brothers, or possibly be tied to a larger issue. Either way, mentioning it was more than likely to evoke an emotional reaction in Joshea Brondar, and Minox recognized it would not serve his purpose.

Minox ate more of the meat, and as he was chewing it occurred to him that he didn't know exactly what his purpose here was. He had already ascertained the key point that he had come to investigate; neither Joshea, nor any of the Brondars were directly involved in the attack on the lockwagon and the abduction of Jaelia Tomar.

Minox helped himself to another serving, while the two elder Brondar brothers continued to torment and berate their younger sibling, as if they were all schoolchildren. Despite the ludicrousness of continuing to sit and join in their dinner, Minox felt compelled to stay. *This is patently irresponsible,* he thought. *You need to devote your full attention to finding—rescuing—Jaelia Tomar.*

And it would be a rescue, if he could find her in time. The likelihood of Jaelia Tomar's abductor being her husband's killer was too high to give other possibilities serious weight. It was also likely that, despite being a notable mage, she would be unable to protect herself. Minox had made a direct magical attack on the assailant that had proved ineffective. Just as Jaelia Tomar had on Satrine this afternoon, when she held the spike used in the murder of Hessen Tomar.

"I'm very sorry," Minox said, getting to his feet. "But I've just had a sudden realization about a case. I really must go."

"What?" Old Mister Brondar asked. "No, sir. You need to eat. You're too skinny, you know, like Joshea."

"Believe me, Mister Brondar, I would find it highly pleasant to remain. I do not have the luxury." He pushed himself through the tight space of the room to the door. Joshea was already there.

"I'll see him down and latch up, Pop."

"Good, good," his father said. "Hurry back."

Minox reached the door to the street before Joshea had been able to get into the stairwell.

"Hold up, Inspector!" He tore down the stairs, bounding three steps at a time. Joshea grabbed the door as Minox was opening it, pulling it shut. "What do you think you are doing?" he hissed out.

"I was investigating something that led me here."

"Investigating me, you mean."

"Not precisely," Minox said. "Though I was attacked by someone well trained in the fighting arts, who was able to block my magical attacks, and the trail led me to this alley. You have to admit that cast some reasonable suspicion in your direction."

Joshea grunted. "But no more?"

"I don't think so, no," Minox said.

"What sort of trail?"

"Come over here," Minox said, leading Joshea down to the end of the alley. The current was weak, but still present. "Can you feel that?"

Joshea's eyes went wide. "What is that?" He ran his fingers through the air, as if trying to touch something that wasn't there.

"My killer has another victim. Another mage. I believe he grabbed her, took her through the sewers and out the alley. This . . . current is connected to her, I think. But it falls apart before leaving the alley."

Joshea walked up the alley. "Right by our door," he said.

Minox nodded. "You can see I had a good cause to think you may have been involved." He followed after Joshea. Then he noticed the current was gone throughout the alley. Right after Joshea had walked through there. "Did you go out in the alley earlier tonight at all?"

Joshea nodded. "I came out to dump the mop bucket." He pointed to the puddle of greasy water by the door. "Why?"

"Blazes," Minox muttered. "I think—it's possible you disrupted the current when you came out."

"What?" Joshea's face turned hard. "Are you accusing me—"

"I don't think it was intentional, Joshea," Minox said quickly. He lowered his voice and moved closer. "Neither of us exactly has perfect control over our . . . ability. I don't fully understand what it was I was following, or what it means, or how delicate it may have been."

Joshea cooled. "Fair enough."

"You should go back in," Minox said. "And there is still a life at stake. We'll talk again later."

"Tomorrow night?" Joshea said.

"Barring my duties compelling me otherwise, I should be at my home," Minox said. "By all means, come by and we'll talk." They shook hands, and Joshea went back inside.

Minox went out to the street. Somewhere out there, Jaelia Tomar was being held, and it was likely her life was in danger. The last thing Minox could do was go to sleep. There was work to be done.

Chapter 15

SATRINE WENT INTO HER BEDROOM. The sick-room. Loren lay on the bed, eyes open. His eyes flashed over to her when she entered. She couldn't tell if it was recognition, or just reaction.

"Evening, love," she said, bending over to kiss his forehead. "You're awake now."

His eyes stayed on her, his mouth opening as if to say something. No words came out.

"You feel all right? Any pain?" She brushed her hand against his face. No fever. The doctor had told her they had to keep a close eye on that. His head shook—no, she only imagined that. It just lolled to one side. "Warm enough?"

She knew he wasn't going to answer. She hadn't heard a word from him since the attack. She still asked the questions. She still talked to him. She had no intention of stopping doing that.

Satrine checked under the blankets, rolling his broken body to the side. He moaned with pain. She touched his ribs. They still hadn't healed. "Today was quite the day, back in Inemar. Hope you were all right with Missus Abernand all day. I know she's brusque. You never really were fond of her." The dressings on his wounds were all clean and fresh. Missus Abernand had done good work nursing him.

"I know you don't approve, but my plan worked. They made me an inspector. Third class. Money will be tight, but I can make it work." She pulled the blankets back over him.

She sat down in her chair next to the bed, pulling off her boots. "So I was given a partner, of course. Quite the inspector, that one. Though no one else likes him, that's clear. Mostly because he's smarter than the rest of them. And he's strange. Like that one I knew back in Intelligence. The one in the map room." She snapped her fingers at Loren, as if he would be able to jog her memory. "Holsing. Knew every town in Druthal, but didn't care when he had said something mortally insulting. Welling is like that guy."

She took off the blouse and pants, draping them over the back of her chair. Loren's eyes were still on her. She imagined he was smiling, watching her undress. His lips had moved open. They shut and opened again. His left hand waved over to the bedside table. In a rush, she poured a cup of water from the clay pitcher and put it to his mouth. He drank readily.

"You were thirsty, I'm so sorry, my love. I should have known." She put the cup back down on the table.

"Quite the day, though," she continued, removing her underthings. She sniffed at them. They still smelled faintly of the sewers. Missus Abernand wouldn't be happy about laundering them. "A dead body, a mage, killed in a ritual. And I saw Idre Hoffer." She shuddered involuntarily just saying the woman's name. "She's a mother of many children. And about as awful as I imagined she would be. And sad." She felt her shoulders tense. "It's not worth talking about. I'll just get upset. You don't need that."

She put on her nightgown and sat back in the plush chair. She touched his hand, gripping it tightly. She needed to reassure herself that he was physically real and there with her.

"You know who else I met today? The grandson of Old Man Plum. The bookstore man. I told him the story about the poetry book. I still have that book here. I could read you some poems. Would you like that?"

She mused to herself. "I remember I used to try and read you poems. You never liked it. You're a captive audience now, though." Her eyes were heavy. She leaned her head over in the chair, so she could look him in the eyes.

His eyes were still bright, and beautifully blue. Still full of life and intelligence. Looking into his eyes, she was sure that the true Loren, the man she loved and married, he was still in there, and he could see her. He could hear her. He could understand her.

She lost herself looking into those eyes, and in moments she was asleep.

———◆———

The night clerk took little notice of Minox as he entered the station. It was highly unlikely that either Leppin or Corrie had told anyone that he shouldn't be returning this evening. It was not quite after midnight, so he was breaking his promise to Leppin. However, the opportunity to save the life of Jaelia Tomar had to take precedence over that.

Conventional means of tracking Missus Tomar and her abductor had failed. This was not a surprise, as the trail was quite cold. There had been a handful of boot tracks in the street outside the alley that had the right mix of mud and waste, and those were accompanied with the wheel marks of a handcart. Unfortunately, a few steps into the street, they became completely enmeshed with every other footprint and wheel mark that crossed through Jent and Tannen. Useful for clarifying how the abductor brought Missus Tomar out of the alley without causing a stir—few would bother questioning a tarp-covered handcart—but unhelpful in finding where they had gone.

He slipped up the back stairs, taking a stop in the commissary for a cup of tea before going to his desk on the inspectors' floor. He put the tea on the desk and lit a few lamps. A pile of fresh newsprints from Inemar, Dentonhill, Aventil, East Maradaine, and Colton sat on his chair. Nyla had, as always, got her usual supply and left it for him to comb through.

He was at a loss. There were no reasonable suspects, at least none that he could determine with the information at hand. Research was his only possible ally at this point. There were the newsprints of the day, of course. They might yield an unknown connection that would clear up the entire matter. But that was a long shot. He had to simply go through the information he had again and hope he would gain new insight.

Jaelia herself, or any of the other Firewings, seemed unlikely, given the unique nature of the spikes. At least, they would have to have a non-magical accomplice. That was worth considering.

For that matter, it could involve a rival Circle, also using a non-magical accomplice. Blue Hand Circle had ties to Fenmere's trafficking operations. It was also worth going down to the file rooms and reading up on the other Circles that had dealings in this and nearby neighborhoods. Especially those involved in the Circle Feuds of 1212. He loathed the idea of reading through all that, but Inspector Rainey was correct on that particular point this morning: he was deliberately trying to avoid the subject of Mage Circles. He couldn't afford to do that, not anymore.

A thought crossed his mind. The spikes, and mage shackles. Were they the same thing, or was there more to the spikes? Another point of ignorance he couldn't afford. There was still a pair of mage shackles somewhere in the stationhouse. He needed to get a hold of them and research them as well. He had known for the past three years that there were two pairs in the stationhouse, but had never investigated what they were, or what they would do to him. He didn't even know why they had two pairs. Was that typical for every stationhouse in the city? Or were Inemar's two pairs twice as many as anyone else's?

He had already been shown that there were elements

of magical understanding that were relevant to the case. He couldn't ignore them. The various Circles in the city—even just the ones that had chapterhouses in the neighborhood—could provide a wealth of other suspects.

Other suspects. Neither the Brondars nor the folk in the barbershop were reasonable. The barbers were half-wits and dullards, not one of them had any spark of cleverness. The Brondars had that spark, for certain, but they weren't the type to do it in such gruesome spectacle. Minox could easily believe that Joshea's father would murder a mage like Hessen Tomar, but he'd do it in an efficient, straightforward matter. No ritual or candles. He'd more likely just hack his victims up and grind them into sausage.

Minox shuddered at allowing himself that thought.

He let it pass. File room first. Then the mage shackles. Research the problem, until Jaelia Tomar was safe. There was no other choice in the matter.

Chapter 14

SOMEONE POUNDED ON THE DOOR. Satrine woke, startled. She hadn't realized she had fallen asleep in the chair, her head tilted to one side. Her neck was stiff with pain. She stretched it to the other side, releasing a series of pops. That gave some relief.

The lamp had dwindled down to the barest ember. It was enough light to see that Loren was asleep.

Pounding again.

It was far too early for anyone to be pounding on her door. Satrine didn't have a clock in her house, but instinct told her it was around five bells, still twenty minutes or so until sunrise. She stumbled from the chair, grabbing a dressing gown as she passed it hanging on the wall. She wrapped it around herself quickly, hurrying to get to the door before the caller began another round of pounding. The girls, hopefully, were still sleeping, and didn't need to be roused.

Her Constabulary belt hung near the door. She took the handstick out of its holder and placed her other hand on the door latch.

"Oy," she said. "Who the blazes is pounding at this hour?"

"Is this Inspector Rainey?" a young voice returned.

"Who's asking?"

"It's Phillen," the voice said. "Phillen Hace."

"Who?"

"I'm one of the station pages. I counted the clock for you and Inspector Welling this morning, remember? You know, when you were . . ."

Satrine rolled her eyes. Was this something she was really going to have to deal with? A lust-struck page pounding on her door in the wee hours because he saw her in her underthings. "Phillen, you shouldn't be coming here in the middle of the night like this. I'm sure there are better places for you to . . ."

"But . . . Inspector Welling sent me, ma'am."

Despite her better judgment, Satrine unlatched the door. There was the boy, standing respectfully a few steps away from the door, hat in hand. "He . . . Inspector Welling told you to come here?"

"Yes, ma'am."

"Why?"

"I don't rightly know, ma'am," Phillen said. "He told me that he needed you at the stationhouse as soon as you could arrive properly. Oh, and there was an incident with Missus Tomar's transfer."

"What kind of incident?" Satrine asked.

"He didn't tell me, ma'am. Though word among pages is she broke out from her lockwagon."

"All right," Satrine said. She had to trust that Welling wasn't about to send a page to her house to collect her for spurious reasons. If there was an actual, legitimate issue at hand with their case, she should get on it. "Run back. Tell Inspector Welling that I'll be ten minutes behind you. Got it?"

"Yes, ma'am," Phillen said. He gave a weak salute to her and ran off. Satrine latched the door shut and went to the water closet.

———◆——

Face washed, hair pulled back, dressed in slacks and linen pullover, Satrine made her way into the kitchen by the light of a single candle while carrying her boots in the other hand. She remembered several times Loren had made similar early morning exits. As well as late nights. This was going to have to be a normal part of her life now.

She cut some bread left over from last night, and took out some soft cheese and salted lamb from the icebox. It wasn't much of a breakfast, but it would do. She mused to herself as she spread the cheese on the bread, that if there was one thing her day probably would not be lacking, it was food. Partnership with Minox Welling would see that through for certain.

Had Welling been there all night? Should she have been? What did he have to go home to? She didn't know. He had no marriage bracelet, nor did he speak of any sort of intended.

She took a bite of bread, cheese, and lamb, put it down on the table, and pulled on her boots. No time for tea. There would probably be tea at the stationhouse, if Miss Pyle was there. If not, would they expect her to make it?

"You up already, Mama?" Caribet wandered into the kitchen in her gown, rubbing at her eyes.

"Back to bed, sweetheart," Satrine said absently. She took another bite of her breakfast.

"What's going on?"

"Don't know," Satrine said. "They sent a page to get me, though. 'Something' happened."

Caribet nodded. "You need anything, Mama?"

"No, dear. Get a couple more hours of sleep before you have to go to school." Satrine went to the door hooks for her belt, vest, and coat. Caribet shuffled back to her bedroom. She stopped at her doorway, looking back at Satrine.

"Let me see you, Mama."

Satrine had the coat half on. "What do you mean?"

Caribet gestured vaguely at her. "Like that. Coat on." Satrine finished dressing. "You look like a real inspector, Mama."

"I am a real inspector, honey," Satrine said. She went back to the table to grab her breakfast.

"I know, Mama," Caribet said sleepily. "It looks right on you." She went back into her bedroom.

Satrine couldn't help but smile as she took the last couple bites of her breakfast. She checked her crossbow and handstick, and went out the door.

The streets were nearly empty, the haze of predawn barely lighting Satrine's way to the bridges, across the river, and back into Inemar.

A handful of boys were gathered in a cluster near the base of the bridge steps. Satrine heard shouts and jeers coming from their circle. They all had matching caps. Satrine didn't need to see anymore to guess what was going on.

"You rats got a flop to race to?" she called out. All heads turned to her, opening up their circle enough to see they had another boy on the ground.

A boy in a Constabulary page coat.

One of the gang rats gave the page another kick. "What's it to you, dox?"

"She's no dox!" another jeered. "She's too old to charge for it!"

"She could get a pence or two," said another. "If I had enough ale in me."

"Doubt a sprout like you could hold your ale, rat," Satrine returned. Her right hand went down to her belt slowly.

"You want to see what I hold, dox?" he said, walking closer to her with a cocky strut. He stopped cold a few steps in. "Holy saints, she's a stick!"

"She's no stick," one of the other boys said. He had the bearing of a leader. He kicked the page again, as if to punctuate his point. The page groaned and rolled over. It was Phillen.

Satrine didn't hesitate another second. She drew the crossbow and shot the boy who kicked Phillen. Her arrow hit him in the shoulder; he squealed in pain and dropped.

"Saints!" the one closest to her shouted. That was all he got out before she was on him, handstick drawn. Two hits, chest and head, and he crumpled to the ground.

"Get the dox!" the one she shot yelled. The other boys—three of them—hesitated for a moment, but then charged at her. As soon as they stepped away, Phillen savagely kicked the leader in the knee.

Satrine dropped her crossbow, freeing her right hand for a hard punch at the first of the three who reached her. He stumbled at the blow, while the second boy of the trio swung a sloppy punch at her. She blocked it easily with the handstick, spinning it around and under his arm. Before he could react, she had his arm behind his back, and forced him around to block the third boy's attack. She gave the boy a shove at his friend, sending them tumbling onto the cobblestone.

She got punched in the side. Two more fast hits on her right arm, which she barely had a chance to react to. The first boy of the trio—a weasel-faced tosser with black teeth—was on her, and he knew how to scrap. She lashed out with her right arm, a wild swing that he easily dodged. He grinned with those nasty teeth. "Stick or dox, don't matter," he said.

She didn't talk back to him. She switched the handstick to her right hand, and drove it hard into his ribs. He swung at her, but this time she could block his punches. She hit him again, center of the chest. He gasped for breath. She knocked him across the jaw. Two of those black teeth flew out of his mouth. She swept up the handstick and drummed it down across his temple. He went down.

A glint of iron out the corner of her eye. One of the other two had a knife, and he was moving in to slide it between her ribs. Satrine spun on her heel and knocked the blade with the handstick, followed with a sharp left hook. Before he could recover, she grabbed his head by his greasy hair and pulled down, smashing his face with her knee.

The last boy standing stared at her in astonishment. She took one step toward him and he took off running.

Phillen was on his feet, now kicking the fallen gang leader. "Now it's you and me, huh? How is it now?"

"Phillen!" Satrine yelled. He snapped to, stopping his attack on the boy.

"Ma'am, yes, ma'am!" He even saluted her. "Should I go for a lockwagon for these miscreants?" The four boys lay on the ground, moaning and coughing. They probably wouldn't stay like that for long, though.

"We haven't the time, Page," she said, picking her crossbow back up. It had gotten a bit banged up, but it still looked functional. Good Druth workmanship. She went to the leader and pulled him up by the front of his threadbare coat. "Besides, these boys won't trouble sticks or pages anymore, will they?"

"Piss yourself, dox," the boy said weakly.

Satrine slapped him twice. "He didn't learn anything," she said. "You carrying shackles, Phillen?"

The page nodded and grinned. He pulled out a set from his coat pocket. Satrine took them and shackled the gang leader's wrists behind his back. "Come on, boys, we're late."

She pulled the boy by the shackle chain, Phillen following her as they walked to the stationhouse.

"Ma'am?" Phillen asked. "Where'd you learn to scrap like that?"

"About four blocks that way," Satrine said, pointing down the road. "You all right?"

"I'll heal, ma'am," Phillen said. "Shouldn't have let them jump me like that."

"You want a hint, Phillen? Next time, if you have a heavy chain in your pocket, pull it out and wail whoever's in charge with it." She yanked on the shackle chain in emphasis. "Gang boys tend to fall apart when their leader goes down."

"Shut it, witch," the boy snapped.

She knocked him across the teeth. "Your mother really failed to teach you any manners."

"My mother's a dox and a waste," he said.

"Poor you," Phillen said. "So's mine, and you don't see me being street trash."

"You shut it, stick lover," the boy shot back.

"And here I thought Inemar was becoming a nice neighborhood," Satrine said absently. "Glad to see my worst opinions weren't proven wrong."

They entered the stationhouse, the gang boy half-dragged inside. There was a minimum of activity, a few regulars working in pools of low lamplight, a few dregs and gang boys sitting chained at a bench near the back. Two officers in horsepatrol uniform chatted in front of the bench—one a young woman, the only other one Satrine had seen wearing trousers. She perked up when she saw Satrine come in.

"What's this blazing noise?" she asked. Her eyes were all up and down on Satrine. "Page and a civ bringing the blasted sewage in here?"

"She's no civ, ma'am," Phillen said.

"If she ain't, I'm a blazing pence whore," the woman said. Satrine caught the name on her badge: Welling. Did Minox say he had a sister who worked the night shift?

Satrine held open her coat. "I'm sure your rolls are worth at least a tick, Corrie."

"Rutting saints," Corrie said. "You're the skirt inspector!"

Satrine stifled a laugh. Welling was proper almost to a fault, and his sister had the coarsest mouth in the station. Might as well match it with her best. "I'm not blazing well wearing a rutting skirt, am I?"

Corrie smirked. "You would know a rutting skirt, wouldn't you?"

Satrine shrugged. "Got two daughters somehow."

The chained gang boy groaned. "Either knock or roll each other, would you?"

Satrine yanked the chain. "You can shut it, unless you want another bolt."

"Just put me in a blazing cell already."

Satrine handed Phillen the chain. "Take him to the desk officer."

"Yes, ma'am," Phillen said. He grinned broadly. "Come on, Hoffer."

"Wait," Satrine said. She moved closer to the gang boy. "You're Idre Hoffer's son?"

"What of it?" the boy asked. "Like I said, she's a dox and a waste."

Now Satrine didn't disagree. Frowning, she said to Phillen, "Favor me, Phillen."

Eagerly he replied, "Anything, ma'am."

"Make sure his mother gets called in for him. And if and when she comes, make sure she sits until I talk to her. Deal?"

"Even if I have to sit on her, ma'am."

"Good lad."

Corrie was watching her intently. Her voice dropping low and husky, she asked, "So why you here before the rutting sunrise? Don't tell me they're having you set up tea and bread up there before they all come in or something."

"I better not be," Satrine said. "I don't know. You're brother had that page come get me to bring me in."

"Minox did—is he here?"

"I think so," Satrine said. Corrie's eyes could have burned a hole through the ceiling.

"That rutting trickster, I knew I should—"

"Corrie!" the other horsepatrolman shouted. "We've got to do another round."

Corrie bared her teeth and turned hard on Satrine. "Listen, skirt. Be good to Minox. Have his rutting back, you hear? Because he's waded in enough sewage. Got me?"

"Got," Satrine said, more than a little spooked at Corrie's intensity.

"Good. Have a fine day, Inspector." She gave a brisk salute and stalked off with her partner. Satrine watched her depart and went upstairs.

The lamps were almost all out up on the inspectors' floor, save the flickering glow in the back, hidden behind two slateboards. Shaking her head in wry amusement, she went back to her desk.

"Morning, Inspector," she said. Welling was sitting on the edge of the desk, chalk in hand, studying his various slate scribblings. A huge pile of newsprints lay out on the desk, ink marks and circles around various stories. Her own desk was now covered with files that were not there the day before.

"Morning, Inspector Rainey," he said flatly.

"Have you slept?" she asked him. He was wearing fresh clothes, but his coat was covered in dust, and there were specks of blood over the front of it.

"A bit," he said.

"Just met your sister," Satrine said.

Welling's hand froze up. "I take it she is aware of my presence in the building, then."

"She expressed some concern on the subject," Satrine said. "Quite colorfully."

"I can imagine," Welling said. "I'm certain to hear quite a bit on our next encounter. I was supposed to go home and rest."

"Which you obviously didn't."

He shrugged and turned back to his boards. "It's been an eventful night. I think our mage killer will strike again."

Satrine was intrigued and sat down next to him on the desk. His notes, lines, and scratches didn't make much sense to her. "What are you basing that on?"

"Someone attacked Jaelia Tomar's lockwagon when we were bringing her to Eastwood."

"Breakout?"

"That was the first thought," he said. "But it doesn't add up. It didn't have the markings of a rescue. Single attacker, excellent combat precision."

"How does that not—"

"Two points," Welling said, making marks on his board as he spoke. "One, the attacker disabled Missus Tomar as part of his strike."

"Give her deniability in case it went wrong."

Welling chuckled. "Inspector Mirrell offered the same theory. It has merit. There is another point, though. When the attacker was escaping with Missus Tomar, I gave pursuit and tried to stop them with a magic blast. It washed off of him."

"I don't see the connection."

"You don't?" Welling said hotly, his eyes wide with excitement. "What did you have in your pocket? The very spike the killer used to subdue Hessen Tomar. With it, the magic didn't touch you. The same thing happened to our attacker. It stands to reason—"

"That he was similarly protected for the same reason," Satrine finished.

"I thought it was especially odd that the killer would

leave such objects of obvious value behind. Unless he had more."

"Strange thing to have a lot of," Satrine said. "I don't suppose you've discovered exactly what they are?"

"No," Welling said absently. "However, I did spend some of the night performing a small experiment." He pointed to a pair of shackles on his desk.

"Mage shackles?"

"One of two pairs we have here. Apparently, our stationhouse is one of the few with two pairs. I'll get to that in a moment." He picked them up. "Now, what's interesting is, when I'm in contact with these, I cannot perform any magic."

"Like the spikes."

"No, not like the spikes. The spikes sap me, physically. The shackles have no such effect. They only block me."

"What does that mean?"

"It means the spikes are different than the shackles. The significance of that is not something I've further examined." He stepped over to the board, placing the chalk on it, then stepping away without writing anything. "Through less than traditional means, I was able to track the killer and Missus Tomar to an alley, through the sewer tunnels, and back out. The path led to the same alley where we found Hessen Tomar."

"That's interesting. But then what happened?" All of this sounded strange, and Welling himself was in an odd state. Which was typical for someone who had stayed up all night, probably drinking more bad tea than anyone would recommend.

"The trail was lost."

"Were these 'less than traditional means' magical, Inspector?"

"They were," Welling said. "But secondary evidence supported their accuracy." He took another step toward the board, drew a single line between two markings. After another moment, he erased it with the side of his hand.

"Fine," Satrine said. "But forget the magical and secondary evidence. It led you back to the alley. That has to be significant."

"We certainly know the killer has been there before," Welling said absently. He was more interested in whatever markings he was writing.

"If the trail was lost there, maybe it ended there. We should be looking at the butchers and the barbers again."

"I am fairly certain that the trail was merely lost at that point, but it did not terminate there. Missus Tomar was not to be found."

"But she might have been in the butcher shop, for instance. I had a strange feeling about that bunch, especially the youngest."

"I am certain they are not involved, Inspector Rainey," Welling said harshly.

"How?" This didn't fit his earlier methods. Welling wouldn't dismiss an avenue of investigation without good cause. "I know you interviewed the youngest outside, and you were upset about it, but . . ."

"I went into the Brondar home last night, Inspector."

"What? Did you get a writ or something?"

"No writ. I knocked and was admitted. I spoke to all of them, at length with Joshea . . ." He stumbled. "With the youngest. I am certain that none of them were involved in the attack on the carriage or the abduction of Missus Tomar."

"Joshea?" That was the first time he had used anyone's given name, save Nyla, who was his cousin. "Is he family?"

"No, of course not." Welling wasn't looking at her, his attention determinately focused on the slateboard. He was hiding something, something personal.

Satrine grabbed Welling by the shoulder and turned him around. "Is he a mage?" she hissed out.

He slapped her hand off his shoulder and grabbed for it, but she pulled away too quickly. It was too late, though. The truth was clear in Welling's face.

"Uncircled?" she added.

"It's not pertinent to the case," Welling said.

"How could it not be?"

He spat out his words with raw anger. "The spikes, Inspector Rainey. We know the killer is *not* a mage. It could not be the Firewings, it could not be me, and it could not be Joshea Brondar. Simple deduction."

Eyes red, nose flaring, he turned back to the slate-board and continued his pattern of making marks and erasing them. Satrine sat down and let him do this for some time.

"What are you trying to do?" Satrine asked after she had decided he had cooled down.

"Determine where the killer is going to take Missus Tomar to kill her." He spoke as if he had never had a heated temper in his life.

"How do you know he's going to kill Missus Tomar? And even presuming that's correct, how can you figure out where he'll do it?"

"The first part is rather simple deduction. Why else would the killer of Hessen Tomar capture Jaelia Tomar, except to kill her as well? Well, no, I did speculate that she might be his accomplice and the whole matter is an elaborate marital squabble. Then I recalled you telling her the news of her husband's death. Her reaction was far too raw, too nakedly emotional to be anything but genuine. Unless I am grossly underestimating her skills as an actor, but I don't think I am. I can speculate any number of motives behind such killing, though my preferred reason is in order to perform another ritualized murder."

"Another?" Satrine was amazed he had taken breath enough for her to get a word in.

"This is only an instinct, mind you," Welling told her. "I can't put any reasonable deduction behind it—save that he abducted Missus Tomar last night rather than killing her then and there—but I have a sense that the killer has, in his mind, a higher purpose that requires ritual, and it is incomplete."

"That's your main theory?"

Welling indicated the scribbling on the slateboard. "I have several theories, of course, as you can see. That's the one I consider of highest probability. Another one, though this is of much lower likelihood, is that the killer had romantic notions toward Jaelia Tomar, and his attack last night was, in his mind, a rescue of sorts. Though

I have little doubt of Missus Tomar's fidelity, and it is highly unlikely she would welcome his advances."

"You've given this some thought."

He nodded. "For the past few hours I've considered every possibility I can conceive, eliminated those that are most unlikely, and examined the remaining for all possible scenarios playing out from here."

Satrine studied the various hash marks, single letters, numbers, and symbols on the board. It was all gibberish to her. "That's what you have written up here?"

"More or less," Welling said, staring at it.

Satrine's head was pounding. "I can't make any sense of your big board."

"This isn't the big one," he said. "That's somewhere else."

Satrine didn't want to think about that. "All right, never mind. How can you figure out where he may or may not kill her?"

"I can't," Welling said, gritting his teeth. He put down the chalk and stalked away from the desks. "I have nowhere near enough information, and little more than second or third levels of speculation, which makes everything I try to build a house of straw."

"So why am I here this early?" she asked, annoyed.

Welling looked up, surprised. "Because I need your help, Inspector Rainey."

Satrine's annoyance blossomed into anger. "With what? You've just admitted you don't know anything! And our one decent lead you insist had nothing to do with it! So what can I possibly add?"

Welling's mouth hung open for a moment, his eyes racing back and forth. Satrine imagined that he was thinking so many things that he was unable to verbalize any of it in a sensible way. Finally he said, "Jaelia Tomar was taken from Constabulary custody, and so we failed in our duties to her safety. I failed, specifically. And as of this moment, she may or may not be alive. If she is, then there is still some small chance of preventing her murder. If . . ." He faltered and looked at Satrine with confusion. "If all we do is wait for her body to turn up, then what function do we serve? What are we, then, but the morbid cataloguers of the atrocities of humanity?"

His words knocked Satrine out of her anger. For several moments, she stood dumb, unable to come up with an adequate response to his oration. "You're right, Welling," she said finally. "I just . . . I need a cup of tea first before I can think."

"It's there on your desk," he said, pointing to the cup she hadn't noticed. "Cream only."

That was a pleasant surprise. Satrine took her chair and sipped at the tea. "You made this?"

"No one else is around," he said. "Nyla usually arrives around seven bells." He took a good look at her. "Were you in a fight?"

"It was an eventful morning. Some Inemar rats had ganged up on the page you sent to fetch me."

"How many?"

"Five," Satrine said, trying her best to sound casual about it. "We only brought in one, though."

Welling nodded respectfully. "That's good work."

"Thank you." The tea helped. She was starting to feel functional. "What's our next step?"

"The best lead we really have right now is what Jaelia Tomar told you yesterday about her husband having a rival or enemy in another Circle. We need to pursue that, find out who that rival was, what Circle."

"Easy to say," Satrine said. "How are we going to do that?"

He pointed to the pile of files on her desk. "Following your rebuke yesterday, I've spent a portion of the evening studying the records we have on Mage Circles in the city, which are woefully inadequate."

She fingered through the files. "These aren't all of them."

"No, I narrowed it to the ones worth paying attention to. The large, nationwide Circles like Lord Preston's or Red Wolf, with major presences in every city are far too decentralized to even be a factor. Minuscule ones who don't even house themselves in this part of Maradaine weren't worth examining."

"But many Circles do have chapterhouses in Inemar."

"As near as I can tell, it is the neighborhood with the highest concentration. So I took other factors into consideration, and narrowed down to eight Circles that, as far as I can tell, are similar to the Firewings. They have chapterhouses in this neighborhood, and that chapterhouse appears to represent a significant portion of their membership."

"That's something," she said, glancing at the names: Four Winds Circle, Circle of Light and Stone, Crimson Crescent Penumbra Circle, and so on. "Is it just me, or do these Circles try really hard for poetical names?"

"There was one I eliminated whose name actually was a poem."

Satrine laughed, despite herself. "So now we have eight Circles to look into. So what's the next step?"

"We're going to have to go back to the Firewings' chapterhouse." Welling did not look too pleased about that idea.

"I don't see them being too cooperative, especially after we arrested Jaelia. And then she was kidnapped from our custody and is possibly in the hands of a murderer."

"I wouldn't expect much cooperation from them in any event," Welling said. "Which means we'll have to take a different approach."

Satrine was intrigued. This was starting to sound more like her old work in Intelligence. "I think Captain Cinellan would disapprove of us breaking into the chapterhouse, even with a life on the line."

"Breaking in?" Welling looked scandalized. "Not at all, Inspector Rainey. Not at all."

"Sorry," Satrine said, abashed. "I was thinking about—"

"The methods in Druth Intelligence. Of course, I won't deny there's a certain ruthless efficiency to such tactics, but the last thing we would want to do is violate the rights of the Firewings."

"If you don't expect them to cooperate, and you don't want to violate their privacy, what do you intend to do?"

Welling gave her a very slight smile, so subtle that she

almost didn't catch it. "I said their rights, Inspector Rainey. I said nothing about their privacy."

"Then how do you . . ."

Pounding footsteps came from the stairs, the fast steps of a young boy running. Welling picked up his coat and belt off the desk. "I didn't send out only one page in the middle of the night."

A page soon came from behind the slateboards, a piece of paper in his hands. "I got the writ, Inspector Welling!"

"Excellent, son," Welling said. "How was Protector Hilsom's spirit at your late night call?"

"Angry as a kicked cat, sir," the page said. "But he did it anyway."

"Did what?" Satrine asked.

Welling took the paper from the page. "Wrote out a warrant to search the premises of the Firewings' chapter-house. And now that we have it, Inspector Rainey, let's drum up a few of the footpatrol to join us on this venture. This is the sort of thing that works best with a show of the color."

Chapter 15

A SHOW OF COLOR turned out to be a dozen Constabulary Patrol, most of whom had just reported for duty with the sunrise. They walked the six blocks to the chapterhouse, with Welling and Satrine at the head, looking more like an organized mob than Constabulary on official business. The streets were beginning to buzz with activity, though most anyone walking about made a point of clearing out of the way of the swath of red-and-green coated Constabulary coming up the lane. Satrine found the whole thing strangely thrilling, the blatant display of authority.

"We should have marched them in formation," Satrine joked. "Leading them on horseback."

"That would have been ostentatious," Welling said.

"Like this doesn't make a statement."

"It does," Welling said. "'We're coming.'"

Welling didn't hang back on the stairs when they reached the chapterhouse. He bounded up, two steps at a time, and gave a resounding knock on the door. "Maradaine Constabulary! We have a warrant for a search of the premises! Open peacefully or the door will be battered in!"

"How much time will you give them?" Satrine asked.

"A count of ten," Welling said.

Satrine was starting to think Welling was enjoying this a bit too much. "They could still be asleep."

"And Jaelia Tomar could still be alive, so I'm not wasting any more time." He snapped his fingers and gave a nod to the uniformed patrolmen. Two of them charged up the steps and smashed their shoulders into the door. It only budged a little. They hit it again. A third time yielded no better results.

"Good door," Satrine said.

"Hmm," Welling said. He pulled his arm back, and his hand shimmered and shone with yellow energy. Satrine grabbed the two patrolmen and pulled them away.

The door flew open before Welling did anything else. The same old man from the day before, now in a dressing gown, came storming out, eyes on Welling. "Let that go, Inspector!"

The glow around Welling's hand dissipated, but Satrine noticed her partner's muscles tense, the wince of pain in his face. Despite that, Welling reached into his pocket and produced the writ for the old man's inspection. "We have a warrant. We will search these premises."

"What for?"

"Either for Jaelia Tomar, or evidence about those who may have wished her harm."

"Who would—the last I saw Jaelia she was being arrested by you!"

Satrine stepped forward, touching the man on the arm. She gave a slight nod to Welling and the patrolmen, who filed into the house. "We know that. However, she was broken out of Constabulary custody."

"Broken out—"

Satrine cut the old mage off before he could continue. "You do understand that there are two possible parties we think would do such a thing."

"Two parties? What do you mean?"

Satrine gave a nod, indicating inside the chapterhouse. "Either she was rescued by her allies . . ."

"You mean us? Preposterous!"

"Or she was abducted by the same people who murdered her husband."

The old man shoved Satrine's hand away. "This is all some sort of ploy to invade our privacy, discredit our Circle. It won't work."

"Why would we do that, sir?"

"We'll have our counselor on the lot of you!" He glared at Satrine, and then stomped down the stoop. After a moment of glancing about, the old man stalked down to the street. "I see you all!" he shouted at the shops and homes across the way. "We will not be bullied!"

"Bullied?" Satrine asked. She came down the steps. "Who has been bullying you?"

"You people are all the same," the old man said, his voice dripping with scorn.

"Who are 'you people'? All I know is a member of your Circle is dead, another is missing and likely in danger! Help me!"

"You come here, invade our home, and ask me to help you?" The man's face was full of anger.

"Your choice," Satrine said. "You can fight us, or try to save your friend."

The old mage snarled, and went back up the steps into the house. Satrine followed after him, but before she got inside, Welling came out with a journal and a handful of papers.

"I have it, Inspector Rainey," he said with a manic look of triumph on his face.

"Those are private papers!" the old man shouted. He lurched toward Welling, his bony hand outstretched.

Satrine noticed a faint glow forming around his fingers. She grabbed the man's arm. "Please, sir, don't give us a reason to arrest you as well."

"As if you don't want to!"

"We don't, sir," Welling said. His voice was full of compassion, the level of which surprised Satrine. "Your house has suffered enough injustice."

The old man huffed and went back inside.

"What did you find?" Satrine asked.

Welling thumbed through the journal. "The Circle of Light and Stone. That's who the Tomars—the whole of the Firewings, actually—were having their row with." He took his whistle out of his pocket and blew hard. One of the patrolmen came out. "Keep the search going. Send someone back to the stationhouse to put in a report.

Inspector Rainey and I will go to the chapterhouse of the Circle of Light and Stone. We will likely need a similar complement of patrolmen to meet us, preferably with another writ of warrant, if one can be provided in due haste. Have it done under my authority." The patrolman saluted and went back inside the house.

Welling bounded down the steps and marched down the street at double time. Satrine ran to catch up with him.

"Where is Light and Stone?"

"Straight shot ahead of us, corner of Jewel and Downing."

"You already know that?"

"I spent the night digging through records. Three years ago there was a feud between several Circles, including Light and Stone. A huge magic-fueled rumble broke out right in front of their chapterhouse."

Satrine nodded, vaguely remembering. It had been an enormous tragedy, several civilians killed, many more injured. But in North Maradaine, it was just another horrible story to remind her to stay away from Inemar. She shook off the thought.

"For someone who hasn't slept, Welling, you seem full of energy."

"I believe I'm about to solve one murder, Inspector Rainey," he said. "And I have the chance to prevent another. For that, I could run the length of the city and back."

◆━◆◆━◆

Minox was too late. He knew this before he even reached the chapterhouse. Half a block away, a horrified scream pierced the air. His gut churning, Minox broke into a run, hoping that Inspector Rainey would follow his example.

He ran around the corner to see Jaelia Tomar dead. Dead in a grotesque and perverse spectacle, killed in the same manner as her husband. Stripped naked, spikes through her hands, heart removed. The only difference was her body was splayed out on the front steps of the Light and Stone chapterhouse, obscured only by a slight haze around the steps.

Pushing the bile back down his throat, he raced over to the gawking and screaming crowd that had already formed. Rainey was at his elbow, shoving people aside to form a path. They blew their whistles and forced their way through to the steps.

Inspector Rainey tore off her coat and covered the body. Minox turned to the ugly crowd, screaming over their shouts and cries. "Who saw what happened? How did she get here? Anyone? Anyone?"

Screams and jeers were the only reply. Inspector Rainey came back up to him, standing close to whisper in his ear. "Public street, all but broad daylight? Impossible!"

"From what you could see, was she killed here?" Minox asked. His eyes stayed on the crowd, scanning it for a face he could connect to the earlier murder.

"Almost no blood here," she said. "We need to clear this mob before things get out of hand."

The crowd was shouting incoherently, Minox able to pick out only a few choice words about dead mages and serves them all right. "We might have some good witnesses in here. If not the killer."

"Not much good if we have a riot," Rainey said. "Earlier you said something about a show of color?"

Minox nodded, understanding her meaning. He pulled out his whistle and gave five hard, short trills as loud as he could manage. Inspector Rainey took out her own and did the same. The Riot Call. Not only would every footpatrol Constabulary in earshot come running, they would repeat the signal. Most people on the street knew what the call meant as well.

Minox drew out his handstick, noting that Inspector Rainey already had hers out. Now that they'd made the Riot Call, they had wide latitude in how they handled the crowd. People knew the call meant get clear or get beaten down and arrested. That didn't seem to intimidate them: they still shouted and pressed forward.

"Stand down and step away!" Rainey boomed out. He was impressed she had that much power with her voice. "You have to the count of ten!"

"Burn out the mages!" someone shouted.

Inspector Rainey did not count. Instead she drove into the crowd at the direction of that voice. Minox blew the signal again, and he could hear other whistles repeating the call in the distance.

Inspector Rainey knocked three or four men in the crowd—not too hard, but enough to get them out of her path and think twice about causing more trouble. She grabbed one man by the front of his coat and pulled him out of the crowd to the steps. He struggled with her, but she knocked him with her handstick across the head.

"Did you yell that?" she asked the man.

Her approach was direct; Minox respected that.

"No, I—"

"You did!" Inspector Rainey snapped at him. She threw the man onto the steps next to the covered body. He scrambled away from the dead woman. "Look at that! You want more of that?"

"No . . . no . . ." the man gibbered in panic.

Rainey turned out to the crowd. "Anyone else?"

The crowd all moved back. Whistles sounded from all directions. Constabulary descended on Downing Street.

"Round up and question!" Minox yelled out to the approaching patrolmen. "I want to know every witness account!"

The patrolmen looked confused, and more than a little apprehensive. Minox deduced that they were not sure exactly how to follow his orders. Inspector Rainey, however, had no trouble.

"You three," she pointed to a group of patrolmen coming from Dockview. "Set up a perimeter around the square and that teahouse. The rest of you, corral the witnesses into the teahouse. Get names, addresses, and witness accounts. Anyone who doesn't cooperate gets the lockwagon!"

The patrolmen got to work herding people into the teahouse. Inspector Rainey released a slow breath and turned to the body. She lifted her coat up off it just enough to look under. "The spikes weren't driven into the steps," she said.

Minox stayed a respectful distance away from Missus

Tomar's body. "But they are completely through her hands?"

Rainey nodded. She reached under the hands. "Bits of powdered stone. So the killer did his whole ritual somewhere else and then brought her body here."

"Why here?" Minox asked, not that he expected an answer from Inspector Rainey beyond supposition. Dead body left here on the steps? How could it be done? There was the haze in the air, the slight sulfurous odor. He glanced at the steps around the body. Fine white powder. Minox dabbed a bit on his finger and tasted it. Sweet, just as he suspected.

A window opened up on the second floor of the Light and Stone chapterhouse, and an older woman stuck her head out. "Will you please remove that filth from our step!"

Rainey took the lead in responding, stepping out to the walkway. "What do these vests mean, ma'am?"

"What?"

"The vests that we are wearing? What do they mean?"

"You're city Constabulary!"

"Right," Rainey said. "Not sanitation. We're here to investigate a murder, not clean up a mess for you."

"Get rid of it, like you did the crowd!"

Minox stepped over so he could address the woman as well. "Ma'am, I don't think you quite understand the gravity of the situation here."

"I understand there's a corpse on our front step!"

"And I need to figure out who killed her," Minox said, straining to keep his voice even and calm. The muscles in his neck were tightening, and his stomach turned in knots. This woman was strangely infuriating, but he could not let that cloud his judgment or impede the investigation. He knew that the fact that he was at his second Mage Circle chapterhouse in as many days was additionally affecting his emotional control.

"That's not my problem!"

"No?" Minox couldn't believe the woman would have the audacity to say that. "Let me clarify my line of thought for you, then. There is a dead body here, on your steps." He stepped up to the stairs and lifted up the coat so the woman could see. "The body of a naked woman with her heart cut out. Not exactly something a person can carry around town and escape notice. So the question is, what's the easiest place one could do that from?"

The woman looked nauseous, placing a hand over her mouth. Minox noted, however, that she did not pull back through the window despite her obvious discomfort. She was a captive audience now.

Minox held up two fingers. "Two places, ma'am. One is right out that front door!"

"You're disgusting!"

"Most likely place," Inspector Rainey said. "We'll need to question everyone in there."

"You can't do that!" the woman shouted. "This is a private place!"

"We've made the Riot Call, ma'am," Inspector Rainey said. "That gives us quite a bit of freedom of action, especially when there's a dead body involved. We will come in there."

Minox knew that Inspector Rainey's interpretation of the rule of law with regard to privacy and the Riot Call was, to say the least, imaginative, if not wholly inaccurate, but he wasn't going to ruin the moment by interrupting her. They did need to investigate this Circle and its members.

The woman stared quietly for a moment. "What's the second?" she finally asked.

"The second what?" Inspector Rainey asked.

"The second place the body could come from?"

Minox pointed up. "Your roof."

Chapter 16

SATRINE COULDN'T STOP BEING ANGRY. She had attempted to curb this by hitting random bystanders when the Riot Call was made, but it wasn't helping. Her first assignment as an inspector had spiraled into a dismal failure. The murderer not only was still on the loose, the murder unsolved, but now another person was dead. A woman who might have been home and safe in her chapterhouse had it not been for Satrine.

The moments when she had spoken with Jaelia Tomar yesterday kept running through her mind. She could have done something different, said something smarter, and kept the whole situation from falling apart and ending in Jaelia's arrest.

Welling was still thinking clearly, in his own way. Satrine had been trying to figure out how the blazes someone could put Jaelia's body on the building steps, and the only thing she had thought of was some fast work with a wagon. The roof hadn't even crossed her mind. Not thinking straight.

Not thinking like an inspector. Because she wasn't one. She was a fraud.

"Inspector Rainey," Welling said. "I think it best that you inspect the body further, while I question the Light and Stone members."

"That's what you'd prefer?" she asked. She was surprised that he'd volunteer to talk to the mages.

"I'd honestly prefer to do neither one," he said. "But given the circumstances that would be the height of irresponsibility. We also need to . . . ah, look." He pointed down the street, noting Inspectors Kellman and Mirrell approaching.

"The blazes is happening?" Kellman asked. "Which one of you made the Riot Call?"

"We both made it," Satrine said quickly, before Welling could do anything to gainsay her.

"Where's the riot, then?"

"Quelled before it started," Welling said. "And it was starting, gentlemen."

"Really?" Mirrell asked. "Why was that?"

Satrine stepped forward, noting that Mirrell flinched slightly away on her approach. "We've got a dead body—a dead naked woman—on the steps of the chapterhouse of a Mage Circle. People surrounded it gawking and screaming. The whole situation was a hay barn on a dry day."

"Funny," Kellman said.

"Where's your crowd?" Mirrell asked.

"Rounded into that teashop," Satrine said. "Footpatrol are taking statements, but they may need some inspectorial guidance. Why don't you go give it to them?"

"You trying to give us orders, Tricky?"

The nickname was sticking. Terrific.

"Oh, I'm sorry," Satrine said. "I thought you two were inspectors interested in helping keep the blasted peace. If you just want to sit around and chat, go back to the stationhouse."

"Hey, hey," Kellman said. "The blazes is your problem?"

"Problem is a dead body, gentlemen," Welling said.

"There's twenty of those problems a day, Jinx," Kellman said.

Mirrell had walked over to the body and lifted up the coat. He yelped and skittered away. "That's—that's our mage from yesterday!"

"That's right," Welling said. "The one we let get grabbed. Our fault, Mirrell."

Mirrell frowned, biting his lip. "Come on, Darreck. Let's go ask some questions." He stalked off into the teashop.

"I would suppose that the teashop owners will be displeased with our commandeering their business," Welling said once the two of them had walked out of earshot.

Satrine shrugged. "Or they'll be pleased by how much tea they're selling today."

Welling gave the barest hint of a smile at that, and turned up the stairs, pointing to the body quickly, and then up to the roof, before going up to the door and knocking on it. Two Light and Stone members opened the door just enough to admit him entrance.

Satrine called for a page on her whistle. The body was going to have to be investigated, but not here on the street. The air was moist, it was going to rain soon. Plus, this was too in the open, too exposed. That was the least she could do for failing Jaelia, preserve some degree of dignity for the woman—a woman whose only crime was not holding herself together when she found out her husband was dead.

Blazes, Satrine was barely holding herself together all this time.

She didn't wreck city blocks when she lost control, though, she smirked to herself. No, she just cracked the skulls of street trash. Not exactly the healthiest way of confronting her problems.

She looked back up at the door of the Light and Stone chapterhouse. The door had a frosted glass panel, so she could make out the silhouettes of Welling and the mages. She really wondered what it was like for Welling and other mages. Were they constantly holding themselves in check?

Was it at all like the gnawing anger in the pit of her stomach over what happened to Loren, threatening to burst out at the slightest provocation?

Satrine glanced up to the roof, three stories up. Like most of the houses in this neighborhood, the roof was flat-topped. Getting up on the roof with an unwilling victim might be challenging, but certainly possible, and once up there the killer could easily perform his death ritual, and then throw the body down to the stairs below.

Satrine crouched down and looked under the coat. The steps were solid stone. Would the impact of a woman dropping three stories do much to them? Satrine had no idea. Leppin would know. Where was the page she called for?

She looked back up to the roof, and the heavy clouds beyond it. It would be a perfect place not only to kill someone without being disturbed, but to watch the chaos unfold on the street.

Two pages came running up to her, but her mind was racing with a need for action. Barely glancing at the pages, she shouted, "One of you, stay with the body, the other one, run for Mister Leppin!" Her gaze darted along the brick face of the building, spotting hand- and toeholds she could use to climb up to the roof. Windowsill, corner block, window lip—the path became clear to her.

It had been a long time since she had climbed up to the roof of a building in Inemar, but old instincts had never died off completely. In seconds she was halfway to the second floor.

"Sweet saints!" one of the pages shouted.

Satrine presumed they were reacting to her climb. They'd probably never seen a mother of two climb up the side of a wall before. Between this and stripping off her clothes in the alley, she was going to become a legend among the pages before too long. The only question was what kind of legend she was going to be.

She pulled herself up over the lip of the roof, and almost dropped into a huge puddle of blood. She was so surprised she nearly lost her balance, gripping the ledge before falling down to the street below.

There was more than a puddle of blood. A boot print of blood led away from the edge of the roof to the other side of the building. Fresh and wet.

Satrine drew her crossbow, quickly checking that it

was loaded. Drops of moisture glanced off her hand and arm. First bits of rain, the rest would start quickly. With it, the trail of blood would be lost.

She followed the trail of blood to where it ended, at the side overlooking a narrow alleyway. The next building over was taller, no way to jump up to the next roof without a rope or other gear. She scanned across the windows a flight down. One was open.

A red stain smeared the sill.

Satrine leaped for the open window.

She landed on the sill and scrambled in to a rough tenement apartment—dingy cracked plaster walls, scrappy bedrolls on the floor—among three kids who were staring at her.

"Stick!" one of them yelled. The kids bolted out of the room.

Satrine didn't bother trying to explain to them. No time. She ran through the flop as fast as she could, knocking into the doorframe in her rush.

Spots of blood on the floor, down the hallway to the stairwell. Wet and smeared. Doors along the hallway slammed shut, bolts clicking. Call went out of a stick in the building, plenty of people don't want Constabulary to see what they're up to. Not something Satrine needed to worry about. She sprinted, knowing that she couldn't surprise her quarry now. Her only chance to catch him was just plain outpacing him.

Fortunately, if there was one thing Druth Intelligence taught, it was how to run.

She bounded down the stairs, three at a time. The wood creaked and groaned with every landing. Someone was running on the stairs below her. It could be the killer, or just anyone running away from the stick call. No way to be sure, but she couldn't take the chance.

"Constabulary!" she screamed. "Stand and be held!"

The runner kept going, which didn't surprise Satrine. She was down one flight, and her runner was on the ground floor, surely about to use the next door.

Satrine jumped all the way down to the next landing, impact jarring her knees. She almost lost her balance, her shoulder knocking into the wall, plaster crumbling from the hit. She gripped the crossbow tightly, afraid to let it drop out of her hand. If this was the killer, then he would have no compunction in taking her life.

She reached the ground floor. No sign of anyone. No blood on the floor. Had she lost the trail in her rush? The door outside was on the other side of the hall; he'd still be running if he went that way. The apartment doors closest to the stairs were closed and—

One door burst open, right next to her. A masked figure grabbed her arm—her crossbow arm—before she could react, wrenching it upward. She fired instinctively, the bolt imbedding into the ceiling, and the figure punched her in the ribs.

Satrine ignored the pain and cursed herself for getting surprised. She pulled her arm back down while driving one knee up into her attacker's gut. She pulled the man closer—he was strong but light—about to crack her head against his nose, when his other hand slammed her in the chin, knocking her backward. Satrine lost her balance and fell to the ground, and lost her grip on the crossbow. Her attacker ripped it from her grasp. She landed on her back, wind knocked out of her.

Struggling for breath, Satrine watched helplessly as he cocked her crossbow and reloaded it, his fingers dancing over the weapon with practiced skill. He took aim at her head and stepped away, a slow walk backward down the hall.

There was no fear, staring at her own crossbow. Satrine only had a vague sense of uncertainty.

He was halfway to the doors, and Satrine couldn't get on her feet, couldn't force herself to draw breath. She rolled over and clawed her way along, trying to get closer to him. Despite the pain, the spinning vertigo of suffocation, Satrine pulled her failing body toward the escaping killer.

"C—C—" She couldn't speak. He was at the door, still aiming at her, a clear kill shot. Why wasn't he taking it?

She drew a small breath, just the tiniest amount.

"Co—" she pushed out. She breathed in again, pushing her legs under her.

The killer broke off, running out the door.

She gasped deeply, a desperate drink of sweet air.

"Come on!" she shouted. She couldn't run, but she managed to gain her feet and stagger forward toward the door.

He hadn't shot. He could have killed her, cleanly and quickly, but didn't.

Why hadn't he?

———————•◆•———————

Minox found the foyer of the Circle of Light and Stone chapterhouse oppressive and intimidating. The walls were painted in bright colors, swirled and splashed in random patterns. It was unsettling. Just standing in the room was making his eyes hurt. The presence of the three Light and Stone mages didn't help his mood either. The woman he had spoken to earlier, and two other women, all glowered at him silently.

This was the best choice, though—he had to leave investigating the body to Inspector Rainey. Handling that himself would have been inappropriate. He couldn't even trust his own unbiased opinion. That was an unsettling feeling as well.

Everything about this particular case was unsettling.

An older gentleman, almost portly for a mage, came in to the foyer. He came bearing a warm smile, even chuckling a little. Minox was not able to read what this meant. Mages always confounded his knack for reading body language.

"So," the old man said, "this is the Constabulary man who thinks we threw a dead, naked woman out our door."

"Or off the roof," Minox said. "Though you would not be the only suspects in that case."

"Good to know," the old man said. He extended his hand genially. "Wells Harleydale, Circle of Light and Stone. Though you knew the last part. What can I do for you?"

"I have a few questions regarding the victim," Minox

said, taking Harleydale's hand. "I understand she had some connections with your Circle." Harleydale's eyes went wide as soon as their hands touched.

"And what Circle are you from?"

"The victim was a member of the Firewings Circle, Mister Harleydale, and I understand that—"

"I didn't ask about her Circle, sir. I asked about yours. No Circle allows its members to join Constabulary."

"I am not the matter at hand, Mister Harleydale."

"Check him," Harleydale said to the three women. One waved her hand absently, and Minox suddenly found himself pinned against the wall. He struggled, but could not move his arms an inch. The other two women tore open his clothing with magic-laden gestures. He tried to summon his own magic, but when he did Harleydale countered with a blast, dissipating his power. "None of that, Inspector!"

"You are assaulting an officer of the law!"

"The law!" Harleydale scoffed. "The law has been no friend of ours, sir. I am insulted that you see fit to try and use your ability while wearing that coat and vest! Do you know what . . ."

Minox pushed hard with both magic and muscle, knocking the three women off balance for a moment. "I will see all of you dragged from here in irons!"

"Yes, there it is," Harleydale said. "Isn't that always how it ends when mages and constables meet?" He left the foyer. Minox was about to chase after him when the women, having quickly recovered, grabbed him bodily and threw him out the door.

Minox rolled down the steps, knocking and bruising his arms and body as he fell. He was able to get his feet under him before he fell onto the body of Jaelia Tomar.

The body was still there.

Three other mages from the Firewings were there as well, marching up to the house.

Inspector Rainey was not there.

"Stand aside, Inspector!" the leader of the Firewings shouted. Minox could feel the crackle of magic being pulled toward the three of them. The same sensation came from behind him; Minox had a feeling of sinking, of dropping down as everything flowed away from him.

There were two pages at the bottom of the stairs, both looking frightened beyond belief. Minox understood how they felt, and had no small amount of pride in them holding their ground. He could barely stand, the sudden shift in magic energy was like the air being sucked away; he had to remember to draw breath.

He was about to be in the middle of a mage war. In his streets.

Not while he wore his vest.

"Stand down, Firewings!" he shouted, pulling out his crossbow and handstick. "Take no action or you will be bound by law!"

That stopped them, if only for a moment. Magic was still primed, like cords tied to Minox's chest, pulled taut.

"What are you trying to do?" Harleydale's voice boomed out behind Minox.

"Two dead!" the Firewings' leader returned. "And your hands are all over it!"

"Our hands?" Harleydale came down the steps, his three women behind him. "Your troubles landed on our step!"

"And now we have as well."

"Quiet!" Minox shouted, not realizing until it was too late he had poured magic into his voice. The word shook across the square, more raw magic than sound. The two groups of mages all stumbled back, while the pages were unaffected.

"Is that the best you can manage?" Harleydale hissed in Minox's ear.

Minox spun on his heel, driving his handstick square into the old man's jaw. He hit the man again, center of the chest, then another blow cracking against his head. He let his attack be savage, let it draw from his anger. He had to be relentless, not give Harleydale a chance to use any magic against him. With all the strength Minox could muster, he flipped the old man down onto the cobblestones and jumped on top of him. He aimed his crossbow a few scant inches from Harleydale's eye.

"Does anyone else want to see my best?"

Magic was being pulled behind him — the three Light and Stone women.

"Step back, ladies!" another voice called out from across the square. Minox glanced up: Mirrell, Kellman, and several of Maradaine's finest patrolmen stood in a phalanx, crossbows aimed at the top of the steps.

Harleydale breathed laboriously, sweat beading across his head. Minox felt a wave of shame and pity; this was an old man he had just pummeled. Even considering that, Harleydale had deliberately provoked and assaulted an officer of law, and had shown intention of continuing to do so. Just action was on Minox's side in this case, the age of the man notwithstanding.

"We demand justice!" the Firewing leader shouted.

"Justice?" Mirrell said. "You've got half the sticks in Inemar working here!"

"Real justice," the Firewing said. Minox felt the magic they had built up was still not dispersed.

Kellman pivoted to train his crossbow on the Firewings; several of the footmen did as well. "Real justice would mean dragging all you lot to Quarrygate right now."

"If not the river," Mirrell growled.

"Always the same," Harleydale said, still wheezing with his face pressed to the ground. "You proud of this?"

"You aren't the victim here," Minox said, grabbing the man by the hair and forcing him to look at the dead body of Jaelia Tomar. "There is the victim." Minox got to his feet, wrenching the old man up with him. "You could have helped her. You chose, instead, to make things worse."

"Jinx," Mirrell called out. "This is your case. What's the call?"

Minox wanted to have every one of the Firewings and Light and Stones thrown in a lockwagon. He'd be within his rights, even though Mage Circle protection rules would mean they'd be released before sunset. Except for the Light and Stone women—he could probably make an assault charge on them hold. None of that, though, would make any blazing difference in solving his murder case. Murder cases. Minox wasn't the victim who needed justice here. Justice needed to be served for both the Tomars.

"I saw him!" A piercing cry from Inspector Rainey. She stumbled out of the tenement apartment next door, blood on her mouth and face, clutching at her sides. "The killer . . . was on the roof."

Minox dropped Harleydale to the ground and ran to his partner's side. "Where?"

"He got away from me," she said. Quieter, she added, "He got my weapon."

"This morning has been full of indignities," Minox said in an equally low voice. "We shouldn't dwell on them."

Inspector Rainey nodded. Loud enough for Mirrell and Kellman to hear, she said, "He just ran out of here, dark clothes and masked face."

"We didn't see a blazing thing," Kellman said. "Our attention's been elsewhere, eh, Tricky?"

Mirrell took in the whole scene, eyes darting glances to the roof of the Light and Stone house. "He killed her up there, and threw the body onto the steps?"

Inspector Rainey nodded, limping over to the body of Jaelia Tomar, clearly not worried about being in the field of fire. The Light and Stone women, the Firewings, and the Constabulary all kept their guard up. She looked up at the whole scene, seeming to drink it in for the first time. "It looks like we all had some excitement."

"Had, Tricky?" Kellman asked.

Rainey flashed a bloody grin at the Inspector. Minox was worried about her state of mind. She looked at the two pages, both of whom hadn't moved an inch since Minox came out of the house. "Where's the wagon, boys?"

"It's coming," one of them offered meekly.

"Good, good," she said. She glanced down at Harleydale, still lying on the ground. "Welling, can we clear the street?"

"You think it's that easy?" Mirrell asked.

"Are we arresting anyone?" Rainey responded. She squatted down next to Harleydale. "Are we going to have to take you in, sir?"

"Don't talk to me that way, young woman!"

She leaned in close to Harleydale, her tone jovial. "Go inside, sir. Bring your wives or whoever they are with you."

"You can't—"

Inspector Rainey's voice dropped to a deathly whisper. "I am an officer of the law who has given you an order in the public square, sir. Comply or you will be jailed."

Harleydale reached his hand out to the Light and Stone women, who came down and pulled him to his feet. The four of them all climbed the steps and went back into the house. Harleydale stopped at the door. "This is not resolved. Mark this, Inspector Welling. You have made a choice today."

"Go on, you all," Kellman told the Firewings. The three of them frowned, but turned away and left.

The magical energy in the area faded, making Minox's ears pop and joints crack.

"End of action, boys," Mirrell told the patrolmen. "Everyone get back on your beats. All of us here, someone is probably stealing the stationhouse." The patrolmen lowered their weapons and dispersed.

Inspector Rainey sat on the steps, next to the dead body. "Is every day like this?"

"Nah." Kellman crossed over to them, Mirrell walking with him. "Some days are bad."

Rainey laughed dryly. "This is going to fall apart, isn't it?"

"Are we going to get another Circle Feud, Jinx?" Mirrell asked.

Minox had the distinct sense that Mirrell thought he ought to have a better idea about what the mages of Light and Stone and Firewings would do than anyone else. Minox had to admit he probably did, but not for the reasons Mirrell was implying—he had no more insight into the Mage Circles than he did any other person, though his insight in all matters certainly surpassed Mirrell's and Kellman's.

Even so, his ignorance was damaging the case.

"If we don't resolve the murders of the Tomars, and soon, I believe the tensions will reach an explosive level. They almost did right now."

"Hmph," Mirrell said. "You two going to wait for the wagon, go back to the station with the body?"

Rainey smirked at Mirrell. "Are you asking if we're fine with you two going about your business? Feel free."

Kellman pointed over to the teashop. "Should we let them all go? We've got a few statements and such, but . . ."

"They reported a sudden burst of smoke, and when it cleared, her body was there," Minox stated and Mirrell nodded.

"That's right. They said the mages did it. You have to admit, it looks like the Light and Stone folks did this."

"Indeed it does, which is why it clearly isn't the case."

"How do you figure?" Kellman asked. He actually looked genuinely interested in the answer, rather than his usual dismissive expression.

"The smoke served as a useful cover for dropping the body off the roof. And the crowd would presume it to be magical."

"It's not?" Mirrell asked.

"Smoke powder, encased in honey-glass. Thrown from the roof, it would leave little trace save the honey powder." He pointed to the dusting of powder on the steps.

Mirrell nodded. "Which any corner chemist would sell for ten crowns."

Kellman smirked. "And forget who they sold it to for another ten. So the killer just wanted it to look like it was the mages?"

"Most likely a secondary goal, but one that suited his needs."

"The folks in the teashop are all fuming," Mirrell said. "What do we do with them?"

"Let them go," Rainey said. "Let's not disrupt anyone's day any further."

Mirrell and Kellman nodded and went back to the teashop.

Minox felt drained. He needed to get off his feet, and sat down on the stoop next to Inspector Rainey. He had never before noticed how the ebb and flow of magical energy around him would affect him. It would be a fascinating thing to study if it didn't make him weak and dizzy.

"You need to eat something?" Rainey asked him.

"Soon," he answered. "I can wait until we've got Missus Tomar on the wagon."

"This all got very hot out here, hmm?" She shook her head. "I should have known it would."

"I fear I'm culpable for some of that," Minox said. Rainey only looked at him with a raised eyebrow. Clearly he needed to explain further. "Inspector, I think my presence here today . . . specifically with me being an Uncircled Mage, caused a further escalation of conflict that could have otherwise been avoided."

"Really, Minox?" she asked.

He bristled at her use of his given name. There was a certain unprofessionalism, he felt, at early adoption of casual address. When Nyla started on the inspectors' floor, she had also quickly taken up the habit of using given names, with everyone save the captain. Minox briefly considered if it was a female trait, or if it was an ingrained habit of Rainey's from a lifetime of not serving on Constabulary or a similar force. Druth Intelligence might well not have standard protocols for rank and address.

He had been lost in thought, and she had continued. "Those Firewings were going to march in here and cause chaos. The Light and Stone were going to respond. I doubt they were, as you say, 'further escalated' by your presence." She sighed and got on her feet. "If anyone messed up here today, it's me."

"I thoroughly disagree, Inspector Rainey. You took decisive action and put yourself in a position to potentially catch our killer."

"He got away."

She was dwelling on her errors. They both were. Not something that would aid in effectively solving this case. Steps needed to be taken to regain focus.

"Immaterial. Certainly, his capture would have been a preferable outcome, but as the bruises sported by me and Inspector Mirrell can testify, our adversary is not lacking in cunning or skill. Failure to subdue him hardly constitutes failure as an inspector."

Rainey looked wistfully out across the street. "Do you think Mirrell or Kellman noticed I had lost my weapon?"

"Certainly not Kellman," Minox said. "The man is largely incapable of keeping his idle thoughts from coming out his mouth. Mirrell, in my estimation, would have made it an issue immediately as well."

Rainey chuckled dryly. "And what will the captain say?"

"He will say something along the lines of 'Blast it, Welling, you're getting sloppy.'"

Rainey turned to him. "Why would he say it to you?"

Minox drew out his crossbow and passed it to her, handle first. "Because I'm the one who will be missing his weapon."

Rainey stared at the crossbow, her hand held away as if she were afraid to take it. "Why?"

"Because I'm gathering that you are operating on some form of probationary basis, and the captain might use a minor cause to dismiss you. As you have been the only partner I've found to be of tolerable intelligence and capacity, the idea of your dismissal over a minor infraction is abhorrent."

Inspector Rainey laughed and took the crossbow. "You have the most fascinating manner of speaking, you know that?"

Minox did not know how to respond to that, and was saved from the necessity of providing one by the arrival of Leppin and his wagon.

"You've all had a blazes of a morning, haven't you?" Leppin asked as he hopped down to the street. He squinted up at Rainey. "How's the second day treating you, Missus Inspector?"

"Full of excitement. Yours?"

Leppin shrugged and pointed at Jaelia Tomar. "I always got something to keep me busy. What's the story?"

"Same as yesterday's," Minox said. "Dead mage, Firewing, heart cut out."

Leppin crouched down next to the body, lifting up the coat. "Bird this time?" He whistled out low. "Same type of spikes through the hands, I see. Same effect on you, Welling?"

Minox had presumed that the spikes had been the same, but hadn't bothered to check. He bent down and gave the spike a glancing touch. The same draining, sinking sensation filled him, and he instinctively stepped away from the body. "The same," he coughed out. That had been a foolish test, given his state.

Leppin moved in closer, changing the lenses on his eyepiece. "Our friend seems to have an unlimited supply of these things."

"At least he's not worried about losing them when he hits his victims," Inspector Rainey offered.

Ideas clicked in Minox's head. "Valuable objects, of rare material and origin. He must have a limited supply of the spikes."

Rainey locked eyes with him, nodding with understanding. "Which means he's using them exactly how he is intending to, in a very specific way."

"It also implies the killer has a very specific plan, and to that end, it's highly likely he has a final goal to his actions."

"A pattern," Rainey said. "Leading us to understand what the killer is trying to accomplish."

"Or say," Minox suggested. He walked around the body. "He didn't shoot you when he could."

"No."

"You saw him?" Leppin asked.

"He got away." Rainey notably did not make eye contact with Leppin.

Minox didn't let the details of his partner's body language distract him from his train of thought. "And he notably did not use deadly force when he struck the carriage last night absconding with our new victim."

Rainey's eyes went wide, and the slightest of smiles played across her lips. "Perhaps he doesn't want to kill anyone who isn't part of his plan."

"He might even consider it immoral—in his own way—to murder outside of his plan. But what is it?" Minox said, half to himself. "Blast, it's nigh impossible to find a pattern with only two points of information."

"You want a third murder?" Rainey said.

"No, no," Minox said. "Leppin, collect the body, bring it to your examinarium, and get me every piece of information you can find."

"What are we doing next?" Rainey asked.

Leppin glanced over at him. "You're going to go sit down somewhere and eat something, that's what. You look like a half-dead man."

Rainey nodded. "You were up all night."

"What?" Leppin snapped. "Blazes, Minox. You're on the verge of collapse, you can't just push yourself on pure willpower. Bodies don't work that way!"

"I'm fine, Leppin."

Leppin pointed a sharp finger at Rainey. "I'm sure you don't want to be anyone's mother here, Rainey, but someone has to make him take care of himself."

"And that's my job?" Rainey asked.

"Did he tell you he collapsed twice last night? Magical Depletion Fatigue."

"Leppin!" Minox said. He did not need to disclose personal matters to Inspector Rainey.

"I told him to go home and get some rest, but he ignored me!"

"I don't need—" Minox started. But he knew Leppin was right—his strength was about to give way. If he let himself fall over here and now, in front of Leppin, it was very possible the examiner would report to the captain and keep him from working for several days. Minox couldn't allow that. "I just need to eat something, and then get back to the stationhouse."

"Other way around," Leppin said. He went to the wagon and pulled out a litter. "Sit in the blasted wagon and I'll take you back over myself. You go get him some food and meet us there."

That was the wrong thing to say to Rainey. "You want your pants pressed while I'm at it, little man?"

"No," Leppin said. "Help me get the body in the wagon, though."

Minox saw no value in fighting either of them right now. His legs were about to give out. He went over to the wagon and sat in the front seat. Leppin and Rainey continued to snipe at each other as they loaded Jaelia Tomar into the wagon. Minox didn't realize he had fallen asleep until he woke up in the stationhouse's wagon hold.

Inspector Rainey was sitting a few feet away, watching him intently. When she saw that he had roused, she picked something up and crossed over.

"I got you three fast wraps," Rainey said, holding out the newsprint-wrapped food to him. "I still don't know what the meat is supposed to be, but if you can eat it, I won't judge too much."

Minox grabbed one out of her hands. "It really doesn't matter." He tore the newsprint open and took several bites, giving no regard to any sort of decorum. He ate it so quickly he barely tasted it.

"I really have to disagree," she said. She gave a light smile, so Minox figured his savage eating had not disconcerted her. "The smell alone makes me nauseous. But if you like it."

"Times like this," Minox said, after finishing the first one, "liking what I'm eating has very little to do with it."

"How do you feel?"

"Functional."

"Good," she said. "I've been thinking about the spikes. We need to figure out what they are, and where they came from."

Minox tucked in to the second wrap, able to eat in a more civilized fashion now. The spikes were a unique element to this case, but he would prefer not to have to pursue that avenue of investigation. "I am concerned that they may prove too obscure to yield fruitful information."

"That's crap, Welling."

Minox wasn't surprised by Inspector Rainey's crudity, but he didn't think she would so bluntly note his dissembling. "I hardly think that's appropriate."

"Yes, I know, your Uncircled status is not up for discussion. But you don't want to look into the spikes because that involves talking to someone who might know about them."

"I think we have well established how Circled mages react to me, Inspector Rainey."

"True," Rainey said. "However, I may be able to call in a favor along those lines."

That was surprising. "Have you been holding back, Inspector Rainey?"

"Don't we all?" She gave the barest of smiles. "Though we're going to have to go over to Laramie. Are there horses we can take?"

He got to his feet. "Certainly. That is an area in which I can call in a favor." More than one officer of the horse-patrol owed him. "Though I must say, even with your assurances, I am not looking forward to this meeting."

Chapter 17

MINOX RELISHED THE PLEASANT serenity of having a proper horse under him. It was the one thing he missed about his position before being promoted to Inspector Third Class. Rainey handled her own chestnut with considerable grace. That had to come from her Intelligence background.

"We're meeting an old contact of yours, aren't we?"

"That's one way of putting it," Rainey said. She glanced about the street. Homes and shops in Laramie were tall, narrow, and stacked up tight together, almost universally gray brick with iron lattice on the windows. Even the people were nondescript and subdued in this part of town. Rainey pointed to one tenement, crammed in between two taller buildings. Paler stone, newer construction. Built over an alley. "That's the one."

"You've been here before?"

"Just know it from description." She dismounted and led her horse over to the edge of the street. "What's the protocol?"

Minox came down. "Normally, I'd call a page, but I don't think they are as prevalent in this neighborhood as they are in Inemar." There was a hitchpost in front of a striker pub, and a nearly adolescent boy leaning against it, shirtless save for his suspenders. It would have to do.

"Tick two pence to hitch," the boy said, not even

looking up as Minox brought the horse over. "Just a tick if you're buying strikers."

"Are you buying a striker, Welling?" Inspector Rainey asked.

"Possibly before we leave," Minox said. "We're here on Constabulary business, boy."

The boy glanced up. "Oh, Constabulary business. Pardon me, your graces, for not taking a blazing knee." He sneered at them both. "Sticks can pay tick *five* pence."

Rainey took hold of her handstick. "You want your five pence?"

"Sure do," the boy said, turning his cheek up to her. "Gimme a nice bright welt right there. Won't that make a nice tale."

Minox pulled three ticks out of his pocket. "Tick five is just fine."

The boy took the coins. "Then hitch away, stick."

Minox tied his horse up, while Rainey did the same with her own. "Shouldn't let him lip to us like that," she said.

"Not going to begrudge a boy a few extra pence," Minox said. "You know any newsboys?"

"Course," the boy said.

"Round up whatever sheets you find in this part of town, for however many days back you can. Two ticks over cost if you do."

The boy looked skeptical, but nodded. "One tick up front, stick."

Minox flipped him another coin and turned to the building. "We're going in here, Inspector Rainey?"

She walked apace with him. "What was that with the newssheets?"

"You'd be amazed, Inspector Rainey, at how many missing pieces from unsolved cases I've found by a casual perusal of the day's newssheets."

Rainey shrugged, clearly dismissing the idea as his own eccentricity. That was fine, as far as Minox was concerned. She went up the stoop and rang the pullcord. "Let me do the talking here."

"Of course."

An elderly woman with a scowling face came to the door. "We ain't done nothing here."

Inspector Rainey put on a smiling face and a soft voice. "We need to see the major. Is he in?"

"Major don't see no one. Especially not a couple of sticks."

"Tell him—" Rainey paused, considering her words carefully. She then spoke with a perfect Waish accent. "Tell him that her Most Honorable Lady, Quia Alia Rhythyn, Jewel of the Ironroot Clan, is here to speak with him."

The old woman scowled even harder, as amazing as that was. She shut the door without a word.

"She'll tell him," Rainey said, her normal North Maradaine accent returning.

"True," Minox said. That much was clear in the woman's demeanor. "'Quia' is a minor noble rank in Waisholm, no? Second daughter or niece to a thane?"

"Something like that," Rainey said. "It's a bit of a joke."

"If you say so," Minox said. "Though I will admit, your history is clearly more colorful than I previously suspected."

Rainey appeared to be ready to comment on that when the old woman returned to the door. "Says he'll see you," she grunted out.

The old woman led them up a very narrow staircase to a modestly appointed sitting room. "Tea?" She spat the word out.

"With cream," Rainey said. The old woman glared at Minox.

"Two spoons honey and cream."

"Two spoons?" The old woman stomped off, muttering about the nerve of some people.

Rainey took a seat in one of the austere chairs, and gestured to Minox to do the same. "This will probably be . . . colorful."

"You haven't been very forthcoming," Minox said, taking his seat next to her. "Though I would imagine that we . . ."

"Shh." Rainey held up a single finger.

A lean gentleman of middle years, wearing a coat similar to that of a Druth Navy officer, though dark gray in color, strode into the room. "Her Most Honorable Lady," he said in gravelly voice. "About as honorable as the mole on my ass."

"Then that's quite an honorable mole, indeed." Rainey held out her hand to the man. With a gruff scoff, he kissed it and took his own chair.

"Wouldn't have thought I'd see you come here, Trini," he said, settling in. "In a Constabulary inspector's vest, at that. I'm not sure I want to know about that."

"It is a tale not worth telling, Major," Rainey said. "Welling, this is Major Altom Dresser."

"From Druth Intelligence," Minox said, standing up to offer his own hand. "Inspector Third Class Minox Welling."

"Hmm," Dresser said, looking at Minox's hand as if it held a dead fish. "Aren't you an interesting one?" After a moment, it was clear the major was not going to shake his hand, and Minox took his seat again.

"Major," Rainey said. "I have . . ."

"Must be something quite intriguing to get you to haul yourself to this part of town," Dresser said. "I don't get too many visitors from the old days."

"I haven't made too many visits," Rainey said. "Or received any."

"Eh," Dresser said. He furrowed his brow. "Whatever your little mystery is, I bet it's not as interesting as this one right here." He pointed a lean finger at Minox.

The old woman rolled out her tea tray. She handed a cup to Rainey. "One just cream." Then she picked up the other two and handed them to Minox and Dresser, muttering something about the price of honey.

Rainey's eyes sparkled with a strange, almost impish delight. "Major, I have to say, she is a jewel."

"Keeps me from being bored."

"Never would want that to happen, sir," Rainey said. "Now, on the subject of interesting things."

"Yes," Dresser said, leaning forward. "So which is it, boy? Failure, hider, or late bloomer?"

"I'm sorry?" Minox asked. "I don't understand the question."

"You're an Uncircled mage, that's clear." He said it like it was pure, inarguable fact. No point in trying to deny it.

"That's true," Minox said cautiously. "But I don't see how . . ."

"Boy, I can feel you, buzzing against the back of my skull, like a fly trying to crawl in my ear."

Minox wasn't sure how to take that.

Rainey coughed. "Major, that's not why—"

Dresser waved her off. "It'll hold, Trini." He got up from his chair and came closer to Minox, looking at him in a way that made Minox feel like an insect in a glass case.

"Have you never met an Uncircled mage before, Major?"

"Course I have, don't be stupid." He moved in closer and actually sniffed at Minox. "In my experience, the Uncircled fall into three categories. Failures, hiders, and late bloomers. You're a working man, inspector in the city sticks. So not a hider. But you've got a hint of that in you, don't you?" He fingered Minox's vest.

Minox beat down his instinct to run out of the room. The last thing he wanted was this man talking about magic, poking at him. "I really must object . . ."

"Must you? Am I upsetting you, Inspector Welling? Making you uncomfortable?" On the last word, a twitch formed in Minox's eye, which ran down the base of his skull until it became a tremor in his arm. His fingers shuddered as his arm shot forward. Sparks and snaps danced around his hand.

"Stop it, Major!" Rainey shouted.

"Me, stop it?" Dresser said in a charade of innocence. "He's doing it. No control, right, Inspector?"

Minox found his own mouth betraying him. He could barely breathe, but forced himself to make the words come out. "No . . . no one . . . controls . . . me."

"I didn't say I was controlling you, Uncircled," Dresser said. "I said you have no control. Do you?"

Another surge hit Minox, like a needle in the eye.

"Enough!" Minox snapped, flinging that surge back out of his eye into Dresser's chest.

"Welling!" Rainey was on her feet, standing between him and Dresser. "Both of you need to calm down!"

Dresser laughed, despite clutching at his chest as he flopped back into his chair. "That's some spirit. Jessel! Bring out a tray of something!"

"Are you all right?" Rainey asked him.

"Fine. Stings a bit. Keeps the heart pumping."

She turned back to Minox. "What the blazes was that?"

"I haven't any idea," Minox said, getting to his feet. "Other than your old friend here doing his best to sabotage this interview." His heart raced, his fingers felt like jam.

"It's quite all right, Satrine," Dresser said. "It's most definitely of my doing. Your friend here has some real kick to him." He leaned forward in his chair. "So he probably wasn't a hider. Failures tend to run away once they're kicked off their campus, so that means he was a late bloomer."

"What are you talking about?" Rainey asked. She turned back to Minox, her expression clearly showing she wanted him to explain what was happening. Not that he understood at all.

Minox couldn't look Rainey in the eye. His knees buckled. "I think I—" Words could barely form. He could hardly breathe. He fell back into his chair.

"It's all right, son," Dresser said. "You've been pushing yourself. Pass out a couple times?"

"A couple," was all Minox could force himself to say.

The old woman—Jessel—came out carrying a tray of pastries. With a wordless scowl, she dropped them on the table and shuffled away.

"Go ahead, you need it," Dresser said, taking a couple of pastries and eating them with no pretense of decorum. Minox wasted no time doing the same.

Rainey had clearly tired of the lack of answers. "Would one of you kindly tell me what the blazes is happening here?"

"I believe," Minox said, once he swallowed, "that your friend is trying to test the limits of my magical ability and my patience. Both of which are in short supply right now."

"And well they should be," Dresser said. "Consider that a bit of an object lesson, Inspector Welling. What you're feeling right now is very similar to what every trained mage feels when you walk into the room."

Rainey came over to Minox, looking him over with more motherly concern than he wanted. "Really, Major? Is this the moment?"

Dresser craned his head to catch Minox's eye. "How old were you when you realized, boy?"

Minox sighed. This was torturous, but if it must be withstood to learn something about the pins, and perhaps make up for failing to save Jaelia Tomar, he would bear it. "Twenty-three. Three years ago."

Dresser whistled low. "Have to admit, ain't never heard of a late bloomer blooming that late. Twenty is the oldest I ever heard before. And a lot of raw ability for one. Most only trickle with magic. You are a rare specimen, indeed." His demeanor softened noticeably. "Blazes, you never had a chance, did you?"

"Is this enough, sir?" Minox asked. "Have I satisfied your curiosity?"

"Pff. I'm a spy, Inspector. My curiosity is never satisfied."

"We did come here with purpose," Minox said.

Rainey stopped fussing over him and sat back down. She reached into the pocket of her coat, produced the spike, and tossed it over to Dresser. He caught it deftly, and immediately cried out and dropped it to the ground.

Rainey laughed. Despite himself, Minox did as well.

"The blazes was that, Trini?"

"What you deserved," Rainey said, fetching the spike. "But that's what we've come to you to find out."

"Saints and sinners," he whispered. "Really, Satrine, what is that?"

She held it up to his eye level. "Something that was used to kill two mages so far. Two each, hammered through their hands."

Dresser set his jaw with grim determination and grabbed the spike. He held on, despite his face turning pale and sweat starting to pour down his face. The veins in his neck bulged out, large and pulsing. Finally he screamed and released it.

Minox had counted fifteen seconds.

"I can only presume," Minox said, "that you feel drained, weak, and sickly."

"Not to mention ravenous," he said, reaching shakily for a pastry. "I've never . . . I haven't heard of anything like that."

"It's not like the mage shackles we have at the station," Minox said.

"Mage shackles?" Dresser raised his eyebrow and then nodded. "Right. Steel manacles with bit of dalmatium mixed in. Uncommon, but effective in dampening a mage's power. But this . . ."

"It's a mystery," Rainey said with a wry smile.

"Which is your job, I suppose," Dresser said. He looked at the spike more closely. "No markings that I can see. It looks so blasted ordinary. But this is something very rare, indeed."

"And yet our killer has left four behind," Minox said.

"I'm stumped," Dresser said, sitting back. "I've never experienced anything like it before. Or even heard of it."

"I've stumped you," Rainey said. "I can cross that off my list."

"You really have no idea?" Minox asked, even though he was rather certain the man was being honest.

"I'm more than a little put out about it."

"Good," Minox said, getting to his feet.

"Trini." Dresser fluttered his hand in her direction. "If you can, leave that here. I'd like to get some further opinions on it, if possible."

Rainey gave a glance over to Minox, as if for approval. "This is evidence in an ongoing investigation."

"We have three others," Minox said. "Any opinions we do get wouldn't hurt." As much as he would like to deny Major Dresser, he had to admit it would be useful to allow him his own investigation.

Rainey nodded and left the spike on the table. "Thank you for your time, Major," she said with a nod.

"Always a pleasure to help the Most Honorable Quia," Dresser said. He turned back to Minox. "Keep your head up, son. Pay attention to what your body tells you, hmm?"

Minox held his tongue for a moment, unsure of how to respond. Finally, he let himself say, "It has been a very . . . instructive experience." That was as honest as he could be without falling prey to stronger emotions. Nothing good would come from that. "Let's be off, Inspector Rainey."

Satrine followed Welling down the stairs to find the shirtless boy holding a pile of newssheets and two steaming strikers.

"Way I figure, stick," the boy said as soon he spotted them, "you owe me one crown six and four."

Welling fished into his pocket and produced a crown and a half-crown. "Well-earned with extra," he said, passing the coins and taking one striker. "I am quite grateful." He bit greedily.

"Welling, I am so sorry," Satrine said. Despite the pastries he ate inside, he was eating the striker voraciously. The ordeal may have affected him more than he wanted to let on. "I knew it wouldn't be pleasant but I thought he would at least . . ." She paused, at a loss for words. She wanted to say that Dresser had been an unmitigated ass, acting like a petulant child because he sat in the same room as an Uncircled mage. Though clearly there was more happening between the two of them than she could perceive. It didn't matter, Dresser was completely inappropriate. Finally she shrugged and said, "Behave professionally."

"It's fine, Inspector," Welling said. "I was aware that any expert we might consult would react to me in a . . . less than cordial manner. I was not prepared for how uncordial it could become, of course."

Satrine sighed. She knew Dresser was Red Wolf

Circle—Red Wolf being a sizable Circle with a fair amount of capital because of their connections with the government. Officially, Red Wolf had a statement of co-operation with the Druth government as part of its charter. Unofficially, from what Satrine had always understood, Red Wolf Circle acted as a recruiter for mages who would serve well as Intelligence agents. Usually this took the form of paying for their education and pledging them to services upon completion. That's how it had gone for Dresser.

Was that what he was doing? Sizing Welling up for his recruitment potential?

"Here, skirt," the boy said, offering up the other striker. Satrine looked at both of them in askance.

"Go ahead," Welling said. "It's worth it."

Satrine took the other striker and cautiously bit into it. "Oh, saints, that's good," she said.

"Best meal I've had today," Welling said.

She took another bite, for once allowing herself to enjoy the savory flavors of lamb, onion, beer, and potato.

"We didn't even learn anything," Satrine said, returning to the previous subject.

"On the contrary," Welling said, before noting the shirtless boy was still looking at him expectantly. "Another task for another half-crown?"

"Listening," the boy said.

"Deliver those sheets to 418 Escaraine, up in Keller Cove."

"Up in the Cove?" The boy's voice almost screeched.

"That's why half a crown. Else I'll carry them myself."

The boy grumbled but nodded.

Welling produced another coin. "Take it straight to the stable in the back. Tell the man it's from Minox. You understand?"

"'Stood," the boy said, snatching the coin away. He took the pile of newsprints and headed away.

Satrine shook her head. "You paid that boy two crowns, plus his hitch fee. Which was probably a hustle."

"And he'll remember at least one stick who paid him

generously for honest errands," Welling said. "Consider it an investment in this neighborhood."

Satrine leaned against the hitchpost and took another bite. "Who's in the stable?"

"My cousin, Evoy. He . . . shares my enthusiasm for researching newsprint articles."

"You're a very interesting person, Minox Welling."

He paused in his eating. "Your husband. Inspector First Class, stationed out of the High Commissioner's Office, over in Trelan. All correct?"

"Correct." Satrine wasn't clear where Welling was going with this.

"Attacked on the West Hetrick docks, specifically outside the customhouses, at nearly midnight on the evening of Maritan the fourth."

"Correct again." Was this punishment, bringing up something unpleasant for her? If so, she'd bear it.

"Maritan the fourth was Fenstide. So the docks were shut down. No legitimate freight was coming in."

"Which may have been the very point of his investigation."

"You don't know what he was specifically investigating." This wasn't a question from Welling.

"No," she said. "We had a small celebration, just the family and Missus Abernand—"

"Your landlady, who lives above you."

"How did you—" She was sure she had never mentioned her.

"Obvious deduction. Continue."

"We aren't particularly traditional or religious, so after dinner, Loren left. Said he had something to investigate. I didn't press or pry."

"Or think it was strange he did that on a holiday?"

"The job is every day," she said, repeating Loren's usual mantra.

"I'm familiar with that." Welling unhitched the horses. "I happened to have read some of the official reports, newssheet articles, and such. Before I met you. Are you familiar with what they claim he was working on?"

"I wasn't paying close attention, frankly," Satrine said. She finished her striker, though her appetite had soured.

"It says he was investigating a smuggling operation. Investigating alone."

"Sounds reasonable." Though she had to admit, it was a bit odd that he was working alone that night.

"I'm not as sure," Minox said. "Onali was full on the fourth. And the sky was clear. Bright night, minimal legitimate traffic for cover. Poor conditions for smuggling. It is also atypical for an inspector of your husband's rank and stature to be investigating crimes of that nature."

"You know a lot about that sort of thing?"

"My cousin Thomsen works river patrol."

She mounted her horse. "What exactly are you driving at, Welling?"

"If you allow, Inspector Rainey. Another point, which may be uncomfortable."

"By all means," she said. He was definitely punishing her.

"Your husband was beaten severely, and supposedly left for dead in the water. By all rights, he should have drowned."

Should have, indeed. It might have been easier for her if he had. Then they couldn't deny her the widow fund. "If you have a point—"

"I am approaching it. He should have drowned, but was rescued, in the loosest sense of the word. In the water just long enough that his mind was lost, but not dead. The window of that rescue is very narrow."

"He was lucky that river patrol happened to be—"

Welling pulled himself up on his horse with surprising grace. "*Lucky* and *happened to be* are terms I find troubling, Inspector Rainey. In my experience, coincidence rarely occurs naturally."

"What are you saying, exactly?"

"The points of record on your husband's case do not add up." Taking up the reins, his face screwed up in thought. "Therefore, I believe my count of unresolved cases is now twenty-six." He kicked his horse and started riding east, back toward Inemar.

Chapter 18

MISS PYLE WAS DOWN in the stables when they returned. "You better watch yourselves," was the first thing she said.

"Are we in trouble?" Satrine asked.

"Hilsom is up there, raving mad. I think you really burned his hair, Minox."

"Does it matter?" Satrine asked.

"It would be ill-advised to build too adversarial a relationship with the City Protector's Office," Welling said.

"He can make our lives difficult if he wants to," Miss Pyle added. "Don't hide from him this time, Minox."

"So you were hiding last time," Satrine said.

Welling shook his head defiantly. "I was engaging in other activities elsewhere. That they occurred during his last visit to our office is merely a coincidence."

"I thought you don't believe in coincidence," Satrine said.

"I said it was rare."

Miss Pyle smirked. "His belief in coincidence changes when it conveniences him."

"I take great exception to that, Nyla." His effect was so flat, Satrine couldn't tell if he was joking with his cousin, or actually offended. Miss Pyle laughed, so Satrine took it to be jovial.

"Come on, Welling. We can't put off facing him too long."

Welling nodded. "Then shall we, how do they say, 'step on the beach'?"

Satrine grinned, remembering "The Ballad of Benson's Best." "And thus we stand, we hold, shields aloft; each inch we claim, we claim with blood and bone."

Welling raised an eyebrow at her. "Is that poetry?"

"You should read more, Welling. Let's go."

Hilsom stalked across the inspectors' floor, pacing back and forth in front of Cinellan's office. He had deep circles under his eyes—Satrine realized hers must look the same—and his fingers twitched like they wanted to get around someone's neck.

"Welling!" he shouted across the floor as soon as the two of them reached the top of the stairs.

Welling didn't break stride, walking past the man. "There is no need to shout, Mister Hilsom."

"A writ of search on a Circle house! You bully your way into another! And you make a Riot Call! And how many arrests did we make from all of this?"

"So far none," Welling said calmly. "The day is not over yet."

"My neck is out, Jinx!" Hilsom snapped.

"Your neck, Mister Hilsom?" Satrine asked. "Welling is the one on the line here."

"As am I," Hilsom said. "The Circles will file a suit, and Justice Review is already screaming at my office over the Riot Call. When they look into the original writ—"

Welling waved Hilsom off, walking past him to the desks behind the slateboards. "Nothing will be out of order, Mister Hilsom. Are you calling into question the grounds for which the original writ of search was justified?"

Hilsom stomped along with them, not letting it go. "It's not a matter of justification. It's a matter of results."

"Indeed," Welling said. "Though as you have said to me a number of times, there is knowing and there is proving."

"If you can't prove it, it doesn't matter." Hilsom raised

an eyebrow. "Do you know something, Jinx? Something at all useful?"

Welling stopped, and Satrine could see his eyes darting back and forth, like the gears were spinning in his head. "I know several things which are relevant pieces of data to solve this case. That said, they are not substantiated enough to warrant discussion with you."

"Oh, no?"

"They're theories, Protector," Satrine interjected. "Sharing them prematurely could bias you, and thus poison your own attempts to successfully prosecute this case."

Hilsom threw his hands up. "Is there anything you can give me, Inspectors? Something I can use in the inevitable moment when the Circle counsel has a suit filed against me. And the two of you as well, I am certain."

"We know that there existed enmity between the Firewings and the Circle of Light and Stone," Welling said. "A point they tried to conceal from us. I haven't intertwined all the connections yet, but I am certain that enmity plays a key role in the murder of both Hessen and Jaelia Tomar."

"You didn't need a writ to learn that," Kellman said from his desk. He crossed over. "Blazes, they almost burst out in a magic fight in the middle of the street outside the Stone house."

"Light and Stone," Satrine said.

"Sure, sure," Kellman said. Mirrell had quietly come over, and Captain Cinellan was watching the whole exchange from his office door. "Two Circles fighting. Plus Jinx in the middle of it."

Hilsom spun on his heel and glared at Welling. "You engaged them? Magically?"

"Not directly, no," Welling said. His eyes went down to the ground. "I did forcefully subdue one of the Light and Stone members, but entirely with standard Constabulary procedure."

"Would that be Wells Harleydale?"

"I believe that was his name, yes."

Hilsom opened up his leather satchel and thumbed

through his papers, muttering the whole while. "You believe that was his name. Rich, Jinx, very rich."

Welling's nostrils flared. "Inspector Mirrell, in your observation, did I use undue force or unorthodox methods in subduing Mister Harleydale when he took aggressive posture?"

Satrine looked over to Mirrell. He looked like he'd rather eat a live cat than answer, but he shook his head. "Not at all. I would have done the same."

Hilsom grunted. "Light and Stone has already sent word that grievances will be filed against you, and me, and the whole Constabulary for his treatment, both at their chapterhouse and anything that happens in his questioning. This is going to be a big problem, Jinx."

"Let them have a problem," Kellman said. "They had a dead girl on their front steps."

"Circle Law protection or not," Mirrell added, "they can't let that slide in the river."

"So charge the man then," Hilsom said. "Don't just let him sit in the cell!"

"I'm sorry, what?" Welling asked. For once, Satrine thought, her partner looked utterly confused.

Hilsom rolled his eyes. "I'm saying bringing Harleydale in for questioning isn't going to do us much good unless I can level some kind of arrest charge on him. When you subdued him, did he—"

Welling didn't wait for the question. "Protector Hilsom, what are you blathering about?"

Hilsom buried his face in his hand for a moment. "All right, Welling. Is Harleydale who you like for the Tomar murders? Are you hoping to get him to crack in Interrogation?"

Satrine couldn't take this man any more either. She put him in his place in the most effective way she easily could. "Zebram, why are you being so obtuse? We haven't brought in Harleydale."

Hilsom stammered, clearly put out of sorts by her casual use of his first name. "Of course you have. It's one of the Circle's key complaints."

Welling opened his mouth, then stopped and walked

away. He took five steps and turned back, looking at Kellman and Mirrell. "Inspectors, did you bring him in?"

"Not our case," Kellman said. "You two dragged us into it enough."

"Nor did we," Welling said, looking to Satrine for confirmation.

"First I've heard of it." She turned to Hilsom. "Who says we brought him in?"

"His own Circle!"

"And . . . is he here?" Satrine glanced about until her eyes found Miss Pyle. "Is Wells Harleydale in the building?"

"I'll find out," Miss Pyle said, and in a moment she was off the floor.

"Do not play stupid with me, Inspector Rainey." He pulled a sheet out from his satchel. "They've already sent unofficial complaints to the Protector's Office of how a patrolman came and collected Mister Harleydale for questioning under the authority of the two of you. I'm sure Olivant is talking to my superior right now writing up the formal papers!"

"We sent no patrolman," Satrine said. "We didn't have him brought in."

Hilsom looked at his paper, then back at Satrine and Welling. He shoved it back into his bag and got uncomfortably close to Satrine. "You better be straight with me here, Inspector Rainey."

"Why would I lie about that?"

"Why else?" Hilsom glanced over to Welling with an open sneer. "Protect your partner."

He stalked off. Captain Cinellan stayed in his doorframe, unlit pipe clenched in his teeth. "So what the blazes are you two going to do now?"

"Go over our evidence again," Welling said quietly. "There's some pattern we're missing."

Cinellan crossed over. "Listen, Welling. I know when the Protector's Office is only stoking the furnace, and this doesn't sound like it. Have you taken too big a bite on this thing?"

Satrine saw doubt on her partner's face. She didn't

need that. She couldn't afford that, not yet. "We've got it, Captain," she said. "Might take another day or two, but we've got it."

Cinellan gave the barest hint of a smile. "Yeah, you've got until the end of the week, Rainey." He glanced over at Welling again. "Where's your weapon?"

"Lost in the scuffle, sir," Welling said. He didn't look at the captain or anyone else, his eyes focused on some empty spot of air in the middle of the floor.

"Damn careless, Welling," Cinellan said. "Have a page bring another one up from the armory for you, all right?"

"Yes, sir," Welling said. Without any sign from the captain, Welling spun around and went back behind the slateboards.

"You both look like you've had a hell of a knocking, Rainey," Cinellan said.

"It's been an eventful morning, sir," she said. He grunted and went back to his office. She felt she couldn't leave it at that. "We will close this one, sir."

He shrugged and shut the door.

Satrine went to her desk to find Welling erasing things from the slateboard.

"Trying to get a fresh look at it?"

He shook his head, "I'm a detriment to this case, Inspector Rainey."

"I don't see how." She sat down on the edge of the desk. "You wouldn't see the likes of Kellman or Mirrell putting in this kind of dedication."

"Dedication or obsession?"

"Does it matter?" She took the rag out of Welling's hand. He stared at the board, not looking at her.

"Makes no difference to Jaelia Tomar," he said. "My devotion to the case made no difference to her."

"Perhaps," Satrine said. "But we might make a difference for whoever the next victim might be. And I think we're both agreed there will be a next victim."

"Certainly," Welling said. "It'll be Wells Harleydale of the Circle of Light and Stone."

Satrine nodded. "Because the killer has already

grabbed him, under the pretense of being a patrolman collecting him for questioning."

"My thoughts exactly. It's impossible for me to be certain, but I am reasonably confident."

Satrine nodded. She had to admit it made a degree of sense. "So then, what's the goal? Is this some sort of new Circle Feud? Is he trying to incite one?"

"The murder of Jaelia Tomar may have set that in motion, but I do not believe that is the explicit goal."

"Because Hessen Tomar's murder doesn't serve that end." Satrine needed more tea to think through this. "I could see it if this were just about the Tomars, but then how might Harleydale fit in? Is the killer part of one of these two Circles? A third Circle? Or not even—"

"Is *Uncircled* the word you want, Inspector Rainey?"

Silence hung uncomfortably for a moment. "Is that why you think you're a detriment?"

"My presence has done little but hinder our investigation. It's caused active hostility among our witnesses. And victims."

"No, Welling." Satrine got between him and the board, forcing him to look her in the eye. "We can't let that be a factor. Your mage status is not relevant to the case. It's not the problem."

"Don't tell me it hasn't caused trouble."

"We're both trouble," Satrine said. She lowered her voice to a whisper. "But don't tell me we aren't the best chance for justice on this case. Don't tell me that the likes of Kellman and Mirrell would give a blaze over two dead mages like you would."

"Or would be as hungry to solve it as you?" Welling returned, giving her the barest of smiles.

"We're both hungry here, Welling. You know I'm right."

Welling nodded, and then picked up his chalk. "Location has to be important to the killer. The question is why."

Satrine got out of his way so he could start writing on the boards.

"Excuse me, Inspector Rainey?" Phillen had come behind the slateboards. She was about to snap when she got a look at his face. In addition to the yellowing bruises on his face from his beating earlier, the young man looked like he had just eaten a live snake.

"You all right, Phillen?" she asked. "Have you slept at all?"

"I, uh, had a nap in the page bunks," he said. "I had left word with one of the other pages, but the message didn't reach you, I think."

"What message?"

"You had put a hold on Ret Hoffer, that his mother couldn't spring him until you talked to her."

"I had?" The events of the early morning seemed like a lifetime ago. "I only said—"

"That you wanted her called in and to keep her until you talked to her."

"Blazes."

"Who is this?" Welling asked.

"The mother of the rat I dragged in this morning. She . . ."

"Is the same mother of our eyewitness from yesterday. The one with whom you have a past history you said would not interfere with your duties." This was said in his usual dry, flat tone, though there was the barest hint of humor in his voice.

"That's the one," Satrine said. "Is she here now?"

"She's been here for two hours, actually. She's down in the holding area screaming a fit."

That amused Satrine. "Good."

"The lieutenant down there is getting blazed up, though," Phillen said. "He doesn't want to deal with her, but he can't do anything until you go down and sign off on her leaving. Unless a captain or protector gets involved."

That wouldn't do. Protector Hilsom already seemed to have it in for her. And as Welling had already said, it wouldn't take much for her probationary status to be wrecked.

"I'll be right back, Welling."

"I'll be here," he said. He was fully focused on his slateboards. That was a good sign he had moved past his crisis and was back on task.

The holding area was on the ground floor, a series of small cells—some of them occupied—surrounding a central waiting room, where a red-faced Idre Hoffer was screaming at two desk officers.

"Are there any blazing charges? If he isn't being charged then you let us both go or I will knock you so blazing hard—"

"I didn't file charges yet, Missus Hoffer," Satrine said. "Though I certainly could."

"For what?" Idre spat out, turning on Satrine with beady, squinting eyes. The desk officers both released noticeable sighs of relief.

"Assault on a Constabulary page, for one. Assault on a Constabulary officer, namely myself, for another."

"You're the skirt inspector who hassled me yesterday," Idre said. "What's your problem?"

"My problem?" Satrine asked. In the back of her brain, Satrine suddenly felt like a twelve-year-old girl again, cornered in an abandoned flat, about to get her face beat in again. Like a mouse, she was ready to run for the door.

"I ain't done anything to you, skirt. Why are you hassling me and mine?"

Satrine bit her lip to not laugh in Idre's face. "Ain't done anything" indeed. If this woman only knew.

"I didn't know I was hassling yours, Missus Hoffer. Your son there was leading a gang of boys beating on a page, which I broke up."

"She means she shot me!" the boy yelled from inside his cell. His wound had been patched up, and he was flailing both arms around with enough energy that he didn't seem seriously impaired.

"You're fine," Satrine said. "You're lucky I'm a good shot."

"Fine, then," Idre said. "Charge the little rat. Let me get home." She made for the door.

"Missus Hoffer!" Satrine said. "If I charge your son,

he's sure to be convicted and send to Quarrygate for . . . how long?" She addressed the question to the two desk officers.

They looked at each other briefly. "Three years at least," one of them offered.

"Three years, Missus Hoffer."

Idre stood at the door. "That's what he gets, I suppose."

"Don't you care what happens to him?"

"A little time in the 'gate, it might do him some good."

"Did it do you any?"

Satrine bit her tongue, regretting saying that.

"You look me up or something?" Idre said, squinting hard, beady eyes at Satrine. "I've got enough to worry about, skirt. You going to charge him or not?"

Up until this point, Satrine hadn't actually been in any doubt about charging the boy. Now she felt a surge of pity for him, having grown up with this monster of a woman for a mother.

"This is how you treat your son, Hoffer? This is how you raise him?"

"What business is it of yours, skirt? Charge him or don't."

"Let him go," Satrine told the desk officer.

"Ma'am?" he asked.

"The boy, send him out in his mother's custody."

"Pff," Idre said. "No stomach."

"Let me tell you something, Hoffer," Satrine said, getting close into Idre's face, so close she could smell the rotten cider on her breath. "I've got my eye on you and yours now. Any one of them gets out of line, steps up a bit too strong, I'm going to know about it. And you'll be the one sitting in there." Despite the hard edge to her words, the stone sneer on her face, Satrine's heart was pounding faster than ever in her life. She bit the inside of her cheek, using the pain to hold back the fear, hold back the contents of her stomach threatening to leap out all over Idre.

Idre's eye twitched, but she didn't get a chance to respond before Phillen came bursting through the door, knocking into the woman. "Inspector! They just found another body! It's your killer again!"

Satrine nodded. "If you'll all excuse me, I have investigating to do. Good day, Missus Hoffer." She stormed out of the room before anyone could say anything else to her. Still, she felt Idre Hoffer's hot gaze on the back of her neck, even as she was long out of the room.

Welling was waiting for her at the entrance hall, furiously smoking his pipe.

"Not good," he muttered.

"We've got another one?" she asked him. "We're sure about this?"

"The report is it's another mage. But I'd bet my next meal it's Harleydale." He drew a large toke of his pipe, his hands trembling. "Three in two days."

Satrine moved in close to him and whispered, "This is getting to you."

Welling jerked back slightly, but didn't pull away from her. "More than usual," he whispered back.

"Is it that it's mages, or that we haven't caught the killer?"

"Both," Welling said. He stepped away toward the door. "Though more the former."

"Where are we going?"

"Saint Limarre's."

Chapter 19

SAINT LIMARRE'S WAS NOT Minox's church. His attendance at services at Saint Benton's in Keller Cove was haphazard, usually out of familial obligation, though he did enjoy joining his mother on her monthly pilgrimages to Saint Veran's in the outskirts of the city. He was familiar with Saint Limarre's, of course, as it was the dominant public timepiece in Inemar. It did not escape his notice that it was also just a block from where the lockwagon had been attacked and Jaelia Tomar abducted.

The place had a humble simplicity, age without ostentation—plain stone walls, no color to the windows. Even the clock tower didn't go very high, barely clearing above the surrounding buildings.

Two patrolmen stood outside the main doors, flanking a cloistress in a dark blue habit. She rocked back and forth on the balls of her feet, not making any effort to hide the annoyance on her face. As Minox and Inspector Rainey came up the stone steps, she bounded forward.

"Inspectors." She spoke boldly and straightly, extending her hand to them both. "Thank you for coming so directly."

"Of course," Minox said. "Inspector Welling and Inspector Rainey."

The cloistress gave a curious glance at Rainey, something approaching recognition. "Sister Alana of the Holy Order of Saint Limarre." She took Inspector Rainey's hand confidently, which Rainey returned. Rainey did not return the look of recognition, however.

"Are the patrolmen barring you from entering the crime scene, Sister?" Rainey asked.

"Exactly," Sister Alana said. "I assure you I can handle seeing everything in there. I found it in the first place."

"The purpose of closing it off is more to maintain the integrity of the scene, as best we can," Minox said. "Though I think most patrolmen misunderstand that. Come in with us; your insight would be most appreciated."

"I will serve as best I can," Sister Alana said.

She led them into the church, where they were first confronted with the statue of Saint Limarre. As opposed to the detailed bronzework image Minox was used to at Saint Benton's, the statue of Limarre was a humble woodcarving. This fit the image of the saint himself: hooded head hanging down, palms outward. The usual collection of prayer offerings, coins, trinkets, and scrips of verse lay at the base of the statue.

The statue was not isolated in an entrance alcove, which was what Minox was used to. Instead, the entire assembly was a large, open hall. The rest of the church matched the humility: muted colors, paint cracking, unstained wooden pews and altar podium.

The body was laid out on the altar, naked like the others, with two patrolmen standing guard over it. A mage, like the others. It was unquestionably Wells Harleydale from Light and Stone.

There were key factors that stood out as different from the other two murders. His heart was not cut out. Instead, his hands were severed and his eyes removed. Massive pools of blood spread out from the stumps of his arms.

"This is different," Rainey muttered.

"Indeed," Minox said. "Why the change?"

"Change?" Sister Alana asked.

"The other two victims had their hearts cut out," Minox said.

"Two Firewings, hearts cut out," Rainey said. "Here we have Light and Stone, hands off and eyes out. We sure this is the same killer? Maybe this was a retaliation from the Firewings."

"Indeed we are, Inspector Rainey, though I had considered that as well." Minox pointed to the damning evidence: two spikes, driven into the shoulders of Harleydale. "Different placement clearly due to taking the hands off this time."

"Sister," Rainey said, turning the cloistress away from the scene. "You were the one who found the body?"

"Indeed I was, Madam Inspector," Sister Alana said.

"And you found it like this? No one else around?"

"I saw no one. I did hear, from my quarters upstairs, a curious clanging sound, which is why I came down here to see what was going on."

"But no one else was here in the nave or the aisles? Even with no services, there's always a few—"

"Not anymore," Sister Alana said. "Most unfortunately— and uncharitably, I'm afraid—in the past months we've been forced to flush out parishioners between services and bolt the main doors. It is not something I am proud of, but we've had several thefts and bodily assaults upon the faithful in residence. The safety of the cloister must take precedence."

"You weren't afraid to come up when you heard the noise," Rainey noted.

"I consider that my duty, Inspector. I've had my share of experience in theft and bodily assaults."

Rainey gave the sister a quizzical look. She shook it off, and then continued her questions. "So you heard the hammering of the spikes?"

"I presume," Sister Alana said.

"And he was like this when you came in? No one else here?"

"As I already said, Inspector."

"Our killer moves like a spirit," Minox said. He glanced at the room for all possible exits. The main door in the front. One behind the altar. Two others on the side. "When you came from upstairs, where did you enter from?" The sister indicated the door on the left side. Minox went over to the doorway. From that vantage, the front door was visible; the other two could not be seen. The body, however, could be seen quite clearly. "Did you enter cautiously, or quickly?"

"Cautiously, of course."

"Taking several moments to step in, take in the whole room." He took similar cautious steps, noting at each point how his field of vision would change. Four steps, he could see the other door on the side. Five more before he could see the exit behind the altar. "You could have been in here with him for several moments without spotting him."

"That did occur to me, Inspector."

"And the victim?" Rainey asked. "When you saw him, was he dead? Or dying?"

The sister moved next to Minox and closed her eyes. "Blood poured out of the stumps of his arms. But he didn't move, didn't scream. I don't know if he was breathing."

"And how long ago was this?"

"Almost an hour."

"And then what did you do?" Minox asked.

"I went to the front door and unlatched it, and called out for a constable. It took only a few moments for a brace of them to come. They saw the body, glanced about for a bit, and then called for pages to deliver you here."

"These two?" Minox pointed to the patrolmen.

"That one," she said, pointing to the one closest to the body. "The other one kept me outside until another pair arrived."

"You two aren't partners?" Rainey asked them.

"No, ma'am," one of them said. "I arrived first with Mickey. Then Dutes and Ossam showed up later." He indicated the other patrolman as Ossam. Both these men looked familiar enough to Minox; he had seen them around the station.

Rainey moved close to Minox. "We know that Harleydale was grabbed by someone in uniform."

Minox nodded. "Have the two of you been in here with the body the whole time? And have there been any other patrolmen here?"

"A few more showed up, I think," Ossam said. "We stayed here while they circled the grounds, checked out the rest of the church."

"All men you recognized? Any of them without partners or brass?"

"Blazes, specs, I don't know every man on foot," Ossam said. His cheeks blushed. "Sorry, Sister."

"I've heard far worse, Constable," Sister Alana said.

Minox continued. "Sister, you were kept outside. Did you see or speak to any of these other patrolmen?"

"Indeed. One circled the grounds and checked the kitchen door, which was still latched."

Minox glanced around the chapel again. "That door leads up to the cloister's cells, and the one behind the altar?"

"To the priests' chambers."

"And that one over there?"

"The kitchens, the back door, the cellars."

"Cellars? Do those lead anywhere?"

"Lead anywhere?" Sister Alana did not seem to understand the question. "It's a cellar."

"No access to the sewers or such down there?"

"Not that I'm aware of," Sister Alana said.

Minox turned to the patrolmen. "Have we searched the entire church?"

"Not yet," Ossam said. "That would violate sanctity."

Rainey glanced over at the naked corpse. "Sanctity is out the door at this point."

"I have not had a chance to talk to the priests at all," Sister Alana said. "I'm sure our head pastor would approve a reasonable search of the grounds, given the situation."

"Where are the priests?"

"One came to speak with us briefly," Ossam said. "He indicated that they would be staying in their cells until we had removed the victim."

Rainey raised an eyebrow. "Sister Alana didn't see him, right? You can't be certain he was a priest."

"He wore the robe and sash."

"Our killer has already murdered a man in the church,"

Rainey said. "I'm sure he wouldn't hesitate to dress in the vestments. Sister, let's go talk to the priests. All of them."

"Of course, Inspector," Sister Alana said, leading Rainey out the back.

"Welling," Rainey said as she left, pointing to the floor behind the altar. "Our guy is definitely taunting us."

Minox went around the altar. Lying on the ground was Inspector Rainey's crossbow.

———◆———

The hallway to the priests' cell was dim, lit only by candles in niches. Sister Alana led Satrine along. She kept glancing back to Satrine, something in her eye annoyingly familiar. "How many priests are in residence here?" Satrine asked.

"Only three," Sister Alana answered. "You're the first female inspector I've seen."

"The only one currently, I think," Satrine said. "It's just my second day."

"Daunting," Sister Alana said. "You must have a few tricks up your sleeve."

Satrine stopped. "Pardon?"

The sister turned back, her gaze narrowing. She spoke with slow deliberation. "A woman would have to be very tricky to reach your position."

The woman's face, the shape of her jaw, the slight scar above her eye, it was all familiar, but Satrine couldn't find it in her memory. "You were a Tannen and Jent girl, weren't you?"

The cloistress shrugged. "Born and raised. I heard you died."

"I guess that was the story out there," Satrine said. "I'm surprised you recognized me."

"I wasn't sure until just now," the sister said. "Plus when I was ten you beat four Bridge Rats off of me in the Puller Flop."

Satrine's memory raced. She had scrapped with Bridge Rats plenty of times; all of those were blurs. Who would she have saved in the Puller Flop? "Lannie Coar?"

"The same." Sister Alana smiled widely. "What happened to you?"

"Too long a story to tell right now," Satrine said. "We should go see the priests."

"Of course," Sister Alana said. "I'm sorry we had to find each other this way."

"Part of the job," Satrine said.

Alana knocked on the cell door. "Graces? It's Sister Alana. The inspector would like a word."

A man's voice came from the other side. "We don't know anything, Sister. We would prefer to stay in seclusion until the matter is concluded."

"I understand, your grace," Sister Alana said. "The inspectors would just like to search the church and grounds, for evidence."

"Of course," the priest said from behind the door. "Our chambers need not be searched, however. Some measure of sanctity must be observed."

Satrine gave a nod. The priests being as cooperative as they were being was almost a miracle, there was no need to push the matter.

"As you say, your grace," Alana answered.

The priest coughed. "Please let us know as soon as things are concluded, Sister. We will want to begin preparation of the evening meal as soon as possible."

Sister Alana gave a nervous glance to Satrine. "Absolutely, sir. I will." She walked away from the door, grabbing Satrine by the elbow. As soon as they reached the end of the hallway, her voice dropped to a whisper. "The priests are never involved in cooking."

Satrine drew her crossbow—Welling's crossbow, truly—and took a quiet step back toward the cell door. "Get the others. Quiet."

Sister Alana nodded and went off down the hall.

Satrine slinked down the hall back to the door, checking the bolt of the crossbow as she approached. She braced herself against the wall and took aim at the door.

Welling was at her side, quiet as a cat. "We think he's in there?" His voice was barely a breeze.

Satrine only nodded.

Welling had his crossbow out. "I'll take the door." He counted to three with his fingers, and then snapped.

The door flew off the hinges.

Satrine bounded in, ready to shoot when opportunity presented.

Two priests were bound up in one corner of the room, blindfolded and gagged. Welling stepped in, moving over to the priests.

Satrine spun on her heel to face the next room in the cells. One priest stood in the doorframe, pure terror on his face, steel blade pressed against his throat. From the side of the door, Satrine only saw the gloved hand holding the knife.

She briefly considered taking the shot at the killer's hand, but she knew she couldn't do it.

"There's no way out," she said.

Satrine heard the barest hoarse whisper from behind the frame.

"He wants you both to lower your weapons," the priest said.

"That won't happen," Satrine said.

The blade slid slowly along the priest's neck, leaving an impression but not breaking the skin. "Please," the priest said.

Welling put his crossbow back in its holster.

Satrine glanced at him, but he shook his head. She hated it, but she followed his lead.

"Weapons are away," she said.

More whispering. "Remove your belts as well."

Satrine unbuckled and let it drop to the ground, as did Welling.

"Anything else?"

There was an extended amount of whispering. Satrine strained, but couldn't make out any words. The priest looked worried. "Which of you is Inspector Welling?"

"I am," Welling said.

"You are to go to the hallway," the priest said, his voice cracking. A tear welled at the corner of his eye. "Please step out now."

"I'm not going to—"

"He says if you do not cooperate, he will kill me, and you, and Inspector Rainey."

"I doubt that," Satrine said.

"Rainey," Welling hissed. "We cannot risk the priest." He stepped out into the hallway.

"There," Satrine said. She hated that they were capitulating, but she would be damned if she was going to let this murderer get past her. "Now you've got just me here." She held her hands up, showing herself unarmed, but ready to grab the killer the moment he moved.

The blade flashed, and blood spurted from the priest's neck. In an instant, the killer shoved the bleeding priest at Satrine and darted past to the hallway. Satrine reacted, grabbing for the priest, instinct drawing her to help him first. She caught the victim, she had him. Welling wouldn't let the killer get past him.

The killer—in the same dark, hooded outfit from before, carrying a bloody sack—threw something at Welling, something soft. Welling batted it out of the way, a cloud of chalky dust erupting from it when he made contact. Immediately, his arm started trembling. He grasped at the killer, fingers only grazing the man.

Satrine laid the bleeding priest on the floor. She knew she should press her hand against the wound, focus on saving that life. Every click of the clock was precious, but she couldn't let the murderer get the best of her. Not again. She grabbed her crossbow off the floor and went out the door.

Welling's tremors filled his whole body, his skin clammy. Despite that, he stumbled toward the killer. Satrine grabbed her partner, held him up with one arm while taking aim. Welling became dead weight, and as he fell, his body burst forth with a wave of energy. Satrine dropped him and was thrown against the wall.

All the candles in the hallway blew out, leaving them in the dark.

Satrine pulled herself up, slightly dazed, unsure if she had lost any time. She couldn't see a blazing thing. She could feel Welling's body on the ground next to her, still but breathing. She had to hope that he would be all right, as well as the priest in the next room, but she couldn't let that stop her. She charged down the dark corridor, toward sound and light.

Her knee screamed at her as she ran. She must have banged it when she fell down. She couldn't think about it right now, she had to keep going.

The only one still standing in the chapel was Sister Alana, and she had blood trickling out her mouth. The two patrolmen were laid out on the ground.

"Got a piece of him," Sister Alana said.

"Where?" Satrine couldn't say anything else.

"He went into the cellars," Alana said.

"They need help in the priest quarters!" Satrine shouted, running out the other way, through the kitchen to the cellar.

Only a single oil lamp hung above the stair landing. No sign of anyone, but a team of horses could hide in the shadows. Satrine checked her crossbow. Still cocked and loaded. She pointed it out into the darkness.

No sound. Not a scuff of a shoe or a hot breath.

She kept the weapon trained at the shadows, ready to shoot at any sign of motion. She reached up to the lamp, keeping her gaze focused at the dark room.

Her fingers grazed the bottom of the lamp. Not enough to get a grip. She pushed herself up on her toes. Eyes still forward, crossbow aimed, not looking away.

She grabbed hold of the lamp, hotter on her fingers than she expected, tried to get it off the hook. It wouldn't come loose. She let go before her fingers burned.

"Blazes," she muttered.

There was—a chuckle? A breath? Nothing? She wasn't even sure. She took a step into the dark.

"Rainey!"

Satrine's heart hammered, and she spun toward the voice at the top of the stairs, almost shooting on instinct. It was Welling, pale and red-eyed, face dripping sweat. He held himself up in the doorframe and looked as if he didn't have the strength to go down the steps.

"He came down here," Satrine said.

"Likely how he got in," Welling said. "He got pinned in the priests' quarters when Sister Alana came down to the chapel. This is where he wanted to go."

"Do we have any patrolmen on their feet?"

"Not sure," Welling said. "Barely on mine." Despite that, he took a tentative step down the stairs.

"Need you in one piece, Inspector. Stay here." She went back to the lamp, now feeling secure enough to use both hands and full attention to get it down. "I'll go."

"This killer is too dangerous, Rainey," Welling said.

Satrine didn't want to hear that. "I can handle it."

"He just made fools of the two of us together. You shouldn't venture after him alone."

Satrine held the lamp high and went farther into the cellar. At a far end, past several barrels, there was a hole knocked through the wall, brick and mortar scattered on the floor.

"There we have it," Satrine said. She looked inside, and seeing no sign of anyone, entered.

"Satrine!"

That pulled her back out. "You can't expect me to let him go."

"I don't want you to take that risk," Welling said. She couldn't see his face in the shadows, but he was looking at his feet, not at her. "The killer is clearly prepared for us, and we are not for him." He started coughing.

Satrine swore and went back to the steps. "What happened to you back there?"

"I don't know," Welling said. "It was like . . . magic just fell into me and then flew out."

"You look awful."

"Appearances do not deceive, Inspector. I'm afraid we should have the body collected and return to the station, given the circumstances."

Satrine glanced back at the hole. "Let's get the blazes out of here, then."

Chapter 20

MINOX HAD TO STOP for breath every few steps. He had never felt like this, never experienced loss of control on this level before. Inspector Rainey came up from the church cellar and supported him on her shoulder. He had every urge to push her away, but he could hardly argue that he could walk on his own.

"Was it poison of some sort?" she asked.

"I can only presume," he told her, though he had a lingering suspicion that wasn't accurate. The killer had targeted that dust at him, after having isolated him in the hallway. Logically, it stood to reason that it had been a weapon to be used on him specifically.

The dust had affected him on a magical level as well. Given that the victims were all mages, and the killer had neutralized their magic, it stood to reason he had an understanding of how to manipulate mages. The dust surely served that very purpose.

Possibly its only purpose.

He glanced at his hand. The chalky powder still coated his fingers, which felt numb and swollen. He should clean the powder off if he had any hope of feeling normal again. But he also needed to know the exact nature of it.

He brushed the powdered hand on Inspector Rainey's cheek.

"The blazes you doing?" she snapped, letting go of him. He fell to the floor.

"Testing a theory," Minox said, pulling himself back up. There was a well basin in the corner of the kitchen, and he stumbled over to it. "How do you feel?"

"Annoyed."

"Not weak? No shaking or shortness of breath?"

"No." Rainey came over. "What does that mean?"

"Confirms that the powder was a poison, at least for mages." He opened the spigot and let the dust rinse away. "We should collect the pouch, but I am confident that it will be dangerous only to me."

Rainey brushed the dust off her face, glowering at him. "I'm so glad I could help you."

Minox got as much of the dust as he could off his hand. The effect was noticeably rapid; while he still felt drained, he no longer felt incapable of walking without assistance. "That does not change the fact that we are significantly stymied. The frustrations of this case are myriad."

Rainey shook her head. "Twice we had him, and he got away."

"Thrice," Minox said. "You forgot about last night at the carriage transfer."

"He has us beat," Satrine said.

"Indeed, he is clearly well prepared for not only his murderous plans, but our involvement. Fortunately, our failures have not been in the realm of inspectors. At least, yours have not."

"He got past me. Twice. Once he stole my crossbow."

"True," Minox said. "But you, at least, found him twice. Forced him to get past you. I've yet to be able to discern anything regarding our killer's identity, motivation, or future intentions."

Rainey shook her head and walked out of the church kitchen. Minox had the distinct impression that something he had said or done had upset her.

❦

"You two look like every saint had dragged you through the coals," Captain Cinellan said as Minox and Rainey returned to the inspectors' floor. Minox wasn't much of one for making theological comparisons, but the idiom was apt. On top of the beating they both had taken, an afternoon cloudburst hit as they returned to the station-house. "Blazes happened to you both?"

"The killer was still at the church," Rainey said. "But he got past us and escaped."

Cinellan raised his eyebrow. This was not an expression that Minox had ever been able to fully read on the captain. "How?"

Minox stepped forward. "The killer was prepared for us, specifically me. He used some form of powder that mages are susceptible to. This resulted in a loss of control on my part, giving him a window to escape."

Inspector Rainey opened her mouth, looking for a moment like she intended to amend Minox's statement. Then she turned away.

Cinellan nodded. "He's got a plan, then."

"One which I fear he is not finished with."

"So where do we stand?"

"As far as the murders of the three mages are concerned, we still are on the hunt for the killer, as well as trying to determine his identity."

"You don't have that sussed out yet, Welling?"

"Unfortunately, no. I fear the situation is outside of the realm of obvious suspects. The killer is of grave concern to me, but I believe we must focus on a secondary matter."

"Three mages dead, two Circles involved, and the second dead on the front step of one of them." Cinellan groaned. "Another Circle Feud?"

"I do not believe that the murders were about a fight between the Circles," Minox said. "However, they may cause one to erupt. In fact, the most logical analysis of the evidence is that the killer wished to instigate such a feud."

"You don't think so?" Rainey asked.

"I believe the killer has a purpose that is far more specific than that. I just cannot discern what that purpose is."

"All right," Cinellan said. "This isn't really my element here, Welling. What do we do about the Circles?"

Minox paused. This was hardly his element either. He had failed more than once now in his deductions about magic or mages.

Inspector Rainey focused back onto the conversation. "Protective patrols around both chapterhouses, full details all night long."

"They aren't going to like that," Cinellan said.

"The Circles, or the night shift?"

Cinellan laughed. "Either one, I'd gather." His expression quickly sobered. "Look, this whole business is getting ugly, and we need to get it locked down."

Minox understood. "I know Hilsom is ready to bite through leather if we don't arrest someone."

"I'll keep Hilsom in check," Cinellan said. "But you two have been knocked by enough stray carts for one day, you hear? Go home. Get some sleep. Saints, Minox, you look like you can barely stand."

That was too close to the truth for Minox's liking.

"As you wish, Captain," Minox said. Cinellan went back into his office.

Inspector Rainey turned around and went straight to the stairs. Clearly she needed no further prodding. Minox followed after her. "Rainey?"

She stopped and stared at him, but said nothing.

Minox stammered a moment, unnerved by her intense eye contact. "Despite our poor results for the day, I do not believe I could have achieved better with any other partner."

Rainey shrugged, clearly not heartened by his attempt at praise. "We certainly couldn't have achieved much worse." She continued down the stairs.

Minox stood still for several minutes at the top of the stairs. The elements of the case were not adding up. There was a pattern, surely, that made sense to the killer. Minox simply was unable to see it. His thoughts were cloudy and thick.

The captain was right, and Minox decided there was

no value in gainsaying his orders. He went back to his desk for his coat, where both Nyla and Corrie were waiting for him.

"Your skirt partner took some blasted hits today," Corrie said.

"We both did," Minox said, noting the slight blush on Nyla's cheeks. "Inspector Rainey gave as good as she was given, however."

"And you, you rutting little cheat." Corrie pressed a finger into his chest. "You were supposed to stay home."

"Slipped away and spent the whole night here," Nyla said, clucking her tongue at him.

"There was a pressing matter of a woman in danger. I was hoping to prevent another murder."

"And did you?" Corrie asked.

Minox sat down, head slumped. He had failed utterly.

Nyla put a hand on his shoulder. "Minox, you can't blame yourself—"

"You blazing well know he will, Ny," Corrie said. "Look, Mine. You're not going to do anyone any good running your head into the rutting ground. Go the blazes home and rest."

"I have every intention to," Minox said.

Nyla scooped up the pile of newssheets he had piled up on the desk. "Come on. We'll take the tickwagon together."

"Make sure he doesn't come back here, Ny."

"Yes, ma'am," Nyla said, giving Corrie a mock salute.

Minox got back to his feet. "Two things, Corrie."

"You're asking me to favor you now?"

"They're business," Minox said. "The captain is going to assign some night shift to patrol duty around two Mage Circle houses. Volunteer for that."

"Really?" She looked disgusted.

"I want to make sure there's someone I trust involved."

She bit at her lip. "Fine. What's the other?"

"There's a pub owner on Silver, who says that some night shift horsepatrol have been rattling him for crowns. Find me some names."

She glanced about nervously and dropped her voice. "I'm not rutting well going to rat—"

"Get me names, Corrie. I'll handle the rest."

"You'll owe me." With a nod to Nyla she went off to the back stairs.

"Let's go," he told his cousin, taking the newssheets from her. "I'll pay for a cab."

"Damn right you're paying," she said. "You're the one on inspector's wages."

———— ◆◆ ————

The walk through High River was long and dreadful. The rains had stopped, or had never started on the north bank. Satrine's wet coat coupled with the failures of the day had given her a completely foul mood. The sight of the fashionably dressed students at the street tables of the High River Wine Club didn't help. They laughed, drank, argued, and generally had a wonderful time, blissfully unaware of all the misery across the river. Or even right next to them. Satrine envied them even as she loathed them. The young couple kissing at one table made her think of Rian. Soon she would be one of the girls at a place like this.

Wait.

Satrine turned back and looked again. That girl wasn't like Rian.

It was Rian.

Rian kissing some boy. Rian sitting at a table with a glass of wine.

Anger paralyzed Satrine, thoughts racing through her head. The first thoughts were about money, irrationally raging over the idea that Rian might waste even a single tick on a glass of wine at the High River. More frenzied thoughts came: Why is this boy buying her wine? Who is this boy buying her wine? Why is the High River selling wine to a fourteen-year-old girl? Why is this boy, who is clearly seventeen if he is a day, kissing a fourteen-year-old girl? Who is he and why is Rian kissing him?

Her anger took voice, as her feet leaped over the low fence surrounding the street tables. "Rian Rainey, what in the blasted name of all the blazing saints do you think you're doing?"

All the people at the street tables startled, but Rian jumped away from her paramour. The boy, for his part, held his ground, barely moving in his chair.

"That's rather rude, ma'am," he said, his accent crisp with privilege and education.

"Rude?" Satrine's voice cracked to a screech. "You're shoving your tongue into the mouth of my daughter—my fourteen-year-old daughter, young man—while plying her with wine!" Satrine took a real good look at the boy, staring him hard in the face. Dark hair, piercing blue eyes, ridiculously pretty. Add in the tailored suit with silver hasps, the boy clearly had money to spend. It was easy to see why Rian was star-eyed for him. "It's damn polite of me not to knock your teeth out!"

"Mother!"

"I should do the same to you!" Satrine snarled at her daughter. "How dare you be here when your father is . . ."

"Missus Rainey," the young man said, holding up his hands peacefully. "I'm so sorry for our first meeting to be marred with this unpleasantness." His voice dripped charm like an overfilled oil lamp.

"That's *Inspector* Rainey to you—"

"Poul Tullen," the boy said, extending his hand to her. "I'm at the Royal College of Maradaine."

Satrine resisted the urge to slap the hand away, instead only glaring at it in disgust. "Is that where you learn to seduce schoolgirls?"

"Mother!" Rian grabbed Satrine's shoulder and yanked.

"You start walking home right now, Rian," Satrine said. "If you're lucky you'll stay far enough ahead of me to avoid getting cuffed across the head!"

Rian took a moment, looking between her mother and Poul, before letting out a scream of exasperation and stomping off.

Satrine turned back to Poul. "I don't want to see you near her again, you hear me?"

The boy flashed a grin. "If that's what you want, Inspector, you won't see me."

Satrine didn't like that answer. She slammed her hand down on the table, knocking the wineglasses over. "I don't want it to happen, Mister Tullen."

"Mister Tullen is my father," the boy said. There was an edge of a threat in his voice.

"Stay away from my daughter, boy."

Poul stood, picked up his empty glass, and walked off, calling to the nearest server. He never lost the self-assured smirk as he left Satrine's view.

The rest of the patrons of the High River were staring at Satrine, making her feel more than a little conspicuous. She had made enough of a scene, and she didn't need any more time wasted. She hurried down the street toward home.

Rian was a good block ahead of her, easily spotted with her red hair and school uniform. Her pace was hard and deliberate, pushing through the crowd of buskers and hawkers with practiced ease that reminded Satrine of herself at that age.

Satrine remembered that at fourteen she was doing much worse than kissing rich boys in wine shops. Not that kissing rich boys in wine shops had ever been an opportunity afforded to her at that age.

At full walking pace, Satrine could barely keep Rian in her sight. She'd have to run to catch up. Her knee flared, her feet screamed—her body did not want to run right now. It barely wanted to walk. Rian had reached Beltner, she would be in the house shortly. Satrine pushed through the pain and sprinted after her.

"Rian!" she shouted as she closed in on her daughter. Rian didn't turn around, just continued stalking to the stairs. Satrine caught up and grabbed Rian by the shoulder just as the girl was getting out her key. "What the blazes were you doing there?"

"What did it look like I was doing, Mother?" Rian snapped. "Now thanks to you, he'll never call on me again. He won't even look at me."

"No, he won't, if he knows what's good for him."

"What did you tell him?"

"I told him to stay away from you, and since you're the daughter of a stick, he'll know to do just that."

"You are such a rutting bully, Mother!" Rian fumbled with the key, trying to get it in the latch despite her hands shaking. Satrine felt her own hands shaking just as much, her anger getting the better of her.

"You do not talk that way to me!"

"Don't you rutting well tell me how to blasted talk to you!"

Satrine's fist raised up before she even knew what she was doing. "How *dare* you talk to me that way!"

Rian had never, to Satrine's knowledge, been hit in her life. Satrine had never done it, nor had Loren, and if it had happened at school, Rian had never shared it with her. At Rian's age, Satrine had been hit more times than she could count, by her own mother and plenty of others. Satrine had long known how to hit back, and would have scrapped anyone who would dare cross her.

Rian was not Satrine.

Rian burst into tears, her face shocked as she cowered behind her hands.

"Baby, I'm sorry, I—" Satrine stammered out, but Rian's cries drowned her out.

The door opened, Missus Abernand scowling at them both. "What are you ruckusing about?"

Rian pushed past Missus Abernand and ran inside the apartment.

"What was that about?" Missus Abernand asked.

"Nothing," Satrine said. She stepped toward the door, but Missus Abernand didn't move, and unlike Rian, she wasn't small enough to easily push past the woman. "Can I get in my own home, please?"

"Maybe," Missus Abernand said. "What happened there?"

"Foolishness," Satrine said. "Rian's and mine." She flexed and relaxed her hand, the urge to strike still in her muscles. If she had swung, it wouldn't have been a simple slap.

"Hmm," Missus Abernand said. "I need to go to the market, anyway." She brushed past Satrine, letting the door swing shut behind her.

Satrine still didn't have her key.

Chapter 21

RICH, MEATY SMELLS and raucous laughter greeted Minox and Nyla as they entered the house. Lamb, beef, and pork, to Minox's nose. That was highly unusual. "Is something special happening tonight?"

"Not that I'm aware of," Nyla said, hanging her coat.

Ferah came into the cloakroom, still wearing her Yellowshield vest. "Minox!" she said, her face bright and warm. "Your friend is so charming!"

"His friend?" Nyla asked.

"I'm at a loss," Minox said.

"Charming, handsome, and no marriage bracelet," Ferah said. Nyla's interest perked up, and she brushed past Ferah to go to the sitting room. Ferah laughed, and looked at Minox again. "You look horrible. What happened?"

"Constabulary work," Minox said. "What friend is this?"

"Joshea," Ferah said. She raised an eyebrow. "He said you invited him here."

Joshea was here? That was surprising. Though it was accurate, Minox had told him to come. He never expected he would call so early. "No, of course. It has been a trying day, is all." He passed the newssheets to Ferah. "Leave those on the back stoop for me. I'll bring them out to Evoy later."

She took them, nodding. "Mother is a bit put out you didn't see him yesterday."

"I will rectify tonight," Minox said. "Solemn promise."

She led him to the sitting room, where Minox's uncles and male cousins—save for Evoy—all howled with laughter while listening to Joshea, who held court in front of the fireplace, beer in hand.

"—and he didn't even realize! He just stood there, proudly, sword in hand, while—Minox!"

"Joshea," Minox said. "I see you've met just about everyone already." He noticed Ferah, Nyla, and even Alma all standing in the archway to the dining room, looking more than a little lovestruck. It seemed almost ridiculous.

"Indeed," Joshea said, crossing over to take Minox's hand. "Your whole family has been quite welcoming."

"I would expect nothing less of them," Minox said.

"He's been telling us old war stories," Uncle Tal said.

"Army stories, Tal," Joshea said jovially. "I may have been in a few skirmishes, but never a war."

Uncle Timmothen shook his head. "If wearing the Gray is like the Red and Green, every day is a war." The room at large nodded in agreement.

"You take a few to the chin, brother?" Oren asked. "Anyone check you out?"

"It's nothing," Minox said. "Though I should clean myself up."

"Don't be too long, son," Uncle Cole said. "Your mother and aunts are cooking up quite the feast tonight."

"Are they now?" Minox asked, looking at Joshea.

"I couldn't possibly arrive empty-handed," Joshea said. "I brought a large selection of meat."

"And we can't stay, Pop," Colm said fiercely. "We've got to go check in."

"We could come late, Colm," Tal said. "Saints know the chief isn't paying attention."

The room launched into raucous jibes, as Minox's various uncles, cousins, and brothers all admonished Tal for daring to say such a thing. "Duty first," was the most commonly repeated phrase. Minox himself almost said it out of habit. There was no need to add his voice to the chorus, though.

"All right, all right," Tal said. "Forget I said it. But I better find some still left in the morning, hear?"

"Can't promise that," Edard said, patting his own father's stomach. "It's been a hungry day for all of us."

Jace piped up, "And I bet Joshea can eat as much as Minox can!"

The room went quiet for a moment.

Colm broke the silence. "Really, Pop, we've got to move along."

"Aye," Tal said. "It's been a pleasure, Mister Brondar."

They brushed past Minox and left.

"You said something about cleaning up," Joshea said quietly.

"Indeed," Minox said. "If you'll all excuse me."

"If I may join you?" Joshea asked.

Minox nodded and went to the stairway, Joshea at his side. Regular conversation resumed in the sitting room.

"I'm terribly sorry if I've inconvenienced you," Joshea said. "But you said—"

"It's quite all right. I did tell you to look me up here. I was not expecting you to be so well received, though."

Joshea gave a weak smile. "Arrive with full hands, be welcomed with open arms. That's what my mother used to say."

"Wise woman," Minox said, leading Joshea over to the washroom. "I have to offer apologies of my own. Today's work was . . . trying."

"The . . . murder in the alley? You haven't solved it?"

"Hardly. In fact, there have been two more deaths. I'm sure the newssheets are already printing the salacious details." Minox stripped off his vest and shirt.

"There's more to it than that, though," Joshea said.

Minox glanced out the door to make sure no one was listening in. "Indeed. But I think we should discuss it at a later point, with more privacy."

"Of course," Joshea said. He gave his own glance while Minox pumped water into the basin. "Does your family know? About—"

"It's not something anyone speaks of," Minox said. Of course they knew. Most of the Inemar stationhouse knew, and that included Corrie and Nyla. The only way anyone in the family didn't know was out of willful ignorance, which was not something he'd put past Uncle Timmothen or his sons. But there was the unspoken agreement throughout the house that no one brought it up.

Minox washed off his face. "How bad do I look?"

"Bit of bruising is all. If you were army, the Yellow would send you right back out."

"Fair enough," Minox said, drying off his face. He tossed the soiled clothes into Zura's laundering hamper and went to his room to collect a fresh shirt. "Though I'm sure Aunt Beliah will say otherwise."

"She's the brown-haired one with the gray streaks?"

"Right." Minox finished dressing. "Nurse at Ironheart, and she can be tireless in her fussing."

"She seems sweet," Joshea said. "The whole household does."

"Who's talking out there?" A sharp, crackling voice called from the back bedroom. Grandmother Jillian.

"Minox."

"I know it's you, rascal. I mean the other voice." With slow stomps, Grandmother came out in the hallway, wrapped in a dressing gown. "Not many strange men come up here."

Joshea saluted her with military crispness. "Ma'am. I had no intention of disturbing you."

"Pff," Grandmother said with a dismissive wave. "He's not here from the asylum, is he?"

"No, Grandmother. He's just a friend."

"Good." She looked Joshea over. "You've got army in you, don't you?"

"Three years, ma'am," Joshea said with a smile.

"We aren't still mucking about in the islands, are we?"

"I spent one year out there, but we're not engaging in direct action. That war has been over—"

"For fifteen years, I know. I'm not mad yet." Grandmother smiled and approached, resting one hand on Minox's arm. "That war took up most of my life, you know. And what was the point of it?"

"My father would say 'principle,'" Joshea offered.

"Hmm," Grandmother said. "You lost people in that, didn't you?"

"None I knew. But there's a whole list. My father even says there was a Brondar among the Twenty at New Fencal."

Grandmother laughed. "Everyone claims an ancestor among the Twenty. They must have sowed a lot of bastards before they shipped out."

"Grandmother!" Minox said. He wasn't entirely shocked; Corrie's salty mouth didn't come from nowhere.

"Oh, hush. He's a soldier, they expect that sort of talk."

"It's quite all right, ma'am."

"You call me Jill or I'll box your ear," she said. "Minox, dear, help me down. Supper at the table seems worth the effort tonight."

After Satrine knocked several times, Caribet opened the door. "What's going on?"

"Nothing," Satrine said, coming in. "Where's your sister?" Satrine asked. Caribet pointed to their shared room. Rian had already closed herself inside. Satrine tried to open it, but Rian must have moved the beds to block the door. Satrine spoke as gently and calmly as she could manage. "Rian, let me in."

"Go away, Mother!"

Satrine didn't have any fight left. She turned back to her younger daughter. "Did you have a good day?"

"Fine," Caribet said warily. "We worked on penmanship most of the day."

"Good," Satrine said. "Practical skill."

"Are you all right, Mother?"

"Far from," Satrine said. "I'm going to check on your father."

"All right," Caribet said.

Satrine went into the bedroom. Loren lay in the bed,

face a blank, as it had been for nearly a month. No change. Never a change.

"Is this what it was like every day, love?" Satrine asked. She sat on the edge of the bed and pulled her boots off. "I don't know how you managed to come home smiling most of the time."

She touched his face. His eyes moved around, searching the room, never landing on any one thing for more than a moment. She leaned in close to him, cradling his face in her hands. His eyes still didn't find hers.

She kissed him. His lips were soft, open, and unresponsive.

She pulled away, tears welling at her eyes. "I don't have much to come home to, do I?"

She stood back up, taking off her coat and belt. "What choice do I really have, though? Second day, and I'm . . ." She didn't let herself finish the sentence. She didn't want to even think about what she was about to say. She took off the vest and held it in front of him.

"I never wanted to have this role, you know. I just wanted . . . I don't even know. I want our girls to not have to worry about the things I had to. Have to." She laughed despite herself. "Maybe I should let Rian run off with that rich boy. Most mothers would leap at the possibility of such an upward pairing. Though I doubt he has noble intentions toward her."

Loren's eyes weren't darting anymore. They held locked and steady on her.

Not on her, no. On the vest.

She threw it down on the bed, and his eyes went lazy again.

"Is that it, Loren?" she snapped, not caring how loud she was being. "Is that what matters most? The vest? The work? Honor to the Green and Red?" That was what she had lost him to. That's why he was in the state he was in, what he cared most about.

And now she was stuck in it too. No other choice.

She stormed out to the sitting room. She wanted to scream, to hit something. She wanted to be back in that church with that maniac five feet away from her so she could get her hands around his throat and tear him down. She wanted to smash her fists into Idre Hoffer. She wanted to pound the smug look off that rich boy's face.

She had been going through shelves, rifling through the sitting room, not even sure why. She opened up her old trunk, pulling out clothes and keepsakes that had been buried in there. She realized what she wanted.

"Mama?" Caribet asked. "What are you doing?"

"I have a book," Satrine said. "A book I want to read."

She got to the bottom of the trunk. No book.

"What book, Mama?"

"It—it should be here." She felt around the clothes, thinking that it might be wrapped inside something. Nothing. She tilted the trunk over, dumping its contents on the floor.

"Mama?"

It wasn't there. "Where is it?"

"What are you looking for?"

"I—I had a poetry book here. I know I had it here. Have you ever seen it?"

"No, Mama," Caribet said. "I didn't know you . . ."

"That I what?" Satrine snapped.

"Read poetry," Caribet said meekly.

Satrine slumped down to the ground. "I don't. Or I haven't, not in a long time."

Caribet came closer, curling up to Satrine, arms around her. "We could get you another book, Mama. I know you're worried about money, but . . ."

"No, sweetheart," Satrine said. "That . . . that book was special."

"I'm sure it's somewhere," Caribet said. "Maybe Rian has it."

Satrine looked over to the shut door. "Maybe. But it doesn't matter." She glanced at her daughter's face. "Are you hungry?" Caribet nodded. "Me too."

Chapter 22

MINOX COULDN'T REMEMBER EATING that much meat in one sitting before. He was hardly the only one. The dining table was covered in dirty plates, with discarded bones picked clean. His uncles and cousins were all pushed away from the table, hands on their stomachs.

"I want to eat another bite, but I just can't," Jace said.

Off all the people at the table, only he and Joshea didn't look like they were stuffed beyond the capacity for movement.

"That was truly excellent, Amalia," Joshea said, directing the comment to Minox's mother. He was already comfortable using everyone's given names. "You have masterful skill in the kitchen."

"It's not all me," Mother said. "Zura is the one with the magic touch." She quickly bit her lip, a guilty look passing to Minox and back to Joshea.

"The both of you, then," Joshea said.

"All right," Aunt Zura said, getting to her feet. "All of you, on your feet. Plenty of washing to do. Let's be about it."

"Have at it," Davis said to his mother. Zura cuffed him across the back of the head.

"Get up, and help out," she said. "All of you, hear? I'll excuse Minox and our guest."

"Hardly fair," Jace said.

"You ate away your fair," Zura said. "Everyone, come on."

"Coming, coming." There was a general grumbling, but the family got up and started to clear their plates. Only Grandmother stayed in her seat. "He's a very charming one, isn't he?" she said, nodding over to Joshea. "And no bracelet. Shame your sister isn't here to note it."

"He's had plenty of note," Minox said, getting up, with a nervous glance around. "In fact, I think I should rescue him from further note."

"Hmm?" Joshea asked.

"Let's step out to the tobacconist," Minox said. "It'll be a bit quieter there."

Joshea nodded. "Everyone, it's been a pleasure and an honor." He went over to Grandmother and kissed her hand. "I was born too late, I fear."

"Very good," Grandmother said. She waved over to Ferah. "You're paying attention, aren't you?"

"Quite," Ferah said. "Do you need help going back up?"

"Please." Grandmother got to her feet. "Very charming, indeed."

Minox tapped Joshea on the arm and led him out to the coatroom. "You weren't overwhelmed, were you?"

"Not at all," Joshea said, taking his coat off the hook. He had a leather case hanging under the coat. "They're all very interesting."

Minox had his own coat on when there was a hand on his shoulder. Aunt Beliah, her face scowling.

"You didn't see Evoy yesterday."

"Yes, I know," Minox said, lowering his voice. "I will go see him."

"Tonight, Minox. When you come back."

"Of course."

"You were gone all night yesterday."

"I won't be this time."

"Promise!"

"I promise, I will come back tonight and speak to Evoy."

Her scowl relaxed. "All right." She put on a large smile and gave a small nod to Joshea. "It was very nice to meet you, Mister Brondar."

"The honor was mine, Missus Serrick," he said. He was hiding the case under his coat. Minox wasn't sure if he was hiding the case from him or Beliah.

Minox got Joshea out the door without further interruption, taking him down the street to the tobacco parlor. It was only a couple blocks away, at the edge of the Little East section of Inemar.

"Can we talk more freely now?" Joshea asked.

"I suppose," Minox said. "I apologize if I am out of sorts. This case has weighed very heavily on me, especially today."

"If you don't mind me saying, you look particularly awful." He smiled wanly. "What was special today?"

"I had . . . several difficult encounters." Minox hesitated. He wanted to have a greater understanding of things that happened to him, and he had no one else to talk to. "Have you ever . . ."

Joshea nodded. "Understandable. Did something happen to you today, regarding your . . . abilities?"

"Several things. Have you ever had an encounter with something that affected you? Made you lose control?"

Joshea screwed his face. "I'm not sure what you mean."

Minox hesitated again. He knew he probably shouldn't talk too plainly about an ongoing case with a civilian. Especially a civilian who had ties, however minor, to that case. It was inappropriate. Even still, discussing it could lead to insights on the case that he'd be unable to reach on his own. That, he decided, justified the discussion.

"The murders we've been investigating—"

"You said there were now three. And all of them . . ." Joshea gave an awkward nod. "Mages?"

"Yes. Two from one Circle, and one from a different one. A rival one, apparently."

"Surely that's significant," Joshea said.

"It may well be. Though both Circles, I fear, will consider me a mutual enemy. I ended up confronting both in the middle of the street, when they were about to get into each other."

"Was that the Riot Call this morning? You were in the middle of that?"

"Indeed," Minox said. "My day only deteriorated from there."

"But wait," Joshea said. "You don't think these murders are some sort of Circle Feud?"

"It's more complicated than that," Minox said. "Plus it would be impossible for the killer to be a mage."

"Why is that?"

Minox hesitated. Still, discussing it might bring about the revelation he needed. "The killer used metal spikes that disabled their ability."

Joshea's eyes went wide. "Disabled? How?"

With a wave of his hand, Minox halted the conversation for a moment. They were at the entrance to the tobacco parlor. The parlor, despite being a typical Maradaine brickwall shop, had a Fuergan flair to it—much like the buildings farther into the Little East. The entranceway was an open arch, with a high and bulbous curve, and thick cords of colored ropes hung like a curtain in place of a door. Minox navigated his way through the dim, hazy establishment until he found his way to the main counter, giving a cordial nod to Mister Hsethir, the long-mustachioed Fuergan proprietor. "*Ushetit sam*, sir."

"*Ushetit sam*," Hsethir said. "Your usual pouch, Inspector?"

"We'll take a table, tonight," Minox said. He glanced over at Joshea for approval. "Two pipes and a pot of *afedhlan*?" Joshea nodded in tentative approval.

"Very good, Inspector," Hsethir said. "Sit over there, and I will bring it to you."

They took their table in a darkened corner, significantly away from the rest of the patrons. The place was quiet, only a few hushed conversations in Fuergan or Druth Trade. Sitting at the low table, Joshea leaned in. "So spikes that disabled their ability. And yours when you touched them, I presume?"

"I'm not sure how to explain it. When I came in contact with one it felt like . . ." Minox struggled to find an apt description. "Sinking into icy water."

Joshea shuddered. "I've heard some stories about metals that affect . . . it. Rumors, old soldier tales, that sort of thing."

"I'm more concerned about something else, though." Minox took a deep breath. Discussing this, even with someone who appeared to understand, was harder than he thought it would be. "At one point we encountered the killer directly."

"You caught him?"

"Unfortunately, no," Minox said. "He had . . . he used on me . . . a powder of some sort. A poison. Just coming into contact with it made me lose all control."

"Control of your magic?"

The word, said blatantly like that, even in the low voice that Joshea used, felt like a blow to the chest. Minox reflexively glanced back to make sure Mister Hsethir or his workers were not in hearing. "Yes, exactly. Like a seizure."

Joshea sat in silence, drinking it in.

Minox kept going. "I'm worried about what that means, especially facing a criminal—an adversary—who knows what I am, and knows how to use it against me."

"I can't imagine what that would be like," Joshea said. "What happened when you lost control, exactly?"

"A pure burst, out of my body. Not focused, not too strong, thankfully. Else my partner might have been seriously hurt."

"That's something to be thankful for."

"Very little," Minox said. "It wasn't even the only loss of control today."

"Another?"

Mister Hsethir came over, putting a tray down on the table. Two pipes, and a small bowl of Minox's favorite tobacco, with a candle and tapers. Next to that, the steaming pot of *afedhlan* and two small mugs. Hsethir poured out the *afedhlan* for both of them, nodded briefly, and went off.

"Afedhlan?" Joshea asked, picking up the mug.

"It's kind of a sharp tea," Minox said. "That's the best I can describe it."

Joshea took a sip. "Interesting."

Minox packed his pipe and lit up. "My partner and I visited an 'expert' she knew, to get an opinion on the spikes."

"By expert, you mean a Circled mage."

"Exactly," Minox said. He took a deep draw off the pipe, holding the sweet smoke in for as long as he could bear, then he released it. "My partner thought he would be civilized, but he was anything but."

"Did he attack you?"

"More like forced me to attack him," Minox said. "Like he was able to manipulate my magic through me."

"Can't trust Circled mages," Joshea said, shaking his head. "The lot of them, they think they're so smart." He lit his own pipe and sat back.

"He did say something interesting, about how all Uncircleds fit into three categories."

"I'm sure they have opinions about us," Joshea said. "We don't fit into their ideas of how we should be."

"My ability didn't manifest until I was already in the Constabulary," Minox said. "I gathered from that man I am an exceedingly rare case."

"I suppose. How did it happen?"

Minox took another toke off the pipe and steeled himself. He had never really told this story to anyone. "It was when I was on horsepatrol. I was chasing a shop thief down in Inemar, and he was gaining ground. I spurred the horse, and at that moment I felt . . ." He paused, deciding the best way to phrase things. Poetics were unnecessary. "Well, that rush of magic, but I didn't understand it at the time. My vision blurred, and suddenly I found myself on the Eastwood Highway. And ravenous."

"Always that part."

"Over the next few weeks, I started to piece together what had happened, what I . . . had become."

Joshea nodded. "I was fourteen. I guess that's typical."

"So did mages from the Circles come looking for you?"

Joshea took a deep draw. "They looked. My father

chased them off with a cleaver, told them they were mistaken. Blazes, I've seen that man all kinds of angry over the years, but nothing like that day. I'm amazed those Circle mages got out alive. Days after they were gone, he was still sputtering."

"So you were hardly about to admit it was true." Minox wondered how his own father might have been had it happened when he was young. He probably would have been angry—not the ranting, violent angry like Joshea's father. Silent, resentful anger was always Rennick Welling's way.

"Not a chance."

"And he's never suspected?"

"Not that I'm aware of. And he is not a man who would keep quiet about such things." Joshea sighed ruefully. "But I've learned how to be pretty blasted careful."

"I thought I had been until today." Minox took another puff. "Between the major, the powder, and the spikes . . . it's clear I don't know anything."

"Like, why us?"

"Exactly!" Minox said. "Is there history of it in your family?"

"None that I know. Not that my father would admit it."

"Nor mine, unless there's some in the Racquin relatives."

"Racquin?" Joshea asked.

"On my mother's side."

"Hmm." Joshea turned quiet and pensive for a moment, and smoked again. "It's just . . . a fair amount of my service was on the Kellirac border. There are places in this world where magic works . . . differently. Kellirac is definitely one of them."

"I hadn't heard that at all."

"Of course you haven't. Who talks about that? We've had to feel around in the dark, you and I. Learn by doing. Learn through failure."

"Failure is definitely the word for today."

Joshea leaned in closer. "I don't know anything about the spikes or that powder. But I have . . ." He paused, biting his lip. "I don't know if this would interest you."

"I need to know whatever I can, Joshea. I fear my ignorance will make me a liability."

Joshea took out his leather case and set it on the table. He looked about, but no one in the shop was paying them any mind. He opened it slowly, revealing small glass jars, powders in each one.

"This is nothing illegal, I hope, Joshea."

"No, of course not," Joshea said. "These are spices. All legal, locally made or properly imported, to the best of my knowledge."

"Spices?"

"A hobby of mine, one of the few things I can connect with the rest of my family over." He reached into the case and pulled out one jar with a deep orange powder in it. "This is called *rijetzh*."

"Poasian?" Minox asked.

Joshea nodded, opening the jar and offering it. "There's a merchant in North Seleth I get this from."

Minox took the jar and sniffed at it. The odor was strongly pungent, but not unpleasant. "Interesting. I presume you're showing it to me for a reason."

"I only have an idea about it," Joshea said. "But I've been using it in my food, in varying amounts, for some time now."

"Does it have a property like the poison I encountered?"

"Nothing like that," Joshea said. "But I believe that, depending on how much I take, it represses my ability."

Minox put the jar down. "You've been using it recently?"

"I actually haven't," Joshea said. "I had run out a few weeks before my army unit was decommissioned. I was starting to think I didn't need it. But after what happened in the alley last night, I thought it would be wise to acquire more. That was part of why I stopped by your home, since it was on my way back."

"But what's the advantage of using this *rijetzh*?"

"Control, Minox! I use that, and I'm the one in control of myself."

"You can't use any magic?"

254 Marshall Ryan Maresca

"I don't feel it. That infernal crackling in my belly, that sense that every hair on my neck is standing on end. It's gone." He opened the jar and sprinkled some into his cup of *afedhlan*. Then he held it out to Minox. "Do you want to try it?"

Minox's hand reflexively went out. Control was a very tempting idea, especially after today's incidents. "You're certain it's safe?"

Joshea responded by downing the contents of his cup.

Minox picked up the jar. "How much do I use?"

◆━━◆━━◆

By ten bells, Rian hadn't come out of her room. Not to eat, not even to use the water closet. Satrine admired her tenacity, at least. She also hadn't let Caribet come in herself, and the poor girl fell asleep on the couch. If nothing else, Satrine was confident that Rian wouldn't be getting any sympathy from her sister.

Missus Abernand had not returned, at least not through their apartment. Satrine went up the back stairs, but found the door latched. She couldn't hear any obvious signs that Missus Abernand was up and about, and didn't want to wake her if she wasn't.

Satrine returned to her apartment. She knocked gently on Rian's door one more time. No response. The girl was probably sleeping. She should do the same.

She went into her bedroom. Loren slept. She envied him. He was allowed to be unaware.

She cursed herself for having that thought. She knew damn well Loren wouldn't want to be unaware of what was going on. He went out, every morning, and he did the job with a smile on his face. If anything, she envied his ability to do that. He may have brought the mystery, the excitement of his work back to the house, but never the burden. He carried that without complaint.

She kissed him on the forehead. If he could manage, so would she. If for nothing else, for Rian and Caribet. She had to work now, for all of them, but she had to bear up as well. No matter how the day went, it had to stay at the stationhouse. Her family deserved no less.

Satrine washed off her face and prepared for bed. Yesterday, she had decided she would get this job, and she had. Tomorrow, she would do it right. No matter what.

———◆◆———

The house was mostly dark when Minox returned. That was as expected, given that it was almost midnight bells. A few lamps could be spotted from the street, including one in the parlor. Minox suspected that was left burning for him. He wasn't going to need it, not yet. He had made a promise to Aunt Beliah, and he would keep it.

He made his way around the back of the house to the stable. They hadn't kept any horses in the stable, not since Father died. On some level, Minox regretted that. Back in his own horsepatrol days, he would have relished keeping his own mount at home. But he knew that was more expense and burden than should be placed on the family. He was already enough of a burden, given how much of his salary he ate.

Though, surprisingly, he wasn't feeling particularly hungry at this moment. Perhaps that was an effect of Joshea's spice. Maybe that's all it did. Minox didn't know anything about Poasian spices—it was hardly relevant to his Constabulary duties. It may have been foolish to sample it so blindly.

Flickering light was visible through the cracks in the door. Minox knocked quietly.

"Not hungry," came Evoy's gravelly response.

"Not bringing food," Minox replied.

The door opened up. Evoy looked wild, hair a greasy tumble, thick beard growth on his chin. The rancid scent of the man hit Minox full in the face.

"Minox! Good to see you! You sent papers from south neighborhoods today."

"You got those all right?" Minox asked. He was glad to see the boy had proven trustworthy.

"Yes, yes. Very good. I haven't gone through everything yet, but . . . I've found a few things of note."

"Excellent. May I come in?"

"Of course, of course." Evoy jumped back, allowing

Minox entry. He wasn't wearing shoes, and his trousers were becoming worn and tattered. Beliah had been worried, and with good reason. He hadn't thought Evoy was getting this bad.

"Look, look," Evoy said, pointing at the walls.

Three of the four walls in the barn were all covered in newsprints, notes, lines of twine and slateboards. Minox knew he was roundly mocked and derided for the notes he kept on his boards on the inspectors' floor. If his fellow inspectors saw this room, knew not only that it was here, but that he was a participant in its creating, they would think him mad.

They might be right.

Minox hadn't been in the barn for several days, and Evoy had clearly been busy, building off Minox's own notes and ideas. Minox scanned over one slateboard, names and questions popping out. Fenmere. Thorn. Blue Hand. Where is Pendall Gurond?

"They didn't listen to you on that one, did they?" Evoy asked. "Two dead horsemen, one dead assassin, case closed! Typical, typical."

"Indeed," Minox said. "Though now that I think about it —"

Evoy shook his head. "I know what you're going to say, and I don't see it." He pointed over to another part of the wall. "Two dead from Firewings. One dead from Light and Stone. Something is missing. Pieces aren't snapping together. But three dead Blue Hands on a garbage scow isn't part of it."

Minox nodded. "Because the methods don't match."

"One's a typical body dump. Yours mean something. I just can't see where."

"Where?"

Evoy jumped up, running to another part of the wall, where a large street map of all of Maradaine was the prominent feature. "The alley, the Light and Stone house, the church. The where means so much more to the killer than the who."

"How so?" Minox asked.

"And then there's the matter of the girls in Laramie,

Gelmoor, Keller Cove, and Aventil. I never would have seen it without those papers you sent, but now it's so clear. The pattern. You need three to start a pattern, but even that can be a coincidence. But now it's five! And no one else has seen it. And why would they? You have to be looking at every piece of the pie."

"There are girls . . . dead?"

"Missing, but most likely dead."

"And this ties to my case how, exactly?"

"Not at all, aren't you paying attention?" Evoy ran over to the first wall. "Of course, that might be a premature pronouncement. I can't see every piece. Where's the north side, Minox? Any newssheets from there? Because I'm sure it ties to the Parliament. Two members, I think. Or the Royal College. And a duchess. There would have to be a duchess involved. Wouldn't there? It only makes sense."

"Evoy—"

Evoy grabbed a piece of chalk and scrawled rapidly. "I mean it's almost comical, isn't it? The obviousness of it all. A duchess. And another noblewoman, I'm sure, so they can have The Lady. All the Grand Ten, you know? That's what they would do."

"You've lost me, Evoy," Minox said. That usually brought him back down, even when it wasn't entirely true. Sometimes Minox was terrified by how much of what Evoy said made perfect sense to him.

"I'm very far ahead of you right now, Minox," Evoy said. He went over to his small table and took the ball of twine. "The tapestry is far larger than three dead mages."

Minox knew not to fight Evoy on this, not directly at least.

"You should be writing this, you know," he said. "Get it in print. Get back to work."

"Ha!" Evoy said. "Like the *South Maradaine Gazette* could handle all this. As if they had enough paper to print it all!" Suddenly he dropped down, sitting on the floor, and his voice turned calm. "Have you seen Rencir lately?"

"He stopped by the station yesterday," Minox said.

"Did he ask after me?"

"Not this time." As much as he was tempted to, there was no point in lying to Evoy.

"You're right, of course," Evoy said. "I should write it all out. And send Rencir just a dollop of it. Just a little bit of the truth. Enough to let him know there is a bigger picture."

"That'd be good, Evoy." Minox knelt down by him. "Your mother would like that."

"Would she?" His tone darkened. "She'd probably like it if I came into the house as well."

"She would," Minox said. "I did promise her I'd speak to you on the subject. And now I have."

"Fine, fine," Evoy said. "You've fulfilled your promise. It's no good for me in there. Not enough space in the house. Too many voices, clamoring about minutiae. Can't hear myself think in there. Saints, you had that big dinner with your friend from the army. Clammer clatter bang bang." He jumped back up to his feet and started writing on a slateboard again.

"Joshea Brondar," Minox said.

"Brondar. Name from Eastern Druthal. Monim, I think. Was he a pikeman?"

"Not sure," Minox said.

"But army family. Probably an ancestor went to Khol Taia."

"It's entirely possible," Minox said.

Evoy pounced on a pile of papers, tearing through them. "Khol Taia is always important. I don't suppose you could get me a roster of every single Druth soldier who was stationed there."

"No," Minox said. "I've told you this before."

"And when the whole city comes crashing down on our heads, dear cousin, don't come crying to me!"

Minox had had quite enough, and he had fulfilled his promise to his aunt. No need to submit himself to any more abuse today. "I would never do that, Evoy. However, I think I should retire."

"True. You've got a big day tomorrow. Rest while you can. If you can, with all that noise. So much noise."

Minox slipped out of the barn and found his way

through the dark to the kitchen door. He briefly considered helping himself to something from the larder before going to bed, but the encounter with Evoy had left him too troubled to eat. Evoy was worse than Fenner had ever been.

Despite that, Minox completely understood what he was doing, and even had the urge to join him.

He touched his face. Stubble had grown. He resolved to shave that off and get to sleep as quickly as possible.

Chapter 23

SATRINE WOKE SHORTLY BEFORE DAWN. Loren had soiled himself in the night, so she washed him and changed him. She washed herself and dressed. She put on her inspector's vest, and for that moment, her husband's gaze was fixed on her. And then it slipped away again. Satrine had the hard thought that every morning in the foreseeable future would follow this pattern, and this was the most she could hope for out of him.

Missus Abernand was in the kitchen when Satrine came out of the room, as was Caribet.

"Morning, Satrine," Missus Abernand said, putting a cup of tea on the table.

"Is Rian awake?" Satrine asked, sitting next to Caribet.

"Already left," Caribet said. "Are you ready to go to work?"

"I suppose I need to be," Satrine said.

"Here you go." Missus Abernand put a bowl of creamed oats in front of her. "Need your strength out there."

"Thank you, Missus Abernand," Satrine said. The old woman shrugged and went back over to the stove. Satrine got up and touched her shoulder. "Missus Abernand? Really, thank you for everything you do."

Missus Abernand glanced at her for a moment, then

turned her attention back to the pots on the stove. "Someone needs to help you out."

"Did you see Rian this morning? How did she look?"

"Looked like a girl going to school." Missus Abernand pointed at Caribet. "Like that, with red hair and taller."

"She's still plenty mad, Mama," Caribet offered. Satrine sat with her and started eating. "But she told me what she did and everything, and it wasn't right, and I told her that."

Missus Abernand snorted. "That's good, Cari. You stay smart, and stay away from the college boys when you're her age."

Caribet crinkled her nose. "Did you really catch her kissing him?"

Satrine nodded. "I really did." She touched her youngest's face, sweet and soft. "You are such a blessing, you know that? Straight from the saints, you and your sister."

Caribet laughed nervously and got up from the table. "I have to get to school, too."

"You see your sister, Cari, tell her I said that. All right?"

"I'll tell her you're not mad, how about that?"

"Fair enough." She took another sip of tea. "I should start walking as well."

"You'll be back at six bells?" Missus Abernand said.

Satrine shrugged. "If I live through today."

"Shouldn't make jokes like that, Satrine. Saints don't like it."

"Six bells, Missus Abernand," Satrine said as soberly as she could. "That is my intention."

The morning was warm, the sky was bright and clear. Satrine's knee still ached as she walked down to the bridge, but besides that, it was a pleasant stroll to Inemar. The day ahead would probably be filled with more dead bodies, murderers, and painful memories, but she pushed those thoughts into the back of her mind. She would bear it.

She had to bear it. There was no other option.

"Minox, are you sick?" Jace's whispered voice pulled Minox out of slumber. Sick? Why would Jace even ask such a thing?

"Of course not," Minox muttered. Opening his eyes, he focused on his young brother. "Why are you in here?"

Jace shrugged. "It's almost seven bells. You're always awake at six bells."

Minox sat up quickly. "Almost seven? That can't be right." It was unusual for him to sleep so late.

"That's the time. Mother thought you had spent the whole night out again, and had me check."

"Of course," Minox said, brushing Jace away. "I'm well. Let me dress in peace, and I'll be down shortly."

Jace left, and Minox began to get ready. Almost seven bells? The last two days had had more of a toll on him than he had suspected. But he felt well rested, even refreshed. So perhaps oversleeping had been for the best.

Washed, shaved, and dressed, Minox went down to the dining table, where most of the family were already having breakfast.

"Getting worried about you," Ferah said as he took his seat. "Nyla already headed out."

"Nothing to worry about," Minox said. "I needed to recover is all."

"You don't take care of yourself," Aunt Beliah said, bringing a plate loaded with eggs and sausage to him. She touched his head. "Running a little warm. You shouldn't work today."

"Nonsense," Timmothen said. "Wellings don't shirk their duty. Pop would go on the job—"

"Even if he was on fire," Timmothen's sons said in unison.

"Blazing right he would," Timmothen said.

"I'm fine," Minox said. "I have no intention of shirking."

"Better not," Corrie said. Minox hadn't even noticed she was at the table. He usually had left before she came in. "You need to clean up that Circle business you started."

"Circle business?" Oren asked. "What's this about?"

"Series of murders," Minox said. "Corrie's shift took a patrol duty to prevent things from escalating."

"Rutting mages killing other mages," Corrie snapped.

"Corrianna Welling!" Mother called out from the kitchen. "I don't want to hear that from your mouth again!"

"Sorry!" Corrie called back. Scowling, she took a bite of her breakfast. "They probably will start another Circle Feud."

"So it was an unpleasant night?" Minox asked. "Did either side start trouble?"

"I spent the night outside the Stonelight house, or whatever they're called. Crazy skirts came out four times looking to scrap someone. I almost wish one of them had made a dash so I could run her down."

Minox leaned over closer to her. "Anything else?"

Corrie's eye twitched, and then, looking down at her plate, she whispered, "Kelsey and Prandt. You didn't hear it from me."

"Of course," Minox said. Ringing from Saint Benton's pealed off in the distance. It was seven bells and thirty. He would barely have time to make it to the station by eight bells, and that was only if the tickwagons weren't held up at all. "I appreciate it." He got to his feet and made for the front door.

"Minox!" Aunt Beliah said. "You barely ate!"

Minox glanced back at the table. His plate was still full. He hadn't walked away from a full plate of food in three years. "I'm running late, it can't be helped." He made for the door and grabbed his coat and vest. Beliah raced over to join him.

"Did you check on Evoy?"

"I did," Minox said as he put on his coat. "Though he's unlikely to come back into the house any time soon."

Beliah gasped, her hand instinctively covering her mouth. "How bad is he?"

"I'm not qualified to—"

"Is he worse than my father was?"

Minox had no urge to lie to his aunt. "In some ways, I believe so. But I do not believe he will take the violent turn that Grandfather did."

Tears welled at her eyes. "Thank you. He . . . he won't even let me in."

Minox glanced out the door. He needed to leave. "We'll discuss this more later."

She grabbed his arm. "He listens to you."

"Beliah!" Minox said. She was right, of course. Evoy listened to Minox because they were more alike than not. "I must go. I will increase my vigilance with Evoy."

"Thank you," Beliah said, releasing him. Minox nodded and left the house before she could stall him any further.

Chapter 24

SATRINE WAS SURPRISED THAT Welling hadn't
yet arrived when she reached the stationhouse. The
whole inspectors' floor had an eerie quiet to it. Miss Pyle
moved about like a hummingbird. No lamps were burning
in Cinellan's office. The other desks were empty, save for
Kellman and Mirrell, who conferenced in hushed voices
at their desks. Satrine was more than aware of the nervous
glances they gave her as she passed them, though Kellman
had the decency to say a brief good morning to her.

Satrine sat at her desk behind Welling's slateboards.
After a moment, she realized that she had barely spent
more than a few minutes at her desk, and had done very
little to make the space her own. It was still covered with
Welling's own mess. Satrine had no clue how to even
start to sort through it.

The same was true of the slateboards. A few parts
popped out as sensible. Hessen Tomar, Jaelia Tomar.
Street names. Single words with question marks. Lines
drawn between those words. Welling had a system, she
was sure it all made sense to him, but she didn't have the
patience or energy to crack it herself.

Miss Pyle came over with two cups of tea, placed
them on the desks and began clearing the old cups.

"I thought you said you weren't going to do that," Satrine said.

"I say a lot of things to Minox," Miss Pyle said.

"I'm surprised he isn't here already," Satrine said. "Or is he already out on another call?"

"He was still sleeping when I left the house," Miss Pyle said. "Which is unusual."

Given the abuse Welling took from the major, and the killer, and the Light and Stone mages, it wasn't at all surprising to Satrine that he slept in. "You live in the same house?"

Miss Pyle laughed. "Three generations of Wellings. My parents, Minox's mother, our brothers and sisters, aunts, uncles, cousins, and Grammy Jillian." She nodded her head to the charcoal sketch on the wall.

"She's one I'd love to meet," Satrine said.

"You should have been at dinner last night, then. She rarely comes down anymore, but she surprised us last night when Joshea joined us."

"Joshea?" Satrine asked. "Do you mean . . . Joshea Brondar?"

"You know him?" Miss Pyle said. "He's very handsome, I think, but Ferah had her eyes on him—"

"Joshea Brondar was at your home last night?" Satrine couldn't believe what she was hearing.

"He's Minox's friend," Miss Pyle said, though doubt was crossing her face. "Right?"

"Of course," Satrine said. She waved it off like it was nothing. "I'm just surprised Minox didn't go right to sleep after the past two days."

Miss Pyle opened up her mouth to respond, but whatever she was about to say was lost in Captain Cinellan's storming through the doors of the inspectors' floor.

"Miss Pyle," he called out. "Tea on my desk. Kellman, Mirrell, in my office."

Pyle jumped to her feet. "Yes, Captain."

Kellman and Mirrell hurried over to the office. Cinellan glowered in Satrine's direction. "Where's Welling?"

"Haven't seen him yet," Satrine said.

Cinellan grunted. "Send him in here when he shows." With Kellman and Mirrell in his office, Cinellan secluded himself inside and shut the door.

Miss Pyle rushed back, tea in hand.

"Is this a typical morning for him?" Satrine asked. Miss Pyle shrugged and let herself into the office. She all but ran out seconds later.

Satrine sipped at her own tea. Without specific directive, other than wait for Welling, she wasn't sure what she should do. And once Welling arrived, she should send him in to Cinellan's closed door meeting, whatever that was about. Though she definitely wanted words of her own with Welling. What the blazes was he doing having Joshea Brondar at his house, with his family? Welling may have dismissed the man as a suspect, but he was still involved in the investigation. If it went to trial, he might be needed as a witness, and that could sour the whole mash.

At least it would put Hilsom's nose out of place. That was something.

Welling came up the stairs, out of breath and wild-eyed. "My apologies," he said to no one in particular as he crossed the floor. "Where is—"

"Captain's office," Satrine said, crossing over to him. "You're supposed to join them."

Welling raised an eyebrow. "Did the captain say why?"

"No," Satrine said, putting as much edge as she could onto the word.

"Ah," Welling said. "I believe I understand."

"Good," Satrine said. "Perhaps you could explain it to me."

Welling glanced around, his eyes finding his cousin, sitting at her desk. "I am not at liberty to at the moment."

"Perhaps you could explain why a person of note in our case had dinner at your house last night, then," Satrine said.

That stopped Welling short. After blinking several times, he nodded and said, "I really should join the captain now." He didn't wait for her response, going straight into the office, shutting the door behind him.

"Well," Satrine said to no one in particular. "I guess I

should clean my desk, or tune up my crossbow or something."

She took two steps before the office door opened and the captain came out. "Miss Pyle, be so kind as to fetch three pages. Specifically Hace, Painter, and Quint."

"Hace, Painter, and Quint," Miss Pyle said, getting to her feet. "I presume this is . . ." She let it hang. The captain nodded, and she dashed off.

Cinellan sighed deeply and said, "Rainey, join us in here, would you?" He walked back in, leaving the door open.

Satrine entered the crowded office, where Kellman and Mirrell were leaning against the wall, and Welling sat in the chair, coolly tapping his fingers on the arm.

"Shut the door," the captain said. Satrine did so, trying her best to ignore the sudden cold sweat that was breaking on her brow. They were all acting strange, being secretive, talking in code. This couldn't be good.

"What's going on?" she asked, forcing her voice to be as calm as she could manage.

"You've been a stick's wife for a long time," Cinellan said. "So I'm presuming you've got a sense how some things work."

"Some." Guarded tone.

"Have you heard of a Quiet Call?"

She had. Quiet Call was when they gathered up a bunch of sticks, the ones they knew they could trust, without letting the word get out to the rest of the stationhouse.

It was what they did to handle corrupt sticks. Someone who had forged orders to become an inspector would do just as well.

"So that's what this is about?" No emotion in her voice, but her head was racing. None of them were making a move on her, not yet. They were probably waiting until the boys Nyla was fetching could block the door. No windows or other way out of here. Her hand inched closer to her belt, ready to draw her handstick, ready to beat her way out once any one of them made their move.

"I wouldn't normally bring someone brand-new in on

one," Cinellan said. "But we're going to need every hand we can pull together, and Welling vouches for you."

"He . . . he does?" She almost jerked her hand away from her stick.

"Stop gibbering, Tricky," Kellman said. "This is what Hennie and I do."

Hennie? "You two are watchdog inspectors." It made perfect sense. The first case she heard about them on was the murder of two horsepatrol.

Mirrell nodded. "We've been putting together some pieces, long-term work. Some of our more . . . morally questionable boys, the ones we've been building a long case on, we hear they're meeting some of their connections at a warehouse this morning. Something large is happening at nine bells, and we're going to crack it as hard as we can muster."

Welling's head was down, scrawling a list of names. "Kelsey and Prandt. Night shift horse. You have your eye on them?"

"Had a whisper," Mirrell said. "You have something harder?"

"Just more whispers," Welling said. "But ones I trust."

"Maybe we'll be lucky," Kellman said. "They'll be on the scene now."

Satrine let herself breathe. This had nothing to do with her at all.

"You have that list ready, Welling?" Cinellan asked.

Welling handed over the paper. "These men are solid for the Quiet Call. Seventeen was the best I could do."

"It'll have to be good enough," Cinellan said.

A knock came on the door, and Miss Pyle entered. "I have the pages. And Mister Hilsom is here with a writ of search."

"Perfect," the captain said. "All right, you four. Heavy coats and caps will be on the wagon. Let's crack some skulls."

◆━━━◆━◆━━━◆

Minox checked the straps on his leather cap. He always hated wearing one when he was horsepatrol. It made his hair soak with sweat, and the straps always bit into his ear. As uncomfortable as it was, though, it was surely more comfortable than an unshielded blow to the head.

Inspector Rainey looked out of place with her cap and heavy coat. Her long red hair spilled out the sides, which then puffed out in a ridiculous manner.

"Tie it back," Minox offered. "That's what Corrie does."

"Tie what back?"

"Your hair," Minox said. He glanced out the alley, half a block from the warehouse they were about to target. They, as well as Kellman and Mirrell, were in the forward positions, ready to move when the bells of Saint Limarre's struck nine. Other men, out of uniform, moved through the street like merchants or beggars.

On some level, the whole subterfuge struck Minox as absurd. Any Constabulary worth his badge would recognize a Quiet Call in motion if he saw what was happening in the street. It would be more plausible if they recruited from another stationhouse. The last two times he had been involved in this with Mirrell, he had suggested having one of his uncles put together a team from their stationhouses, but the captain wouldn't hear of it. This time he made no such attempt, instead opting to argue for having Rainey at his side. The past two days had been especially trying, and were only tolerable due to her presence. He looked back to her. Her hair was now tied back, one of the leather cords of the heavy coat sacrificed to the cause. "Are you ready?"

"Is anyone really ever?" She drew out her crossbow, checking its readiness. "I've never really done anything quite like this before."

That was surprising. "You have shown yourself to be a capable combatant."

"Street scrapper, Welling. I can hold my own in a brawl, but an organized raid? We never did anything like that on my corner. Or in Intelligence."

"Stay alert," Minox said. "This is Mirrell's engagement, so give him deference. We're here as support." He pointed to the warehouse, notably the large wagon doors on the south wall. "At the first chime, we all make our move. South doors are ours." He pointed to two footpatrol, dressed as streetsweeps. "They're our lampmen. They'll be right behind us."

"What are we going after, exactly?"

"Not sure," Minox said. "Mirrell was deliberately obtuse on the matter. Whether that was out of ignorance or a desire to hold knowledge over me, I am not sure."

"What's your guess?"

"I haven't been studying this case—"

"Welling," Rainey said, touching his shoulder. "What's your guess?"

Minox repressed the grin. "Warehouse is two blocks away from the riverfront, which makes a pure smuggling operation less likely. Large building, almost half a block. Solid brick walls, few windows. A fair amount of noise could come from inside with little notice." He took a deep sniff of the air. "Interesting."

"What?"

"The stench of human and animal waste is noticeably stronger here than, say, a block away. But closer to a kennel than a stable or a backhouse."

"Dogfights?" Inspector Rainey asked.

"Sensible deduction, Inspector. Though puzzling, as dogfight rings would hardly bother in bribing multiple constabulary officers to cover their operations. Such establishments thrive on being an open secret."

Rainey bit her lip in thought. "Maybe the dogs are the cover."

The idea clicked in his thoughts. "Scent of the dogs covering a different odor? Intriguing. But covering what?"

Rainey was about to answer when the first bell rang. She closed her mouth and held up her crossbow. Minox drew out his own. They moved out into the street. Kellman and Mirrell were already charging at the western doors. Rainey ran out ahead toward theirs, and Minox chased on her heels.

All the scattered footmen in disguise moved at once, converging on the three sets of warehouse doors. Rainey reached the barn doors a full forty feet before he did. She didn't stop, ramming her shoulder at the door at full speed. The door splintered and cracked, but didn't yield.

At the same moment, Mirrell and Kellman kicked open their door, shouting out, "Hold fast! You are all bound by law!"

Rainey stepped back, waiting for Minox to reach the door. Out of pride, he couldn't allow himself to not make the same attempt to knock open the door that Rainey had. He charged at it with full strength, and she hit it again in the same moment. This time, the doors flew open.

At least a score of men were in the warehouse, knocking down lamps and snuffing candles. Minox's eyes couldn't adjust to the darkness fast enough to see more.

"Hold fast!" Rainey shouted, crossbow up. The two lampmen took a place right behind them, holding their lanterns high. Soft beams illuminated the dark corners of the warehouse, while several bodies scrambled and darted for the shadows like the rats they were.

The twangs of crossbow fire came quickly. The lamp over Minox's head shattered. Rainey fired into the darkness. A man cried out, so in all likelihood she shot true.

Minox stepped ahead of her as she bent down, one foot in her cocking stirrup. Another shot flew past, taking out the other lantern.

There were definitely Constabulary inside, making a point of taking out the light instead of the man. They didn't want to hurt fellow officers if they could help it, but they didn't want to get spotted either.

Snarls and barks rushed at them, and Minox barely had a chance to shoot before he saw three sets of jaws flying at him. One dog dropped with a sharp squeal. The other two were on him, clamping hard on the sleeves of his coat.

Rainey dropped her crossbow and pummeled one dog with her handstick. The lampmen tackled the other. Minox wormed his arms out of the coat and pushed forward, staying close to the ground. He couldn't see anything. More light was needed.

He focused his concentration on creating a ball of light in his hand.

Nothing happened.

More crossbow shots whistled past him. One brushed the top of his cap. No time to mess around with magic, or do anything that might make him an attractive target.

He lifted up his hand to shoot back. No crossbow. He must have dropped it.

Men with lamps came streaming in the other door, behind Kellman and Mirrell, where at least ten officers held up their weapons. "Cease fire now!" Kellman's voice boomed. The light hit several men, who were in the process of loading the bows or opening dog cages. On Kellman's voice, they all dropped what they were doing and put their hands up.

"Goddamn bastards," Rainey said. Minox looked over to the cages and saw why. Not all the cages had dogs in them.

Some cages had children. Two or three per cage, covered in rags and filth.

Minox started to get to his feet when a man—someone in the shadows he hadn't seen—burst past him and knocked him down. He slammed hard onto the ground. Flat on his back, he was barely able to see the man barrel through the lampmen into the open street.

"Bastard!" Rainey screamed again, and ran out after him.

Chapter 25

THE BASTARD WAS RUNNING NOW, out in the open street. The lampmen had been useless in stopping him, so all he had to do was get out of sight and he'd be free as a lark.

Satrine would be damned if she let that happen.

She pounded after the man. He had a strong lead, but she would close that distance once she got her feet under her. He stumbled as he ran. Drops of blood on the ground. He must have been the one she hit with her crossbow. Despite that, he had good speed, but he wasn't fast enough to beat her.

Only a few feet separated them when he crossed around a shopkeeper's table, kicking its leg out as he passed it. Brass trinkets and glass careened onto the ground, forcing Satrine to jump out of the way, losing her stride. By the time she found her footing, he was down the next alley.

She turned the corner. The alley was a dead end, but he was beating on a door, his only possible escape. He looked back at her. Despite the bleeding wound in his shoulder, he grinned at her.

"I thought the Jinx was chasing me," he said. "Not the skirt."

Satrine didn't bother with a response, other than charging at him. For a moment, his grin was about to become laughter, and then his face froze, melting into fear.

She had him.

He kicked at the door again. This time some fool opened it to yell at whoever was hitting the door. The bastard knocked him down and ran into the building.

Satrine tried to go right after him, but the fool who had let him in grabbed at her legs, dragging her down to the ground with him.

"How dare you!" the man shouted.

"Constabulary!" was all Satrine responded with, wrenching herself away from his hands. She reined in the urge to kick the man in the face.

"Rutting sticks!"

She pulled away and got back on her feet. Where was she? Looked like the backroom of a tailor. She ran through the separating curtain to the shop floor. Drops of blood led to the front door. Satrine followed, to see her quarry chasing after a tickwagon.

"Hold fast!" she shouted, running after the man. She knew that wouldn't stop him, but it might stop the wagon driver. If she still had her crossbow on her, she could take him down now.

He ran away from the wagon, and she went right after him, shouting again and again for him to hold fast. The street opened up, people clearing out of her way.

She closed the distance, drawing out her handstick. Once she caught him, she'd have no choice but to drop him hard. She wasn't carrying irons. She had her whistle, but she'd be damned if she could remember the page call.

He tried to dodge behind a pedalcart, but his coat caught on a handle, tripping him up. That was all Satrine needed to catch him. She grabbed his shoulder with her left hand, and slammed the handstick into his back with her right. He dropped to the ground.

Satrine didn't give him a chance to strike back, wailing on his arms and head before dropping one knee onto his back. She locked her handstick against the back of his neck, pressing his face into the ground.

"Stupid skirt, do you have any idea who I am?" he snapped.

"Not a clue," Satrine said. "You're bound by law, though. You will be held and ironed, and brought to trial for your crimes."

"I'll see you burned for this!"

Satrine dug her knee deeper into his back. He screamed out, but offered no further comments. She glanced up at the small crowd that had gathered around them. "Could one of you call for a page? I seem to be lacking a set of irons."

⬦——◆◆——⬦

Minox's head was swimming, still recovering his breath from being knocked to the ground. He sat against the barn doors, able to watch the business inside the warehouse and the street outside. The raid was done, twenty men apprehended. They were kneeling in the street, hands in irons behind their heads. Kellman strolled back and forth in front of them, swinging his handstick as if he was hoping one of them would give him an excuse to use it. Minox could hardly blame him for that.

He felt sick to his stomach. He hadn't eaten much this morning, and he was glad for it. The sight of the children, locked in their cages, the scent of them sitting in their own filth, it was more than Minox could easily stand. Footpatrol were busy getting the cages unlocked, which was taking far too long for Minox's taste. He had half a mind to blow the cages apart with a wave of his hand. He resisted the urge, though, as he had no idea if he could do such a thing without injuring the children.

Four of the twenty men were Constabulary from their stationhouse, including Kelsey, the night horsepatrolman. Corrie would be glad to know that she didn't target him in vain. He was deeply involved in whatever atrocities were occurring in the warehouse. The other sixteen were an unsurprising collection of the usual dregs of society, more than a few of them bearing tattoos from street gangs or Quarrygate.

"Where's Tricky?" Mirrell stood over Minox, taking a drag off his pipe.

"I'm not sure," Minox said, forcing himself to stand up. "Someone ran, and . . . she—Inspector Rainey went after him." He knew he shouldn't give her nickname any more credence than the one they insisted on using for him.

"Hmm," Mirrell said. "Good luck to her, then." He glanced over to the cages, puffing away. "So what's your reckon on this? Slave trade of some sort?"

"Possibly, but I would think such an enterprise would require being closer to the river. I cannot even fathom what horrors occurred here."

"Is that an official statement?" Minox hadn't noticed that Mister Rencir had approached the two of them. "Quite an action, Inspectors?"

"Official statements will come from the stationhouse," Mirrell said, all but spitting on Rencir. "I have to help open those cages." He stalked off.

"Always a pleasure, Inspector," Rencir called after him. He turned back to Minox. "Any unofficial statements?"

"I'm still recovering from being knocked on the ground," Minox said. "You can print that if you really wish."

"Heroically injured inspector saves tortured children," Rencir said. "That should sell some sheets."

"We all do our part," Minox said. He lowered his voice. "I'll make sure to get details to you once I have them clear."

"I appreciate it," Rencir said. "Though this whole thing must be making a stir throughout the city."

"The whole city?" Minox asked. "That seems premature."

"I'm not sure," Rencir said. "I just know that Constabulary Commissioner Enbrain was spotted coming across the bridge into Inemar. He doesn't do that every day."

Minox's mind whirled. No, the commissioner certainly did not. Four men were caught here, embroiled in whatever corruption was involved. But there was no way the commissioner could have received word and already come across the river so quickly.

"Did I miss everything?" Inspector Rainey came around the corner, dragging her quarry in irons. "No more excitement?"

"Caught one more, Trick?" Kellman asked. "Add him to the pile."

"You can't prove a blasted thing," her prisoner said. She pushed him on the ground next to the others. Minox recognized him: Lieutenant Haimen, a ranking patrol officer for the day shift.

"Haimen," Kellman said, his face a strange combination of rage and pleasure. "I was so very disappointed that we didn't have you in our little group here. I was certain we'd drop the hammer on you today."

"Hammer ain't on me," Haimen said.

Kellman grinned. "Tricky has you caught and ironed, Haimen. That's quite the hammer."

Haimen's mouth trembled, as he looked down the line at the others ironed up. "I'll talk and walk."

Inspector Rainey knelt down in front of Haimen. "I don't think we need you to talk, Lieutenant. So I doubt you'll get to walk."

"We'll see what the protector has to say," Haimen said. He had a strangely smug smile, which turned Minox's stomach further.

Inspector Rainey shook her head and came over to Minox. "Missed you back there."

"I was in no condition to follow, Inspector," Minox said. She gave a slight smile. "I'm still a bit dizzy." Minox noticed Rencir had slipped away.

"You going to be all right?"

"I just need a few more minutes. I'm impressed by the relative ease with which you apprehended Haimen. I would hardly think a Waish princess would need to do such things."

She chuckled. "I was a *quia*, not a princess. You'd be surprised what the Waish expect out of their nobility." The hint of deception on her face.

"Are we done here?" Rainey asked. She reached out to his head, reminding Minox briefly of Ferah or Aunt

Beliah, but then she pulled back. "Unless they need us here, we should get back to our own cases, right?"

"Right," Minox said. "Inspector Mirrell, do you still require our assistance?"

Mirrell strolled back over to them. "Not specifically. Though we need to figure out what to do with all these kids."

"They'll end up at an orphanage, won't they?" Rainey asked.

"Unless we find specific places for each of them," Minox said. "Though we would be negligent if we didn't send them to Ironheart Ward first. A Yellowshield call would not be out of order."

"Do you need a Yellowshield, Jinx?" Mirrell asked.

"I am fine enough," Minox said, which was only a minor bit of dissembling. He was capable of performing his duty, and that was fine enough. "If you'll kindly excuse us."

"Sure, go," Mirrell said. He glanced back over to the group of prisoners, clearly noting Lieutenant Haimen. "That's a good catch, Tricky."

"Just doing the job, Mirrell," Inspector Rainey said. Mirrell only shrugged and walked back to the cages.

━━━━◆◆◆━━━━

"I probably shouldn't expect more gratitude," Inspector Rainey said as they walked back to the station. "Civility from those two will have to do."

"Civility from Inspectors Mirrell and Kellman is probably the best either of us can hope for," Minox said.

"We need nicknames for them," Rainey said. "It would improve my mood."

"I would prefer not to engage in such behavior," Minox said. There was no need to discuss such things. A fair piece of the morning had been spent assisting those two on their case; Minox had no further desire to waste valuable time not in consideration of their own case. "We need to find out if our killer struck again."

"You think there will be a fourth murder?" Rainey asked.

"I have not determined how many murders our quarry intends," Minox said. "However, I am confident that he has not yet finished with whatever he is trying to achieve."

Rainey stopped walking. "You think that when he's done, it will all be clear?"

"I think the patterns will be easier to determine in hindsight," Minox said. "Not that it will be helpful to his potential future victims."

"Maybe that's what we need to figure out," Rainey said. "Who might be next. Get one step ahead."

"A valid idea," Minox said. "Though I'm not sure what we can do to determine that."

Inspector Rainey pointed over to Missus Wolman's stand. "We should probably get you something to eat."

"That's probably true," Minox said. They walked over to the stand, though Minox had to admit that he wasn't exactly in the mood for one of her fast wraps. Between the blow to his head and the thought of those poor children, his stomach was hardly ready to handle any heavy food.

"Two Firewings, followed by a Light and Stone," Rainey said. As she said it out loud, she had a vague sense of something familiar in the names of the Circles. Almost a memory. She shook it off, unable to connect it to anything solid. "I suppose it would be too easy if the next victim would be another Light and Stone."

"It would be foolish to presume that the specific Circles of the victims mean that much to the killer. There must be a thread of connection that we are unaware of."

"All right, maybe this is magic politics. I mean, Harleydale appeared to be the leader at Light and Stone. At least in that household. And the Tomars, what sort of influence or rank did they have?"

"We don't know how devastating an impact these murders have had on the Circles as a whole."

"It could be one or both Circles have been crippled by the loss."

"Or not affected beyond personal grief. Given how still-tongued both Circles are about their membership, we can't even speculate."

Inspector Rainey sighed and rubbed her shoulder. "We're really just stabbing into the shadows."

Minox nodded, noting that Missus Wolman was slapping together several wraps for him, despite the fact he hadn't ordered any. "We should walk through each murder, figure out the details of how each one was accomplished. Perhaps then we can—"

"This might be some news," Inspector Rainey said. A page—Hace, Minox noted—came out of the stationhouse and hurried over to them. His face made it clear that whatever news he might have, it was unpleasant.

"Inspector Rainey?" he said when he came close. "I need to take you to the captain's office. He and the commissioner are waiting for you there."

Chapter 26

SATRINE'S HEART ALMOST STOPPED. It was over.

Welling may not have known the specifics of Satrine's fabrication, but she knew he had divined enough—he was investigator enough—to know that if the commissioner had crossed south to see the captain, and they wanted her escorted to them, then it had to be because her house of paper had crumpled. It was clear on Welling's face that he had indeed figured it out.

"Well, then," she said. There really was nothing more to say. She patted Welling on the shoulder as she passed.

"You deserve this position," Welling said. "I hope they know that."

He turned away, clearly having said his piece on the subject.

Satrine went into the stationhouse, Phillen walking right behind her. She didn't need the escort. Where else would she go? It's not like the commissioner didn't know where she lived. "Go about your business, Phillen. I'll be fine."

"It's going to be bad, isn't it, ma'am?"

"I'm getting used to bad, Phillen. Run along." He saluted her, and walked off.

She went straight to the stairs and up to the inspectors' floor.

Miss Pyle was standing at her desk, her eyes shifting nervously as soon as she spotted Satrine.

"Inspector Rainey, there's . . . you need to . . ."

"It's all right, Nyla, I already know," Satrine said, giving her warmest smile possible. "But thank you."

The door to Cinellan's office was open, sweet smell of Fuergan tobacco seeping out into the work floor. Through the haze, the captain and Commissioner Enbrain sat silently, pipes in hand.

"You wanted to see me, Captain?" Satrine asked lightly, on the off chance that she wasn't five clicks away from being kicked out to the street.

Cinellan's head came up, but his eyes were low and dark. "Missus Rainey. I'm sure you know the commissioner."

Wendt Enbrain was a burly man, with more hair than he knew what do to with. The large gray mop of it was loosely pulled back, and his face was overrun with a shaggy beard. He kept his head down, as if he couldn't bear to look up at Satrine.

"Morning, sir. Surprised to see you here so early." Satrine wasn't going to give either of them an easy time of this. If they wanted her to break down and confess, or beg forgiveness, or even acknowledge she had done anything wrong, then neither of them knew what kind of woman she was.

Enbrain spoke, a low, quiet voice that barely masked the broiling anger underneath. "My door was pounded on at eleven bells last night, Satrine."

"Always is the risk in this job," Satrine said. "I've lost track of the number of door pounds Loren got over the years. Blazes, yesterday—"

Enbrain burst open with anger, jumping out of his chair. "A city alderman, Satrine! Alderman Tullen—"

"Tullen?" That name sounded familiar.

"Alderman Tullen wanted to know why there was an inspector harassing his son. A woman inspector."

Tullen. The boy kissing Rian last night.

Enbrain continued. "Of course, I know this is ridiculous, because there are no women who have been made inspector anywhere in the city."

"On the north side," Cinellan said under his breath.

Enbrain continued as if he hadn't heard. "But he insists. His son said this crazy red-haired woman who claims to be an inspector broke him up kissing her daughter. Suddenly it all fell into place."

"How long did you think it would last?" Cinellan asked. "Your name would have ended up in a newsprint. Sooner or later the news would have drifted up north."

"Was hoping for later," Satrine said.

"So late that I wouldn't care that you tricked me? That I'd think you indispensable?"

"Something like that. One week here, and you would know I can do this job damn well."

Enbrain growled and sat back down. "I tried to help you out, Satrine. And this is what you do."

"Help me out?" Satrine said. "A pittance five-crown position?"

"I did what I could—"

Satrine couldn't stand it; if the paper house had crumbled, she might as well burn it down. "What you could, Wendt? Don't even sell me that oil. You did just enough to push your guilt aside."

"Blazes, Satrine! I have to answer to the Council of Aldermen and the duke—"

"I'm so sorry you had someone knock on your blasted door at a late hour," Satrine sneered. "That must have been terribly inconvenient for you. Do you want to know what I was doing at the same time?"

"Missus Rainey—"

Satrine ignored Cinellan's futile attempt to cut her off. "I was changing my husband's soiled clothes. Like an infant, sir! That is what he has been reduced to."

Enbrain had the decency to look a bit ashamed. He should. Saints, Satrine and the girls had eaten in his home. "I really am trying to help you, Satrine. Loren was a—a good friend, and a great inspector. He deserves . . . you can't say that I would have left his family to the dogs. I couldn't . . . I wouldn't do that."

"Five crowns a week! You think I could live on that,

with the state Loren is in? With what I need to do to take care of him? And with our daughters?"

"It's good money, Satrine! You could—"

"You might as well take me down to the docks and introduce me to sailors!"

Cinellan's eyes went wide, and he got up from behind his desk and walked close to the commissioner. "Sir, despite Missus Rainey's . . . tone, as far as this stationhouse is concerned, I am open."

"Open to what?" Satrine snapped.

Enbrain sighed deeply. "Captain Cinellan, astoundingly, is still willing to have you serve in a clerk's capacity, with the possibility of earning your way to an inspector's path. I'm leaving that in his hands, but—"

"The possibility?" Satrine couldn't really believe what they were saying. "My family would starve on the street while waiting for that." She went for the door.

"Damn it, Satrine, I'm trying to—" Enbrain reached out and grabbed her arm.

She slapped his hand away. "Don't try, goddamn it. Help me or don't." This conversation wasn't going anywhere useful. She took off her vest and belt, dropping them at her feet. Cinellan looked at the heap they made on the floor and nodded. Enbrain sat back down in his chair, clearly having nothing more to say.

Satrine left the office, feeling every eye on the floor boring into her. Kellman and Mirrell had already returned to the floor, and had placed themselves along her path to the stairs.

"Didn't take long," Kellman said.

"Were you expecting it to?" Satrine asked, though in the back of her mind she was cursing herself for even engaging with them.

Mirrell gave her a look something between a grin and a sneer. "I thought 'Tricky' would at least last a week."

"You weren't the only one." She brushed past the two of them and went for the stairs.

As she passed, Kellman muttered, "Looks like the Jinx strikes again."

Satrine turned on him, shoving the huge man in the

chest. "You want to knock me, Kellman, knock me. But leave Inspector Welling out of it. He's the best thing this house has going for it."

Mirrell pushed her shoulder. "You want us to knock you, Rainey? Knock you to the floor?"

"Take your best, Mirrell!"

"Stop it!" Miss Pyle marched up to them. "You two need to let Missus Rainey get off the floor."

Both the inspectors stepped away, giving a final glare at Satrine before going back to their desks.

"You didn't need to do that," Satrine said.

"I most certainly did," Miss Pyle said. "This floor is for the inspectors and support staff, or civilians here on official business. You, Missus Rainey, are not any of those things."

There was venom in her voice. Satrine went toward the stairs, ready to leave the building completely. She was halfway down when she heard Miss Pyle hiss at her from the top.

"Missus Rainey, there will be a woman—my cousin Corrie, perhaps—who earns that vest that you tricked your way into wearing. And her life is going to be that much harder because of what you did."

Satrine had no response to that, and Miss Pyle didn't stay around to hear it.

◆━◆━◆

From across the street Minox watched Inspector Rainey—correction, Missus Rainey, as evidenced by her lack of uniform—leave the stationhouse. If she had looked, she would have seen him sitting at the counter of Missus Wolman's cookstand. She had left with her head hanging low, not observing anything of the world around her.

Minox's potato-and-meat-filled roll sat in front of him, cooled and congealed. He didn't have the appetite for it.

That was a strange development.

Minox contemplated that, focusing his attention on his stomach. He did not have an appetite.

He briefly considered the idea that this was an emotional reaction to Missus Rainey's dismissal. She possessed an exceptional mind, and was an incredible asset for the MC, and he could not deny that loss angered him. This theory did not hold, as a variety of emotions had never stayed his hunger in the past.

In addition, he had barely eaten all day. He hadn't thought about it, though it was clear that something more was happening to him.

It had to be Joshea's Poasian spice.

There was also the moment in the warehouse, when he had failed to create a magical light. He had attributed that to being unable to concentrate in the moment, but given the other evidence, that must not be the case.

Minox held his fingers out in front of his face, and tried to make flame, one of the few things he could do reliably. A pitiful fizzle of sparks spurted from his hand.

Joshea's theory held. The Poasian spice had given him mastery over his magic, removed it from his concern.

A thought jolted across his mind. He had been focusing too much on the magic with these murders. The fact that the victims were mages was important, certainly, but the other specific elements might be just as important. More important, even. He needed to move past the loss of Missus Rainey and consider every possibility.

He went back into the stationhouse, and bounded up the stairs to the inspectors' floor. "Nyla," he announced as soon as he saw his cousin. "I will be in need of your deft and able assistance."

She stood up straight, her sour expression quickly melting away. "Of course. What can I do for you?"

"Can you acquire a map of the neighborhood?"

"Of course," she said.

"Bring it to my desk, with all possible haste." He went back to his slateboards. It was time to work out each murder, every step, until the illuminating details became clear.

Chapter 27

SATRINE DIDN'T WALK BACK HOME. She didn't even cross the river. She just shuffled through Inemar, every familiar sight burning a hole in her throat.

She didn't have a plan. She needed to figure out how to survive. She had to work, that was clear, but her options were poor. Up on the north side, she might be able to get a clerk position of some sort, or secretary. At best something like that would pay ten crowns a week. Seven or eight was more likely.

She'd have to pull Rian from school, put her to work. Apprenticeship of some sort. That might bring enough in to pay for Caribet's tuition. At least one of her daughters might get to university. Move out of the apartment and take a low-rent flop in Inemar, or saints help her, somewhere farther west. Maybe Rian having the Tullen boy's attention wasn't the worst thing.

The real truth was most of her problems could be solved by smothering her husband.

She shook that out of her head. She'd choose meeting sailors on the docks before that.

Satrine looked up. Her feet had led her over to Saint Limarre's. That was surprising. Why had she wandered this way?

Three cloistresses swept the front steps, including Sister Alana. She stopped her work and approached Satrine. "You here as a repentant sinner, or as a stick?"

"I don't know about repentant."

Alana smiled. "We all have a bit of sinner in us. So why are you here?"

"Not sure." She sat down on the steps. "I don't know what the blazes I'm doing."

One of the other cloistresses gasped. Alana shooed them off and sat down next to her.

"I notice you don't have the vest on. Have you already quit?"

"Failed. Caught for the fraud that I am."

"Hardly. I know all about frauds. You definitely are not one."

"You don't know what you're talking about."

"Then tell me," Alana said. She closed her eyes for a moment. "May our voices be heard only by God and the saints, for our words are for no one else."

Satrine bit her lip to keep herself from scoffing. "I wasn't looking for absolution."

"You didn't realize you were," Alana said. "But the saints lead us where we need to be."

This time Satrine did scoff. "I seriously doubt this is where I need to be."

Alana sat quietly for a moment. "How did you first leave the corner?"

"I can't talk about that," Satrine said.

"I'm bound to silence by the rite," Alana said. "And I doubt you want to risk damnation by ignoring me."

Satrine couldn't argue with that. At least, she didn't have the urge to. Alana was right about one thing, she needed to unburden her soul. "I was . . . recruited by Druth Intelligence."

"Interesting. Why did they choose you?"

"What do you mean?"

"It seems the obvious question. Even presuming Intelligence needed a tough street girl for some reason, why were you the one they chose?"

Satrine pulled at a lock of her red hair. "A Waish

quia—princess—died suddenly while studying in Maradaine. And I was her perfect twin."

Alana's eyes went wide. For a moment, Satrine saw the little girl she had known years ago. "They replaced her with you?"

"As the *quia*, I gathered information, charmed lords, and slit a few throats when asked to."

"Why?"

Satrine hadn't thought much about those particular days for a while. "I'm told that I kept the right clan on the Waish throne."

"'Right' according to whom?"

"According to Druth Intelligence. We were at war at the time, remember?"

"I remember," Alana said. "It's why I had no father or brothers."

Satrine mused. Her father had always been a mystery that her mother had never shed much light on. Satrine imagined he might have been a Waish trader, or even a nobleman. After all, how else could a Maradaine street girl look just like a Waish princess? In her years in Waisholm, she often idly wondered whenever she talked to a man of a certain age if he had been the one.

"Same," she lied. Dead soldier had always been her mother's story, until she found a new living one to run off with. "And I did my part, too. By tricking our closest allies. Not exactly the authority of God and the saints, hmm?"

"You were Tricky Trini."

"Wasn't much worse than life down here, really. Did what had to be done. Instead of getting by and keeping my stomach, I flirted and listened and killed. As a Waish noblewoman."

"How did an Inemar street girl pull that off?"

Satrine put on her highborn Waish accent. "After intensive training."

Alana cackled in delight. "That's incredible."

Satrine switched to a regal Druth accent. "It really is quite amazing. With the right tone and manners you can fool just about anyone into believing that you are a person of substance."

"Is that what they taught you?"

A thought crossed Satrine's mind, and her heart sunk. "It would be so easy, you know," she said, returning to her current normal accent. "I could just walk away, invent some documents, become a baroness or something. Live off the good graces of a fellow noble."

"It just occurred to you." Alana stated it as a matter of fact.

"I could only do it if I were alone. Abandon Loren and the girls. I would be—I'm probably damned just for thinking it."

Alana shrugged. "I never took stock in sins of thought, myself. Saints know, it is our actions that define us."

"My actions are pretty damning. Falsified documents, pretended to be a stick."

"From what I've heard, you didn't pretend that. You did the job well."

"What did you hear?"

"I heard some dirty sticks were running a blood pit, children fighting dogs."

"Sick bastards," Satrine said. Her stomach twisted again just thinking of it. She knew people loved to see fights, but making children do it? That was grotesque.

"And that a skirt stick called Trick chased down the boss of it and dragged him off the street." Sister Alana giggled. "That's what they're saying. And that, in my opinion, is what a real constable does."

"Well, you and God and the saints. The commissioner has a different opinion." Satrine got to her feet. "So, Sister, you've heard my plea. Do I get absolution, or am I damned?"

Sister Alana stood up, brushing off her cloak. "A long time ago, a thirteen-year-old girl pulled four boys off of me and chased them away with a piece of glass. As far as this earthly agent is concerned, that girl will always have absolution." She kissed Satrine on both cheeks.

"I appreciate the blessing," Satrine said.

"Good." Alana looked back at the other two cloistresses, who had finished the sweeping and looked put out. "I should return to my more mundane devotions. And you to yours."

"Thank you," Satrine said. "I still have to figure out what I should do."

"Do something for yourself," Sister Alana said. "I think you deserve a small ministration of selfishness."

Satrine laughed. "I just might." As soon as she said it, she realized exactly what she wanted.

———◆·◆———

The maps did not help. Minox had noted the three murder sites, and while he could note patterns, there were too many possible patterns to be of much use. He drew circles of equidistance. He drew out four-pointed crosses, five- and six-pointed stars. All he was able to narrow down was that the killer, and the next murder, were likely to be in the southeast of Inemar.

This was not helpful.

Walking through the necessary actions was not helpful, at least doing it alone on the inspectors' floor. Nyla did her best to help him, but she did not have Missus Rainey's instincts. Also she had other duties that she needed to attend to.

Sketches of the three murder sites, provided by Leppin's charcoal-man, did not bring further insights. The fact that the killer made use of sewer tunnels to move about the city without notice was clear, but did not make narrowing points down any easier.

He did work out that the killer could perform each murder alone, given sufficient strength. Again, this did not yield any revelations.

Minox's head pounded. The knock to his skull was not helping his thought process. And he wasn't hungry. He had always considered the hunger a distraction, but now its absence was even more so. He didn't feel like he was in his own skin.

He needed to stop thinking in spirals. Focus on the specifics he had, go through every detail, piece by piece. He tacked the maps and the sketches up on the slateboards and sat back down.

Evoy would probably look at the board and announce the killer's name in half a click. Minox wondered if he could let his mind drop into the same snakehole, just for a moment, and see things the way his cousin did.

He shook the thought off. He had to stay focused, clear of purpose.

The killer had a purpose, a plan. The information had to be in what he already knew. Two killed by removing their hearts, both in the same Circle. One, from a different Circle, hands removed and eyes cut out. An alley off Jent, a private house on Downing, and a church on Silver. The connections had to make logical sense to the killer.

The killer. Knowledgeable about magic. Meticulous planner, well prepared. Clear of purpose.

Very clear of purpose. He could have killed Satrine Rainey if he had wanted to. For that matter, Minox himself. Or the wagon driver and Inspector Mirrell. The priest he used as a hostage he had only injured, just enough to cause distraction. He had quite deliberately not taken more lives than the ones he specifically intended. He was able to fight past two patrolmen—and a cloistress—without using lethal force. The man was clearly gifted in the fighting arts. Minox had seen plenty of evidence of that in the carriage.

Not gifted in fighting arts. Trained.

A memory clicked. Joshea had said it last night.

His unit had been decommissioned a few weeks ago.

Which meant Joshea wasn't the only soldier who had recently come back home.

Nyla came to his desk with a cup of tea. "Have you figured something out?"

The revelation must have been clear on his face. "Perhaps so. Please tell the captain that I am off to follow up on a lead. If my theory holds, I should return with a short list of potential suspects." He gave a brief nod of thanks, and raced out of the inspectors' floor.

◆━◆━◆

After some searching, Satrine found Plum's Books. The narrow shop was easy to miss—a tiny, faded sign hung over a plain wooden door, the rest of the storefront featureless brick. Absently, Satrine opened the door, jangling a hidden bell, and went in.

She realized that in her childhood, she had never entered the shop. There was something funny about that, she thought, since she owed so much to Old Man Plum and his book-throwing temper. The place was crammed with books, every shelf nearly bursting, and the multiple shelves forming a small maze that obscured the back of the store from her view.

"Can I help—oh, Inspector!" Nerrish Plum emerged from the shelves. "Why are . . . is there something you need?"

"Not inspector right now, Mister Plum," Satrine said. No need to burden him with further details.

"So you are here as a customer!" His face brightened. "There are never enough of those."

Satrine glanced around the shelves. "Business not what it should be?"

"No, it's exactly what it should be, given that I have a bookshop on this corner. It's just that it's hardly what I would like it to be."

Satrine noticed Plum's marriage bracelet. "Enough for you and your family to get by, though?"

Plum apparently felt her gaze, and he wrapped his hand around his bracelet. "It's just me, but yes. My wife passed a few years ago." He let out a deep sigh, and then widened his smile. "No need to go into that, though. You are looking for a book."

Satrine knew she shouldn't be buying anything. Every coin in her pocket was sacred at this point, not a tick should be wasted. But then she realized what she wanted, what she needed, and she knew she deserved one last frivolous expense. Something to save her life again.

"I cannot find my copy of *Lost Poems of the Sarani*," she said. "I was hoping to get a new one."

Plum's eyes widened, just for a moment. "Yes, of course. We discussed that briefly the other day. My grandfather threw that book at you."

"So perhaps it's finally time I pay for it," Satrine said.

Plum nodded, and went in the back. "It is a powerful book," he said as he disappeared from view. "I can imagine the words had quite an effect on you."

"You have no idea," Satrine said.

Plum came back out, book in hand. "But I do. I have found . . . I found quite a lot of solace in this book." His nimble fingers danced through the pages, well-practiced at finding his place. He smiled—a sad, melancholic smile—as he looked at the page. "But I think I've gotten what I need from it, and it needs a new home. I have a feeling that you are the right person for that." He closed the book and handed it to her.

"How much?"

"I would like to tell you no charge—"

"I couldn't possibly take it for free."

"And, unfortunately, nor could I afford to pass up a paying customer. Seven ticks, I think, is a fine balance of generosity and necessity."

Seven ticks was only a hair above outright theft, but Satrine wasn't in a position to insist on paying more. Even the seven ticks were more than she should be spending.

"Deal, Mister Plum." She held the book close to her chest, while taking the coins out of her pocket. "Thank you."

"I hope you get as much out of it as I did," he said.

Satrine gave him a final nod of her head and left the store, the bell jingling as she opened the door. She started walking with purpose, toward the bridge and back to home, all the while thumbing through the worn pages, catching snippets of the familiar verses.

◆━━◆�◆━━◆

Minox ran at full tilt to the Brondars' butcher shop. It was crowded this morning, customers shouting out their orders while all four Brondars shouted back, chopping and cutting meat.

"Joshea!" Minox called, trying to push through the crowd. Joshea was focused on his work, as were his brothers.

Minox didn't want to waste further time. He pulled out his whistle and gave it a shrill blast.

Everyone stopped.

"Blazes, Inspector!" the elder Brondar shouted. "What you trying to do?"

"I really do apol—"

Joshea's father's face turned deep red, and he shook his knife in Minox's direction. "You think you can come into a man's business and just disrupt—"

"Pop," Joshea said, stepping forward. "I'm sure—"

"I'm blazing well sure that the sticks aren't leaving us alone!"

The customers all cheered, far too heartily for Minox's taste.

"I didn't mean to cause—"

"It don't matter what you meant to do!"

"Get out, stick!" one of the customers shouted.

"Leave them be!" another followed.

Minox's hand went reflexively to his belt.

"I just have some questions."

"More questions," Brondar said. "For Joshea. Still hassling him?"

"No, it's not—"

"Pop, it's fine—"

"Get out!" a customer screamed, grabbing Minox by the vest.

Minox drew out his handstick, ready to club down the citizen, but Joshea had leaped over the counter and tackled the man to the ground.

The crowd lunged at Joshea and Minox, hands clawing and pawing at both of them. Minox couldn't understand how the situation had turned so ugly so quickly.

He brought down his handstick on one arm that had gotten a grip on him, a resounding crack that dropped its owner. Another person got in a blow at Minox's head, soft punch glancing. Minox struck back across his jaw.

Two more people grabbed hold of his shoulders, tried to push him at the door. A fist came rushing past Minox's head, knocking one of his attackers clean down: Joshea at his back. A smile naturally came to Minox's mouth as he grabbed his other attacker and spun him out of the shop.

"Oy!" Brondar senior shouted. "Stop brawling in my shop!"

Joshea's brothers had jumped into the fray, grabbing

the patrons and casually tossing them out the door. They both had expressions of solid glee on their faces, as if they could hardly care about why they were fighting, as long as they got to fight. In moments, Minox and the Brondars had cleared the shop floor.

"Now we got no customers!" the father shouted.

"Oy, Pop," Jonner said. "Serves you right for raising a smell over the inspector coming in here."

Joshea brushed off Minox's vest. "You all right?"

"Fine," Minox said. "I really had no intention of causing such disruption."

"Folks are in a state," Joshea said.

"And they don't like sticks," the father said. "For good cause."

"I assure you, I only am looking for information that I hope Joshea can help me with."

Joshea's father scowled, and put down his cleaver. "Go ahead, then."

Joshea's face froze. Minox understood his fear, especially since his friend had no idea what Minox would ask. Minox also understood that he had to phrase things delicately, as Joshea's family might have no idea that they met the night before.

"I believe that the murders I've been investigating were committed by someone with military training. A former soldier."

"Come on, now, stick!" Gunther said. "You're not really not going to keep at us—"

"Please let me finish," Minox said, holding up his hands. "I am making no accusations to any member of your family."

"Go on," the father said.

"Joshea, when you were discharged, was anyone else discharged at the same time? Anyone who came back to this neighborhood?"

The other Brondars looked to Joshea. Joshea nodded. "Yes, there are a few others."

"Then I'll need their names."

Satrine didn't reach her home until after the noon bells. The door was unlatched, which Satrine was grateful for, as she still wasn't carrying her key.

"Missus Abernand?" Satrine called out. "Are you here?"

Missus Abernand came out of the kitchen. "What are you doing here this early?"

Satrine shrugged. "Things didn't work out today."

Missus Abernand scowled. "That's not too good."

"No, it's not. How is he?"

"He just ate some broth. Half the bowl got down his throat, at least."

Satrine nodded. "Good." She managed to put on a smile. "I know I owe you some money, Missus Abernand."

Missus Abernand walked over to her stairwell. "I'll be up on the roof hanging the laundry. Go sit with him."

"But—"

"Sit with your husband, Satrine."

Missus Abernand left Satrine alone.

Loren lay awake in the bed, propped up with pillows. He looked comfortable, even as his dead eyes hung toward the corner of the room. She placed the poetry book on the bedside table and kissed his forehead.

"So I'm back," she said. "I thought it would . . . it doesn't matter. I rolled it up. I wanted . . . would you believe, it was Rian and that stupid rich boy? I got up in his face, and he went to his father. And his father called on Wendt. So my whole web fell to pieces."

Her stomach churned. The memory of the morning drummed again and again in her skull.

"And they thought they were doing me a favor, can you believe it? Sitting there in the captain's office, smoking and laughing. Offering me a clerkship. Five rutting crowns a week. I told the captain and Wendt to go roll themselves."

Loren made a gurgling noise. She wanted to believe it was laughter.

"So that's it, then," she said, sitting on the side of the bed. Loren's head turned toward her, most likely just from her weight shifting the bed. She smiled at him, as if that meant anything to him. "But the day over in Inemar wasn't a complete failure. I did get a book. I know I shouldn't have, but . . . I needed something for me. You couldn't blame me for that. Tomorrow we'll . . . I'll figure out tomorrow when tomorrow comes."

She picked up the book. "Would you like me to read one to you? When I was a girl I must have read all of these a hundred times." She opened the book, it naturally falling on a page where the spine had cracked slightly. One of the love poems, possibly a favorite of Plum's. He had even written a note on the margin.

> *Our love, our passion,*
> *Lasts beyond this lifetime*
> *Life everlasting, love everliving*
> *Paired hearts lifted up on wings of fire*
> *You hold me, hands as strong as stone*
> *You gaze deep into me with eyes of light*
> *No ring keeps us apart,*
> *Body and blood forever joined*
> *Reborn in the blaze of a setting sun.*

Satrine stopped reading. The words, ancient and familiar, suddenly clicked into new patterns.

Paired hearts. Wings of fire.

Hands and eyes. Light and Stone.

Plum had crossed out the word *ring* and written in *circle*.

No circle.

Uncircled.

Welling.

———◆———

The bell above the shop door jangled as Minox came in. The third and final person Joshea had given him—the first two Minox had easily dismissed as being unlikely suspects as soon as he met them—worked in a convenient enough location to all three murder sites. That alone wasn't damning, as Minox could say the same thing about Joshea, or anyone else in this block of the neighborhood.

"Can I help you?" a voice called out from the back of the shop.

"City Constabulary, sir," Minox responded. "I have a few questions for you, if it's no trouble."

"No trouble at all, Inspector." Nerrish Plum emerged from behind a shelf of books. "In fact your timing couldn't have been more perfect."

Chapter 28

"**M**ISSUS ABERNAND!" SATRINE POUNDED up the stairs to the roof. "Missus Abernand!"

"What is it?" The woman was already in the door-frame, wet shirts in her hand. "Is Loren all right?"

"He's fine," Satrine said. Of course, that would be what Missus Abernand would think would be wrong. "I'm going to have to go back out."

"Something happen? Another job?"

"No, it's . . . I think my partner is in danger."

"Partner?" Missus Abernand clearly didn't understand what Satrine was talking about.

"Inspector Welling."

"I thought you weren't an inspector anymore."

"No, but—"

"You need to worry about your own right now." Missus Abernand went back out to the roof. Satrine followed after her.

"Look, I figured it out, the murders, the poem . . ."

"I just don't see why it concerns you. They got rid of you."

"It's not about the job, it's about—"

"Remember you do still owe me, Satrine."

"Why am I arguing this with you?" Satrine said. "You'll get your money, don't worry. Please just keep an eye on Loren. I'll be back as soon as I can."

Satrine didn't wait for a response. Missus Abernand

had enough of guilt-driven sense of responsibility that she would do the job, regardless. She'd be resentful as all blazes later, but she would do it. Satrine raced down the steps and out the front door.

———◆◆———

"You just recently finished a stint in the army?" Minox asked. Plum nodded, only giving Minox a portion of his attention.

"If three years could be considered a 'stint,' Inspector," Plum said. "I'm not entirely sure of the semantics."

"And on your return, you opened up the bookstore again?"

"My mother had, technically, kept the store operational, though she had been rather negligent in its care. It has taken quite a lot of work on my part to get things back to where they are now." He slumped around the shadowed stacks, his body hunched slightly. Probably spent inordinate time reading at a desk.

"A family business, then?"

Plum nodded. "Indeed, Inspector."

"A family passion, even?"

"For books?" Plum shrugged. "For knowledge, definitely. You know, Inspector, we met briefly the other day, if you don't recall."

Minox's memory did not fail him. "Your grandfather was instrumental in Missus Rainey starting an education."

"Exactly. He threw a book at her. Did she tell you about that book?" He giggled slightly and went to another bookshelf. The man's spindly fingers danced along the shelf, even as his feet shuffled idly along the row.

"I'm afraid not, Mister Plum." Minox was shocked that this slight, scholarly man had ever lasted in the army. "What drove you to—"

"It's a very interesting book, you see. Most people don't realize, the poet didn't actually write the poems."

"Very interesting, I'm sure. You were in the army for three years?"

"Yes," Plum said. He came out from the shelves, a

thick metal-spined book in his hands. "I enlisted shortly after the death of my wife."

"My cond—"

"Did you know how she died, Inspector Welling?"

Minox wasn't sure how this was relevant. "I am afraid I didn't even know . . ."

"Of course you didn't. That's not your fault. You had no reason to know."

"If I may continue my questions—"

"No more questions," Plum said. He threw the book at Minox, with surprising speed.

Minox raised his hand and instinctively drew on magic to deflect the book flying at his head.

There was no magic to draw on. Nothing happened.

The book cracked across his head. He dropped to his knees, dazed and spinning.

Plum was already on him, any sign of stoop or hunch now gone. He slammed a hard boot into Minox's face.

Blackness encroached Minox's mind; he couldn't force himself back up. He couldn't make his body react.

He was vaguely aware of Plum flipping his inert form over, quick hands binding him with a rope. "You are not at fault, Inspector. But you are exactly what I need."

Then it all went dark.

———◆◀▶◆———

Satrine didn't walk or trudge back to Inemar; she ran. She ran like Intelligence had trained her, years ago. Slow breathing, steady pace. Scanning ten steps ahead, dodging or leaping anything in her way. Get as far as she can, as fast as she can, without wearing herself out.

If she was reading the poem right, if she wasn't crazy, the killer—Plum, Nerrish Plum, damn it all—would kill an Uncircled mage by sunset. And Plum knew Welling was one. The pieces lined up.

The usual hawkers and buskers at the Inemar bank of the bridge must have seen her coming; no one got in her face or tried to sell her any blasted thing. She leaped down the stairs and hit the cobblestone running.

Her knees were really going to hate her for this later.

She raced, weaving through people and horses and pedalcarts and stacked crates. She didn't slow down one bit as she approached the stationhouse. Her eyes moved past the outer gate, focused on the door, so she didn't notice until it was too late that the patrolmen at the gate had grabbed her by the crooks of her arms.

"What do you think you're doing, Missus?" one of them asked.

"Let go!" Satrine yanked her arms free. They didn't give her any fight, but moved in front of her. She stepped toward the door, but they blocked her, hands resting on their sticks. "I need to get in there."

"Oh, I don't think you do, Missus."

"I do, I'm—"

"We know who you are, Missus Rainey," the blond one on the left said. Iorrett, by his badge. "We know what you've done."

Satrine didn't have time for their petty junk. "You don't understand."

His partner, a doughy, meat-faced stick with Leckly on his badge, gave an ugly smile. "She prob'ly thinks, what with us being just footpatrol, we don't understand much."

"We understand plenty, we do," Iorrett said. "Lieutenant Haimen is one of ours, you know."

Leckly nodded. "He's a good man, wife and family. Not that you'd care."

"He was dirty—"

"We understand dirty, Missus Rainey. You're a cheat and a fake," Iorrett said. "Thinks she's too good to work as a clerk."

"My sister clerks the front at the Gelmoor house," Leckly said. He shoved Satrine's shoulder. "You think you better than my sister?"

Satrine beat down the urge to smash her fist into Leckly's face. "No, I—"

"Course she does." Iorrett stepped in close, nose almost touching Satrine's. She made a point of not cringing away from his hot onion breath. "Fake thinks she should skip the street and get specked right away."

"I didn't skip the street," Satrine muttered.

"Right, Tricky. Being a rat gang's doxy don't really count."

Satrine let her old accent flow through. "I ain't never doxied. But you'll want to get your nose out of my face."

"Make me," Iorrett said in a hot whisper. "And we'll have an excuse to iron you for the night."

Satrine took a step back. "I just need to talk to Inspector Welling. Then I'll go."

"You don't get nothing you need," Leckly said.

"What about Inspector Welling?" she asked. "He needs to know what I've got to tell him."

Leckly laughed. "Whatever you got to say, Jinx has probably figured out already. He's a stick who's earned his specks."

"Look, I just . . ."

"Really simple, Trick," Iorrett said. "You're only getting in one way. Ironed and heading in the box."

Briefly Satrine considered the merits. She could make enough of a ruckus that Welling would hear that she'd been put into holding. Or Captain Cinellan. It wouldn't be pleasant, but at least she'd be able to get them to hear her out. And it would be very satisfying to give these two street sticks a real reason to throw irons on her.

That was assuming it wasn't already too late. She couldn't risk it. She took two more steps back. "Iorrett. Leckly. I'll remember that."

"Remember well," Iorrett said.

She turned back to the street. Blazes.

Missus Wolman was in her fast wrap stand across the street. The woman glanced over at Satrine, and with a flick of her cooking tool, waved her over. Skeptical, Satrine took a step closer. Missus Wolman gestured more stridently. Satrine approached the cooking shack.

"Can I help you?" Satrine asked.

"Doubt it," Missus Wolman said. She pointed to the ground. "But I've got this one hanging about my skirts here."

Satrine leaned over the counter. A Constabulary page crouched at Missus Wolman's legs.

"Phillen." Satrine put on her voice of bemused chastisement. "What are you doing down there?"

"Can't let them see me talking to you, Missus Rainey," Phillen said. "They'll give me the haze if they do."

"I understand, Phillen," Satrine whispered. She already knew she had a black mark on her name; even though Phillen had to be exaggerating its severity. Still, if he was willing to help her, she'd take it however he could give it. "I need to talk to Inspector Welling. Can you get him out here?"

"I think so," he said. He slipped out through the back of the shack.

"He's a good sort," Satrine told Missus Wolman after an uncomfortable quiet moment.

"Mmm," Missus Wolman grunted. "It ain't kidneys."

"Pardon?"

"The meat. It ain't kidneys. Or rancid for that matter."

"Then what is it?" Satrine asked.

"That's my secret."

Satrine leaned in. "So it's horse, then."

"Don't you insult me, lady," Missus Wolman added a mutter. "Horse ain't cheap, you know."

Phillen returned, sliding out of sight under the counter again. "Inspector Welling ain't inside."

"Are you sure?"

"Miss Pyle said he went out on a lead a while ago. She's actually surprised he's not back."

"A lead on what? The mage killer?"

"I think so," Phillen said.

Blazes. Welling might have already walked into it. Welling might already be dead.

"All right, Phillen, this is what I need you to do. Get back in there, and give word to whoever. The captain, Miss Pyle, Mirrell, or Kellman. Whoever you can. Tell them that I figured it out."

"But if I—"

"I know, Phillen, but Welling's life and reputation are on the line here. You've got to risk it."

"Fair enough," Phillen said. "So what do I tell them you figured out?"

"Two things. One, I think the killer is Nerrish Plum,

the bookshop owner. Two, I think that Inspector Welling is the next intended victim."

Phillen's eyes went wide. "I'll do whatever I can. Count on me, Inspector." He ran off.

Satrine was surprised at how much her heart swelled at being called inspector again. Even if it was a mistake.

She did count on Phillen, but she couldn't imagine getting much help from any of the other inspectors. She had to figure out where Plum would be, where he would take Minox, in the hope of stopping him. She thanked Missus Wolman for her help and left the stand.

There had to be a logic to the locations: alley, chapterhouse, church. It had to be a set, if it only made sense to Plum. Like the poem, a pattern laid out in the ancient text.

Perhaps there was a different poem, one that explained the where of the murders as much as the first revealed the murderer and the victims. She started walking to the store, thumbing through the book, hoping to find some secret treasure in the ancient verses.

She didn't notice the meaty fist until it connected with her face.

She fell onto her back, the book dropping onto the ground.

Satrine's vision was blurred for a moment, until it came into focus on the pudgy face of Idre Hoffer.

"Hello there, Tricky," she said. "It has been a while, hasn't it?"

Chapter 29

SATRINE GOT BACK ON her feet as quick as possible, as Idre picked up the poetry book.

"Still got your nose in this, after all these years?" Idre asked.

"I'm busy, Idre."

"With what? I've been on you for two blocks now. The sticks don't want anything to do with you. Took your vest away."

Satrine lashed out for the book, and Idre tried to pull it away, hold it out of reach. However, Idre was no longer an older girl with speed and muscle over Satrine. Satrine grabbed the woman's wrist and held her fast, plucking the book out of her grasp.

"I don't have time for you." Satrine shoved Idre away, but the large woman did not move easily.

"You don't have time?" Idre spoke with an exaggerated North Maradaine accent, unsubtle in her mockery. She swung a heavy punch at Satrine's face, but Satrine was more than ready this time. She blocked the punch and countered, square in Idre's face.

That felt good.

Idre barely blinked.

"Must have thought it was so funny, lecturing me about my boy. Thought I wouldn't place you, Trick? You think I'm that dumb?" She swung several more punches—

surprisingly fast for such a large woman—Satrine could only block and dodge, unable to get her own shot in.

"Didn't think you cared that much." Satrine shoved the book into the waistline of her pants, and dove under Idre's arm. She didn't have time for this, she should just run the blazes out of there. The sun would set in an hour at most, and if she couldn't find Welling—

She snapped out of her reverie as Idre's heavy boot nearly connected with her chest.

"Cared about those six months," Idre snarled.

Satrine couldn't run. She couldn't hunt down Minox while looking over her shoulder for Idre.

"Six months?" she said. "You mean your little trip to Quarrygate when we were kids?"

"Yes!" Idre snapped. She leaped onto Satrine, hands going for the neck.

Satrine landed a solid punch across Idre's head, but the woman's momentum took them both down into the street. Satrine was vaguely aware of a horse braying, the crunching noise of cart wheels coming to an abrupt stop. Shouts rose up from a crowd circling around them.

Satrine was on her back, Idre straddled over her. She couldn't get any leverage to force the large woman off her, though her arms were free enough to stave off her attacks.

"You got me pinched, you rat!" Idre shouted, swinging wildly. "You ruined my life!"

Satrine landed a hard punch in Idre's chest, followed by another to her chin. This was enough to knock Idre off balance. Satrine rolled to the side to force her off.

"Damn blazes I did!" Satrine shouted, getting to her feet. There was a wall of people circled around them, cheering and hollering.

Idre was up, swinging her fist like a hammer. "I heard you were dead, slag. When I came back, they all said you were dead."

"I just went away." Now Satrine was in her full sense, ready to brawl. Idre wasn't going to get the better of her again.

"Ran away, eh? Couldn't face me." Heavy, wild punches. Nothing touched Satrine.

Satrine dashed into range, throwing two hard jabs at Idre's side. "Never was about you."

She didn't get out in time. Idre got a solid hit across Satrine's jaw. Satrine lashed back, a hard swing out that connected across the side of Idre's head. The big woman went reeling.

The crowd cheered for more.

Satrine leaped at the dazed woman. Despite Idre's bulk, Satrine was able to knock hard against her, throwing her further off balance. Idre took another wild swing. Satrine was nowhere near it.

"All I wanted was you out of my life!" Satrine shouted. "Let it alone!"

She threw another punch, everything she had left in her arm, knocking most of the sense out of Idre. Her old rival dropped to her knees. Satrine kicked Idre in the back, pushing her the rest of the way to be facedown in the street.

Two whistles blew all around her.

"All right, break it up," the familiar voice of Inspector Mirrell droned. He and Kellman came through the crowd, a couple of footpatrol with them.

Kellman nudged the insensible Idre with his boot. "Iron and box this one. Overnight for brawling. She gives you trouble tell her we might pink her for interfering with an inspector's investigation." One patrolman chained Idre's wrists, while the other looked expectantly at Satrine.

"What about her?"

Mirrell and Kellman both had card-playing faces as they circled around her. She couldn't get any sense off of them. "What about her, indeed?" Mirrell said. "You boys don't mind if Darreck and I take something of a personal interest in her, do you?"

"No, sir," said one of the patrolmen, his grin a little too wicked.

"Good," Mirrell said. "And, boys? Let's keep her involvement quiet, all right?"

"Mouse quiet, sir."

"Then let's be about it," Mirrell said. He grabbed Satrine by the arm, and Kellman took the other side, and they led her off into an alley.

If this was what they wanted, Satrine wasn't out of fight yet. As soon as they were out of sight from the street, she wrenched herself free from Mirrell's grasp and pulled up her arm to drive her elbow in his face. He caught her arm again before she could deliver the blow.

"Hey, hey," he whispered. "None of that, now."

"You think I won't fight back?"

"Blazes, Tricky," Kellman said, letting go of her arm. "We already saw what kind of fight back you can give."

"Then . . ."

"Kid said you think Jinx is in trouble. Bookshop guy is the killer?"

Mirrell nodded. "So tell us what you've got."

Satrine pulled the book out of her waistline and started to explain.

<hr />

Consciousness came slow and ugly for Minox, pain coursing through his head. Bit by bit, he became more aware of his circumstances. He had been stripped of his clothes. He was strapped to a metal table, hanging head down at an uncomfortable angle. He felt the same draining sensation he had experienced when he had come into contact with the killer's spikes, but he did not feel like any spikes had been driven into his body. He wondered if the magic effect of the spikes was so profound as to cause actual numbness.

When he finally opened his eyes, he was surprised to see sunlight. Glancing around, best he could, he could not quite determine where the light was coming in. He was in a stone chamber of some sort. The masonry reminded him of his earlier trip through the sewer system.

He finally spotted the source of the sunlight. There was a mirror, lined up with a chimney shaft of some sort, aligned to send the light at him. Meticulous. Ritual. The killer—Nerrish Plum—had his fourth victim.

Minox found his voice. "Plum! Where are you?"

Plum's face appeared in front of Minox's eyes. "No need to scream, Inspector. Also, no purpose. No one other than me will hear you."

"So your purpose is to kill me in another of your ritualized murders," Minox said.

"Indeed," Plum said. He moved around so he could sit on the stone in front of Minox, as if they could have a friendly chat, despite Minox hanging nearly upside down. "You do have a sense of what I'm doing."

"I have a sense it means something to you," Minox said. "But killing four innocent people is nothing but senseless."

"Innocent, really?" Plum gave an uneasy chortle. "I'll grant that you, dear Inspector, probably do not deserve this fate. But the others? They could hardly be called innocent."

"So they did something to deserve what you did?"

"More or less."

"That's why it was easier to kill them, correct?" Minox knew he was trying to catch a rabbit out of the hutch attempting to reason with the man, but he had little other choice, not if he hoped to survive.

"Easier than what? I mean, Harleydale was a challenge, sawing through those hands. Took longer than I thought. But it had to be done. All has to be done."

"But you're hesitating with me."

"Hesitating? Saints, no, Inspector. I'm waiting. There is a difference." He pointed to the mirror. "You have until the sun sets."

"Why, Mister Plum?"

"Well, the ritual has to happen at sunset. I don't make the rules."

"But why the ritual, Mister Plum? What purpose does it serve?"

"Yes, of course," Plum said. "Even facing death, you need to figure out the reason behind it all. It's only natural, I suppose. And an answer is the least you deserve."

Minox struggled to keep himself awake, the draining feeling threatening to pull him back down to inky blackness. He had Plum talking now, and that bought him some leverage. And he did have a morbid curiosity to know how all the murders made sense in Plum's mind.

"Do you know how my wife died, Inspector? It was three years ago, during the Circle Feuds. It happened right on those steps of the Light and Stone house. You did know several local people had been killed in the crossfire of mages fighting each other on the streets."

"I knew, but I didn't know details," Minox said. "So that's why you killed Jaelia Tomar there. Where your wife died."

"Well, that's what it had to be, of course." Plum got to his feet and walked out of Minox's field of vision. "Met and married, dead and buried. That's what I figured out, you see. She died on those steps. Not that anyone was held accountable."

"Charges were filed, and successfully prosecuted—"

"For the whole feud, not for the lives lost, Inspector. Not the individual, precious life ripped too soon from me!"

Plum was agitated. Minox needed to change the tone of the conversation. "Met and married, you said. You met her in that alley?"

"Six years ago. Would you believe, both heading to the backhouses? What a way to start a romance."

"And married at Saint Limarre's?" The locations all made sense now, fitting the mad logic behind the killings. All that remained was his own death here . . . and buried. "Where are we?"

"The underground world beneath our city is fascinating, Inspector. I must confess, I've only scratched away a tiny portion. But this mausoleum dates back to, I think, the fourth century. I may be wrong. And to think, it's a mere thirty feet underground, nearly below my shop." He moved back into vision, taking another look at the mirror. "I will admit, it makes timing the sunset a challenge, but what can you do?"

"Your wife wasn't buried here," Minox asserted.

"No, not originally," Plum said. "But she's been here long enough, I would think." His eyes went to a spot under Minox's head. Minox strained to crane his neck to see. On the ground underneath him lay a shamble of bones, laid out over a chalk-drawn symbol. The symbol, drawn with long, elegant lines, had four points marked with circles. Glass jars sat on three of the circles: two with hearts, one with hands and eyes.

"What the blazes are you doing, Plum?"

"Two hearts, on wings of fire. Hands of stone, eyes of light." Plum approached Minox and ran a finger along his bare chest. "No circle keeps us apart. Body and blood."

The man had clearly lost his mind.

"Mister Plum, I realize that you've suffered a great loss, and it's understandable you wish to enact vengeance upon the Circles that caused your grief. But this won't change what has occurred. Killing me won't bring your wife back to you."

Plum crouched down, face to upside-down face with Minox. "Oh, no, Inspector Welling. That's exactly what it will do."

"That's the craziest thing I've ever heard," Mirrell said.

"I don't disagree," Satrine said.

"It's batty as all blazes," Kellman said. "But it does kind of work, you know?"

"It sounds like one of Jinx's theories, is what I think," Mirrell said. "But these mage murders have been so strange, it would need a Jinx theory to work."

"I'm not saying the poem is anything more than a love poem," Satrine said. "But an unhinged mind might have sought meaning in it, and came up with action to match it."

Mirrell raised an eyebrow. "So you're arguing that this crazy idea is sensible because the killer is crazy?" He glanced over at Kellman.

"That's good enough for me," Kellman said.

"All right, then," Mirrell said. "Let's check out the bookstore."

The door was latched and shades were drawn when they arrived. Satrine looked at the sun. It would be setting in less than an hour. "We don't have a lot of time."

"That may be," Mirrell said. "But we've got limits of what we're allowed to do based on a crazy hunch. Shop is closed."

"It is odd for a shop to be closed this early," Kellman said. He looked around the street. "Nothing else is."

"Odd, sure," Mirrell said. "But not actionable. Sticks got to play by the rules, Tricky. We can't just go into a house or shop without just cause."

"Then it's a good thing I'm not a stick anymore," Satrine said, taking off her coat. She wrapped it around her hand and punched through the glass. She reached through the broken pane to unlatch the door.

"Why, Inspector Kellman," Mirrell said in a flat voice. "It appears we are observing a possible robbery in progress."

Satrine opened the door and entered the shop. It looked much the same as it had this morning.

"It certainly appears that could be the case," Kellman said from the street outside, matching his partner's tone. "Perhaps we should investigate more closely."

"We would be negligent in our duty to do otherwise," Mirrell said, and entered the shop. "Anything?"

Satrine scanned the floor. Something caught her eye, and she picked it up. "The proverbial nail in the shoe." It was the broken nib from Welling's pipe.

"Not distinctive or damning enough," Mirrell said.

Satrine's eyes went back to the floor. Lines in the dust. Something heavy had been dragged into the back room. Something like a full-grown man.

"This way," she said, following the trail to the back room.

The back room was a cramped office, with a tiny desk and a hole torn into the floor. A rope was tied around the desk that led down the hole. On the desk was a pile of clothes: Constabulary coat and vest, and a belt with crossbow and handstick.

"Blazes," Kellman said. "Jinx really is in trouble."

For once, Satrine wished she hadn't been right.

"Look at all this," Mirrell said, pointing at the wall. Satrine had been so focused on Minox's situation she hadn't even noticed. The wall was covered in papers, small notes and diagrams, maps of the city and the underground tunnels, charcoal sketches of the Tomars, Harleydale, and Welling, other notes in characters Satrine couldn't recognize.

"Blazes," Kellman said. "And I thought Jinx's slateboards were crazy."

Mirrell went over to the rope, drawing his crossbow. "Come on, Darreck. Let's go save our guy."

"Your guy?" Satrine said. "You don't even like him."

"I don't," Mirrell said. "But his heart's Green and Red, and that's all that matters today."

Kellman pulled out his own weapon. "I'll take point."

"I should do that," Satrine said.

Mirrell shook his head. "As you already pointed out, you're not a stick. We can't let you go with us."

"Don't you dare—"

"I'm serious, Rainey. We can't let you go down there with us."

Kellman took the rope and dropped down.

"This isn't right," Satrine said.

"A lot of things aren't," Mirrell said, and he followed after his partner.

Satrine heard them go down, reach the bottom, and walk off. After she couldn't hear them anymore, she decided enough time had passed that she wouldn't be going down with them. She grabbed Welling's belt off the desk, drew his crossbow, and went down after them.

Chapter 30

"LIFE EVERLASTING, LOVE EVERLIVING. It took me so long to understand exactly what the words really were. What had been mistaken as flowery poetry for centuries!" Plum cackled. Minox had never seen someone in such an obvious maniacal state.

"I don't know what you're talking about, Plum, but you can't think that the dead can be brought back."

Plum scrambled over to the metal table, his eyes boring into Minox. "Why not, Inspector?"

"Magic doesn't work that way."

"How do you know that, Inspector? Do you really understand magic, uneducated as you are?"

"If it did, people would bring back the dead all the time."

"All the time?" Plum scoffed. "Because what I'm doing here is just so easy?" A solid punch cracked into Minox's ribs. "Do you have any idea, Inspector, of the amount of work I've done here? The research? The attention to detail? I alone had the awareness to see the power in those words! Words written with divine inspiration. Ritual magic to bring back a lost love!"

Minox struggled to catch his breath. Talking out the lunacy of Plum's intentions was not going to get him anywhere. He had to try a different tactic. He had to do something to escape. At the angle his body was bound, his head hanging down, he couldn't get a good look at how he was held. Getting himself free would prove impossible without knowing the details of his bondage. Even with the knowledge, it might prove he lacked the strength or means to liberate himself. He still felt weakened.

A different tactic. Appeal to the man's pride. "Finding those spikes must have proven quite difficult. And they clearly were necessary to fulfill your plan."

"Spikes?" Plum's voice and demeanor returned to that of a man having a civilized conversation. "Ah, you mean my pins." He chuckled lightly. "My eight fallen pins."

"So there are eight." Minox focused on the number, ignoring the strange bowlpin game reference that Plum made. "You used two of them on each of your other victims, but left them behind."

"No need to be greedy, all things considered. I wasn't going to need each pair after I had used them, and trying to retrieve them would have just put me at risk. Put my plan at risk." He paced away from the table, moving through the beam of diminishing sunlight. "And this was my plan. My knowledge. My research. I took the pins and did what I needed with them."

"Took them?" Minox pressed. "From whom?"

Plum looked at the beam. "I'm afraid some questions must remain unanswered, Inspector Welling. It's just about time for you."

He came over to the table and did something out of Minox's vision. There was a momentary release of the weak feeling running through Minox's body. Plum crouched down in front of Minox's face. He was holding one of the spikes and a hammer. "I really am sorry, Inspector. But I do need your precious blood."

"Wait, Plum. Wait!"

Plum set the spike at Minox's left arm, on the muscle right above the wrist. "Please, Inspector, I need to concentrate. Shallow cut."

He slammed the hammer on the head of the spike.

Minox screamed as he felt the bone crack, though the spike only sliced through the side of it.

"And that's one," Plum said.

A hard snap cracked in the distance, followed by the jangling of a bell.

"Company," Plum said dryly. "Possibly the former Inspector Rainey, if she's clever." He leaned down, cheerily smiling in Minox's face. "I did hate to hand her such vital evidence, but I couldn't afford to pass up a sale. After all, I'll have a wife to support soon."

Struggling, frustrated voices shouted in the distance — male voices. Two of them. Missus Rainey was not present, then. Despite facing his imminent demise, Minox felt some relief. He would hate for Missus Rainey to risk her life, especially as a civilian, in a vain effort to rescue him.

"Not Missus Rainey," Plum mused. His face went pale. "The Brotherhood couldn't possibly have found me, not so soon." He frowned. "It's no matter. Whoever was coming is now trapped."

The voices yelled some more, but not with enough clarity for Minox to make out what they were saying. But he was able to recognize the pitch and timber of the voices: Inspectors Mirrell and Kellman.

Minox would have to reassess his opinion of their investigative skills, even if he was unlikely to survive the next few moments.

— ◆ —

Satrine had been expecting sewer, but she had climbed down nearly twenty feet to a clean, dry tunnel that smelled more of lime and chalk than filth and waste. It was also dark as all blazes, save the thin trickle of flickering light from above. Two pitch-black passages were her only options; from one direction she thought she could hear hushed voices. It might have been Kellman and Mirrell, or something more, or only her imagination. She had Minox's crossbow cocked and loaded, and ventured down the passage.

She had only taken five steps when she heard a horrific snapping sound ahead. The jangling of a bell. Then shouts. Kellman and Mirrell, most definitely this time.

More cries from the two inspectors. Not pain. Not fighting. Annoyance.

That would confirm she was on the right path, then. If they set off some sort of trap or alarm, it would stand to reason Plum would have been the one to set it. It also stood to reason there would be more than one.

More annoyed yells from the inspectors. She could make out a few words from Mirrell. They were definitely trapped somehow.

Each step became cautious and deliberate, every sense open for the brush of a tripwire or slightest shift in the stones. She couldn't afford to get stuck. Not if Welling was still alive.

She let the shouts lead her. The blackness lightened slightly up ahead. She hadn't triggered anything.

Mirrell was still shouting, making demands to be released. Satrine thought this was futile until she was close enough to see the situation. The two of them had been pinned into an alcove by a large spring-loaded grate. Neither of them had much mobility, but Kellman was trying to crack the wooden edge of the grate. Mirrell shouted to cover the sound of Kellman's kicks.

Satrine came into the light, putting a finger to her lips. Kellman pointed to the grate, signaling her to try to find a release of some sort.

"I have to finish this," Plum shouted from the lit chamber nearby. "If you stop me, you'll never get the list. You understand?"

Satrine glanced around the mechanism of the grate. There wasn't enough light to see a way to release it, and she didn't dare start poking things, lest it trigger another trap.

"List?" Mirrell shouted back. On Kellman's confused look, he shrugged. "I'm going to list every bone in your body I'm going to break!" Kellman brought his massive leg down on the wooden frame, but he couldn't move enough to make much use of his strength.

Satrine kicked the frame in the same place, splintering the wood some. It didn't make much difference.

"No, Plum, please."

Minox's voice.

Kellman and Mirrell would have to wait.

Gingerly, she stepped to the edge of the passage before it opened up to the lit chamber. Crossbow up, she reflexively checked it one more time. She peeked her head around the edge of the wall.

Minox was bound, naked, to some strange table, hanging upside-down. One of those blasted spikes had been driven into his arm, and his blood was dripping onto a pile of bones and other human parts. Quite a lot of blood already.

Plum had his back to her, but he was about to drive another spike into Welling's other arm.

No time, she spun out and took the shot. She hit Plum in the upper shoulder, forcing him to drop his hammer. Satrine charged at him as he cried out. He turned toward her, snarling. She hurled the crossbow at him as she closed the distance, drawing the handstick.

"No!" Plum shouted, dodging the crossbow. He quickly turned back to Welling, placing the spike in position as he crouched to pick up the hammer.

Satrine crashed into him, battering his side with the handstick as they fell to the floor, sliding in blood and bones.

"You can't . . ." Plum wheezed. She grabbed his bad arm and tried to force it behind his back, get her weight on top of him. He was too strong, too wiry, and he flipped around to face her.

She drove her stick into his chin. "Stay." Again. "Down."

"Please." Plum's tone mixed desperation with rage. "Don't."

Too late, Satrine saw he still had the spike in his hand. She tried to grab it, but he wrenched free and stabbed it into her leg. She lost her grip on his other arm, and he pushed her off of him.

He tried to take the spike back, but she pulled her leg

away from him, rolling away from Welling. Despite the pain, she yanked it out of her leg.

"Give me that," Plum snapped, coming closer.

Impulsively, she threw the spike down to the passage she had come from. Plum lashed out, striking her across the chin, and ran after it.

He had gone into the passage. "You've ruined it! You've ruined everything!"

"Sorry," Satrine said, grabbing him by the back of his coat. She yanked him off his feet and threw him onto his back. He swept his leg out, knocking her right where he had stabbed her before. She fell back against the wall.

"You've lost this fight before," Plum said.

"Still breathing," Satrine said, throwing a feinted punch to his right side, making him dodge to the left. "Still here."

Another feinted punch, but he grabbed her arm and twisted it behind her. "Not much longer, Missus Rainey."

She kicked her feet up off the ground, gaining purchase on the wall. With everything she had in her good leg, she pushed back, slamming Plum up against the grate.

Kellman's arm shot out, wrapping around Plum's neck, holding him fast to the grate. Mirrell, from his vantage, was able to grab one of Plum's arms. In a moment, he had his irons out, one shackled on Plum's wrists.

"You got him?" Satrine asked.

"Get to Minox," Mirrell said. "Go!"

Satrine wasted no time, limping back to the strange table. More blood had pooled up under the table. Minox looked pale and drawn. Satrine fumbled at the straps, unbuckling Welling until he was loose. "I've got you, Minox," she said. "I'm getting you out of here."

"Spike," Minox whispered.

Satrine grabbed hold of the head of the spike and tore it out, fresh blood coming with it, and threw it to the other side of the room. She helped him onto the ground.

"Are you all right?" she asked. "You look . . ."

"Horrible, I'm certain," he said. "Is Plum dead?"

"Kellman and Mirrell have him," she said. "Look at

me, Minox. I'm going to get you out of here." She tore off a strip from her slacks, already ripped from being stabbed, and wrapped it around his arm. She glanced back at her leg. Blood was flowing from her own wound. She'd need to bandage that as well soon.

His eyes focused on her. "You aren't wearing a vest, Missus Rainey," he said woozily.

"No, I'm . . ." She wrapped her leg. "I'm not an inspector anymore."

"The facts do not agree," Minox said, glancing around the room. He looked back at her. "You found Plum."

"Just in time, too," she said. She stood up. She could put weight on it, but it hurt like blazes. "Can you walk?"

"Give me your coat," he said weakly. "Allow me some small degree of dignity here, Missus Rainey."

She gave it to him, and he wrapped himself in it as best as he could. He glanced at her again. "You're not wearing a vest, Missus Rainey."

"You said that already," she said. "We need to get you to a doctor."

"Yes, I believe that's right," he said. He shook his head slightly as they both stumbled down to the passage. "Quite extraordinary, indeed."

Chapter 31

ONCE OUT OF THE BOOKSHOP and in the street, Kellman and Mirrell didn't even bother calling the lockwagon for Plum. Keeping him ironed by wrists and feet, they half dragged him to the stationhouse, making a shameless public spectacle of the event. Satrine fashioned a sling for Welling's arm out of his vest and helped him walk a few paces behind them. Satrine suspected he did not wish to be assisted in any such way, but he voiced no objections. Given the condition of her leg, she needed his assistance as much as he needed hers.

"Call the Yellowshields," Minox said. "For both our sakes."

Mirrell blew the call on his whistle, but their march to the station continued. A small crowd formed around the parade, people shouting and calling out. One man stepped out from the crowd. "Inspector Welling! Inspector Welling!"

Welling whispered low in Satrine's ear. "Mister Rencir from the *South Maradaine Gazette*."

"Nothing right now," Satrine said, holding up a hand to the man.

"But what's happening, who have you arrested here?"

"This is not a matter for the press yet," Satrine said.

"You're Satrine Rainey. Tricky!" Rencir said, pointing

an accusing finger. "The woman who faked her way into being an inspector!"

"Word gets around," Satrine muttered.

"Surprisingly fast," Welling responded.

"If you're a fraud, why are you helping the Constabulary with—"

"She's not a fraud."

Satrine had expected that Welling would say something along those lines. Which was why she was so surprised that Inspector Mirrell was the one saying it. He had left the escorting of Plum in Kellman's hands and crossed back to confront Rencir.

"Three murders were solved, and the life of an inspector was saved, thanks to Missus Rainey. She's blazing well a model citizen is what she is." He poked two fingers into Rencir's chest. "And I blazing well better not see anything different in your newssheet."

Rencir nodded and slunk away, and Mirrell grabbed Welling's arm. As they continued, Satrine noticed another face in the crowd, hanging back from the action but far more intense in gaze. It was the youngest of the Brondar sons from the butcher shop. Joshea. He was entirely focused on Welling. Satrine glanced back to her former partner and saw that he was giving Joshea the same degree of attention. There seemed to be an unspoken moment between the two, and then Joshea nodded and slipped off into the crowd.

He didn't figure into the case anymore. If he and Welling were friends, that was their business.

Yellowshields finally arrived. They went to work laying Satrine and Welling out on the shields. There was a brief argument between the Yellowshields and Mirrell over where to take them, which Mirrell won out, insisting that Satrine and Welling be brought to the stationhouse's infirmary ward.

Once in the stationhouse, there was a whirlwind of clamor and action, shouts from the desk clerks and floor sergeants and all three inspectors, everything happening in such rapid succession that Satrine didn't entirely realize when Plum had been taken off to the holding cell, or when she and Welling had been escorted to the infirmary ward. She had barely been aware of the cup of Fuergan whiskey that had been shoved into her hand before the dour ward matron started sewing up the gash in her leg. She glanced over to the cot next to her, where a surgeon was hard at work setting Welling's arm. They had already stitched the gash in his head, but the bruise surrounding it was ugly. The ward nurse muttered something about how Welling must have a thick skull.

"Lucky the break was clean," the surgeon grunted. "Else we'd have to cut it off."

"Let's avoid that if we can, Doctor," Captain Cinellan said, approaching their two cots with Protector Hilsom right behind him. Mirrell and Kellman hung back by the doorframe, both waving off the attempts by the other matrons to tend to their scrapes.

"I'd prefer that as well," Welling said.

"So we now have our mage killer caught and locked up," Cinellan said with an appreciative nod. "Tomorrow morning he'll be escorted to Quarrygate. You'll be excused from that duty, Welling. Though, technically, his arrest will go to the credit of Mirrell and Kellman."

Cinellan hadn't even glanced at Satrine, and she didn't speak up. Mirrell and Kellman both looked distinctly uncomfortable with the credit.

Welling, apparently, had focused on another point. "Quarrygate? Without trial?"

"No need," Hilsom said. "Fortunately, Mister Plum has spared us the trouble by giving us an eager confession. I'm recommending ten years of incarceration, which I'm confident the city court will uphold."

Welling sat up hard, only prevented from getting off the cot by the clamp holding his arm in place. "Ten years? For three murders and the attempted murder of an MC inspector?"

Hilsom shrugged. "Not ideal, but it saves us from public trial that would inevitably involve members of various mage Circles."

"And no one wants that," Welling growled, staring hard at his clamped arm.

"Keep still," the surgeon said. "Or you will lose it."

Cinellan clapped a friendly arm on Welling's good shoulder. "What no one wants, Welling, is another Circle Feud."

"Was that an issue?" Welling asked.

Hilsom spoke up. "It was possible. Mister Olivant tells me that the two Circles were in a state, and Light and Stone were incensed by losing their chapter leader. Things could have gone badly, but the arrest of Plum has appeared to calm both Circles."

"At least in terms of wanting to fight each other," Cinellan added.

"That was quick," Satrine said.

Cinellan only gave her the slightest of glances, and then returned his focus to Welling. "The point is, this case is closed, good and solid."

Welling turned back to Hilsom. "Plum confessed everything?"

"Murder of three mages, attempted murder of you."

"That's all?"

Hilsom shrugged. "There was a bit about why—revenge on the Circles for the death of his wife, some sort of attempt at ritual magic to bring her back. It was all a bit fantastical, but the salient points were covered."

Welling frowned. Satrine sensed there were elements of this result that didn't sit right with him, but she wasn't sure what.

"Good, then," Cinellan said, stepping away from the cot. "It's good work, Minox. Take some time to heal. No new cases until the doctor says. We'll let you rest now." He made for the door, gesturing to Hilsom to follow him.

"I don't think so," Welling said.

"Pardon?"

"You're not leaving, Captain, as our conversation is not over yet."

Cinellan raised an eyebrow and returned. "You have something else to ask?"

"There is the matter of Missus Rainey."

"What about Missus Rainey?" Cinellan finally looked at her, really looked. Satrine couldn't get a read of his face.

"As the saying goes, we're not talking about the dead mouse on the floor," Welling said.

"I'm a dead mouse?" Satrine asked.

"I'll talk about it," Kellman said. "Tricky there did some smart thinking, letting us find Jinx. Then she fought like blazes to save him. He'd be dead if it weren't for her."

"Blazing well good," Cinellan said. "We'll patch her up and not let the city charge her a tick."

"Not good enough," Welling said. "Missus Rainey is an extraordinary individual with a singularly adroit mind."

"I don't doubt her talent," Cinellan said. "But what do you want me to do about it, Welling?"

"Failure to appoint her with an inspectorship would be a severe error on your part."

It may have been from the whiskey, but Satrine burst out laughing.

"You think this is funny?" Welling asked her.

"No, I . . . I don't know what to think anymore. I'm touched, Inspector Welling."

"Touched in the head, maybe," Hilsom said.

Welling turned back to Cinellan. "If you don't, I'd be forced to turn in my vest."

"Minox, don't say that," Satrine said.

"Really, Minox?" Cinellan said. "You'd resign? Let's say I did take her on. After what she did, every other inspector would resign."

"I wouldn't," Kellman said.

Cinellan turned his attention to Mirrell. "What about you, Henfir?"

Mirrell spat on the floor. "I wouldn't like it, Cap. But I can't deny, I ain't seen a heart as Green and Red as hers."

"Hmm," Cinellan said.

Hilsom coughed. "I would remind you, Captain, that even if you are considering this, you do not have the authority to appoint a civilian to the rank of inspector."

"That's true," Cinellan said. He gave a quick glance at her and Welling. "All I can do is remind you that the clerkship offer from this morning is still on the table."

Satrine had a hard time believing that. "That's very kind of you, Captain, all things considered. But that doesn't—"

"Take the clerkship, Satrine," Welling said.

"What?" She couldn't believe he'd change his attitude that quickly. "But you said—"

He turned his head to meet her eyes, a hard trick considering he was still clamped to the cot. "Just take it."

Satrine ground her teeth. The weekly crowns of a clerk wasn't going to cut it, but it was better than no crowns at all. "Fine. I'll take the blasted clerkship."

"Good," Cinellan said. He went over to the ward matron. "Have you written up your report on treating Missus Rainey?" The matron nodded. "Deliver your report to her for filing."

The matron, looking utterly perplexed, handed the scribbled piece of paper to Satrine. Satrine took it, and equally confused, started to get to her feet. She then noticed the sly half-smiles on the faces of both Welling and Captain Cinellan.

"Where does this get filed?" she asked.

"I believe it gets delivered to the ward matron on duty," Welling said.

Satrine handed the paper back to the woman.

"Excellent work," Cinellan said. "So now that you have served so ably in your clerkship, I have the authority to promote you to the position of Inspector Third Class." He extended his hand to take hers. "Congratulations."

"Thank you, sir," Satrine said.

"You're still partnered with him, of course," he said, pointing to Welling.

"Wouldn't have it any other way," Satrine said.

"Good," Captain Cinellan said. "Since you two will be the ones getting all the freak cases."

"I prefer to think of them as special challenges, sir," Welling said.

"You would," Cinellan said.

Hilsom looked especially out of sorts.

"There a problem, Mister Protector?" Cinellan asked.

"Legally, no. Inspector Third Class is the highest rank that you have the authority to promote someone to," Hilsom said. "However—"

"Anyone who does have a problem can report to me," Cinellan said. "And I'll tell him to roll his own hand."

"But—"

"Including the commissioner. But I'll tell it to him more diplomatically."

"Very well, Captain," Hilsom said. "It's no business of mine, anyway, as long as all the inspectors stick to proper procedure."

"We're all agreed," Cinellan said. "Are we done now, Welling?"

"I believe so, sir," Welling said. He looked to the surgeon. "Are you done?"

"You all don't shut your mouths ever," the surgeon said. "But it's set. You're free to go." He undid the clamp and went off to his office.

"Home. Rest. Both of you." Cinellan gave a small point of his finger to Satrine. "See you tomorrow, Inspector." He left the ward, Hilsom in tow. Kellman gave her a wide grin as he left. All Mirrell managed was a slight nod of approval.

Satrine and Welling sat alone in silence on their respective cots for some time.

Satrine finally said, "So they're really getting the arrest credit?"

"I've never done this for the credit," Welling said. He flexed the fingers of his broken arm and winced. "And that isn't the point for you, either."

"All things considered, it's probably best I keep my head down for a while."

"No, that's not it." His eyes danced over her face. "When you first came in, you were holding back, lying for the sake of getting the work, working for the sake of the salary."

"The salary's the whole point, isn't it?"

"Never was for me," Welling said. "And if it was for you, you'd never have come down to that mausoleum."

Satrine laughed, despite herself. "Still, getting paid is important."

Welling got to his feet. "I suspect I will not be too useful a partner for the next few weeks."

Satrine stood up. Her leg screamed when she put weight on it, but she could bear. She could always bear. "Hardly. Your arm is not your most useful feature."

"I'm presuming that's a compliment on my mind, Inspector Rainey."

He was calling her Inspector Rainey again. For some reason, that made Satrine incredibly happy. "It was indeed, Inspector Welling."

"You'll be all right getting home, then?"

"I won't be running any time soon. I could ask the same about you."

"I'll be fine. Though I'll count on you being at my back tomorrow, Inspector."

Satrine went to the door. "How many do you consider unresolved?"

"Twenty-seven now," Welling said.

Satrine caught an edge to that. And she recalled it being twenty-six yesterday. "We'll start whittling that down in the morning."

"Satrine," Welling said. "I wanted to . . ." He came up to her by the door. For once, his face showed a glimpse of warmth. "You have a uniquely gifted investigative mind, Inspector, and that is something I am quite grateful for."

"Just glad I get to use it," Satrine said. "I think I've been out of practice too long."

Welling reached out briefly with his good hand, clasping her gently on the shoulder. "Until tomorrow."

Satrine smiled. "Looking forward to it."

She left the ward and navigated her way through the twisting corridors to the main doors. She was about to step into the night air when she heard a woman calling her name. Miss Pyle came running up with a tied bundle.

"The captain wanted me to give this to you before you left," Miss Pyle said, handing over the bundle.

"What is it?"

"Your vest and belt," Miss Pyle said. "Apparently you'll be needing them again." Her eyes were locked coldly onto Satrine.

"Thank you," Satrine said. She still felt the harsh stare on her. "Is that all, Miss Pyle?"

"I told you, someday a woman would earn this vest, and she was going to have a harder time because of what you did."

"And now?"

"And now you've earned it," Miss Pyle said. She turned away without further comment.

Satrine wasted no time undoing the bundle and putting on the mantles of her position. If she was going to have to limp home, she'd at least do it in style.

Chapter 32

"**Y**OU STUPID BLAZING BASTARD," was the first thing Corrie said as she entered the ward.

"Our mother is not to be denigrated," Minox responded. The doctor had released him, and he was already dressed and ready to return home. "You can rebuke me as you wish."

"If you weren't half crippled I'd knock you in your rutting head."

"I assure you, I am at most a quarter crippled," Minox said. "Do not underestimate my ability to knock you back."

"You fought for her?" This was Nyla, standing in the doorway.

"Indeed I did," Minox said.

"For who? His skirt partner?"

"His lying cheat partner," Nyla said. "Did you hear what she did?"

"Save your gossip for my absence," Minox said. "Inspector Rainey saved my life tonight, and I will not hear anything against her character."

Nyla shook her head. "Can you get home all right? I have a caller tonight."

"I'm capable," Minox said. "I'll catch a cab."

Nyla turned away. "Stay safe, all right?"

"Always," Minox said. Nyla left.

Corrie cuffed him across the head. "Lying cheat? What did she—"

"I will not hear it, Corrie. She is an Inspector Third Class and will be given her due respect by you."

"I've got streets to ride," Corrie said. "Sleep well."

Minox was able to bear the pain in his arm as he walked down to the street, though he suspected the whiskey was playing a role in that. The morning would be the real gauge of how hard it would be to deal with the break. It did seem that the surgeon had done a competent job repairing the damage, and it would hopefully heal cleanly.

No matter how inconvenient his injury was, Minox found it far preferable to the fate he avoided. He had never felt so powerless in his life. Despite that, at this very moment, he still had no gnawing need crawling up his gut, no jittery energy coursing across his arms. He couldn't deny that he enjoyed finally feeling like he had control over his own body, even damaged as it currently was.

It was just a question of finding the balance.

Minox hailed a passing cab and jumped in. As the driver was about to press the horses, Joshea jumped in next to him.

"Cab is claimed, friend," the driver snarled.

"We ride together," Minox said.

"Are you all right?" Joshea asked as the cab started to roll, reaching over to Minox's arm.

"Nothing that won't heal," Minox said.

"I am so very sorry, Minox," Joshea said. "I mean, I had no idea, but I should have . . ."

"I was careless," Minox said. "I failed at my job, it wasn't your fault."

Joshea's hands fidgeted. "Nerrish always was a bit away from the center, though. I should have warned you, or . . ."

"Don't worry about it, Joshea."

Joshea's eyes went everywhere, as if he couldn't bear to look at Minox. "It's just . . . I finally find someone that I can, you know . . ."

"Actually talk to?" Minox asked. "Part of what happened to me today happened because I was careless. Because of that spice."

Joshea's face hardened. "You took that—"

"Of my own accord, and I don't blame you at all."

Joshea eased and nodded. "So what do you mean?"

"For the first time in my life, I let my guard down. I didn't have to be aware of myself, be in constant control."

"Was that a good thing or a bad thing?"

"It felt good," Minox said. He held out his hand, and made the barest of flames dance across his fingers. Enough that Joshea could see, but not to get the driver's attention. Now the magic was flowing, enough that he could use it, but not so much that it held sway over him. No hunger, no restraint. Just power at his fingertips.

Joshea blanched. Minox extinguished the flame and put his hand in his coat pocket.

"Sorry," Minox said. "It's just . . . this experience, this whole case I just finished . . . it's driven home the idea that I have a significant gap in my knowledge."

"About magic?"

"About myself. Ourselves. Think about it. This is a part of who we are, as much a part of our body as breathing and eating." He reached into his pocket and took out his pipe and put it in his mouth. Then he took out his tobacco pouch.

He quickly realized trying to fill his pipe and light it with one good arm would prove challenging. Joshea noticed his difficulty and took the pouch, holding it open for Minox to grab a pinch.

Minox got the pipe lit. "This is my point," he said once he had a few puffs. "Not understanding how magic works, how I work, was used as a weapon against me. But relying on it as part of doing my job, without understanding it, almost cost me my life."

"I've tried just ignoring it," Joshea said. "But sometimes things will just . . . happen."

"Exactly my point," Minox said. "I've never ignored it, but I did try and pretend that I understood it as well as I needed to. Our—my ignorance caught up to me this week. The same might happen to you soon."

"What do you mean?"

"I think . . . we both need to learn. We need each other."

Joshea raised an eyebrow. "Like a Circle?"

"Not in the legal definition," Minox said. "But that's hardly the point. At its core, what is a Circle but a group of mages who help and teach each other? I think we both could use someone at our back, don't you?"

"A Circle of two?" Joshea asked, a bemused smile on his face. "I think I might like that a lot." He extended his hand to Minox.

"Done, then," Minox said, shaking Joshea's hand. It felt like a solid step.

Joshea glanced around nervously, not that the driver or anyone on the street noticed. "I should head back, before my family wonders what the blazes I'm up to."

"I understand," Minox said. "We'll meet up soon."

Joshea said his final good-byes and jumped out of the cab.

"You're still paying for two passengers," the driver said.

Minox stood in front of the house. Surely, word of the day's events had preceded him. Mother and Aunt Beliah would fuss, Zura would pray, and Oren or Timmothen would make some speech on the necessary dangers of the Green and Red. Minox did not look forward to any of these things.

He went to the barn.

Surprisingly, Evoy was asleep, curled up on the floor with a low-burning candle next to him. Minox had no intention of disturbing him. He didn't need to talk, he only needed to study Evoy's work. Carefully. He needed to understand something, not get drawn in too deep.

Nerrish Plum had said something that Minox had heard before: the Brotherhood. His "Eight Fallen Pins," if Minox was inferring correctly, were stolen from this Brotherhood. Plum was also willing to give a quick confession and go straight to Quarrygate. Men rarely chose Quarrygate unless the alternative was more frightening.

Minox searched across the slateboards along the wall

until he found the part he was looking for. With three question marks around it, in quickly scrawled letters: The Brotherhood of the Nine.

He drew a dashed line away from the Brotherhood to a clear space on the board, and wrote in "Nerrish Plum." Under that he wrote "Eight Fallen Pins—stolen."

He glanced around the board. Every time he came out here, he took a good hard look at every name, every clipping, to see if some new inspiration would jump out at him. This newest addition brought no epiphanies with it.

There was something brewing in this city. He could feel it. Evoy constantly spoke of it. It was breathing and building, simmering under his feet.

That was the other thing Plum had said. He had only scratched the surface.

He drew two more lines, from "Brotherhood" and "Nerrish Plum," and then wrote "Underground?"

That felt right.

Maybe with that, Evoy would make a new discovery. Maybe in time, Minox would make his own.

Minox blew out the candle, slipped out of the barn and made his way back to the house. With any luck, he would make it to his bed with a minimum of fuss. He had a feeling that, despite the pain in his arm, he would sleep quite soundly tonight.

<hr>

It was well after nine bells by the time Satrine returned home. The door was latched, and Satrine had to knock three times before Missus Abernand finally responded. "Who's there?"

"It's Satrine, Missus Abernand."

The door flew open, Missus Abernand's face a mix of anger and fear. "You've been gone for hours! We had no idea what had happened to you." Her eyes fell on Satrine's leg, bloody and bandaged. "Oh, sweet saints, are you all right?"

"I'll be fine," Satrine said. The woman, standing dumbstruck, hadn't moved from the doorway. "Are you going to let me in?"

"Yes, of course," Missus Abernand said. "Girls, your mother is here!"

Satrine went into apartment, where Rian and Caribet were sitting at the table. Caribet jumped up and ran into Satrine's arms.

"Where have you been, Mother?" Caribet cried. "We hadn't heard anything, and we . . ."

"It's all right," Satrine said. "I should have sent a page with word a few hours ago. But I'm fine."

"You aren't fine," Rian said, not getting up from the table. "How did that happen?"

"Catching the bad guy," Satrine said. "It is my job."

"Is it?" Rian asked pointedly. Satrine wasn't sure how much Missus Abernand had told them.

"It certainly is," Satrine said. "And I do it pretty blazing well, you know."

"Well," Missus Abernand said, brushing past Satrine to the back staircase, "I've been doing this job all day, and I need to get to bed." She stopped at the foot of the stairs. "I'll expect extra pay for today."

"Absolutely."

Missus Abernand left. Satrine sat at the table, Caribet still clinging to her side.

"Are you hungry?" Rian asked sullenly.

"Famished."

Rian went to the stove and ladled out a bowl of stew. "Beet and onion and bitter greens," she said as she put the bowl in front of Satrine.

"Thanks," Satrine said. The stew was perfectly acceptable fare. "How are you, Ri?"

Rian slumped in her chair. "College boys are horrible."

"Good," Satrine said. "Why?"

"He said he went and got you in trouble. Did he really?"

"He really did," Satrine said. "It's fine, though. Everything is going to be fine."

"Really, Mama?" Caribet asked.

"I'm certain of it."

"Good," Rian said. She went back to her earlier thoughts. "Also he was really strange about me drinking wine. He takes it really seriously. Like, he kept wanting me to taste all these different things, and they all were the same, and even if you hadn't shown up I would have left soon."

Satrine finished her stew listening to Rian rant about the boy and Caribet talk about classes. They finished up and she sent the girls to bed. After a few minutes of straightening up, she blew out all the lamps, save one candle, and went into the bedroom.

Loren lay awake, his eyes found her vest as soon as she came in. He moaned softly.

"I got it back," Satrine said. "So we'll do all right for a while." She put the candle on his table and poured him a cup of water. He drank readily, eyes staying on her vest.

"We got our man. I got him, actually, but Mirrell and Kellman are getting the credit." She sat on the bed and took off her boots. "It was a dice of a fight, though, Loren. Two fights, actually, since Idre Hoffer notched me. That was the real dice. Taking down Plum, it was almost sad. Locked him down, saved a life, like you always used to say."

Another soft moan from Loren.

"Yeah," she said. "Looks like I'm getting the job done."

The moan turned into a wheeze.

She got up and turned to him. "Looks like I have your attention, as long as I have this on?" She held open the vest.

"Ree . . ." he wheezed out.

"What was that?" she asked, moving closer.

"Reen . . . an . . ." He trailed off.

"Green and Red?" she asked. Of course that was what he was thinking. She took off the vest and let it drop on the ground. "No more of that in here."

His eyes stayed on her. No lolling, no flailing about.

"Ree . . . Satree . . ."

She dropped to her knees.

". . . Trine," he finished hoarsely.

She almost fell over, and then scrambled to his side, cupping his face. "Loren? Are you? I'm here. I'm here."

His eyes went away again. The moment passed.

She kissed his forehead. "All right, my love. That was good." She stood back up and continued undressing. "I want you to know, Loren, I won't stop fighting for you. Working for our family."

She got in the bed next to him. She hadn't slept properly in days. "Every day, for as long as it takes."

She turned and wrapped her arm around his warm chest. "I can do it, because I know you're here, waiting for me." The tears formed at her eyes, and she didn't bother trying to stop them. "I'm at your back. Until the saints come for you. And even then, I'm going to give them a blazes of a fight."

She leaned up and blew out the candle.

"You don't have to worry about anything. I'm on it."

Marshall Ryan Maresca's
Novels of Maradaine

begin with

The Thorn of Dentonhill

"Veranix is Batman, if Batman were a teenager and magically talented. His uncompromising devotion to crushing the local crime boss encourages him to take foolish risks, but his resourcefulness keeps our hero one step ahead of those who seek to bring him down. Action, adventure, and magic in a school setting will appeal to those who love Harry Potter and Patrick Rothfuss's *The Name of the Wind*."
—*Library Journal* (starred review)

"Maresca's debut is smart, fast, and engaging fantasy crime in the mold of Brent Weeks and Harry Harrison. Just perfect."
—Kat Richardson, national bestselling author of *Revenant*

ISBN: 978-0-7564-1026-1

And don't miss

A MURDER OF MAGES
A novel of *The Maradaine Constabulary*

978-0-7564-1027-8

To Order Call: 1-800-788-6262

www.dawbooks.com

0371

E. C. Blake
The Masks of Aygrima

"Brilliant world-building combined with can't-put-down storytelling, *Masks* reveals its dark truths through the eyes of a girl who must learn to wield unthinkable power or watch her people succumb to evil. Bring on the next in this highly original series!"

—Julie E. Czerneda

"Mara's personal growth is a delight to follow. Sharp characterization, a fast-moving plot, and a steady unveiling of a bigger picture make this a welcome addition to the genre."

—*Publishers Weekly*

"*Masks* is simply impossible to put down."

—*RT Book Reviews*

MASKS
978-0-7564-0947-0

SHADOWS
978-0-7564-0963-0

FACES
978-0-7564-0939-5

To Order Call: 1-800-788-6262
www.dawbooks.com